THE KNOWING

THE KNOWING

SHARON CAMERON

Scholastic Press

New York

Library of Congress Cataloging-in-Publication Data available

ISBN 978-0-545-94524-0

10 9 8 7 6 5 4 3 2 1   17 18 19 20 21

Printed in the U.S.A.   23

First edition, October 2017

Book design by Becky Terhune

For those who long to know
what has been forgotten

I am one of the Knowing.

I was three years old the day my memories came. I had my arms stretched out, my brother, Adam, flying me up and around and over his head like the bluedads that dart through the linen fields. I was laughing. And suddenly there were voices in the rush of air. Images. Swirling color. And so much feeling. Cold on new skin the moment after my birth. Hunger pangs before I knew how to ask for food. Fear. Shame. I knew the number of painted stars on the ceiling over my bed. I knew how many pins held back my hair. I knew because I remembered.

And then I sank, deep inside my mind, and I was two seasons younger, standing before my mother's chair, tears running wet on my cheeks, skin hot on the back of my hand. "We do not show what we feel," Mother says. "When I cannot see your fear, there will be no slap." And then she slaps my hand. Stinging. Again. And again.

I lived the memory eight more times before rising back into the present, kicking and screaming while Adam stroked my hair. "Don't cry, Sam." I can hear his voice now, soft in my memory. "You are one of the Knowing. Special. Like me."

Fifteen years have passed since that day, and my memories are like words piled on words on pages that are infinite in ink that is indelible. As sharp and fresh as the day they were written. I saw Adam die, and I have lived that death a thousand times. I will live it ten thousand more. When you cannot forget, pain is a fire that never stops burning.

I am one of the Knowing. The privileged. Special.

What have we done to be punished with this life?

FROM THE HIDDEN BOOK OF SAMARA ARCHIVA
IN THE CITY OF NEW CANAAN

SAMARA

Always I thought it would be my Knowing that killed me, when actually, it's going to be this rope.

I lower myself down, hand over hand, the sheered, sparkling rock of the cliff face slipping by at a pace that is agonizingly slow. I saw a boy from the Outside scaling a rope once, snatching fruit from the top of a spicemelon tree like he was running up a set of stairs. Down, I'd thought, would be so much easier. But I, Samara Archiva—the girl who is Knowing, who remembers so much—had no idea my body could feel so heavy. Or that rope could eat skin. My palms are tearing, muscles seizing, and I can't look down. I don't want to Know how far it is to the bottom.

And then the rope jerks and I drop, quick. If I didn't Know that rope could eat skin, it seems I was also unaware that rock can eat rope. Where my line hangs over the edge of a jutting stone, I can see the strands snapping, frayed ends lit by the lowering sun. I drop again, twisting, dangling in the air. Terror uncoils in my middle.

"Knowing," my mother always says to me, "is the pinnacle of human evolution and the birthright of the people Underneath. Doing is for those Outside." But when Nita's grandpapa is Outside with a ten-centimeter cut on his leg, then it seems to me that someone ought to be out there actually doing what they Know. And so, instead of being where I was supposed be, ordering my mind in my bedchamber, I was climbing up an unused supply shaft. To the Outside.

And when Grandpapa's stitching was done, there was a group of supervisors in the old supply hut, standing around the boxes I'd used to cover the entrance to the shaft. I watched through the wall cracks as one of them picked up a thin scarf, beautifully dyed in blues and greens. What was supposed to be wrapped around my unbraided head when I slid back down to the city Underneath. And because Outsiders only wear undyed cloth, this was obviously a scarf of the Knowing, and because supervisors are the only Knowing allowed Outside, this was obviously a scarf that had been hoarded. Stolen. Held back from the requests of the city.

And then the supervisors were in the streets, metal-capped sticks breaking open doors, searching the houses of the dyers, and Nita was telling me to run. I did, hood pulled low to hide my face, flitting past furnace fires and workshops, carts, curtained windows, and cesspits, and up through five levels of harvested fields, terraced into the sides of the mountain. Across orchards stripped bare of fruit, and up again, pushing back the branches of thick, untended fern trees to the cliffs that separate what is Outside from what is not. To the rope I had hidden, dangling down a sheltered crack in the rock face, hung for just this sort of emergency.

It's really not a very good rope.

The rope jerks for the third time, and I loosen my grip and let myself slide. It doesn't just hurt, it burns. Enough to make me scream, ripping my hands, shredding my leggings. When I hit the ground, I hit it hard, pain shooting up my shins, air knocked from my lungs. I stare into the bowl of an empty purple sky, bruises spreading, hands bleeding onto the scattered stones. Amazed that I am alive. That I'm not in pieces. Amazed that I am not caught. Yet.

My breath comes back in a wheezing gasp. I get to my feet and stagger to a rivulet spilling down its own pale, encrusted path from the cliff face. Salt water. I examine my palms. Bloody and blistered, each missing a wide strip of skin. I heard and therefore I Know every word of the recitations on wound healing—eighth week, second session of my physician training—and I won't be able to do any of it. Not in the medical rooms. Not without being seen. I grit my teeth and thrust both hands into the waterfall.

I yell with my mouth closed. A shriek inside my head. And the sound brings a memory pulling at my mind. A tugging weight. I Know what memory this is, and I don't want it. I close my eyes, breathe. Fight. But the memory yanks, dragging me downward. I sink into my mind, and then I fall . . .

. . . into the dark of a corner behind an open door. Someone is screaming. A deep voice. Full of pain. Adam. I don't understand. My father is crying in the corridor, but Mother says the Knowing never show what they feel.

I creep out from the corner. This is Adam's room. But it doesn't feel like Adam's room, and when I tiptoe across the rug, push onto my toes to peek over the edge of the bed, what I see is not my brother. This Adam is sweating, frothing. Broken. His fingers twist in the wrong direction. Then he opens his mouth, his back arches off the bed, and he screams and screams . . .

. . . and I shove the memory away, cache it back to a high shelf in the darkest corner of my mind. I'm beside the salty waterfall, on my knees with burning hands.

"To cache is to organize your mind," the tutor said, "and is the special privilege of the Knowing. Visualize a place to put your memories, a place far away and inaccessible. When you cache a memory there, it may only be retrieved when you choose to retrieve it. Cache both the very distressing and the very happy. The first is unpleasant, the second addictive, and both may interfere with daily functions . . ."

I was three years old when I heard these words, on my first day in the learning room. I was terrible at caching then. I'm terrible at it now.

And I Know what's going to happen to me next. I close my eyes, and pain rips through my chest, tearing, slicing, cutting its way through my insides. Like needles. Like knives. This is separation from my brother, the grief I felt when I first understood that he was never coming back to me. And it is agony.

I lift my eyes, panting, my gaze sliding down the grassy slope to the tamed trees and the empty, shaded groves. The cliffs are over there, much higher than the one I just came down. A long drop into nowhere. Aunt Letitia went that way. And Grandfather Archiva was so afraid of the memory of helplessness from his infancy that he threw himself into the River Torrens rather than grow old. He could not cache, my mother said, and that was the end of him. It may be the end of me. The absence of pain, the absence of memory, sounds a lot like peace. And then the idea that death is the only way to peace makes me mad. Because it isn't. There is another way.

But for all my Knowing, I am not supposed to Know about that.

I push myself upright, wipe my cheeks with the back of a burning hand, and peel away the undyed shirt of the Outside, trying not to bleed on the embroidered blue-green tunic I'm wearing beneath it. The matching leggings are a little torn from the rope, but Nita's clothes have taken most of the damage. If I keep to the shadows, to the lesser-used corridors, I may escape some notice. But I'll still have to pass through the Forum, full of the Knowing, and I will be spotted, with my loose hair and injured hands, and this is a twelfth year. A year of Judgment. When the Council weighs our accumulated sins. When the worthy of the Knowing are kept, the unworthy condemned and . . . removed.

I'm as unworthy as they come. But most of what makes me unworthy the Council doesn't Know about.

Unless they catch me today.

I hide the torn clothes behind a clump of bluing grasses, sidestepping down the slope and into the upland parks. The parks are a table of land cut off, like the Outside, sheltered by the mountain on one side and the long drop over the cliffs on the other. The one place the Knowing are allowed to go open air but don't. Mother thinks the parks are beneath our dignity. That to stand in the presence of the sky is to act like an Outsider.

I wonder what she'd think if she knew where I really spent my time.

I Know what the Council would think. And I Know what they would do.

The air dims, cooling in the shadow of the mountain, and then I am slipping through an arched door cut into a smooth face of shining rock. I leave the light and enter the dark, feet tapping down winding stairs of black stone, taking me to the Underneath. The temperature drops, hanging lamps making shadows, the spiced perfume of the city inside my nose. It's quiet, the stairway deserted. Until Level Twenty-Two, where I see Nita on the landing, beckoning to me, frantic, her blue eyes bright against the undyed cloth, a sky-purple scarf trailing from one hand. Nita has been our family's help for seven years now, since I was eleven and she was fifteen, and I think she's just risked a flogging to bind my hair. This is not our level, and she is definitely out of bounds.

"I used your note and came in through the gates," she whispers. "Your mother's come back! Turn around . . ."

Mother never comes back before the middle bell. This is her time to order her mind. Like I was supposed to be doing in my chamber. My stomach sinks.

"Oh, Sam, you're a mess," Nita says, gathering up the mass of my hair, long, black spirals hanging halfway to my waist, wrapping it all up quickly in the scarf. "Where are your shoes?"

Hidden beneath the stack of boxes that had supervisors all around them. I'm still wearing Nita's sandals from the Outside.

"Here, use this to cover up." She whips a cloak of dark, shining purple around me and fastens it at my neck. "I'll try to distract your mother so you can get through the door. And do something about your hands!"

"What happened to the dyers?" I ask, but Nita's already shoved me forward, disappearing back through the doorway. She must have an agreement with the Outsiders in this level's kitchens. I wish I did. The way would be much shorter.

I hurry down the black stone stairs, Level Eighteen, Seventeen, passing more doorways and landings without seeing another soul. No one ever comes this way, because the Knowing never go open air. Except for me. Of course, the Knowing never break the law to put on undyed cloth and dress the wounds of their help, either. Except for me. And they definitely do not consider their help family. Except for me.

When I'm not so afraid, I feel good about my unworthiness.

Fifteen levels down, I duck through the arch on my right, into the dull, flickering lamplight of the medical section. It's as empty and quiet here as in the stairwell, and that, I think, is at least one thing I do exactly like the rest of the Knowing: Never get sick.

There's a door open on my left, a storage room, with shelves of boxes and bottles on one side, and on the other a back, a male back, in a sleeveless green tunic, brown hair braids hanging past his shoulders, injecting a clear liquid into tiny glass vials. He has ten scars on each of his arms, one for every year of his life. Reddix Physicianson. The sharp scent of our wellness injections springs to my nose.

I take one silent step inside, reach up for a roll of bandages, and Reddix says, "Can I get something for you, Samara?"

I glance back. He hasn't turned or twitched or even stopped filling his vials. But he Knows it's me. I snatch the bandages with my fingertips. "No, I don't need anything." My hands are hurting enough to make tears well in my eyes. Or maybe that's Adam.

Reddix's voice is low. Composed. "Then I suppose I'll be seeing you later."

I dart out the door. There's a shadowed corner on the landing at Level Eight where I stop to bind my hands, wincing while I do it, ripping the cloth with my teeth, uneasy. I can't think of one reason why Reddix would be seeing me later. When I'm done, I run down seven more levels, through a short tunnel, and then I straighten my back, adjust the cloak to hide my feet and my hands, and enter the noise of the Forum.

Water gushes from a high black arch in the cavern wall, the River Torrens, rushing down a channel that winds through a mirrored floor of dark and glossy rock. Seven bridges span the channel, water echoing against sporadic columns of blue-black stone, natural features now honed and polished, rising to a ceiling I cannot see. But there are lamps up there, glittering, hanging from terraces and balconies like the stars I've seen Outside. In the long stretches of the dark days. When the sun is gone.

I slow my walk to something calm and unconcerned as I cross the first bridge, edging along the fringe of the crowd, cloak held together, trying to blend with the sea of bright fabric and elaborately pinned braids. I want to run. There's a platform on the far side of the cavern, a high piece of rock hugged on three sides by the Torrens, bare and smooth on its top. Where we will be Judged. And reclining on its carved steps is my father, Sampson Archiva, skin and eyes a rich brown, hair twisted into ropes strung with red. Waiting for someone.

A mural rises beyond my father's head, meters high and stretching the length of the cavern wall, images shifting as I weave through the columns. The first section is titled "The Legacy of Earth," green mountains and an impossibly blue sky fading into a smoking, flattened land. Then the color blends to pale, into the circular walls of a city of white stone, a silver-white sunrise sparkling above it. This is "Canaan. The Cursed City." And to the right of that, reaching to the curve of the wall is "Journey to New Canaan," showing a long line of beautiful people on a road to a black mountain, the white city in the distance, each with a hand extended to a smaller, stunted figure with a blank and empty face.

The beautiful ones are supposed to be my ancestors, 379 years ago, the Knowing, the people of memory, leading those without it to a refuge safe from the destruction of a coming Earth. Only there is no Earth. Earth is a myth. A story to make us afraid. To make us think we're special. To keep the Outsiders out and the Knowing Underneath. Adam told me that.

And he was right. Because I Know the real reason we left the Cursed City. And it has nothing to do with a myth . . .

Memory grabs at my mind, heavy, trying to drag me downward. I struggle. I cannot do this here. I will not. I've stopped walking, heads turning to stare as I dam the flow of people like a stone in a stream. The memory pulls. Hard. I pull back. And then it wrenches me down and I plummet . . .

. . . *into a room of gray pine, herbs drying in bunches from the ceiling, yellow flame from a heating furnace showing me the face of an old man drinking tea from a mug. Cyrus Glassblower. Nita's grandpapa. I sip from my own mug, hugging my knees, on the floor at his feet. There are sixteen scars on my arms.*

"Nita tells me you're writing the truth in a book," Grandpapa says. "That's good. Memories last when they're written. They can be given to someone else. So here's a truth I want you to write. I can't remember being a child. I just opened my eyes one day, and the memories were gone . . ."

I hesitate. "So different from . . ." I'm looking for words that aren't "different from the way you usually forget." Outsiders don't have memory, and I don't want to be insulting. I want him to like me. Grandpapa smiles.

"It's a natural thing, little girl, to let a memory fade. Like chiseling stone. If the carving is shallow, then the picture just wears itself away.

And even if it is chiseled in good and deep, the edges still smooth out, soften. Time has a kindness like that. That's as it should be . . ."

Meaning that we of the Underneath are not as we should be. I watch Grandpapa's forehead fold up like cloth.

"But this wasn't the same. This was like the mason had never picked up the tools. My life was Forgotten. Nita's grandmama, she had to tell me my name, tell me hers. I had to pretend I knew my own mother. And we never told, because there have been others. Even a supervisor, once. And they whisked him belowground fast enough. But the Outsiders, now they just disappear. And then we see the smoke, coming out from Underneath . . ."

Three moons are rising, shining white light through the window-panes. How could a supervisor, one of the Knowing, Forget his own name? And how could I not Know about it? I couldn't Forget a face if I tried. If one of us had gone missing, I would Know. Grandpapa puts a hand on my head.

"But you, little girl," he says. "You Know. You remember. And you could do something about it . . ."

. . . and I go soaring, up through my mind, and my eyes snap open, blinking at the bodies moving through the Forum. At Thorne Councilman, our Head of Council, now standing next to my father on the steps to the platform. The one who will be Judging me, standing where I will be Judged, his black-eyed gaze making a straight path to mine. Fear stabs inside my chest. There's a jerk inside my mind, and I plunge, down . . .

. . . into the Forum of twelve years ago, full of the Knowing in their finery. It's dark. Silent. Judgment. And Ava Administrator has just been condemned. My father holds my hand, a rare gesture, and I watch a blank sort of shock steal over the serenity of Ava's face. Thorne Councilman reads her transgressions: funneling the best of the goods to her own level, numbers that do not rectify, an improper relationship.

And then Thorne condemns Ava's bloodline, all three of her children, because her oldest, a rebellious thirteen-year-old, has been refusing to cache. My father's hand slips up to my face, covering my eyes so I will not remember the sight, but I can hear the children cry, and Ava's soft protest of "No." And a louder "No." And then, "No!"

. . . and I rise through my mind, and this time when I open my eyes both Thorne Councilman and my father are staring at me from across the Forum. As are others. Because I have just shouted the word "No," the echo still bouncing back and forth between columns. And then someone screams, and it's not me. I look up.

A body is falling, down through the dark of the Forum, legs and arms outstretched, hair fluttering in the wind. And while my eyes track the descent of a long silver dress, all I can think is that I want to be like Grandpapa Cyrus.

I want to be cursed like the people of Canaan.

I want to Forget.

I am Beckett Rodriguez, and I am flying through the stars.

The ship is big, but I think it feels smaller than it's supposed to. We spent a year on the fake *Centauri III*, in the middle of a California desert without ever seeing the sun. They say this ship is the same size, but I'm not sure I believe them. Maybe it's because I've grown. Or maybe it's because this time I know that there's no sand, no sun, no air, and no Earth out there. Nothing outside the hull of this ship that could keep me alive. I don't like to think about the void.

We'll be on the *Centauri III* for thirty-one more months if everything goes okay. If the ship doesn't stop working. If we don't run out of food. Or air. If we don't get bored and kill each other before we get to Canaan.

I'll be eighteen before I stand beneath a sun again. And when I do, it will be a sun in a sky that isn't mine.

FROM THE LOG BOOK OF BECKETT RODRIGUEZ

Day 1, Year 1

The Lost Canaan Project

2

BECKETT

Two and half years I've been dreaming about this sun, and now I'm going to die under it.

"Beckett! Come on!"

Jillian yells down at me from the top of the cliff like I'm fooling around, making us late for a training session. At least I know she's not dead. I pull myself up the rope, arms on fire, sweat slicking my hands inside their gloves. It took some time to get used to the gravity on this planet. For my feet to stop feeling like the weight bars in the exercise cube back on the ship. I don't think I'm done getting used to it. Or the heat. It's a long drop to the bottom of the cliff.

"Everything okay?" says a voice in my ear. It's my father, Sean Rodriguez, eminent doctor of human anthropology, a man who right now is not having to scale this wall of rock. He's only watching me scale it. Through my glasses. He can see what I see, hear what I hear. I wonder if he can hear me sweat.

"Fine," I grunt.

"Does Jillian see anything up there?"

If Jill had found a lost city, I'm thinking she would've said so. Dad's next words are amused.

"Use the safety harness and rest if you need to."

He knows I won't. We have equipment on the ship that makes all of this unnecessary, but the rules of protocol say no visible technology. Even the basics. And anyway, Jill climbed it. Jill, of course, weighs next to nothing no matter what the gravity is. I pull for all I'm worth.

Another five meters and I get a boot on a rock and push myself over the top. I roll away from the edge and lie there, panting while my muscles scream. I hear Dad chuckle. Jill peers down at me, blond hair sticking out in a spiky halo. She looks like she's falling from the purple sky.

"Made it, huh?"

"I think you impressed her," Dad says through the earpiece.

I wince. Jill can't hear him, not unless she's really close. Lately she likes to be really close, and lately my father likes to tease me about this. And only lately has it occurred to me that Jillian might have been brought on this mission for reasons other than her triple-digit intelligence and equally brilliant archaeologist parent. We could be on this planet for years, and out of one hundred and fifty team members, there's no one else here under the age of thirty. I wonder if my parents know she was chosen for me. If they had any say in it. If Jillian did.

I really am stupid to have never thought of this before.

Jill, who I'm guessing has not been as dense as me in this area, holds out a hand. I take it, and let her haul me up.

"Here," she says, "you've got dirt on the lenses." She snatches the glasses off my face and gives them a scrub on the back of her jumpsuit while she kisses me. The idea of Jill plotting to have my babies means I enjoy this less than I should.

"Exhaustion looks good on you," she whispers, before sliding the glasses back on my face.

It might be easy to make exhaustion look good when you're the only eligible human in a galaxy.

"Beck," my father is saying. I adjust the earpiece. He's amused again, which is embarrassing. He's also in a hurry. "We only have forty-eight hours before the sun sets, so stop fooling around and let me see where you are."

I unlatch the harness rope and safety, straighten the lenses, and gaze around us, making a slow sweep of the clearing while Jillian goes back to documenting the finer details for our map. "Vegetation," I tell him, confirming what can be seen on his screen at the base camp. "No visual on any life-forms . . ."

We're in a forest, as far as I can tell. The plants are all one kind, but in different sizes, new growth on finger-thick stalks all the way to massive trunks three and four meters around, weirdly pliable. Leaves flutter, pale yellow and as thin as a layer of skin, the tips darkening to deep purples and blues. But what I can't describe to my father is the sense of space, a ceiling of sky too far away to touch, a vast, empty openness that until four days ago, I hadn't known since I was sixteen. Wind moves through my sweaty hair, laced with a sharp, fresh smell that I think is life. I close my eyes, breathing air that hasn't been breathed. And then I hear a short, clipped noise. A sound that is Jill holding in a scream. I spin around.

She's exactly where I left her, eyes squeezed shut, cartographer in one stiff hand, and something like a beetle, hard-shelled, yellow as the leaves and as big as my fist, is crawling up the back of her leg. A long, pointed needle of a tongue darts out, probing, testing as it goes.

Correction, I think. I have a visual.

"Don't move," I tell her. I don't think she was going to. Our jumpsuits are thin but weapons grade. Metal can't pierce them and neither can this thing. Or I don't think it can. The only life we've encountered so far on this planet is vegetation and what I choose to think of as insect, and so far none of it has been dangerous. It's why Jill and I were allowed a scouting trip. But how can we really know what these things are, or what they'll do? Carnivorous insects is one of the more gory theories about what happened to the lost colonists of Canaan. I pick up a piece of the long, peeling tree skin.

"Careful," says my father.

I approach Jill slowly. Her breath is coming fast. I place the tree skin on the back of her leg, directly in the crawling beetle's path, watch as it pauses, flashes its yellow tongue. It moves onto the waiting bark. I lift bark and beetle, and set them carefully in the leaf litter. The beetle probes, tests, takes a few awkward steps, and settles onto a fallen bloom. And then Jill's boot comes down once, twice, crushing it. I straighten and step back. The noise makes me sick.

"Beck!" Dad's voice is sharp in my ear. "That stone by Jillian's foot," he says. "Let's get a close-up on that."

I don't look at Jill, or at the dead beetle's twitching legs. I just reach past her for the rock. I turn it over in my hand, holding it up so Dad can see. The stone is blue gray, metallic with a sparkle, sheared off almost square on one side.

"Are those tool marks?" he asks.

"No."

I know I sound mad, and I am mad. Just not at him. It was only a beetle, if that's the right thing to call it. One of millions, probably. And killing it was stupid. Pointless. Jill turns away from me and the conversation she can hear only one side of, grabs the sanitizer spray from her pack, and douses herself with it.

"No," I say again. "The break is natural. Not man-made."

My father's sigh blows static across my ear. He wants that colony. Bad. Dad is good at what he does. His work documenting the nomadic tribes of old Russia already has his name in the history files. But finding Canaan is his passion. Ever since he was a kid, he's been hanging out with the equally obsessed, forming groups, swapping theories, and sending signals into space. Solving the mystery of the lost colony would be the pinnacle of his career. Of his lifetime. Of ten careers and ten lifetimes. The reason my parents risked their lives and mine to fly across a galaxy.

I want it just as much as they do. And not the echoes of it. I want a living city. To see what the lost colonists have become. But Earth hasn't picked up a signal from Canaan in more than five hundred years. The only other expedition, in the *Centauri II*, went dark just after landing almost two centuries ago, and now the scans of the *Centauri III* have come up completely, thoroughly, and depressingly empty.

If I can't know what they've become, then the next best thing is to know what became of them.

I toss the rock back onto the forest floor and go to release the spike we shot over the cliff to anchor our climbing ropes. There's a sweetness in the air as I pack our gear, heavy, like the alive smell on the wind, only stronger. I think it's coming from the crushed beetle. History is my specialty. I leave the bugs to Roger, back at base camp, who stepped straight off the *Centauri* into some sort of entomological nirvana. But even I know that smell means the beetle was after sap, not blood. When I look up at Jill, she's got the cartographer again, and she's grinning.

"Done," she says. She's fast on that thing, and she knows it. "And we're going this way."

I follow her through the dense growth, slow, careful, observant, and with little noise. Like we've been trained for two and a half years. Unlike the astrophysicists, here for the planet's coming comet, and the geoanalysts exploring for mining, the anthropology team's strategy is low impact: small scouting parties and a protocol of minimal, mostly invisible, basic tech. Just in case.

The Canaan Project was the most infamous social experiment of all time: a group of people sent to a new planet to regress rather than advance, to live pretech—without any technology—creating a society capable of existing in harmony with its world rather than against it. We're here to observe what they've made, not to interfere or change it, and we don't know what they remember. People are frightened by what they don't understand, and frightened people, Dad says, are the ones you have to be scared of. Jill and I have orders to avoid interaction at all costs, to leave any initiation phase to the experts. If there's anyone left, that is. And we already know there isn't. The team wouldn't have let us out on our own for two seconds if there was.

I keep my head turning in broad sweeps so Dad can see all the forest that I do, and so I don't stare at Jill pushing ahead of me through the foliage and heat. Her hair is plastered to her head, curves obvious even beneath the heavy pack and the jumpsuit, and the last thing I need is to force Sean Rodriguez to watch me watching her, and to hear about nothing else in my earpiece for the next two hours.

And then, because it's just my day for revelations in this area, I wonder if the lost city was the only reason my parents decided to take me from Earth. The whole crew of the *Centauri III* has had every test that anyone can think of, and our blood is clean. No contaminated DNA. A zero percent chance of catching or passing on the Lethe's mutation. Maybe my parents weren't just pursuing their dreams. Maybe they were protecting their bloodline. Maybe that was half the plan all along.

I only know I'm not walking when Dad says, "Stop staring, Beck." Even Jillian has noticed, looking back at me from partway up a steep slope, one eyebrow arched in question, a hint of sly at the corner of her mouth. I swear inside my head, where Sean Rodriguez can't hear, wave Jill forward, and start climbing after her, ignoring my father's chuckle.

What if I don't want their plans? Has anyone ever thought of that? I think of the way Mom's face goes a little smug every time I mention Jill's name. But what if I'm just not interested? What then? How do you get rid of a girl when she's the only option on an entire planet? Or should I even want to? Maybe I'm the one who's being stupid, ditching the one available female in thirty-nine trillion kilometers just because my parents didn't ask my opinion about it when I was fourteen. I can guess what I would have said about the options at fourteen. It would have been something like, "Cool."

"Beck!"

I think it's the third or fourth time Dad has said my name.

"You're killing me, you know that? Could you please not waste the last two years of training and give me a visual instead of staring at your hands?"

This isn't fair, since I'm having to use my hands to climb. But I slow down and do a sweep of the surroundings anyway. Stats roll across one corner of my vision, air temperature (34 Celsius, 94 Fahrenheit), heat sources (sun, and somewhere deep in this mountain, a thermal spring), radioactivity (nonexistent), power sources (nonexistent), the distance from base camp (14.1 kilometers). But I'm looking for things our scans would miss: cleared paths that have grown over, a piece of worked wood or stone, a planted field too small to identify from the air. Or a sign would be nice. "This Way to Canaan."

"Beckett!" This is Mom now, coming through the earpiece. "Are you hydrating?"

Really, Mom?

"*Yuàn dé yī rén xīn, bái shǒu bù xiāng lí.*"

Fourteen kilometers away and she thinks I'm going to forget Chinese.

"And monitor your body temperature!"

"*Ài,* Mom."

I really think we should just all stop talking.

"About two and a half more hours," Dad says.

And this is where Jill and I had planned to start sweet-talking my father into letting us camp instead of hiking back to base. If we camp, we had reasoned, we could strike out even farther after we rest, use the sun while it's here, cover more ground. And after all, Jill had whispered, her breath in my ear, the glasses can't be on my face every second, can they?

But I don't say anything, not yet. The climb is hard. Even Jillian is winded. Rich, loose soil slides beneath my boots, and another mountain peak is coming into view, towering up on our right. And then static buzzes sharp in the earpiece, a stab of hissing noise.

"Dad?"

"What is it?"

"Is Jillian okay?" This voice is Vesta, Jill's mother, close by or on one of the nearby screens.

"We're fine," I say. "Just a glitch."

"Beck, go . . ."

The buzzing jabs my ear, and then the connection is back again.

". . . show us what Jillian is looking at," he finishes. I crawl around a boulder and stand beside her, boots on the edge of a sharp drop into a shallow canyon. A stream is falling several meters down into a pool on one side, sunbeams shooting across the spray, making the droplets shine like crystals. It's spectacular, but wild. Nothing human.

"Let's go down," Jill says. Her voice is hushed, excited. She's thinking this would be a good place to camp. Maybe swim. I know her face well enough to understand as if she'd said the words. I wonder if she knows me well enough to get that I'm mad at her.

I follow her down, hanging on to the trees as we slide through the leaves, dirt sticking to my sweaty skin. Something says *chick, chick* as we pass, more of them taking up the song. The roar of the waterfall is amplified by the surrounding rock, so that when we reach the bottom, the noise is deafening. I do another sweep for Dad's benefit, but really it's for mine. It's beautiful here. Pristine. A whole empty planet of pristine.

We climb over tumbled rocks, Jill in the lead, heading toward the pool. She drops her pack beside it, then looks back, face pink with sun and heat, waiting for the glasses to analyze the water. For me to tell her if it's poison, or acid, or full of those dangerous, sap-sucking beetles.

"Go ahead," I say.

She grins, dips her hand, and instantly pulls it back, mouth turning down in surprise. "It's hot!"

I raise a brow at her scowl, and she throws a rock at me. Dad probably enjoyed that. Along with everyone on a screen at the base camp.

But Jill wasn't really trying to hit me, that water wasn't hot enough to burn her, and the result is we're both feeling a little better about things. Jill gets out her hydrator, unzips the suit, and splashes herself anyway, lifting her chin to catch the cooling breeze, little streams running down her neck, soaking her shirt. Maybe camping isn't that bad of an idea. Then I remember where I'm looking and give Dad and the base another circular view of the canyon.

"Nothing obvious here," I say to my father. "Though that break in the cliffs on the other side looks interesting. Very regular. Why don't Jill and I set up camp so we can take a closer look? This is a sheltered spot, people could have easily been here. We could get some rest, then strike out farther . . ."

I pause, surprised not to have heard a protest. Dr. Sean Rodriguez isn't a man known for keeping opinions to himself.

"Dad?"

The stats are scrolling, but there's no noise. No muffled conversation from back at base. I turn to Jill.

"We're out of communication."

Her eyes snap open and she straightens beside the pool. "Really?" Then her voice goes crafty. "Really?"

"No, I'm not kidding. We've got no connection." I look again at the canyon. What could be blocking our signal? I didn't actually know anything could. I don't think anyone did. And it's gone quiet, silent. No more of the *chick, chick*. This place doesn't feel sheltered anymore. It feels dangerous. I turn back to Jill.

And the pool behind her is pulsing. Like a living thing. Like it has a heart. The water trembles, sucking in and out, and there's a rumble beneath the rocks, a shaking beneath my feet. An explosion, a roar. Like the engines of the *Centauri*. Like a bomb.

"Jill!" I yell. "Move!"

One of the first recitations we hear in the learning room is the story of Earth. How Earth is a place in the sky (suspicious), so far away the kilometers are too many to count (suspicious), and how we, in ancient times, were once the best of its people, sent flying past moons and stars (unbelievable) with the task of building the perfect city.

Because Earth was not a perfect city. Earth was full of greed, lies, violence, cruelty beyond imagining, and something called technology. Machines, like the water clocks, only these machines were made of poisons (ridiculous), fouling the water and ruining the land. On Earth, our teacher said, no one used their hands or their minds, because technology not only did their work for them, it did their thinking for them, too (silly).

And so we, the best of the best of Earth, accomplished our task, and with our own hands, not technology. We built Canaan, the city of white stone. A place of beauty, peace, justice, all the things that Earth was not (flattery). But Earth had lied to us, sent agents among us, ready to send a signal through the skies when our work was complete, so that Earth could come back and take our city for themselves. Use their technology to enslave us, steal the best of our best, the Knowing (more flattery), and take them away again, so that they would have to make the Earth beautiful again, too.

But the agents were discovered, and Earth waited for a message that never came. And we of the Knowing, the best of Earth and the best of Canaan (even more flattery), left our white city and built another, deep beneath the mountain. New Canaan, the city of black stone. The city Underneath. Where our memories and our Knowing would be safe. Hidden. So that when Earth came looking, they wouldn't find the perfect city or the best of its people, they would only find ruins, and fly away again (ridiculous). And then the teacher would whisper *how Earth was still out there, waiting to come and take the Knowing, never to see New Canaan again (fearmongering).*

It was at this part of the story that I raised my hand, interrupting our teacher's recitation, to ask why, then, we didn't all live underground? Why did some of us live Outside, where Earth could get them? And the teacher said Earth would not care about the Outside, because Outsiders were not of the Knowing.

There is a sign hung in the learning room, huge white letters on the black of the walls. "The Truth Is What We Know."

I disagree. I think that much of what we Know is a lie.

FROM THE HIDDEN BOOK OF SAMARA ARCHIVA
IN THE CITY OF NEW CANAAN

3

SAMARA

There's a sign above the murals in the Forum, above the platform of Judgment, where my father and Thorne Councilman were standing until the falling body hit the stones just a moment ago. Tall letters, bright white against the black rock walls. OUR TRUTH CANNOT BE FORGOTTEN.

This is wrong. Truth can be forgotten. When it's hidden. Or when you die.

I feel a hand on my arm, a shake to wake me up. I move my eyes away from the lies painted on New Canaan's wall. It's Reddix.

"Go home, Samara," he says.

There's a crowd around us, a babble of noise, but I like the blur of sound. It washes away the words, so I don't have to remember what's being said. I let my gaze glance over the body, lying bloody and contorted two meters from my feet. I knew who she was when she was falling. I recognized the dress. I helped her choose the cloth. Sonia Tutor.

Reddix nods his head toward the doorway that leads to my level, and I go, threading my way through the throng just as Thorne Councilman and my father cross the bridge closest to Sonia. I can feel Sampson Archiva's eyes tracking my progress across the Forum. My very public lapse is not forgotten, of course. Sonia has only delayed how it will be dealt with. Seclusion, probably, until I'm fully in control. But since I'm never fully in control, my time in seclusion has tended to be indefinite.

It is easier to think about this than about Sonia. I'd thought she was doing well. But we are nearing the time of Judgment, and there will be more of this.

I pass a row of stone niches, alcoves curtained off that anyone can use for caching, and Jane Chemist comes out of the last one, snapping the curtain closed. One glance takes me in, including my hands, which are out of the cloak, crimson stains on the bandages. I tuck them away, keep my shoes covered, and mark the time as we pass each other by. Three-sixteenths past the middle bell. If we had a bell, which we don't, because the Knowing don't need them. Our memories keep better time than the water clocks Outside. I pick up speed, through an arched doorway, up a set of stairs that lead out of the Forum, thinking what I'm going to tell Mother—or Father, or the Council, if it comes to that—about what I was up to before Sonia Tutor took her life.

My lies will have to match what they remember.

I'm glad I'm thinking about this, and not what I just saw. The memory of Sonia's fall is going to come back to me.

I hurry down the corridor, past the learning rooms, where a teacher is reciting the methods of caching, up some stairs and through the Level Three entertaining rooms, where the mind can be stimulated, or occupied, and pleasant memories created—though not too pleasant, or you might prefer your memories to your life. Then into the dimmer residential passages, a left turn, and I am through the door of the Archiva chambers.

The latch clicks, soft. Only two lamps are lit in our receiving room, reflecting in the many mirrors and the backs of silver chairs. And it is silent. Empty. I breathe, and rest my forehead on the door planks. My hands hurt, body aching from my fall, the pain of Sonia and Adam very near the surface. And then the terrace doors open behind me.

"Samara. Good."

It's my mother, Lian Archiva, and she sounds pleased. With me. That can't be right.

She says, "We are having a guest this resting meal."

I keep my hands beneath the cloak, facing the door like I'm about to walk back through it. As if her words are unimportant.

"Reddix Physicianson has agreed to join us."

And now I understand Reddix's comment in the storage room, and why Mother is overlooking my absence. She's struck a deal. For my future. With Reddix. I have many opinions about this, and I will say none of them. Words become weapons when you cannot forget them, and they go on cutting. But that doesn't mean I won't do anything about it. What could Mother have done to Reddix to make him agree to this? I hear the tattoo of long, painted nails tapping against stone.

"Samara." The pleased tone is gone. "Turn around."

I spin slowly, holding the cloak together, Nita's sandals well hidden beneath the hem.

"Where have you been?"

"The upland parks. Swinging on Adam's rope." This is the lie I've chosen, explaining both my route and the rope burns on my hands. It also has the added benefit of being something I actually do. But I see the tiniest purse of Mother's brightly painted lips, and I Know I've disappointed her. There's no surprise in it, and yet, I feel the sting. A sting on a pile of stings in a bed of pricking thorns.

"Samara. You are exposing your feelings to the memory of others."

I put a calm expression back on my face. How does she do it, I wonder. Mother is tall, made taller by an intricate concoction of braids, graying white ends falling against skin that is the smooth tan of the potter's clay. And she can choose memories and feelings at will, caching away what is inconvenient. Like her grief for Adam. Her love for me.

"You will be in control tonight?" Mother asks. "The Physiciansons do not have difficulty caching."

I nod. I might be lying.

"And you will be . . . friendly? As is appropriate?"

I nod again. I am definitely lying.

"You are lucky to get this meeting. Considering the circumstances . . ."

Meaning that since the Council closed the Archives, the Archivas no longer have a name or profession to offer a potential partner. Meaning I will have to take my partner's name and profession. Meaning my decision to train in a small and specialized field like medicine without a partner in place has dangerously limited my options. Which was the point. But Mother is never going to accept my decision on this subject.

". . . and his father is Council," Mother is saying. "And Reddix will be, too, when the time comes. You cannot afford any . . . embarrassments."

She has no idea what just happened in the Forum.

"And I don't need to remind you that this is a year of Judgment. You should consider that a good partnership might very well outweigh other deficiencies."

I blink one time, and hold the serenity of my face.

"In fact," Mother says, "I believe that it will. And I think you will find that beginning a partnership without emotional entanglements is preferable. It is easier, Samara."

Which, strangely, might be the softest thing she's ever said to me. Mother runs a finger beneath a large silver necklace, the engraved letters "NWSE" winking in the lamplight.

"There can be no forgiveness Underneath," she says. "But it may be possible to find a compromise. I hope we understand one another."

We do. I turn and leave the receiving room, calm, like Mother taught me, careful to stay covered with the cloak. As soon as I escape into the corridor, I run. Down the passage and into my bedchamber, where I throw the cloak and then myself onto the silky gold of my bed, a move I see reflected over and over in the mirrored walls.

So Mother thinks the Council wants more of the Knowing, and will overlook my faults if I'm willing to provide a few. With Reddix Physicianson. She could be right. There are empty chambers on every level. But I think it would be cruel to make a child live like this. Too many of us make the choice that Sonia did . . .

And there is the memory of the falling body, lurking just below the surface of my mind. I close my eyes and cache. But the sadness is still there. Caching emotion, like Mother does, is not one of my skills. When feelings come, they cannot be forgotten. Like love. Love can never fade, or die, or switch to someone else. Even when it should. Love is once and forever, and so is the pain that comes with it.

Mother was right about one thing. Love ruins you. And life is easier without it. Which is exactly what I had planned. To live without it. Until now.

Maybe I should choose Reddix. There's no danger of loving him. And the Council might need every reason to keep me that they can get.

Then again, regret never dies, either.

I throw an arm over my head, starting up the ache in my palm. I think Mother's doing her best for me. But she's wise to protect herself. Both my parents are. The wound that is Adam's death has been oozing for nearly twelve years now, and will stay as raw as the day it was inflicted. And I'm the only other person in the world with the power to hurt them just as much.

I need to cache. I can feel the swirl of too many thoughts, too many feelings. I search for the memory of stitching up Grandpapa's leg. A bad, gaping cut from a broken pane of glass becoming a neatly sewn wound that can heal.

There was something I could fix.

I lift my head. Nita is coming through the door, a long red dress draped over her arms, thin and shimmering, a new pair of earrings dangling from her fingers. For Reddix. From my mother.

Nita shuts the door, takes one look at my face, and says, "What? Did you think it would be one of my old shirts?" I only just keep from sticking out my tongue at her. And then she says, "I heard about the Forum."

I think our level's kitchen help must be the most efficient means of communication the city can provide.

"Are you okay, Sam?"

"I've been talking to my mother, so not particularly." I don't want to think about the Forum. "What happened to the dyers after the supervisors came?"

"Nothing," Nita says brightly. "I told them I'd seen a goods box stored in there and that the scarf probably fell out. And Mum was so grateful you came today. Grandpapa's leg will heal so much better now."

I stare at the star-painted ceiling. Nita shouldn't lie to one of the Knowing, because I Know exactly what she sounds like when she's doing it. Just a little too nice. Maybe I don't want to think about what happened to the dyers, either.

"Don't look like that, Sam," Nita says, misinterpreting my misery. She lays the red dress carefully on the bed, then pushes me upright, leads me to the stool at the dressing table, and drops a bottle of kojo oil in my lap. For my hands. "So what are you going to do about it?" she asks, with a nod at the red dress.

"I haven't decided."

"Do you like him?"

"I don't dislike him." I frown, wincing as I unwind one of the bloody bandages. And then Nita spins the stool until I'm facing the mirror and puts a cheek against mine, smiling at our reflection. I am the brown of the linen fields at the end of the days of light, while Nita is a sunset, all pinks and reds, flushed from running up and down from the kitchens.

"Well," Nita says, "whatever you decide, I'll make sure you look extremely lovely and very spoiled while you're doing it."

Now I do stick my tongue out. "Fetch my dressing gown, would you, Nita?"

"Fetch it yourself."

I smile, and she laughs. She's been refusing to get my dressing gown since I was fourteen. Nita is an expert at manipulating my moods, at distracting me from the memories that hurt. But she is from the Outside, able to partner with any kind of person she likes, do as she likes, as long as doing as she likes means serving the city. She has memories that will fade. Soften. She can be whatever she imagines. I can never be other than I am, because I can never stop remembering who I've been. I was born special. Privileged. And I would trade this life for Nita's in half a heartbeat.

"Here," I sigh, wincing as I pass her a plate with my fingertips. The kitchens sent down dewdrops for the middle bell refreshment, silvercurrants baked inside the tiniest spirals of sweetened dough. I always pass these delicacies to Nita and her brood of siblings Outside. Smuggling food out of the city is very against our laws. But so is smuggling out myself, and Nita is good at both. She takes the plate with a wrinkled forehead.

"Didn't you say we need to be more careful?"

"But they're Nathan's favorites, aren't they?"

Nita pops a dewdrop in her mouth, winking at my reflection. Her eyes are so very blue. Such an unusual color. And dewdrops are her favorite as well as her brother's. I'm halfway through unwrapping the other bandage, thinking of Reddix Physicianson, when the sound of shattering pottery makes me spin on the stool. Nita is on her knees at the edge of the rug, dewdrops rolling across the floor.

"What's wrong? Are you sick?"

I'm at her side before I Know I've moved. She's choking, spitting, the remains of a dewdrop cupped in her hand. Only what I see is no half-eaten silvercurrant. This is smaller, shriveled, dark like the water bugs we skim from the baths. Bitterblack. Something cold trickles through my chest. And then I shake her.

"Did you bite it?" I yell. "Nita! Did you bite into it at all?"

Nita lets the dewdrop that is not a dewdrop fall to the floor, a move I see reflected from every mirror on every wall and from every angle, like a bad memory. Then she's on her feet, staggering through shards of plate to the washing table. I think once of Marcus, Reddix's father, but I Know the timeline of bitterblack poisoning as well as any other physician. If Nita has gotten the juice in her mouth, there's not one thing any of us can do for her. I run to the table and push her head over the washbasin.

"Put your finger down your throat," I order. "Now!"

I hold back her hair while she retches, my other hand on her back. When she's done she wipes her mouth on a sleeve, lifts her streaming eyes to my face. They are wide with terror. "They Know," she whispers. "Sam, they Know what you've done!"

She's right. No one could mistake a silvercurrant for bitterblack. It was put there. For me. The cold spreading through my chest burns like fire.

"The book!" she says. "Where is the book?"

Hidden. No one could have seen it. I pour water into a glass, spilling half of it. "Rinse your mouth," I say. "Can you feel your fingers? Do your arms and legs hurt?"

Nita spits in the basin and then sinks to the floor. This time when she looks up, there is a certainty there that freezes me to the core. She grabs my injured hand and pulls me to my knees. I Know there must be pain, but I don't feel it.

"Sam," she whispers, "when this is over, you have to get rid of me. Swear it. My family . . ." If Nita is caught eating food from the city, even if it's food that has killed her, Grandpapa; Nathan; her mother, Annis; the children, they will be the ones to pay. "Get rid of me," she says, "and then . . . you have to run. They'll try again, until they get it right. Promise me . . . you'll run."

I can't think. I can't even breathe. Only a moment ago I was trying to decide whether partnering with Reddix would save me from Judgment. But Judgment has come now. And it's fallen on Nita. Her voice is shaking.

"Sam, I swear, I didn't know. I never thought . . . they'd hurt you . . . Not you . . ."

The Council? Why wouldn't they hurt me? And then the first spasm hits, sudden and violent. Nita's back arches, lifting her from the floor, and I have to wrench away my hand before she breaks it. Memory tugs, and then yanks me down, and for a moment I am six years old, in the corner behind a door, listening to Adam die of bitterblack.

I thrust the memory back so hard it leaves me dizzy. Nita's body is easing. I cradle her head, use the sleeve of my tunic to wipe away the blood and tears from her face. She's bitten her tongue.

"Go out . . . on the terrace now," she whispers. She's shuddering so hard the words are difficult to understand. "Shut the . . . door and don't . . . listen. Please . . ."

I shake my head. I'm not leaving her.

"I don't want you . . . to remember . . . this. Sam, do not . . . remember this . . ."

The second spasm hits, more violent this time. Nita's body goes rigid, writhes, and goes rigid again, and with all my Knowing, I cannot fix it. No better than the child crying behind Adam's door. I hear a snap, a sharp crack, and when Nita's flailing subsides, her left arm is limp. Her humerus is broken.

There will be more broken bones, many more. But Nita isn't screaming like Adam did. She only sobs, her right hand stifling her cries. She doesn't want them to hear, to realize that the wrong person is dying. She's giving me time to run.

I do leave her then, but only to go to my bed and throw back the coverlet. The dress for Reddix slithers down into a red puddle on the floor as I grab a pillow and hurry back to her. The spreading cold has numbed me inside, a chilly kind of fog, clouding my thinking. Nita stares at the pillow, frightened. And grateful. Tears run down her cheeks.

"Don't . . . let them find you," she whispers. "Take the book . . ."

I nod, clutching the pillow. I don't think I can do this. She grabs my arm with her good hand.

"Go . . . to the city. Find the Cursed City, and make yourself . . . Forget . . ."

The next spasm is coming. I can see the trembling.

"The Cursed . . . City. You have . . . to Forget this. Swear it, Sam!" she yells.

"I swear!"

She lays back her head. "Then do it now. Please, Sam. Hurry . . ."

I press the pillow over her face. Hard. The thin scabs on my palms break, soaking the fabric, and when the third spasm hits I have to use my body to keep the pillow in place. Nita struggles beneath me, seizing, both wanting and not wanting to die, and the cold inside me has spread until I am numb with it. I listen to Nita's voice. Over and over in my memory.

"Go to the city. Find the Cursed City, and make yourself Forget . . ."

I loved the desert. Not the one where we trained on the fake *Centauri III*. The one outside the fences of Austin, Texas, where I grew up. Especially the bomb craters. Mom said I shouldn't go out there, that the deserts were dangerous, but Dad pretended to be reading every time she brought it up, so I went anyway. There was nothing biological left, not after so many years, and it was a great place to take a bike. Plenty of sun to hold a charge, ten- and twelve-meter holes to jump, no people to avoid running over. And it's not like a bike will let you fall off or get lost.

Channing used to go with me. We were both ten years old, same housing complex and same school, though I was two grades ahead of him. He didn't care. His bike was at least three grades ahead of mine, zero to eighty so quick you'd think you left your guts behind you. I was eating his dust when I saw Channing's shirt flapping, sliding up with the wind, a web of black bruise spreading down from his neck.

I knew what it meant. I knew what I should do. But an hour later, lying with our arms behind our heads on the hot sand, I didn't want to. Did he even know? Having a parent or grandparent with Lethe's meant you should, but lots of people don't know who their families are since the war. Did the tests miss it? Or did he manage to miss the tests?

I did what I was supposed to. I told Mom, and then Channing wasn't at school the next day, or any day after, and his family moved away from the complex.

I don't know why I'm thinking about Channing today. Maybe because I still don't know if I did the right thing. Or because this ship is nothing but metal, and I miss dirt. Maybe because the tutor program gave me this assignment. Or maybe I'm hoping that we will find Canaan, and it will be the world they meant for it to be. One where we haven't made so many mistakes.

FROM THE LOG BOOK OF BECKETT RODRIGUEZ

Day 89, Year 2

The Lost Canaan Project

BECKETT

J illian!" I yell again. "Move!"

She grabs her pack and scrambles, but not fast enough. The pool explodes with a boom like an audio file of World War IV, erupting in a fountain of white water and spray.

Jill screams. I think I do, too, both of us tripping over the rocks to get away. Water shoots four, then seven, maybe eight meters straight into the air, flying jets arcing across the waterfall, the pool roiling beneath it. I get one quick glimpse of the planet's most perfect rainbow before water comes down from high in the sky, dousing the two of us like somebody emptied a bucket.

I pick myself up and splutter, shake out my hair, snatch the speckled lenses off my face. Jill is standing statue-still, openmouthed, pack still in her hand, hair flattened to her head and water dripping down the end of her nose. Chaos spews up from the pool behind her.

"That water," she says, "was hot!"

I laugh, hard, and after a minute, so does she, running a hand to spike up her hair. Whatever turned the pool into a geyser is still happening. The spray isn't quite as high as before, but everything is wet with falling water drops and mist. I decide to remember this planet is not always as innocent as it looks. And that kills my laugh, because we do not have a signal.

I unzip the suit, clean the lenses with my still-dry T-shirt, and check again. Still no connection. I look at the geyser with the glasses. At the center of the fountain the water is boiling. I guess it's a good thing it was too hot to think of swimming. It's not a good thought. "Is the cartographer working?" I ask.

Jill looks up from her pack. The packs are waterproof, like our jumpsuits, just not waterproof if you upend a bucket inside them. She fishes out the cartographer, unlocking the case that hides the screen.

"Yes," she says slowly, standing up to face back the way we came, and then, "No." She holds the cartographer up toward one side of the canyon. "I can only see back to what I've already mapped. Could something have gone wrong with the satellite?"

I shake my head. The cartographer doesn't need the satellite. "Something must be messing with our signals . . ."

Jill's brows draw down, and I look with the glasses, trying to see inside the mountain we just climbed. But I can't scan its subsurface at all. Which is weird. Then I really can't see anything, because the lenses are wet. I wave a hand.

"Grab your pack," I yell, shouting over the noise of the geyser. "And let's climb out the other side."

"Why the other side?"

Because it was back the way we came that our signal first stuttered. And because I want to stay, not get yanked back to the base camp. "Because it's half the climb," I say. "Let's get out of the canyon as quick as we can, and see if the connection comes back."

Jill doesn't like this plan. I see her glance over her shoulder. She looks scared.

"Come on," I say. "That break on the other side of the canyon needs an eye on it anyway. And the longer they think we're dead, the less they're going to want to let us camp."

It's the word "dead" that does it. Jill shoulders her pack, and we leave the erupting pool, heading at a fast clip toward the canyon break.

When I was on the ship, all I wanted was to be off it. The *Centauri III* is big, almost too big, but there's something about being with the same people in the same space when you know you can't open the door. I couldn't wait to be out here on my own, and Jill was the same. And now, for a few minutes, we really are on our own, and here I am, practically at a run without that umbilical cord of a signal. We thought we trained for everything, but we didn't train for this, and I think that's what has me so off-kilter.

But deep down, it also feels just a little bit good not having Dad call the shots.

There's some thick growth to push through, more of the bizarrely bendable trees, and then we find the break and we're climbing again, pushing up against the gravity of the planet. I was right about the way we're following. It really is regular and wide, just like I tried to tell Dad, rising at a steady, even slant. Water could have done it, maybe, but so could hands.

I pause every now and then, trying to see if the rock is showing any evidence of human cut marks, but Jill huffs, impatient, and finally she just grabs my hand and pulls. She wants that signal. I wonder just how many times in her life Jill has been out of connection with Vesta. Maybe not often. Maybe not ever. Jill was with her mom all the time on the ship. When she wasn't with me.

We're both winded when we get to the top, the land going grassy, still rolling and undulating its way upward. I've got our connection status visible in the corner of the lenses, so I'll see the change when we get the signal back, but there's nothing yet. Jill still has my hand, and suddenly we tug on each other. We've tried to walk in opposite directions, Jill circling the canyon, back the way we came, while I've spotted a wide, shallow depression in the landscape that might match the trajectory of the canyon break. She frowns at me.

"You said we were headed up high, to get the connection back."

"I just want to see whether that depression is natural. How it's cutting through . . ."

"Beckett, first priority has to be communication!"

"Actually, first priority is fulfillment of the mission."

"You know we're not cleared to move forward, no matter what our objective . . ."

"Forward is only about fifteen meters that way, Jill." I watch her eyes narrow, and sigh inside. "Look, we're going that way to look at the evidence, because looking at the evidence is why we came. It'll take ten minutes."

She drops my hand. "Are you pulling rank?"

I ought to be scared of that look she's giving me, but right now I'm just annoyed. I could pull rank. Technically. I'm older by a year and I've trained longer. Jill and Vesta didn't join the project until we were six months in. And now, in view of my earlier revelations, I'm suddenly wondering if Jill and Vesta were brought on in the first place at the direct request of my parents. Not for the good of the mission. For me. Does the Lost Canaan Project have requisition applications for "female, suitable mother of my grandchildren"? Because Mom just might have filled that out. I'm irritated with all of them.

"Beckett," Jill repeats. "Are you pulling rank?"

She is definitely scared. "Jill, you know I don't operate that way. But once we get that connection, they're probably going to pull us straight back to base camp, and then somebody's going to have to hike all the way out here to look at that depression. Or, we could take ten minutes and check it out now." Jill bites her lip. "Look, you don't think the Commander would ignore the objectives of a mission for a technical problem, do you?"

I regret this argument the second it's out of my mouth. Dad doesn't like Commander Faye, and the feeling is mutual, so two years on the same ship and I've never had more than a curt nod out of her.

But Jillian loves the Commander. Admires her. She's risen fast through the ranks, knows how to get things done, and how to deal with the military, which is what most of the *Centauri*'s crew is. But I've heard stories about Juniper Faye. Most of them fact. And Dad says the way she dealt with the Canadian rebels was ruthless. Patient. Like a spider. And with all the ethics of a patient spider, too. A brilliant success if you're interested in crushing your enemies. A disaster if you're interested in cultures and history. Or humans. I don't plan on running anything the way the Commander would.

But the idea has worked on Jill. She readjusts her pack. "Okay, let's just hurry and get it done, then."

I look back to the canyon break and take some measurements with the glasses, then start along the depression, doing the same, sometimes from the vantage point of my stomach on the ground. I am getting a regular width sometimes, which is exciting until I lose it. But that could be erosion. Seismic activity. And then the depression crests the final ridge and we're at the top of a gentle slope, tall grasses flowing down into a valley that is surrounded by mountains.

I squat down to look, searching, but the depression has disappeared, and that makes me think water or erosion after all. Disappointing. Or maybe I just can't see it beneath the ground cover. I take one step forward, and a cloud of tiny, lace-winged mothlike things rises up suddenly from the grasses, thousands of them, making swirling patterns in the air as they fly. I turn my face from their dusty wings, wait for my vision to clear, and then Jill's hand is on my arm, pulling.

"Oh," she breathes. "Oh, Beckett . . ."

The valley is a shallow scoop in the land, and in the center is a forest, trees spreading their limbs like a canopy. But it's a circular forest, unnaturally so, and clear along the edges, reflecting the sunbeams here and there, are gleams of shining white.

A wall. A wall of white stone.

What I'm seeing is a city.

5

SAMARA

I stood for a long time on the edge of an overhanging rock, a green river running slow beneath me. Deciding. I'd climbed down as far as I could, lucky not to have fallen before I meant to, but it was still a long drop, and I had no Knowing of how deep the water would be. I felt my heart beat, and beat, breath pumping in and out of my lungs. I couldn't see a path sideways. There was no way back. Only forward, and I'd promised her I would run. That I would find the city. Forget. I held my breath and stepped off the rock. And the feeling was like falling into memory.

I hit with pointed feet, and the whistling air became a gurgle and a roar. I slowed, the world going quiet, and when I opened my eyes, it was peaceful beneath the water, sun streaking down in bright beams, surface sparkling above me. Like being inside a drop of green molten glass. And I was alive.

And now I am running, skirting the edges of thick-growing groves, skimming the rims of deep clefts that open like cracks in the land, water gurgling in their depths. It's been three days and nine and a half bells since Nita died in my bedchamber. Since I left the note for my parents, telling them I'd gone into seclusion. Since I jumped the cliffs.

There's little more than a day left to find the Cursed City, the Canaan we abandoned, before the sun sinks and the sky stains red and the dark days come.

They have a day of light left to stop me.

I look over my shoulder, without slowing my steps, at the sunbaked plain I've just crossed. Dust rises against the backdrop of the mountains. They're coming. Someone Knows I'm not in seclusion, maybe everyone does, and the Council seems to have a better way out of our mountain than jumping cliffs. But they can't come much longer. It's dangerous to travel in the red light of sunset, foolish to attempt in the long dark, when the rains fall and the last of the wild-growing food will be gone.

I've been gathering what I could find as I go, fallen breadfruit and the occasional spicemelon. The Knowing can live on very little when we have to, and it's a sick sort of irony that we of the city are overfed while the Outsiders, who need every bite of their rations, are the ones who go hungry if the harvest is bad. But fifty-six days is a long time to live on a few pieces of breadfruit.

I'll just have to live as long as I can.

I wonder how long it took them to realize that Nita was missing. If Annis and Grandpapa know. What did the Knowing tell them when Nita didn't come back from the Underneath?

And then I drop to my knees, as if a hand reached up and snatched me to the ground. Memory clutches at the edge of my mind, dragging. I fight, and then I fall . . .

. . . *into the light of many mirrored walls, to my crumpled red dress and broken plate scattered across the floor. Nita is seizing, writhing beneath me, and it's taking all my strength to keep the pillow pinned over her face. And suddenly, there is no struggle. I'm relieved to feel her go still, then so revolted by my own relief that I scramble away on my hands and knees, retching. The pillow falls away and Nita's blue eyes are open, empty, staring at nothing. My stomach heaves, and the cold inside me melts, boils, burns beyond belief, and I am consumed by a single, silent scream . . .*

My eyes snap open and I gasp. I'm on my knees in the orange shade of a pine tree, still panting from my run. But I can feel the scream inside me, and when the grief comes, it doubles me over like a blow.

I squeeze the hair on either side of my head. Breathe in. Out. Wrestle for control. Always I've been taught that Knowing is everything. That the truth of my memory is what makes me special, the lack of it why people like Nita are not. But I have lived Nita's death twenty-seven times since I left the city, three during the four bells I dared to sleep, and I am tainted by it. Made dirty by what I've done. And I will have to live with the memory of it. Like Adam. Again. And again. For a lifetime.

I don't think I can exist this way. Why should any of us have to exist this way?

And on top of my grief comes another sensation. Not anger or outrage. Not even fury. Those are emotions I can remember. This is something new. Simple. It is rage. I lift my head, and when I look back, the dust cloud has moved a little closer.

I wipe the dirt from the shiny new skin of my palms—quick healing is another one of my privileges—get my feet on the ground, and run, drying my cheeks with the passing air, rattling the leaves like the hot, gusting breeze.

I need a memory. A certain memory. But my mind is like the Archives of my city, a deep, forbidden place crammed with books no one wants or will ever use. I shuffle carefully through the volumes in my head, sifting and sorting while Nita's old sandals pound the soil, staying well away from that high, dark shelf in the back of my mind. And now I Know the number of heartbeats since I left the shade of the pine tree, every centimeter of the landscape I've run through. I feel the soft color of my father's lip paint, tried on when I was two. I hear the twelfth day, seventh bell recitation of surgical training. What I'm looking for is the memory of a map.

The map was inside an ancient book being conserved by my uncle Towlend—when I was young and the Archives were still being tended—a book for Council only, while Uncle Towlend was still Council. But Aunt Letitia had just died, and Uncle Towlend was falling into memories when he was supposed to be doing something else. Like working or eating. Walking. Mother said Uncle Towlend needed to cache his memories of Aunt Letitia, that they were too pleasant for him to be of any use. The Council thought so, too, eventually, and Uncle Towlend mostly stayed in his rooms after that, and there was no one to represent the Archives in their meetings at all.

So while Uncle Towlend was staring at the wall, lost in his head with his dead wife, I pushed a chair up to his workbench. And there was the book. Heavy and tattered, mysterious and beautiful. My mind turns to it now, like Uncle Towlend flipping to a page. I see the inked drawings of the valleys and the mountains, the three peaks that are to my left, the hot springs steaming on my right, watch my small finger trace the unfamiliar words. The handwriting was old, too difficult to read when I first saw it. But I can read it now. In my memory. I find the dot marked "Canaan. The Cursed City."

I look up, fully in the present. I need to veer left, toward that pass between the mountain and the hills gathered near its feet. I turn my steps, breath coming hard. What if the map is wrong? What if there is no curse? What if I'm running toward a story just as fantastic as Earth?

And with no warning, I plunge . . .

. . . into the bridges and columns of the Forum, where huge swaths of yellow cloth are festooned between the upper balconies, lamps behind them, shooting glowing rays of fabric light from an enormous, sparkling glass sun. The false sun hangs high over our heads, lit with fire inside, filling the shadows with unexpected color. It's the Changing of the Seasons, when the Knowing gather to eat, drink, and celebrate the rising of a sun in a sky that we cannot see. And the Forum is loud. Full of people and finery.

I huddle in the darkest corner I can find. I am painted and shimmering, hair twisted and tamed, because I have just received my eighteenth scar, and now every male in New Canaan needs to look at me. I am supposed to do as I ought: choose a partner with a profession I prefer, train for no reason, and provide my city with more of the Knowing. I hate it.

Sonia stands at my elbow, hair wound high on top of her head—she's still not quite as tall as I am—dress cut away to show her own wellness scars in rows down her upper arms. Twenty-two of them, her arms say. Safe to look at. But she's not hiding. She's using this spot as a vantage point, darkened eyes scanning the crowd. She loves this sort of thing. Craves it, I think, every glance and smile and stolen moment in an unlit corridor. I think she relives it all later, in her memory, each new conquest like some kind of never-ending sweet. I don't understand her form of addiction, but who am I to judge, if someone else has found a way to cope? Judgment is the Council's job, and we're all only a step or two away from insanity anyway.

I see Martina Tutor, Sonia's mother, chatting with the Chemists, who grow and mix the medicines we hardly ever need, and all six of the Administrators from across the passage milling through the crowd. And there is my mother, exquisitely dressed, gesturing with bright nails, speaking to Thorne Councilman, while my father has a lively discussion with one of the Philosophers, debating ethics we are never, ever going to change. I watch Thorne smile at my mother, an expression imitated by Craddock, who is also Council, representing the supervisors of the Outside, overseeing the plantings and the harvest. I don't think there's one person within a twenty-meter range who does anything useful except for Craddock. And he, Nita tells me, is cruel about it.

Sonia sticks an elbow in my ribs. She's excited, animated, the exact opposite of how I feel. "Smile, Sam," she says beneath her breath. "I'm the only person here who isn't afraid to speak to you. Relax and you could have your pick of this room. Just enjoy yourself, and if you don't, cache it later."

Since my memories seldom stay cached, this isn't a valid plan for me.

Then Sonia says, "Look at that . . ." Her smile has gone dazzling, and when I search the crowd for her target, I see Reddix Physicianson standing not far away, eyes closed. He's not with us. He's in a memory, a loss of control that is unusual for him. I hope he doesn't drop his plate.

But Reddix was not where Sonia's smile was aimed. Beyond his shoulder is an Outsider serving a platter of sweetbreads, a young man, a laborer in the fields from the shape of his arms, newly chosen, evidently, for work in the city. And he just raked Sonia with a glance that was unmissable.

"Sonia," I hiss. The corner of her painted gaze swings up in my direction. I say one word. "No."

Sonia rolls her eyes. She'd pat my head if she could reach it. Mother swirls a red-painted finger at me, telling me to circulate, but I fix my gaze on the spray of the gushing Torrens. I can feel myself being looked at. Evaluated. If I can't do something to distract my mind soon—run, jump, possibly scream—then memories are going to come, and this will get much more embarrassing than it already is.

But once I have successfully offended every potential suitor Underneath, I'm telling Mother I'm going for physician training. Without a physician for a partner. And that should take care of any ideas of partnering off Samara Archiva. What I'm not going to tell her is that I plan to smuggle my new Knowing Outside. Where people actually do get injured. Where there are things I can change. Where there's a sickness the city doesn't want us to Know exists. A sickness I plan to cure. For once, my Knowing will do someone good. And my mother's disappointment in me is going to remain razor sharp from now until the end of time.

"Sam," Sonia whispers, shoving a glass into my hand. Thorne Councilman is climbing up the steps to the platform, dark-eyed and handsome, hair going to early gray, turning to stand in front of the mural of lies that is supposed to be our history, OUR TRUTH CANNOT BE FORGOTTEN bright in the artificial sunbeams over his head. Nineteen more Council members gather around him. He has a glass. Everyone has a glass. I can smell the amrita. Then he recites the words we all Know and couldn't stop remembering if we wanted to, his deep voice echoing across the Forum.

"And so we who remember now remember the sun, because the light of our truth is written in our memory, and is just as enduring. Truth cannot be forgotten. When we remember, we preserve the truth."

"Preserve the truth," the crowd replies together, raising their glasses. There's a silence while the room drinks in unison. And then a cheer. Amrita will get you a little drunk.

I sip mine until Mother catches my eye, and then I drain it like I'm supposed to. And when I lower my glass, Thorne Councilman's gaze is on me, like the ray of a dark lantern beaming directly down into my eyes. And he is judging me, slowly, from head to toe. And I don't think it's because he wants to have a partnering conversation with my parents. My annoyance melts into fear, pure and primal. Does he Know what I've done? Where I've been? What I've read . . .

And just like that, the floor of my memory opens, and I fall again, drifting through my mind, deep into the mountain . . .

. . . to the steps that lead down to Uncle Towlend's office, sliding a key from a ring into a rusty lock. These are keys I am not supposed to have, because they are keys I've stolen from Uncle Towlend's flat. And they're keys Uncle Towlend is not supposed to have, because he hid them from the Council before the Archives were closed. The lock turns, creaking in the silence, and all my memories of yellow light, old paper, and my uncle's comfortable chairs are instantly stained with dark and the smell of rot. Papers litter the floor in the dim, dust thick on my uncle's desk. I go to the next rusting door, jiggle the lock, and when it opens, pull the cover off my lamp. And for the first time in ten years, I am looking at the Archives.

Books cover every surface, shelves spiraling around the inner walls of an enormous circular shaft, one hundred meters from bottom to top, pierced through the heart of the mountain. The wooden balcony rings the walls right along with the shelves, and I hold up my light and follow it, down through the dark, books on my right, a long, black fall beyond the rail to my left.

The quiet is deep, heavy, the kind that won't be bothered, the air stale, and when I brush my fingers across the passing spines, I can feel the damp. I Know the Council says books clutter our minds, make it difficult to cope with the masses of information piling up inside our heads. Even my father, who has few opinions on anything, agrees. "Do not look at your mother's books, Samara," he said to me when I was small. "And if you have, promise me you'll cache them. Don't read. Just cache . . ." But surely the books don't deserve such an agonizing death.

At the end of the balcony is the smooth rock floor at the bottom of the shaft, another locked door, and an empty booth where an attendant used to sit, usually an Archiva, guarding a room that was only for the Council. For the special books. I pause. There's a sign above the door. "Knowing Is Our Weapon."

I'm looking for a weapon. Against sickness. And today, I'm going to read the books. I want to find out if what Grandpapa Cyrus said could be true, and I don't think any teacher is going to recite this kind of Knowing for me. I find the right key and put it into the lock. The hinges open smooth, and the lack of rust or noise makes me wary. I tiptoe down a tunnel cut straight through the thick wall of the shaft, and then I'm standing in a room I've never seen.

It's tiny when compared with the Archives, books lined sparsely on shelves that hug four rectangular walls, another closed door directly *opposite. But there's no dust here. No rot. A brazier of biofuel burns in the center of a matted floor, throwing shadows against ten sets of reading tables with cloth-covered chairs. One of the chairs sits askew, a book open on the table, lamplight shining on the pages. As if someone has just stepped away. Only just pushed back the chair.*

My lamp is shaking. I blow out the flame, the Council words that so devastated my family, that took our profession, running loud through my memory. "The books of the Archives are no longer a beneficial resource. The recitations of the learning room will be sufficient for acquiring information." Clearly the Council does not believe its own rhetoric. But what would they do with someone who Knows this and shouldn't?

I Know they have floggings Outside. I've seen the bloody post in the Bartering Square. But there's nothing like that in the city. The Council waits for a twelfth year, for Judgment, when the gates are locked and sealed. Only then would they condemn the one who had stolen Knowing, and choose a needle from the smaller tray. Not a wellness injection. The injection that meant my eyes would never open again.

I should turn around. Now. But the pages of the open book flutter in the draft and my feet move until I am in front of it, running a finger along a thick, coarse page in the lamplight. This book is old. And then my gaze lands on a single word, upside down, in faded ink. "Forgetting."

I spin the book around and let my eyes skim the pages, turning each with delicate care. I'm not reading. The text is sometimes difficult to understand. But I can study it later, in my bedchamber, in my memory. The important thing is to put as much of this book in my head as I can before someone comes back into this room. But it's impossible not to catch meanings here and there, and I can see that this is a book of Canaan, the Cursed City. And the author is describing the effects of a sickness called the Forgetting.

A key scrapes in a lock. I turn the book the right way around and stumble back into the shadows, bumping into a corner of shelves, dropping to the floor behind a covered chair just as the door beyond the reading table opens. A new wedge of light cuts bright across the matting, very bright, and I resist the impulse to shrink back, to move. To breathe. Two slippers pause in the doorway.

Then the slippers come fast across the floor, silent on the matting, the black robe of Council swinging around the ankles. They stop beside the brazier, someone bends, and for one panicked moment I see Thorne Councilman through the legs of the chair, his face in silhouette, hair braids streaked with gray. I imagine what would happen if he glanced once to his left, and my stomach twists, pulse thudding in my chest.

But he doesn't look to his left. Only drops the lid on the brazier. The room shadows thicken. I don't think he can see me now. My tunic is dark. But there's not a single thing to keep him from sitting in the chair I'm hiding behind. To keep him from taking a book from a shelf that is right above my head. I let out a silent breath, and then hold it again. Thorne straightens, moving with the same abrupt speed to the table with the book about Forgetting.

And my mind is processing, working in the background, like it was while my eyes scanned the ancient book, like it has been ever since the key turned in the lock. Words weave together, giving me their meanings. I read them from my memory, sentences jumping forward in my mind like suncrickets in the rain.

"The Forgetting is a disease of the mind, interrupting an individual's ability to access information, effectively erasing memories and wiping personal information from conscious thought . . . Learned skills are often retained, while emotional connections are severed, only occasionally reinstated . . . Identity is lost . . . The onset of Forgetting is traumatic . . . symptoms of fear, panic, disorientation, and paranoia that can lead to unwarranted violence . . . The curse of the Forgetting *does not respect age or social stature and is so deeply embedded in our city that it cannot be rooted out. Canaan, we have decided, is no longer safe for any person to live in."*

And that was all about the Forgetting. Nothing else.

I stare at our Head of Council, standing thoughtful, stroking his chin in the light of the lamp. I have read the book. I have been to the Outside and listened to the truth. And now I can see the lie. That we of the Knowing—the people of memory, the special, the privileged—that we who remember were the people who Forget. All of us. Not just the Outside, like Grandpapa Cyrus tried to tell me. And not just the fading sort of memory, either. The Forgetting erased our existence from our own minds. And this was the real reason we abandoned Canaan 379 years ago. Why we built this city of safety underground. Not to hide from the evils of a mythical Earth. It was to hide from the Forgetting. And now, the ones we have left Outside are beginning to Forget again. The Council Knows it, and so do I.

They cannot Know that I Know it.

Thorne leans forward, almost gently, and blows out the lamp. And I feel myself float, upward, with a curl of smoke . . .

. . . to the sun and the slope I am climbing. To sweat on my face, the glinting blue rock of the mountain peaks rising tall in my path. I look back. I'm high in the hills now, and there are specks on the plain, black dots in the nearly horizontal rays of the lowering sun. I double my speed.

I'm going to do what Nita said. I'm going to find the Cursed City. Find the way to Forget. But not just for myself. Because I don't think the Forgetting is a sickness. Not anymore. I think the Forgetting might be a way for the Knowing to be healed. A way to peace that does not lead through death. And I am going to bring that Forgetting back to the Knowing like a gift, so that none of us have to live this way ever again.

And what will the Outsiders do when they can see that the Knowing are not special? That there is no Earth for our Knowing to be kept safe from? That we can Forget just like they do? I think they will rebel. I think they should rebel. There are more Outsiders than Underneath. Many more, and this, I think, is what our Council really fears. That the Forgetting will strip their power. That what I Know will give me the ability to strip their power.

The thought blows hot across my insides, and the rage inside me glows. They should be afraid. Because stripping them of their power is exactly what I'm going to do.

I don't Know exactly what I'm looking for yet. Germ or toxin. I don't Know if I'm going to Forget first without meaning to. It doesn't matter. I have my book, and the truth is written in it. If I Forget, I will read the book, and I'll Know the truth and understand what to do. My feet climb the slope, and I try to imagine the bliss of Forgetting. A mind without grief, without pain, without Knowing what I've done. And all this, I think, is why Nita sent me. Whether she knew it or not.

But first, I have to get there.

When I finally crest the pass I am tangled and ragged, winded and thirsty. I lean on my knees, panting, looking down across a valley that is like a shallow bowl surrounded by peaks, a scoop in the center of a ring of mountains. There's a forest in the valley, oddly shaped, circular, little glints of white reflecting in the sun along the edges. And then I feel my thudding heart beat harder. Once, twice. And again. Speeding. Stealing the last of my breath.

I don't think the Council can stop me now. They will not.

Because what I am seeing is a city.

6

BECKETT

I put my hand on the white stone, hot from weeks of soaking in the sun. I can't believe I'm touching it. Something slams inside of me. Again. And again. I think it's my own heart, trying to fight its way out of my chest. Canaan. The lost city.

Whatever Jillian is thinking, she doesn't tell me. She hasn't even moved. She just stares at the vine-covered wall towering over us, then turns two Earth-sky eyes on me. "Do you have communication?"

I adjust the lenses on my face, then the earpiece, and shake my head. I'm not sure what to do about that. Actually, I know exactly what to do about that. I should take Jill and turn around right now, climb back up that mountain to where we had communication last. But the stones of Canaan are beneath my hand and I can't go back now. Not yet.

"Let's walk the perimeter," I say. "See if we can find the way in."

Jill agrees. Or at least she doesn't argue, though a second look makes me think she might be doing some arguing soon. The wall moves by at a gentle curve, the blocks smooth and well fitted where the roots haven't broken them. I can feel that this stone has been printed, not quarried, and that's as it should be. 3-D printing was part of the Canaan Project's original city planning, to build without detriment to the environment before forgoing tech altogether. I could recite the strategic development files on this verbatim if I wanted to. I don't think Jill wants me to. But a perimeter wall, that was not to plan. Were they keeping something out? Or the people in?

And why didn't our scans find this? An enormous wall of human-printed stone is exactly what they were designed to see. Not to mention the topographical and geoanalytical surveys made while we were still on the *Centauri III*, the ones that came up so thoroughly empty. All the unease from our absent signal comes back now and doubled. If our scans missed this, what else did they miss? An overgrown wall doesn't mean the city is deserted, and we weren't trained for initial contact. Not really.

Correction. We were forbidden it.

Maybe Jill is thinking the same thing because she reaches out and grabs my hand. "First sign of life and we go back, Beck," she whispers.

I nod. Of course that's what we'll do. Maybe. And then I see why she said it. There's an opening in the wall.

We approach carefully, quietly, observing like we've been trained. There are more trees now. Huge and all the same kind, thick with heavy buds that look like they're ready to bloom, roots twining together across the gap in the wall. Branches have pushed straight through massive gates made of a metal I can't name, slow growth lifting one right out of its hinges. I duck beneath the limbs, buds brushing my hair, Jill still hanging on to my hand, and then we are inside Canaan.

Only it's not a city of people. It's a city of trees. White stone showing here and there in the dim of a sun lost beyond a thick canopy, buildings crumbling between massive trunks. But it's the silence that really makes me think this place is empty, a full kind of quiet that is wind and leaves and nothing human at all. But you can feel that they've been here, the humans. Once. And now they're gone. It's eerie.

The ground is uneven, easy to trip over, and I realize it's because we're on a street, now dirt covered, roots pushing up the stones from below. On one side is an enormous pile of rubble, practically a mountain, a few stunted trees growing in pockets of dirt on the sides and top. But to my right there's a smaller building. A house. No, a row of houses, now that I'm looking farther, lining both sides of the street. The nearest one looks at me, a two-story front wall stained but still intact, a pitch-dark doorway, and a hole for a window like an empty eye.

I've stopped walking. I'm like my mom in the university vaults right now, like Roger with his bugs. I can't look fast enough. And Sean Rodriguez is going to be so mad I saw all this before he did. And that makes me grin. I shake away the bad feeling I had at the gates, steer Jill toward the open doorway of the house, and stick my head inside, careful not to brush what might be fragile walls.

A second story and maybe even a third has fallen in, though only on one side. On the other there's an undamaged ceiling, a shelf on one wall print-molded from the stone. I want to know if a lamp sat on that shelf. I want to know what happened to the person who lit the lamp. I let go of Jill and step through the door, careful where I plant my feet, squat down and look at the overgrown rubble without touching it. Some of it is decorative, more ornate than I would have guessed, carved vines, curving moldings. Arches? That wasn't part of the city planning, either.

Jillian makes a soft cooing sound. She's on her knees, holding up a shard of pottery in the uneven, dappled light. It's about the size of her finger, still coated in a thick green glaze.

"Bowl," she whispers, "handmade, about twenty centimeters, but of a clay I've never seen . . ."

Considering we're on another planet, I'm not that surprised. Jill reverently sets the shard back where she found it, too well taught to remove any sort of artifact before it's been documented. She looks around the ruins. "Decay, do you think?"

I nod. I'd already decided that. I can't see any obvious signs of breakage that would mean violence, flood, or any other kind of natural disaster, no charring from fire. No bones. At least not here. Everything I'm seeing smacks of slow death, a slide into disuse, the ecosystem eventually moving in to take back its own. And that would be half the theories about what happened to the lost colony of Canaan gone within the first five minutes of setting foot in the city.

A cautious step back through the door, and I tilt my head to look at the front wall, at a set of exterior steps climbing to nowhere on the other side of the window. It could still be disease that killed them off, like what's been happening on Earth. Though I doubt the people of Canaan did it to themselves, not like we did, and the initial explorations of the planet showed no incompatible biology. Not that anyone could convince Jill of that. She's been sanitizing twice a day since we landed. Or maybe the answer is simpler, and they didn't have enough children. Maybe they just died out. Like we are.

I think how it would feel to be the last one. The only soul left in a rotting city. The final member of my race on an alien world. The thought makes me cold inside. But there's something else here, too. Something wrong, and not just with the signal and the scans. It's a wrongness I can feel deep in my gut. If I hadn't been raised by scientists, I'd say this city was haunted. Which is stupid.

I don't want to know what happened here. I need to know, like I need food and water and occasional sleep.

"Hey," Jill says. "Remember me?" I look down and find Jill, a huge smile on her face, running her arms around my waist. She seems to have been trying to get my attention. "I was asking what kind of housing you think they'll give us."

"What?"

"Our housing!"

Not only have I never given this one thought, I'm a little thrown by her use of "us" and "our." She means the whole team, right? Where will they put the housing complex for the team? Not a house for . . . us. Jill smacks my chest.

"I'm talking about Earth, Beck! When we get back! Don't you get it? We found it first. You and me. The lost colony! The investors are going to give us anything we want. Los Angeles, New Canada, we could go anywhere!" She gives my chest another whack. "Our careers are made!"

I smile, because I don't know what else to do, and I can see from Jill's face that my expression is a little weak. "Let's get a quick look at what we can before we go," I say, turning a circle, like I'm taking in the view. Jill drops her arms. "We need to get back into communication, let them know what we've found. Your mom is probably telling off half the ship by now."

"She'll forget to be mad once she hears about the city." Jill's eyes go big and bright. "Our names will be in the history files!"

She kisses me once on the cheek, goes bouncing off to the next ruined house to check for pottery. She really is pretty, and I don't know what she thinks she's talking about. The investors aren't going to be giving us anything. Not unless they put it on a ship. There's years of work to be done just within the radius of my vision. A lifetime of it. Digging, interpreting, documenting. Solving the mysteries. That will be our life. My life. Here. Not on Earth.

I wonder if it will be enough. I think it will. But I'm not sure Jill is exactly in agreement with that. But she is right about one thing. Bringing the team this news is going to be fun, and might even smooth over a sin or two, like moving forward without supervision. Even the I've-never-smiled-and-never-could-have-been-a-child Admiral Commander Juniper Faye ought to be pleased, and she's about as scary as they come.

No. Joanna Cho-Rodriguez is as scary as they come, and nothing is ever going to shut Mom up about moving forward on a scouting mission without supervision. This also makes me cold inside.

I start taking detailed mental notes, imagining the questions Dad will ask, so I can tell everything to the—and then I stop. Like I've been smacked again. Which I deserve to be. No one should have let me off Earth, much less the *Centauri III*. I stare at the control board in the corner of the lenses, watch as it brings up the functions list, and with the tiny, deliberate movement of my gaze, choose the settings that will enable visual documentation. I've never even used the visual recording function of the glasses. What I'm seeing is always being archived by signal at the base camp. But now, when we get back, I can do more than tell them. I can show them.

I get a wide, sweeping shot of the surroundings: Jill on the ground, staring at a bit of a broken pot, the row of ruined houses, back to the metal gates with the tree growing through one side, down at the white paving stones pushing up through the dirt. Then I start walking, over a small, shallow watercourse, still flowing in a formed aqueduct of stone, scanning the sides of the mountain of collapsed rubble.

If this was just one building, it was massive before it came down. The project had planned to build a Council Hall, for governing, and I wonder if . . .

I lift my head. Something changed in the quiet, something subtle, like an extra layer in the breeze. Jill is where I left her, oblivious, and the fullness of the silence comes back. It was probably only wind through stone, but we should go. Soon.

When I turn back to the rubble mound, the glasses focus on a huge chunk of white stone, jutting out from the pile four or five meters up, tree roots twined around it. I glance at the zoom icon and look closer. Flat, half-buried, and . . . Yes. There is writing.

I take off up the side of the rubble mountain, holding on to the trunks of trees, going from broken stone to broken stone, nearly falling before the glasses adjust back to normal vision. My chest is pounding. I don't know what I think the writing is going to say. But it has to be a clue. A piece of the puzzle. Something Canaan wants to tell me about the perfect white city built by humans in another galaxy.

"Beck!" Jill calls. "What are you doing?"

Climbing something I shouldn't be, obviously. I find a footing just below the carved writing, brushing away the dirt and leaves and clinging plants, digging out the words letter by letter. The carving is clear, the words in English, and I am reading a sign that hasn't been seen since the last colonist died in Canaan.

"Remember Our Truth."

I feel a smile break slow from my face. I don't know the truth of Canaan yet. But I'm really, really sure I want to remember it.

My head comes up. There's a noise again, but different this time, soft on the wind, like a cry. And now that I am up high, closer to the canopy, I can see that the whole city is actually sloping downward, the treetops becoming more and more visible the farther I let the glasses zoom. In the distance, a flock of the little lace-winged insects are rising like a cloud from the treetops. Disturbed.

And then the stone under my foot shifts, loosens, rocking to one side. I look down, hear a rumble, Jillian's scream, and before I can move or even think, the whole world drops away from beneath my feet.

SAMARA

I put a hand on the hot white walls of the Cursed City, and the relief is like the first deep breath after a long swim. Like leaving a bad memory. I don't even bother to look over my shoulder. There's only a day of light left, and the Council won't dare enter a city that could make them Forget. They can't stop me. No one can.

I hoist my pack and climb, fast, and I wonder if I'm already Forgetting, because I hardly notice my aches and pains or the fact that I'm tired. The suncrickets have seen me, though, chanting *chick, chick* while I shinny up a low, thick vine, louder and louder, dustmoths rising as I step onto a tree limb, up the trunk, and plant my sandals on top of the white stone wall.

But I don't see a city. Not even a ruined one. I see a lake, like the Darkwater, where we boat beneath the mountain, only this water glimmers with the sunlight. Trees grow thick along a faraway shore, roots twisting down into the water. Where I stand, the lake laps the wall stones. No buildings, no streets. Just a wilderness inside walls.

I don't Know what I was expecting, but it wasn't this. If there's no city, then maybe there's no Forgetting, either. Maybe I've come here for nothing. And the rage inside me flares. Blazes. I am so angry. That Adam is dead. That Nita is dead. That I can't fix it. That I'm standing here, in the middle of nowhere, alone with memories I will never, ever escape in a world I cannot change. And so I shout. With everything I've got. Like the Knowing are never allowed. One word that sums up my life.

"Why?"

The word comes back to me like another question, bouncing over water and trees and stone. I decide I like yelling, and am thinking about doing it again, but when the last echo of my word comes back to me, it carries something else. A distant, desperate, and very human scream.

I jump, startled, eyes darting over the lake and trees. But there's nothing to see. The sound fades, the breeze blows, dustmoths settle, and the suncrickets take up their song. Like the scream never existed. But it did. My pulse races.

I drop my pack off my shoulder, pull out my book, and unwind the scarf Nita used to bind my hair. Holding my balance on top of the wall, I work the scarf through the book's inner stitching, tying the ends together to make a loop that hangs over one shoulder, resting at my hip. This book is the truth. Everything I would need to understand about Samara Archiva. In case I Forget.

And then I turn, and start working my way along the top of the wall, using the spreading limbs for balance, all the way around the curve and to the shoreline of the water, thinking about that scream. How could there be people here? Maybe I'm not the first to survive jumping the cliffs. Maybe we're not the only ones on this planet. Maybe these people can explain the Forgetting to me. Or maybe they've already Forgotten.

The limbs grow thick on both sides of the wall now, and I'm walking mostly on trees instead of stones, like traveling through a forest, only ten meters in the air. Branches snap, scratching at my face, leaves obscuring my vision. I've never seen anything like these trees, but what do I Know about things that grow in the sun? They're fat with buds. I think that means they bloom. This place might be beautiful when the light comes again. A good place for Forgetting. Or it could be that this isn't Canaan at all, and the Cursed City is only a story.

Maybe lies can be written, as well as remembered.

And then I see something white, far off and to my right, peeking through the foliage. Stone. The white wall of a building, and buildings are in cities. I take a deep breath, choose a branch, and climb down it, hanging for a moment before I drop to the ground, pack on my back and book bouncing against my thigh.

It's darker here beneath the buds and leaves. Hot and damp, almost misty. Even the mud squelching between my toes is warm. I'm sweating in an instant, and not just from the heat. I've been careful not to dwell on my isolation until now. Having memory can make a negative emotion reflect over and over, like a feeling caught between two mirrors. But here, in this place, it's impossible not to sense the solitude.

When I Forget, will I remember that I am alone?

Or am I not alone?

The wall I saw through the trees is an ancient building, stained and overgrown, a huge, white circle held up by columns carved with flowers and what I think are plants of the fields, living vines twisting down from the roof and around the carvings. A doorway yawns beyond them, and in the swath of light I can see a room I almost recognize. Broken stone benches, rotted cabinets, the sound and smell of water trickling. This is a bathhouse, like the ones beneath my city, built on a hot spring, which would explain the mist and the mud. And it is empty. So very empty.

Grandpapa Cyrus told me a story once, about how a piece of a person can go on living even after they've been burned. An invisible piece, floating unseen, doing either good deeds or bad, though usually bad, he'd said, because it was the bad ones that tended to not die properly. This was supposed to be a story from Earth, so I knew it wasn't true. But that scream, and this place, this feeling of people that were and now are not, makes me step back.

A branch cracks somewhere behind me, and I turn, startled, but there's nothing there. Just trees, thick with hanging buds and the thinnest veil of mist. I decide not to run, but I do hurry, thumbs under the straps of my pack, through a natural gap in the trees, sloping upward, deeper into what must have been Canaan. And then I realize I'm not following a natural gap. I'm on a road.

I pass more white stone, piles that might have been buildings once, and then the road narrows, the trees encroaching. I take another step, pushing aside the branches. But there's no ground beneath my feet. I scramble, gripping a handful of wood and leaves, only just keeping my balance. I let out a breath. I've nearly stepped off a cliff.

Or not a cliff. I've nearly stepped into a hole. Deep and maybe twenty meters across, semicircular, hidden by the foliage until you're nearly in it. The sides of the hole are terraced, like stair steps, or the tiniest of mountain fields, a waterfall running from the rim and into a channel, dividing the hole neatly in half. And at the bottom, where the ground flattens, straddling the flow of the stream, stands half a stone tower. A spike snapped off in a pile of rubble. The land falls away beyond the tower, and when I look back the way I've come I can see the tops of trees, the blank space that is the lake, the hazy air beyond the wall. What was this place? Whatever it was, it's just as abandoned as the rest of the Cursed City.

But there is something lying at the base of the tower. Something different, long and flat among the pieces of jagged stone. I climb down the terraced steps, careful in case they should break, but the closer I get, the faster I go. There's carving. Words. I take the water channel in a leap, scale the fallen rubble. It's a sign, like the ones that hang in my city. Broken, and with letters that remind me of the ancient map. But I can still piece together the meaning.

"I Am Made of My Memories."

And these words, I think, are truer than any that hang in New Canaan. I am made of my memories. And I am made less by them. I wonder why the Council can't see that. Why they wouldn't want to stop living this way just as much as anyone else. I look up at the clear violet sky, thinking of those black specks, and the dust cloud across the plain. That hazy sky beyond the wall.

The hazy sky. My pulse jumps, skitters in my veins.

I climb the broken tower. Quick. The white stone was laid like an open net, with holds for my hands and feet, and soon I'm above the level of the trees, slowing as I near the top, in case the structure is weaker where it's fallen. But I don't need to go farther. The breeze is blowing, tangling my loose hair, the water falling behind me, my book hanging at my side, and in the distance, beyond the wall, is the swirl of thousands upon thousands of lacy wings. Dustmoths. Disturbed. Rising from the mountain pass between the hills. The same pass that brought me here.

The Council isn't going to stop for sunsetting, and I don't think they're stopping at the wall. They're coming into the Cursed City.

I think it must be very important to kill me.

8

BECKETT

When I open my eyes I'm lying on my side. It's hard to breathe, dark except for one shaft of light beaming down through a mist of dust. I can't think what's happened.

And then pain hits me like a wave of granite, straight up from my left leg to push the air from my lungs. For exactly two seconds, the shock is bigger than the agony. The third second I'm yelling, whether I want to or not. The noise echoes, sudden and wrong in the silent space, and a dark spot appears in the hole letting in the shaft of light, way above my head. It's the hole I've fallen through.

"Beck!"

The dark spot is Jill's head.

"Beck, are you all right?"

I thought the tortured shouting might have clued her in to the fact that I am not, in any way, all right. I try to sit up, but only make it as far as an elbow. The slightest jiggling of my left leg makes me sick with pain, and when I look down I'm even sicker. My foot is not at an angle it should be. I let out a stream of cussing that makes me glad we're out of communication.

"So . . . not dead," Jill observes.

"I think . . . my ankle's broken," I reply between the foulness. "Maybe . . . my leg."

Now it's Jill's turn to cuss, and she's much better at it than I am. Always has been. I lay my head back carefully where it was, panting while she abuses me from on high. We've had medical training, of course, and mending a broken bone is not much of a problem, but this . . . The bone needs to be set, and even if we did know how to do that right, the medical kit is in Jill's pack.

We weren't supposed to be separated. We weren't supposed to be in a position to need a medical kit. We've been in quite a few positions we were never supposed to be in on this trip. But planning for the scenario of being alone and hurt and out of communication, that would have seemed like planning for this planet's sun to rise and set every single day. And it most definitely doesn't. Jill's voice comes again, down through the hole.

"Can you get to the rappelling gear?"

My pack is still on my back, and twisting or reaching around to get it is going to hurt. A lot. It hurts a lot when I don't move. My fingers curl into a thick layer of soft dirt, dirt that must have been sifting in through the cracks of this room for season after season, which is probably what kept me from breaking more than I did. I bet there's a stone floor underneath here, maybe decorated. I wonder what kind of mortar they used. And then my leg hurts and my brain recharges and starts running at full speed again. That rubble is not only too unstable to rappel from, it's too unstable to be standing on.

"Jill," I shout, "get off that pile of rocks!" The dark spot that is Jill's head doesn't move. "Get off before you come down here the hard way, okay?" Or before she starts the rockfall that kills me. "See if you can find another way in. There has to be an entrance."

Jill hesitates, then her head disappears from the opening.

A coughing fit from the dust leaves me no choice but to yell again, and when I'm done my face is running with sweat. I drag an arm across my forehead, and the sleeve comes back red. Fantastic. This is all just fantastic. And what was that I saw, right before I fell, for just a second, when the lenses were zoomed as far as they could go? It almost seemed like a tiny figure, standing on the wall, but that can't be right. The zoom hadn't had time to focus. The eeriness of the place is making me paranoid.

I check the glasses. They're still on my face and working, which is some kind of miracle. I fish around and find the earpiece, stick it back in my ear, but there's no static, no connection to the base camp. I didn't think there would be.

I make myself sit up, grunting while I grit my teeth, and when I'm propped on my hands I look at the analytical menu in the lenses, choosing and adjusting the settings, then stare at my dangling foot. An image comes into focus, a picture of the bones of my lower leg. The ankle is dislocated—I think I'm lucky the tibia didn't come right through the skin—and there's a crack in my fibula, and when I look close, two smaller fractures in my foot.

I turn off the image, wishing I could turn off the pain just as easy. We have to get back into communication. I think of Dad's field set, a piece of ultra low-tech gear he rigged up himself to use on sensitive sites, so his communications couldn't be hacked. Mom thought it was weird, but we used to play with it all the time on the ship. I bet I could get a message out on that. If I'd brought it. Of course, if I'd brought it, the thing would probably be in a thousand pieces right now, like everything else in my pack. I breathe deep and slow, fighting for calm. Then I switch the lenses to the night function, looking through the darkness, beyond the beam of light and scatter of debris I'm sitting in.

The room is circular, like the city, the outer wall studded with decorated half columns, an inner ring of columns I can only hope are still strong, supporting a ceiling with a beautifully curved dome that has a brand-new hole in it. There are no windows, but shelves run along the back wall, empty and broken, and straight ahead is a partially open door, whether just propped up or still on its hinges I can't tell. It looks like there's another room beyond it, a big one, also interior, no windows. Except for the door, and a lack of bodies, and shelves too small for dead people, the place reminds me of a tomb. I don't like that thought.

I lean my head back as far as I can without disturbing my leg, looking upside down and behind me, and then I see the words. Bigger than the ones outside, much bigger, still in place and taking up the entire curving back wall. The glasses show me the letters in shades of green and gray.

"Without Memories, They Are Nothing."

I wait for Jill, pain like a parasite I can't pull out, thinking about those words, and the sense of wrong they give me. Like the whole city. What happened to these people?

I should probably be wondering what's going to happen to me.

9

SAMARA

I run up the terraced steps, deeper into the Cursed City. If the Council is moving as fast as I was, they'll reach the walls in about one and one-third of a bell. I'm going to have to hide, elude them in the tangle of buildings and trees until they give up and go home. Until the dark days come. Or until we all Forget who we are.

I don't Know if I'm going to live through this.

Tumbled buildings line either side of what is recognizably a street now, a broad lane, water still running in a leaf-and-stone-choked channel down the center. I move quick and silent, careful not to disturb the dustmoths. The trees are old here, with branches thicker than my waist, smaller, budding offshoots springing up everywhere to crumble the house stones. And the feeling comes again, of people gone away, and I realize that the quiet is wrong. Not the busy kind of silence, with wind and rustling leaves. This is an absence of sound. All the small creatures holding still.

I come fast around a corner, eyeing a dilapidated house, wondering if it or a tree would conceal me better, and then I stop so abruptly I nearly make myself fall. There is a person. About fifteen meters away, pulling down rocks from a mountainous pile of tree-clad rubble. And even though a human being is exactly what I jumped down from the wall hoping to find, the sight of this one is so shocking I just stand there, staring.

The figure is small, slight, and with the oddest color hair, bright yellow, almost silver, so short it sticks out. I've only seen hair that short on a baby. And this person is scrabbling, pulling down rocks, digging frantically with their fingers, trying to tunnel their way inside a rubble pile. Which seems insane.

A small slide of stones comes down, shaking me to my senses, and I dart behind a partial wall, peering through a hole that might have been a window. Broken pot crunches beneath my sandals, one shard snapping with a crack that shoots through the open space. I duck into the safety of the wall shadow as the person turns sharply, looking around in a quick arc.

It's a girl. Her clothes are plain and shapeless, and she has a pack at her feet, not that different from mine. But her skin is so pale, paler even than Nita's, and she looks . . . scared, unsure as she searches for the source of the noise. She doesn't know this place. No more than I do. Then where does she come from?

I watch her work, pulling out chunks of stone, and then I see that she's uncovered an opening, that she's squeezing through it, yelling words I have difficulty understanding as she goes. But I catch enough to Know that she's looking for something. Or someone. Someone she can't find.

And then the beat inside my chest picks up again. This girl doesn't know where she is, because this girl has Forgotten. I slip out of the ruined building and follow her.

10

BECKETT

It seems like forever, but I know it hasn't really been that long before I see Jill through the night function of the glasses, dusty and with her face pinched, peering through the darkness beyond the half-open door. She pushes on it, just a little, and the door goes crashing to the floor with a puff of dust. I wince. We've been drilled most of our lives on how to observe, not disturb, historic sites. Yet somehow we're managing to destroy this place piece by piece.

"I'm sorry," Jill whispers, kneeling at my side.

I don't know whether she means the door or me. She ought to mean the door, because my condition right now is 100 percent my own fault, not hers. I can see her not looking at the angle of my foot.

"Where else are you hurt?" she asks.

I shake my head. I can't even tell. There's no room in my mind for other kinds of pain, and it's taking everything I've got not to yell. What she needs to do is get the medical kit out. Now.

Jill drops her pack to the ground, digging through the contents like she heard my thoughts. She comes up with an infuser in her hand.

"Tell me where to do it."

The pain has centralized to a single torture in my ankle. Wherever she shoots, she needs to block all my nerve endings in one go.

We've only got four infusers with us, and I'm going to have to get out of here. "Exactly where it looks broken," I tell her, "and a little below."

Jill sets the infuser back in the kit, moves down to my foot, and gingerly begins the process of unfastening my boot. She tries to take it off, and the shout I've been holding back echoes in the hollow places of the room.

"I'm sorry! I'm so sorry!" Jill says.

I'm unreasonably angry at her. Not because she hurt me, but because now she's crying about it. "Can you get to the broken place without taking the whole thing off?"

She bites her lip, nods, and then the cool metal tip of the infuser is sitting just below the bulge of bone that should not be in the area of my ankle. I hear a whoosh, feel tiny stings as the air pushes the medicine deep through my skin. Numbness begins to creep down one side of my foot, spreading to my toes, then to the other side and up my leg. Bliss. I lay my head back on one arm, sighing with relief. Jill is still wiping her eyes.

"I'm going for help," she begins. "We need the—"

"No." I lift my head and see that Jill is beginning to frown through her tears. The "danger" expression. I ease my tone. "The first rule is to not split up."

"The first rule is to not move forward unsupervised, Beck! And you were the one not so worried about that."

I can't really deny it.

"I don't have to get all the way back to base camp," she says. "Give me the glasses and I'll go back through the canyon and up the mountain until I find communication. They can come on the air bikes, since there's no one here. Fly you . . ."

Jill's voice trails away at my shaking head, the frown deepening between her brows. "And why not?" she asks.

"The glasses are set to my DNA. They won't work for you."

This would have been such an easy fix if we were in communication with base camp, just switch the security to Jill, whose DNA is already in the system. It was stupid not to have set the glasses to both of us before we started out, but our protocol was so careful. Locals should never experience unfamiliar technology. If someone else put the glasses on right now, they'd just be clear lenses.

But who could have imagined having no signal? And me, the wearer of the glasses, incapacitated in a room inside a mound of rubble that any son of Sean Rodriguez could only characterize as a ritual site? And who could have imagined a city at all, sitting right here, where our scans showed an empty valley? The feeling of wrong hits me again, full force. I don't want Jill out of my sight. We have to get out of this together. But she's not going to like it.

Jill has her knees pulled up to her chest, staring at the ceiling and the shaft of light. I tread gently. "Jill, I need you to set my ankle."

I read the injury first-aid information from the database inside the glasses while she was gone. Not nearly as detailed as what I could have gotten if we were connected to base camp and the *Centauri III*. But it should be enough. Maybe. Jill is staring at me like I grew another head.

"I can't do that," she whispers.

"Yes, you can. I'm going to read the instructions to you."

She shakes her head. "You need Dr. Lanik . . ."

"I don't have Dr. Lanik. I've got you. And we should do it now, before it swells any more, and while the infusion is working." I really want it to happen while this infusion is working. I might need the other three to get back up that mountain.

Jill is still shaking her head. She wipes her eyes and stands, coming around to look down on my face. Her frown is a deep, straight line between her eyes. I know I'm in trouble.

"You're not fit to call this one, Beckett. I'm going to hike back to base camp."

"I don't think we—"

"I don't care what you think! You're not having your way, not this time."

"Listen to—"

"You listen! I'm not going to set your ankle because I don't know what I'm doing. I'll ruin it! And there's no reason not to wait for the air bikes and Dr. Lanik. So you're going to lie right there like a good—"

"No!"

The word came out harsh, stopping Jill in her tracks. I hadn't meant to sound like that.

"Look, I really don't think we should split up. There's something . . . wrong about this place . . ." I stare into the empty room and its shadowy columns, trying to think how to explain the feeling without sounding like I'm eight years old. Jillian's hands go to her hips.

"What do you mean 'wrong'? Just because the scans weren't calibrated? There's no one here. You're safer where you are than—"

"Jill, the scans don't need adjusting; they were dead wrong. We don't know anything about where we are! And we . . ." And then I stare harder through the darkness, let the night function pierce the shadows.

"Jill," I whisper. I sit up and grab her hand, pulling her down to my side.

"What—"

"Shut up."

"Oh, fine . . ." She is so good at cussing, but I don't have time to admire it.

"Quiet! And don't move."

She jerks her hand away. "What is wrong with you?"

"Something moved," I whisper. "In the other room."

11

SAMARA

Why can I never do what's good for me and just not look? Why can't I turn around and walk the other way? The yell that came ripping through the darkness a few moments ago—deep, male, and full of pain—has my memories churning. I'm afraid of what's out there, moving toward me in the ruined streets of this city. And now I'm afraid of what might be happening inside this bizarre hidden place. I found my way through two inner chambers, all dark, windowless, and now this third room is vast, empty, full of a wood dust I can smell, something, someone, waiting at the end of it. And yet here go my feet, moving me through air that is like spilled ink, taking me straight to a fading in the blackness and an open doorway. I put an eye around the edge.

There are two of them, bickering in an accent that is unusually clipped, the girl with the odd hair, and a boy, a young man, lying on the floor in a beam of murky light. He wears the same baggy clothes as the girl, but his hair is black instead of yellow, not nearly as short as hers, the ends curling into his jaw and neck, and where he isn't dirty his skin is a sunshine brown, like the harvest workers Outside. And I can't stop looking at him. Because I've seen him before.

I never dream. The images that come to me during sleep are reality. Memory. Knowing doesn't leave room for imagination. But I can remember dreaming, when I was small, before my memories came, hazy, fractured thoughts that reflected what was familiar to me as a baby. And there was one dream, of being swaddled tight in my mother's arms, of lights so bright they hurt my eyes. And there was a young man, standing far away from us, his clothes a little like what I see now, only dark blue, his hair shorter. He was talking to everyone at once, though the words were muffled, as if I had the blanket wrapped around my ears. And then my mother put her hand on my head, palm covering my skull, bent down close to my cheek and whispered, "You are dreaming."

But I Know it was his face I saw. The face that is turned to the girl right now. He's wearing something that reminds me of the magnifiers Uncle Towlend used for doing delicate work on parchment, though these are thinner, lighter. Different. He's also dusty and bloody, hurt, his foot not where it should be.

The pages of my mind turn instantly to the drawings of "dislocations, legs and ankles" shown to us in the eighteenth recitation of physician training. It must have been his yell I heard earlier. The pain associated with such injuries was described as severe. And while I'm trying to decide if his tibia is actually broken, the boy raises his voice and says, "We don't know anything about where we are!"

I feel a relief almost as intense as when I put my hand on the wall stones of the city. They've Forgotten. They must have come from Outside, escaped the supervisors and the ring of mountains like I did. How often does this sort of thing go on? I don't understand how his face could have been in my dreams, but I need these two. If they can't tell me how they Forgot, then I need to study them. And we all need to be hidden before the Council comes.

My feet move once, but then I stop. Stiffen. The boy's face has turned, and he's looking straight at me. I've grown up with darkness, and I Know he can't see me in the deep shadows around this doorway, not while he's in the light. But the way he's staring, intense, unwavering, makes me think he can. The girl kneels beside him now, arguing, then slowly turns her head toward the door. Four beats of my heart go by before the boy raises his voice and says, "Hi."

I stay still. I think he's talking to me. The girl waits, wide-eyed, and I glance up once at the ceiling, at the hole letting in the light. What is he trying to tell me? That he fell? From up high? The girl whispers, but he ignores her. Just watches me, expectant. He must have incredible vision. Maybe he's asking for my help. I can see that he needs it. I take a step more fully into the doorway.

The girl gasps and spins around on her knees, stuffing some kind of box back into her pack. Like I might try to take it away from her. Her fear gives me confidence. I don't want them to be afraid. Or maybe they can't remember why they should be. The boy is calm, gazing at me through the magnifiers, so I talk to him.

"I am Samara Archiva, from Underneath. I'm not with the Council, but the Council is coming. Are you from Outside?"

I realize too late that they might not remember where they're from. Outsiders are not taught to read or write, so they couldn't have a book. The girl holds her pack behind her back, but the boy's dark brows come down, thinking. One side of his forehead is still bleeding from a shallow gash, but he's handling the pain from that ankle well. Impressively so. I can see that neither of them knows how to answer me. I take another step forward.

"Have you Forgotten?" I ask. The dark brows deepen, and the girl edges closer to him. I try again. "Do you know your name?"

This time his face eases. "Beckett Rodriguez," he says. It's a low voice. Resonant in the echoing chamber. I look at the girl. Her hand is on his shoulder now, squeezing.

"Do you remember your name?" I ask.

She startles like a dustmoth, but eventually says, "Jillian." It's barely a whisper.

I'm pleased. These aren't names. They've made them up. Because they've Forgotten. I have so many questions, but first I have to get them to hide. And before that, I think, they will have to trust me. I take another step toward Beckett.

"Could I examine your leg? I have physician training."

They both stare at me, and then the girl, Jillian, shakes her head no. But Beckett smiles. It's a friendly smile, a little guilty, somehow, like he got caught doing something he shouldn't. I see the same smile in my memory. But it's not an expression that goes with his injury. Can you Forget to feel pain? He doesn't move as I approach, but he doesn't take his eyes off me, either.

I set down my pack, get my loose hair out of the way, and kneel at his feet. He's wearing an odd, heavy sort of foot covering, sewn from a material I've never seen. I can't imagine how he's managed to make such a thing for himself, and when I move his legging up a little higher, the silver cloth is thin, yet curiously solid between my fingers. Maybe Forgetting actually spurs creativity, I think, when you have no memory of how a thing should be done. It's an interesting idea that I will leave to the arguments of the philosophers. I touch the ankle gently, bending down to look at it from all sides.

"*Luxatio pedis sub talo*," I mutter. "*Antero-lateral.*" They look at me like I've been babbling. "The ankle is dislocated . . . out of position," I explain. "Probably with some small fractures." And I don't like the color of it, as if the blood isn't flowing. "It will heal if I set it, but that should be done soon. An artery may be restricted, and the ankle is swelling. Will you let me set it?"

I can tell the last part of this has gotten through, because I see them exchange a look, Beckett's clearly saying, *I told you so.* This doesn't seem like a reasonable reaction, either. Maybe he doesn't understand what setting a bone means.

"It will be painful," I say, "but will hurt much less when I'm done. Will you let me?"

The girl, Jillian, asks, "Are you a doctor?"

I stare at her. How could that word be in her head? I've only ever seen that term in disintegrating manuscripts in the Archives.

She looks back at Beckett and shakes her head again, hard, but he just says, "Go ahead." When I hesitate, he says, "Yes."

I get to work. It's difficult to take the sandal, or whatever it is, off his foot, and I Know I must be hurting him. Or at least I should be. But this familiar, bloodied, Forgetting young man of abandoned Canaan tolerates pain better than I've ever seen. And he's strong. I can feel the calf muscle beneath my fingers. He's definitely been in the fields. Or maybe at a furnace. Though the magnifiers speak to something smaller, like fine metalwork. It doesn't make sense.

When I drag a piece of fallen rubble to put beneath Beckett's leg, the girl gets the idea and helps me move it, positioning it beneath his calf while I hold the dangling foot. Her eyes are large and very blue, and I have to take a moment to cache, to banish Nita's memory back to the high, dark shelf.

When I open my eyes, Beckett is still watching me. I wish I'd brought a sleeping draught for him, so he wouldn't have to remember this, but his face is steady, his concentration on me intense. Maybe he hasn't Forgotten physical pain. Maybe he can cache it. That would be an amazing skill. But probably not good enough for what's coming next, and we have very little time. The Council could be here in less than a bell.

I turn to Jillian.

"You should sit on him."

Her face is blank.

"He'll move . . ." I try to think how to explain simply. "It will hurt too much for him to be still. Sit on his chest, and hold his other leg, like this . . ."

She does what I tell her, straddling Beckett's chest, leaning forward to wrap her arms around his other leg, to keep it in place, her only words a whispered, "Shut up, Beckett," which makes no sense. I plant my feet, get a strong hold on Beckett's heel and the top of his foot.

I Know how to set an ankle. But Knowing can be different from doing. The Outside taught me that. And the rope on the clifftop. I reexamine the recitation in my mind, go over the details, then meet Beckett's dark gaze through the magnifiers, watching me from over Jillian's shoulder. There's something a little different from my dream, I think now, something about the eyes. But his expression is straight out of my memories.

"I will begin," I tell him.

12

BECKETT

She cannot be real. Tall and lean, with a mass of curling dark hair hanging in loose coils down her back. And the eyes . . . the lightest brown, a shade or two lighter than her skin, glowing, so that they look . . . amber, maybe. Her clothes are dirty, embroidered with tiny blue and green stitches, handmade from the cloth to the thread, like the sandals. Like the book she's wearing tied across her chest.

This girl has walked straight out of a history file on the early civilizations of . . . Where? The Southern American continent? Pretech Asia? But Samara is not from Earth. Not really. She is of Canaan, and I don't know what she's talking about half the time. But when she came out with what I think are ancient Latin medical terms and "physician," a word I've only seen in manuscripts, all I could think is how both my parents might break an ankle to put themselves in my position right now.

Samara has my foot, ready to set the bone, Jill on my chest, bracing me more effectively than I would've thought. She's been incredibly gentle, this girl, and she looks like she knows what she's doing. I hope she does, because either way, I'm about to let her do it.

"I will begin," she says.

She's speaking English, but with the occasional unfamiliar word and an odd cadence, a lilt that goes unexpected places, so that sometimes

I'm slow to catch the meaning. It's pretty, though, fascinating, and then the girl wrenches my leg like she's wringing the neck of a turkey. It doesn't hurt, exactly, but it's uncomfortable enough to make me flinch, and I thank every deity of every civilization I've ever studied that Jillian got that infusion in me. She's making it hard to breathe, squeezing me with her legs she's so tense, her head turned and eyes screwed shut. Samara frowns, gives my leg another killing twist, harder, this time with an audible pop. I feel my leg and foot go back together. Which is weird, and a little disgusting.

"That is done," Samara says. She seems relieved, but she's got her head to one side, looking at me with those amber eyes. I realize way too late that I should have been in excruciating pain, and that I have no way of explaining why I wasn't. Why I'm not. Jill lets go of my other leg, scrambles off my chest.

"Are you okay?"

I hadn't realized until this second how scared she is. I smile at her, and watch Samara watch me do it. She lowers her gaze and goes back to examining my foot, I think feeling for a pulse. Where did this girl come from? Are there parts of the city still inhabited? The way she looks around this room . . . I don't think she's ever been here before.

I have a million questions, and I can't think of one way of asking any of them that doesn't show the truth. That I don't belong here. That Jill doesn't belong here. That we are from somewhere else. How was initial contact supposed to work? The gist of Mom and Dad's training was to not overwhelm with knowledge or the unfamiliar, to not show surprise or judgment at pretech cultural norms. Making allowances for a civilization that is less developed. Now that I'm here, all that sounds like a kind of talking down. Assuming that their society would want to be like ours if it could. Samara may not understand technology or the culture of Earth, but she doesn't seem stupid, and we are going to ruin this, Jill and I. Cause irreparable damage, change the course of a world, just because we—correction, *I*—can't follow protocol and turn back when I'm supposed to. Samara looks up.

"There has likely been a fracture as well. Talus, or malleous."

It's both, I think.

"You will have to immobilize the leg until it heals."

Then Jillian says, "Who trained you? As a . . . physician?"

I shoot Jill a look of respect. She asked a leading question, gave nothing away, and used the terminology. But Samara doesn't answer, only stands. She seems agitated. Nervous.

"Do you understand that you are in danger?" she asks. When we don't answer, because we don't know what to say, she goes on. "The Council is coming. They will be here soon, perhaps half a bell, and . . . Beckett," she stumbles over my name, "will not be able to move well. Perhaps not until sunrising."

I'll be moving twenty minutes after Jill gets the medical kit back out, but Samara has no way of knowing that. I say, "Why is the Council coming?"

For some reason, this stops her dead. "Do you remember the Council?"

I don't. At all. She looks relieved at my expression, though I don't understand why. She sits on a fallen stone next to us, her hair a cascade, eyes rimmed with dark lash, and now that she's closer, I see that one side of her face shows a faint, almost faded bruise.

"Let me explain," she says. "You are from the outside."

I feel my stomach sink, see Jill's eyes go round. She knows already. She knows we're from Earth. And I think that was supposed to be phase nine or ten of contact. She goes on.

"You are out of bounds. The Council will kill you for that."

Out of bounds, I think. Could that mean beyond a boundary? Out of the atmosphere? Or beyond the wall? But we're inside the wall. Jill isn't concerned with an ancient turn of phrase.

She says, "What do you mean, they'll kill us?" Samara looks at her like she's an idiot.

"I mean they will end your life, because you have forgotten."

"Wait. What?" Jill looks to me for help. I'm watching Samara. She has her elbows balanced on her knees, which are also showing bruising, and when she holds out her hands, I see that they are newly healed, a little pink, as if her palms recently lost most of their skin. Culture files move past my memory: self-mutilation, torture, the labs of the Fourth and Fifth World Wars. Something has happened to this girl. But I can't decide if she knows we're from Earth or not. So I gamble.

"Are you from the outside?"

Samara frowns. "I said to you before, I am from Underneath. From the city." She tries again when we don't seem to get it. "From the city of New Canaan."

Jill's hand tightens in mine, and then my brain is racing. There is another city on this planet. New Canaan. They didn't die out, they just packed up and moved. But why? And why are the *Centauri*'s scans turning out to be so incredibly, amazingly worthless?

I've been trying to watch Samara's face. Both my parents trained in the psychology of expression and body movements, the silent language that can tell you so much about another person without having to ask. And now I'm drawing my own conclusions. Samara is a facade, like this building, hard on the outside, mysterious inside, with only the occasional glimpse showing through the cracks. Like right now. Sadness. I gamble again.

"Are you out of bounds?" I ask. "Are they going to kill you, too?"

She looks at me funny, her head cocked to one side again, and then the amber eyes fall closed. And Samara just . . . goes away. The facade comes down in a landslide, and I see raw emotion moving across her face. Uncertainty, fear, and is that anguish?

I don't know what's happening. I don't know what Jill and I have walked into. I don't know if we can walk out again. But I do know that the decades of studying tool marks on a rock or the break patterns of a piece of pottery are never going to be enough for me now, not when the solution to every mystery is sitting right here at my feet. Samara has a head stuffed full of answers, and my need to know those answers might very well take priority over my personal safety. Which is completely unfair to Jill.

I think these things in a few blinks of an eye, and then Samara's snap open. She's with us again, her breath coming fast. She looks to Jill.

"They will be inside the walls soon. We need to hurry. I'll help you hide him, and when the Council is gone, in return, I ask that you tell me everything you know about forgetting."

Jill doesn't respond until I nudge her, and then she says, "Okay."

Samara almost smiles.

"I'll go for water and something to brace his leg. We should move him into the next room, where we cannot be seen if they climb the mound. And then you must help me block up the door."

"How long will they look for us?" I ask.

Samara shakes her head as she stands, picks up her pack. "I will hurry." And then she's halfway to the door, moving like she's melting into the dark.

Jill waits, watching me watch Samara through the glasses. I see her in grays and greens, sprinting through the vast, dark room that is beyond the doorway like she can see it. As soon as she's out the other side, I say, "Gone."

Jill immediately relaxes her stance, then jumps to her feet and starts her expert cussing.

"You know I've got the recording function on," I tell her. It doesn't improve her mood.

"I don't believe you, Beckett, I really don't! She is pretech! A local!" She says it like it's something to be ashamed of.

I get up on my elbows, carefully lift my leg to the floor while she rants. That infusion is starting to wear off a little. Jill doesn't even slow down.

"You know this changes everything. And someone is coming to kill us in 'half a bell,' whatever that means. And what is she talking about, 'forgetting,' and asking if we remember our names? Who wouldn't remember their own name . . ."

I think about the wall behind me, and the carved sign that brought me up the pile of rubble in the first place. "Remember Our Truth" and "Without Memories, They Are Nothing." I have to know what happened here.

"And why would someone want to kill us, anyway?" Jill goes on. She's not slowing down for breath, making the domed room echo. "I mean, I know why I want to kill you, but—"

"Jillian," I say. "Shut up." Her mouth closes, her eyes wide. Then they narrow. "Listen, you can yell at me later. You can call me every name you can think of and scream for a week straight. But right now we need to talk about getting my bones mended before she gets back."

Jill just looks at me, then snatches up her pack. "Fine." She's already pulling out the medical kit. And the sanitizer. "But as soon as you can stand, we're out. Agreed?"

I don't answer. Because I'm not sure I agree with that at all.

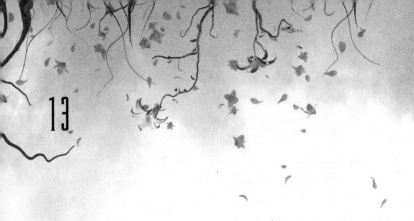

13

SAMARA

I search through the street outside the mound of rubble, scanning the ground for broken branches to make Beckett a splint. And all the while I'm listening, for a rustle, a shout, a change in the wind, I'm not even sure what. My own heartbeat thuds in my ears. Those two are going to show me how to Forget, or the Council is going to end this, and I'm not sure which will happen first.

And what if the Council had come before Samara Archiva? What would the Outsiders have done then? I'm not as naive as I used to be. Nita told me what happened to Sonia's boy from the Outside, the one she couldn't leave alone after the Changing of the Seasons. Craddock made an example of him. At the post in the Bartering Square, and he did not live. It makes me sick to think of it. I never told Sonia. I wasn't sure how good she was at caching guilt. As things turned out, maybe not good at all. Or maybe that boy was more than an addiction. Or maybe she just feared Judgment.

But the two inside the rubble mound seem to have Forgotten danger completely. They are strange, like children. I never thought the Forgetting would make me like a child. I'm not sure I want that. But then again, children are innocent. And they can grow up again. Right now, I need for them to trust me. To help me. I need for all of us to live through this. And then I will take the Forgetting to the Underneath, destroy the Council, and let the Outside rebel. Heal everyone else. For Nita. And Adam.

If only Sonia could have waited a little longer.

And then a shadow flits across the sun. Not a person, or any other creature. The shadow of something large. Silent. High in the air.

I leap to my feet, spinning, eyes to the sky. But there's nothing. Nothing at all. Just the empty violet beyond the treetops, now beginning to show a few telling stripes of pink. The sun is setting. And yet, I can hear that wrong kind of quiet again, the waiting stillness. I wait with it, holding my breath, and when I look back the way I came, dustmoths are rising in a line, from one end of my sight to the other. Moving toward me.

I grab my pack and Beckett's splints and run. A careful run. Silent, no brushing of the branches. When I reach the mound I throw my things inside and start to do the same with pieces of rubble, placing them in the doorway without noise, so I can barricade the opening from the inside. I don't have time. But if I don't get this blocked up, we're going to be found, and we're going to die.

Someone shouts, not in the distance, but in the mound, noise reverberating through the empty interior. Beckett. So now he yells. Now, when the Council is here. When he's going to bring them straight to us. I hesitate, glance at the stones that need to be stacked, then start the same careful, silent run through the darkness of the interior rooms. Beckett needs to breathe, cache, bite something, whatever it takes to stay quiet and give us time to block the door.

I hit the dark inner chamber at a full sprint, but then I slow my steps. There's a glow coming through the broken doorway. Light like I've never seen. Green. Bright. So bright it's startling. Unnatural. Wrong. My feet stop, well inside the darkness. On the other side of the open doorway, Jillian and Beckett are talking, still with the short, clipped words, but very differently from before.

"Fibula, Jill, toward the heel."

"Is it a revelation to you, Beckett, that I can't see your fibula?"

"That should be the angle, right there."

"Are you sure?"

"Yes."

"Please let me do the infusion first. I don't want to miss again."

"No time! Just do it."

I get an eye around the edge of the doorway, but Beckett doesn't see me. He's sitting up, concentrating through the magnifiers on his injured leg. Jillian is on her knees, looking at his injury, too, but with something in her hand, a smooth, metal cylinder, shiny, and it's from one end of this that the unnatural greenness is coming. The other end she holds against Beckett's ankle, and whatever happens, he doesn't like it. I watch him wince and hiss.

"Don't move!" Jillian instructs him. Then, "How are we doing?"

"The crack is almost filled. Just a little . . . There." I hear his relief. "She did a good job setting it, didn't she? Okay, one more, a tiny one, hurry . . ."

I step back, disoriented. Their words, tone, and that odd light. It's all wrong. And Beckett talks as if he can see his own injury, which is impossible. Then Jillian says, "Are we still alone?"

I find the wall and press myself against it.

"I think so . . ."

"Scan and make sure."

"Right this second I'm looking at a cracked metatarsal. Go two centimeters left, no, my left. Angle about fifty degrees . . . Now." I hear him grunt. "You've got it."

"Okay. Ten minutes to set the gel, and we're out."

"Jill . . ."

"Ten minutes and we're out, Beckett."

"What about . . . what she said?"

"What, the locals coming to kill us?" Jillian's voice sounds a little hysterical. "I don't know, that seems like, oh, a really good reason to break contact and go!"

"And what about her?"

"You know the protocol."

"So your idea of protocol is that we leave her to die?"

"Beckett . . ." Jillian's voice pauses, drops. I have to lean forward to hear. "We can't interfere in her life, or her death. You know that. We're lucky to have gotten this far without completely messing up. And we took an oath, remember?"

His voice comes low beneath his breath. "Well, the oath looks a little different in Canaan than it did on Earth."

Jillian says something about how this is exactly where his oath isn't supposed to look different, going on about commanders and ships. I'm hearing, but I'm not listening. I'm sliding down the wall, sitting in the dust of the floor, paying attention to only one word inside my mind. Earth. Beckett said "Earth."

I go back in my memory, quick, frantic, and feel that cloth between my fingers, that shoe covering, hear the clipped speech. I see the confusion, hair the wrong color, the wrong lengths. That eerie green light. Could that be . . . technology? And that shadow in the sky. That's where Earth comes from. The sky. Where they swoop down and take us. Lie to us. Use their technology to enslave us.

I don't understand. But I think I do understand. What an inexplicable feeling it is, when your world breaks, turns upside down, and the pieces shake out all over the floor. It happened when Adam died, and when I found out about the Forgetting. When I killed Nita. I didn't think it could happen again.

But it has.

I remember all the things the Council said, made sure we were taught. Not myths. Not lies. Truth. They taught us truth. I can't believe it. But I do believe it. That's the incredible part. After what I've just heard and seen, I don't Know how not to. Earth is real. And just on the other side of this wall.

The reality slides through my head, like the pebble that starts a rockfall. If Earth is real, and the recitations of the learning room are true, then what are those two here to do to us? To my city? I see the blue sky and green land of the mural in the Forum, fading into the flat and ruined brown. My people, Outside and Underneath—they have to be warned. I shouldn't be running from the Council. I should be running straight to them. But would the Council even listen to me? Or would they just kill me on sight?

I put my head in my hands, fingers digging into my hair. Giving myself up to the Council, giving them power over me, when I was going to take their power from them—it makes me cringe. It makes me furious. And afraid. I was going to fix so many things. But the problems of Knowing, Forgetting, the injustice of the Outside, none of these things matter if we're dead. Taken. Our planet ruined.

And then I lift my head. I told them there was another city. A city underground. My breath stutters, stops, and I close my eyes in the darkness. The ruse begun 379 years ago was actually working. They were fooled. And I stripped the protection of my people with a sentence. Earth knows to look beneath the surface. They will find New Canaan. Soon.

I have to tell the Council what I Know. No matter what they do to me.

I Know what they're going to do to me.

I push myself to my feet, start back across the black and empty room. Jillian and Beckett are still arguing. There's a kind of haze coming down in my mind, clouding my thoughts, like the cold fog when I killed Nita, and when Jillian says, "Did you hear something?" I'm sure it was me.

But the words aren't significant. Nothing is.

I don't look back through the dark.

"We observe, we study, and we record, but we never influence, alter, or interfere with the emerging history of a developing culture."

I had to sign that today, swear it on my life's blood or something. But now I'm wondering. What if the culture we observe is actually smarter than we are? Maybe they should be the ones influencing us.

FROM THE LOG BOOK OF BECKETT RODRIGUEZ

Day 17, Year 1

The Lost Canaan Project

14

BECKETT

"Did you hear something?" Jill asks.

It takes a second to switch the glasses to the night function, but before I can even begin to pierce the gloom, text starts rolling across the lenses. "I've got a message."

"Do we have a signal?"

"No." I'm reading fast, summarizing. "No, they broke protocol and sent in a skimmer to find us. They got the position of the city, but not until the skimmer came back. They had to fly it in low to send the orders. There's no long-range communications, and . . . Wow. It looks like the scans have been . . . reflecting somehow. They're going to have to go back and relook at everything, the whole planet, to find the holes . . ."

"Are the air bikes coming?"

"No. They . . ." I hesitate. But it isn't right not to tell her. "They say ten humans are inside the walls, twelve including us. Our orders are to avoid interaction at all costs, but if interaction has already taken place, follow protocol to break it and get back into communication, beyond the mountain range." I stop reading, and look at Jill through the lenses. "They're coming for her. Like she said."

"So, nine of them?" says Jill. "And we have to get ourselves out? But they know where we are! Message back and tell them we're in danger, that we have a situation . . ."

"I can't. There's nothing within range. The skimmer must have come in and out."

She puts her hands on her head. "She changes the whole mission. You know that, right? Everything . . ." She looks around the room. "What do you think this place is? Ritual?"

I don't want to answer. Jill starts pacing.

"I mean, they can't really want to hurt us. Whatever this is about, we don't have anything to do with it . . ."

Samara thought different. And those bruises, her palms . . . I don't know what we're dealing with, but it's bad.

"What do you think they'll do to us?" Jill whispers.

"I don't know. Maybe nothing . . ." My words don't mean a thing. I can see her thinking occult practice and human sacrifice. Jill snatches up the medical kit and starts putting it away.

"Can you stand? Try out your leg. It should've been long enough."

"And then what?"

"What do you mean, 'and then what?' " she snaps. "We get ourselves out of this place and back to the base camp."

Hope is a frightening thing to feel. The pain of losing it is deep and forever.

FROM THE HIDDEN BOOK OF SAMARA ARCHIVA
IN THE CITY OF NEW CANAAN

15

SAMARA

I stand in the doorway of the rubble mound, beside the pile of rocks I'd meant to use to block the entrance. The cold in my mind is almost a comfort. It makes it easier to do what I have to. I lift my book over my head and leave it on the ground, piling rocks on top of it. I don't want the Council to have it. And then I step out, into the middle of an overgrown street in the Canaan my people abandoned, a city they left so they could hide from Earth.

The moth clouds are rising, a long, stretching line, advancing both before and behind me, and I think of the Council walking through the city like a fan, trying to flush me out, trap me in the middle. It won't be hard. They aren't afraid to walk these streets, because I think maybe they already Know how the Forgetting works. Or maybe there is no Forgetting.

If the stories of Earth are real, maybe everything I've thought was real is only a story.

I wander between the rows of ruined houses and think about how the Council will do it. Something quicker than bitterblack this time. A blow to the head. A knife. Or maybe they'll flog me until I die, like the Outside boy that Sonia liked so much. I wonder if they'll listen to me say one sentence, "Earth has come." Or if they won't, and I'll die for nothing. Like Nita died for nothing. Like Adam. I close my eyes, and I don't even try to resist the weight of my memory. I let myself sink, plunge, down . . .

. . . *and Adam is painting his eyes while I jump on his bed, my braids trailing up and down through the air. "Why do you have to go Outside?" I ask between bounces. "It isn't safe Outside. That's where Earth can get you."*

"There's no such thing as Earth, Sam. And who says I'm going Outside?"

"I do. Supervisors go Outside."

"Supervisor training won't start again until the sun rises, and that's not until tomorrow, so I'm not going Outside."

"You're going Outside because you're wearing your Outside sandals," I tell him.

He raises a brow at me in the mirror. "Why are you so smart?"

I roll my eyes, let myself land flat on my back on the thick, soft mattress. Like six-year-olds shouldn't be smart. Six-year-olds can be just as smart as seventeen-year-olds when you're Knowing. Or almost. I ask, "What does the sun feel like?"

"Hot. And bright. And the sky is so big and empty it's like you could fall off the ground and get lost in it."

"Then why are you going Outside if you could fall into the sky?" Suddenly I'm afraid that Adam won't come back.

Adam puts down the paintbrush and comes to the bedside. He's tall, like I will be, with the same brown skin, only his eyes are darker, his hair braids twisted into a long tail in the back. He holds out his arms and I leap into them, making him "umph" and then laugh. He hugs me, and his arms are so strong I Know nothing can happen to him.

He says, "Would you like to see the sun, Sam? Because the next waking is a special sunrise. A white sunrise, and I'm going to take you to see it."

"Open air?"

"Yes. Open air."

"But the gates will be locked, and Mother says I have to go to the party after Judgment. To celebrate being Knowing."

"There's nothing to celebrate after Judgment, Sam. That's not a party worth going to. So listen to me carefully. I want you to lock your door after Judgment, okay? For the whole resting while everyone is at the party. Don't let anybody in, no matter what you hear, and then I'm going to come and take you to see the white sunrise. It's our secret. Just you and me."

I say, *"So, I shouldn't tell Mother and Father about the sandals."*

"No," he replies. *"You shouldn't tell anyone about the sandals."*

"Don't let Mother see you, then. She'll notice." I hug him harder, feel the roughness of his chin on top of my head.

"Don't worry, Sam," he whispers. *"I'm coming back. And when I do, you'll see the sun, and I'll hold on to you tight, just in case you jump too high and fall into the sky . . ."*

He throws me into the air, and I am flying, up and backward, giggling, closing my eyes just before I hit the mattress . . .

. . . and I open my eyes, and I am still falling backward, though now I'm stumbling in the leaf-dappled light of the ruined city. Someone has me by the arm. I bump into a body, and a voice whispers, "This way. Hurry!"

I'm being shoved across the street, still half in my memory. I wish I was all the way in my memory. It was the last time I saw Adam whole and well, and the pain of it is so bitter, I only rarely allow myself to remember the sweet. Adam loved me, even though I could hurt him.

When people love me, they die.

I'm through a doorway now, my back against a white stone wall, leaves and branches and bits of violet sky where the ceiling should be. There are plants growing through the floor, pepper and tomato and oil, like Nita showed me in the fields of the Outside, and in the center of the room is a fallen door of sparkling metal, still whole. A door made of mountain rock. Who would make a door out of mountain rock?

The other body is in front of me now, a hand still on my arm, and then I see the strange silver cloth. This is Beckett. He's taller than I'd thought he'd be, taller than I am, and somewhere in my head, I can't believe he's standing on his feet. He has me by both arms now, trying to get me to look at him.

"Samara. Are you here?"

I nod. His words are short, cut off, like in my dream. Except for the eyes. The eyes are different. I can see the shape of them now they're so close, through the clear glass of the magnifiers. Dark brown and angular.

"Shhh," he says, listening. And then, through the hole that was once a window, the first member of the Council comes into view. Craddock. Of course it would be Craddock. He has a thick stick in his hand, capped with metal. I think it's for my head.

Beckett slides me down the wall, a finger to his lips, crouching beside me, out of sight. I Know it's time now. And it will be easy. One word, and they will have me and this boy from Earth. The city will be warned, and I will die. I close my eyes. I'm shaking.

"Anything?" Craddock asks. And part of a face joins him. Marcus Physicianson. More dirty and dust-coated and unpainted than I've ever seen him. I wonder if Marcus realized he would be killing me when he approved me for physician training. When Reddix, his son, accepted whatever deal was offered by my mother.

"No, nothing," Marcus replies. "Did you come underground?"

"Yes. It's secure, the side entrance is being watched."

"Where are the others?"

"Spread from here to the wall."

I take a deep breath, ready to shout.

"And Lian and Sampson?"

"Thorne has them," says Craddock. "In seclusion."

Marcus laughs once, and I hold my breath, the shout held just inside my mouth. What do they mean the Council "has" my parents? Lian Archiva has never needed seclusion in her life. Beckett catches my eye, gives my shoulder a little push that means *Stay here*, and begins creeping down the length of the wall.

"This is not the way it was supposed to happen," Craddock whispers. He sounds nervous. "It would've been better to let the girl be."

"And that is Lian's fault, isn't it?"

"Shhh," says Craddock. "Don't tell me your family didn't have any interest."

"If we'd done what we should have and Judged her at the proper time, we wouldn't be in this mess. It was a weak decision. We'll have to make an example of them all now."

Craddock makes another hushing sound, and for the moment there's only the wrong kind of silence. An example . . . of my family. The Council is going to condemn my parents. The whole family. Like Ava Administrator. Because of me. The shout inside my mouth stays there. Beckett takes silent steps, half-bent, to just below the empty window.

"You need to be careful what you say, and who you say it to," Craddock hisses. "You Know it wasn't going to be unanimous. And Thorne thinks condemning still might not be necessary."

"Why?"

"The appearance of the thing. If nobody Knows, then . . ." His voice trails away.

Then, what? If they can come up with a good lie to account for my death, like accidental poisoning, then it might not be necessary to make an example of all the Archivas? Is that what he means?

"Either way," Marcus says, "we have to end this before we lose the sun. Before we have more than her to deal with . . ."

My shout is still sitting there, and I'm thinking, thinking . . . If I could get back to the city, keep what I've done from becoming public, would Thorne spare my parents? Or do I give myself up and warn them all about Earth? Right now? I look at Beckett. He's holding a chunk of broken wall, weighing it in his hand. I draw another breath.

Craddock says, "She might not even be here."

"She's here," Marcus replies.

I draw breath again, ready to shout, and then Beckett stands for a quick moment, heaves the stone, and ducks back down again. The rock goes sailing, over branches, over broken walls and out of sight, landing far behind Marcus and Craddock with a clatter. Two shadows pass beyond the empty window. Then Beckett is up, grabbing handfuls of plants growing from the floor dirt, ripping them up by the roots and tossing them onto the fallen door.

"What . . ." I whisper.

"Creating a distraction," he says before I can finish. He clears the growth away from the edges of the metal door, making a good-size pile of plants in the middle of it. "Five more are coming from the other direction," he says. "Can you see them?"

My gaze darts to the window, and when I look back, the pile of plants Beckett has made is on fire. An instant, roaring fire. And there's no more time for thought. No time for hiding or decisions. Those are oil plants burning. And that door is mountain rock. I leap to my feet, yank Beckett by the arm.

"Wait for the smoke . . ." he says.

"Run," I tell him. This time I push him. "Go!"

We jump over the remains of a collapsed back wall and sprint full-out around trees and saplings, angling back toward the rubble mound. I glance back, and a boom hits my ears like a fist, rattling the hidden paving stones of the road. I stumble, leaves and wood and chunks of blue-gray metal exploding upward in a cloud, and then I drop to the ground beside Beckett, hands over my head, back pelted with a stinging rain of broken stone and pebbles.

I look up when the shower stops. A plume of smoke is billowing into the sky, and there's shouting all around us, voices calling from both sides. Close. I meet Beckett's startled eyes. The ones I didn't dream. We get to our feet and run.

I see the wall, just a few meters away through the trees, ruined gates open to the grasslands, and then the rubble mound is on our left. We circle it, toward the hole in the other side, and there are the backs of Marcus and Craddock, their hair braids tied for travel, hurrying away down the overgrown street toward the explosion, three more figures running with them. We slide through the hole and into the darkness of the mound.

"Quick," Beckett says. He's grabbing one of the stones I piled inside, blocking up the entrance to the mound. Like I had intended to. I hesitate, and then help him do it, uncovering my book as I set the rocks in place. But if Beckett thinks that's strange, he doesn't say anything about it. We stack the stones in silence. If the Council notices the mess Jillian left when she tore open this hole, they'll find the opening and we'll be trapped in here, and I don't Know how many have come. I saw five just then, Martina Tutor running with Marcus and Craddock. But Martina isn't Council. What is she doing here?

I need to think.

When the opening has enough rocks to make the room almost completely dark, Beckett whispers, "Okay, grab your stuff."

I don't Know what that means. But he's holding out my book and my pack, so I take them, and we feel our way through the first room, the small second one, and then the vast, black, open space full of dust to the inner chamber where I first saw him.

Jillian is waiting with both Beckett's pack and hers, one on each shoulder. And she's angry. Very angry. "What did you do?" she demands.

What he did, I think, is set fire to mountain rock. And he's lucky not to have blown up half the city and us along with it. But how? How did he start that fire?

Beckett doesn't answer. He just points to the hole in the ceiling, then puts a finger to his lips. There's shouting in the distance, beyond the mound. Jillian's eyes dart up and she takes another step back, away from the dim light shining down from the hole, while Beckett stands still, on the ankle I just set, magnifiers on his face, listening.

Aliens. That's what Grandpapa Cyrus calls the Earth people. Alien invaders from another world.

I back away, to the other end of the room, clutching my pack until I feel one of the decorative half columns that ring the room's outer wall behind me. I can't believe I'm alive. That I'm here, in the Cursed City, with two aliens from Earth. That I didn't tell the Council, shout out that Earth was crouched just on the other side of that wall. But all my options were terrible. They still are. How dare the Council throw my parents on my own funeral pyre? Those were my sins. Not theirs. They had no control over my choices, no matter how much my mother might have wished to. And cutting off the Archiva bloodline is pointless. Mother isn't going to have more children. This is all about fear. The Council keeping their control of the Knowing. The rage inside me smolders. Flames.

But even if I did go back to the city, attended the Changing of the Seasons celebrations like I'd just come out of seclusion, removed the need to make an example of my parents, warned them about Earth, the Council is never going to let me live. Not even until Judgment.

Unless I have something to bargain with. Something they would want.

I look up and find Beckett watching me. He glances away, grinning a little, like he's been caught at something. The shouts outside the rubble mound are distant now. Fading. Jillian hoists her pack.

"Time to break contact, Beckett," she whispers.

I don't know what she means, but Beckett does. He walks to the edge of the light, the last sunbeam of the season, his smile gone, staring down at the stone I set his ankle on. I watch him think, letting one idea inside my head knock the next into existence.

What would the Council give to talk to two aliens from Earth? Maybe anything I ask. Like the life of my parents. Maybe even my life until Judgment. And if I could live that long, I still might be able to find the Forgetting.

Hope is a treacherous feeling, and yet here it comes again, sprouting in my chest. Clearing my head. I think the Forgetting is real, and I think the Council must Know how it works already. And that means my answers are in the city. If I could get the keys, get back into that room in the Archives, like I did before, it's still possible that I could heal the Knowing. That I could break the illusion of the Council's power. I could still fix this. But I'd have to convince these two to come with me.

I have no idea how to do that. I breathe, my air unsteady, and I think I must actually be homesick, because I can smell the Underneath.

"Beckett, time to break contact," Jillian says again.

He's standing in the exact same spot, eyes closed, magnifiers off, arms stretched up and on top of his head, face dirty and bloody, the ends of his dusty black hair sticking against his sweaty neck. I hadn't realized he was quite this lovely an alien. Or at least, not when I was an infant. How can I have dreamed him? A boy from Earth? But I did. Everything but the shape of the eyes. I don't understand it. Or him.

Why pull me out of the street, save me from the Council, if he meant me harm? But he hasn't admitted where he's really from, has he? Neither of them has. They lied about—or at least hid—that fact, just like they waited until I was gone to use the technology that healed Beckett's foot. Why hide, if Earth isn't a threat? If I asked him about Earth right now, would Beckett lie to me, or tell me the truth?

It shouldn't matter. I need him to come with me, either way. Both of them. To keep my city safe. To save my parents. To buy me time to heal the Knowing.

But it does matter. Somehow. He's been in my head since I was a baby.

I think I will have to test him.

He's standing perfectly still in the sunlight. I don't Know what's happening, but he needs to say something. Something he doesn't want to. I can see it on his face.

"Beckett," Jillian says. "You have your orders."

Beckett opens his eyes.

And then a shadow flits across the last beam of the sun.

Rule one in initiation contact training, according to the eminent Dr. Sean Rodriguez: Establish trust, but never trust them. Because you cannot trust what you do not understand.

FROM THE LOG BOOK OF BECKETT RODRIGUEZ

Day 98, Year 1

The Lost Canaan Project

16

BECKETT

I catch the quick shadow moving across the light, and I know it's a skimmer. I'm not sure if Jill saw, but there's no time to figure out a way to tell her. I slide on the glasses and write, fast, choosing letters with my gaze. I don't know how long we'll have communication, and I need to tell Dad that I'm breaking orders. That I'm with a local, and will stay to continue establishing relationship. That Canaan is still a living city, only moved somewhere underground. That I need help getting Jill out.

Jill is not going to understand this. I think I'm going to hurt her. But Samara is exactly what we came for, and this is an opportunity that won't come again. And when I glance to the side, I find her amber eyes on me. Beautiful, in a smooth mask of a face. I need to write, but I can't help searching her for cracks like before, for a hint of what's beneath.

"The dark days are coming," she says, out of nowhere. Her voice lilts with the words. "It must be difficult to know how to live through the dark when you've forgotten."

Forgotten. That's what she said had happened to us, before she set my ankle. That we were from "outside," and we had "forgotten." It really would be nice to have the first clue about what's been happening on this planet.

Samara asks, "Will you go on living in the Cursed City? When the Council has gone?"

I'm processing "cursed" when a message slides across the lenses. One word. "Don't." The signature is Dr. Sean Rodriguez. Something must be glitching. Jill comes to stand beside me, close against my elbow. Like she's closing ranks. It's time to tell her. I take a breath. "Actually, we—"

"Yes," Jillian says abruptly. "That's right. We'll stay in the city. That's exactly what we're going to do."

Samara's gaze flows over Jillian like a chilly stream. "And have you gathered and preserved?" she asks both of us. "Do you have seeds for the sunrising?"

"Of course," Jillian replies. She smiles, all bright hair and innocence, but I'm watching Samara, and I see one of those cracks I was looking for. A quick fracture. She knows Jillian just lied to her. I don't know how or why, but she knows. And when those eyes flick to me, what I see is . . . disappointment. I wish I were as good as Jill at cussing, because right now I feel like I just failed an exam I never took.

"Wait," I say. "I . . ." Then another message scrolls fast across my eyes:

"Situation understood. Revised orders: Maintain contact according to protocol. Find and report position of subterranean city as soon as possible."

And this time the signature is not my father's. It's from Admiral Commander Juniper Faye.

I turn away from Jill and Samara, hands back on my head. Base camp must have uploaded my files the last time the skimmer came through. I was already set to transmit. Which means they've seen all the visuals, probably up to Samara setting my ankle and right after, and now, I bet, they've just uploaded the rest. The thought of Commander Faye hearing my opinions on protocol and watching me maintain contact with a local directly against orders is enough to make my stomach turn. But maybe I won't be held responsible for not following orders when I was about to get the opposite ones anyway.

Okay, there's not much chance of that. It might be almost as bad as Dad seeing me blow a chunk out of one of the most important archaeological sites since Tokyo.

"The dark days can be dangerous on your own," says Samara.

I wipe away the first message, spell one word, "Understood," and send. Then I turn around. Those eyes are on me.

"Come with me," she says, "to my city. Until it's light again. I can help you remember."

Come with her. That's exactly what I want. What I've just been ordered to do. But why now? The mask is back, hard and impenetrable.

"No, thanks," Jill says, her hand on my arm.

I really do need to find a way of telling Jill to shut up without yelling, *Shut up.*

I take my pack from Jill and sling it over my shoulder, keep my gaze on Samara when I say, "How far is it to New Canaan?"

Jillian goes still, frozen, like she opened the door of the *Centauri III* and got left floating around in space. And then the lenses flash red. The perimeter alarm. I look up and turn around.

"What is it?" Jill asks.

"Someone's close," I say. I scan for heat and I find it, hold up two fingers. "Walking along the edge."

Jill stares at the wall, tense, while Samara holds that book to her chest, backed up against one of the half columns, ready to run. Like me. I scan again, and one of the heat sources is a meter in the air and rising. Climbing up the mound. What has this girl done?

"They're coming up," I whisper.

Jillian spins, like she's giving it one last try to find a door we missed, and I grab my pack and move to get Samara, and Samara is . . . gone. Eyes closed, face open, lost somewhere in her head. Great. Just great.

I shake her once, like I did in the ruined house. She frowns, but doesn't come back. Jill tugs at my arm.

"Leave her!" She's barely containing her voice.

"Orders, Jill." She backs off, startled, glances up at where the sky should be. I scan again. Our climber is taking their time, more cautious than I was, but still halfway, and I'm more than a little worried the ceiling might come down on us. I grip Samara by the shoulders and shake her again. Hard.

Her eyes pop open. She has the tiniest sprinkle of freckles across her nose. "We should go underground," she says.

"Oh no, we shouldn't!" Jill hisses. "We go out the door!"

Then Samara reaches behind her, pulls a latch, and the column swings open. Like a door. Leading down to a damp and hollow dark. Okay, so the glasses missed that one.

"Beckett, no," Jillian breathes. "We can't trust her. She could be leading us straight to them!"

These words are not exactly phrased to promote healthy relationships across cultures. I keep looking at Samara. "Do you know the way?"

"Yes. I have remembered."

"And how did you even know that door was there?" whispers Jill.

The amber eyes swing to her. "Because I smelled it."

Fine. I don't know what that means, but fine. Jill is spitting mad, we have about ten seconds before someone's head comes through that hole, and now that the door is open, the glasses show a long, straight river passage, with at least one branch. "In!" I say beneath my breath. "Go!" Samara slips through the door with her pack and I practically shove Jill.

I shut the door with a soft snick. There's no lock, and I consider fusing the latch with the laser, but I think messing up one more thing in Canaan might actually kill me. If the glasses didn't find that door, it's not likely they will.

Unless they're trying. Or they already know.

I hurry after Jill and Samara, down black, winding stairs that are worn and slick, sometimes choked with fallen stone. There's water running down there, and I think I understand what Samara meant by smelling it. Some kind of spice or perfume is in the air, a scent like water, soil, and something else I don't have a name for. The sound of gushing gets louder, weirdly colored light flickering against the last two or three winding steps, and when I scramble over the final set of fallen rocks, I don't see what I thought I would at all.

We're in a cave, a river rushing fast to our right, and every nook, every angle of the ceiling and walls is completely covered with some kind of flower. Green and purple and the occasional red, each one of them lifting a set of long feelers, waving them in the air as if they were underwater. And the flowers are glowing. Bright, luminescent, the feelers making the light seem to move and dance. It's kind of beautiful, and peculiar. Like celebration decorations gone crazy wrong.

I use the glasses to check the room above us, but I can't see through this rock. At all. Only the empty spaces, like the passage and the opening up the stairway. I reset the perimeter alarm anyway. Samara is already moving down the passage, looking back to see where we are, but Jillian is still standing at the bottom of the steps. And I know that expression. Even in the flickering light of alien glow flowers.

"Jill," I say. "Come talk to me."

She doesn't at first. And then a green flower reaches out a feeler, just brushing her cheek. She jumps like the thing bit her, closes her eyes, and I can almost see her longing for the sanitizer. But she does take a few steps toward me, arms crossed, putting some distance between us and Samara. I bring her up to speed in a whisper, short and quick, watch her face go from mad to a different kind of mad.

"I don't believe it. I just don't believe it . . ." She glances at Samara, who's tying that book back over her shoulder, the flowers brushing at her arms. "Why would Commander Faye send us? It doesn't make any sense."

I shrug. "Until they get the scans figured out I guess the ship is blind, and we're the ones who made contact. So we're elected."

"But they saw your visuals, Beckett! We had locals that were hostile, and nobody even knows what the situation is in this city, except that it's obviously not good where she's concerned." She jerks her head at Samara. "And so they send in two kids from the anthropology sector that haven't even trained in contact? And you think that makes sense?"

No, it doesn't make sense. But I want this. I want it so much it hurts. And I know Jill doesn't. She's more archaeology than anthropology. More comfortable with the dead than the living, learning history instead of living it. She was thinking she'd camp with me, fly back to the team in a cloud of glory, spend the next few years hunting nice, safe, uncomplicated artifacts in those half-fallen buildings, and see her name written in the history files. But this is messy, and dangerous, and nothing like we planned.

"You know there's something wrong with her," Jill whispers. "It's like a trance or something . . ."

"I was thinking maybe a trauma disorder. Did you see her palms, and the bruises?" I glance at Samara again, a long, lean shadow against the light. She's either smelling the flowers, or letting them tickle her face.

"I think she has psychiatric issues."

"We don't know a thing about her culture. For all we know, this could be normal. And she must be mostly okay. She seems to know her medicine."

"She's too young to be a doctor, Beckett! And what is she doing, taking us with her? Who does she even think we are?"

"She said we were from outside."

"Well, there's an understatement."

I laugh once. A breath of humor. Jill smiles a little, and then she's not smiling anymore.

"You were going to leave me back there," she says. "If the orders hadn't come. Weren't you?"

The one thing about Jill is she's never, ever stupid. Exactly the opposite. I don't want to look at her face. "I would have made sure you got back safe."

Jill bites her lip again.

"What she's offering is once in a lifetime," I tell her. "Everything I left Earth for. You can't blame me for wanting to take that chance."

Actually, I think she can blame me. And she's probably going to blame me for a lot before this is over, because when you get down to it, I don't think Jill and I want the same things. But there's no point in talking about it. Not now. We have our orders—maintain contact, get the coordinates of the city—and we don't know what we're about to walk into.

I look over Jill's head and see Samara standing in the greenish-purple light of a glowing flower, her hair curling everywhere, as much like an image from the historic culture files as it's possible to look. It's hard not to stare at her. Because she is history. Only she is also real, right now, and she is taking me to her city.

And she could answer all of my questions.

I had five scars on my arms the day I discovered that my mother had a hole in the wall behind her mirror.

Mother sent me to get the box of picture tiles. I'd only been inside Mother's chamber once, when I was a baby. And so I looked quickly at the face paints, the row of elegant clothes, at one black wall hung with items that were odd and interesting: spoons; tools I didn't Know; a knife, long and thin. All with the letters "NWSE" stamped in the metal. Like Mother's necklace. I let myself smile in the mirror. I am allowed in Mother's room, I thought. I can be asked to bring the picture tiles. I think Mother must love me now.

And then I saw that her mirror was crooked. It hadn't been like that when I was a baby. And there was a spot of tarnish on the silver frame. A finger mark. I reached out my own finger, pushed in the direction that the frame was crooked, and the mirror slid up and to one side. There was a hole in the rock. And inside the hole were two books. Secret books. Mother must miss the Archives, I thought. Like me.

One was plain, with pages written by different people. The other had a title pasted onto the cover: "The Notebook of Janis Atan." They were both very old. I looked at every page, just like Uncle Towlend taught me, turning quickly and carefully, so I could read them later, in my memory. But one sentence got read with my real eyes. "The elimination of all technology was shortsighted. The technology of Earth will lift the best of us to the pinnacle of our evolution." I wasn't sure what it meant, but it sounded like an idea that would get your hand swatted in the learning room.

And then I was afraid. Father said not to look at books. Maybe these books were hidden because they're bad. If Mother Knows I've looked, she'll Know I'm bad, too. Again.

I put them back, exactly as they were. Left the mirror perfectly crooked. Ran from the room with the tile box. And while I was playing in the receiving room, making pictures with the tiles, I asked Father, "Can technology be used for good things? Or only bad?"

It was my mother who answered. "You're asking the wrong question, Samara. Because there is no good or bad. Only better."

I knew after that day that sometimes my mother didn't tell me the truth. You don't hide books in a wall because they're better. And she had spent my lifetime showing me that I was not better in any way at all.

FROM THE HIDDEN BOOK OF SAMARA ARCHIVA
IN THE CITY OF NEW CANAAN

17

SAMARA

The two aliens follow me down the cavern, river spraying on our right, wafting flowers on our left. They're coming to the city. Both of them. And I don't even understand it. I can't see Jillian's expression, but whatever Beckett said to her, it must have been good. Hope blooms inside me like a poisonous flower. Pretty, but dangerous.

I need to be careful. Because that was much too easy.

Beckett lied to me, or at least he let Jillian do it for him. And what was he looking at through those magnifiers while she did? For a moment, it seemed like he was reading. Words I couldn't see . . .

I sift through my memories, fast. Beckett spotting me in the shadows, looking at his own bones. That fire. And he seemed to know exactly what was on the other side of a wall. My stomach twists, turns over, a tingle of fear trickling through my insides. I think those magnifiers are technology. And that Beckett is hiding that fact from me, too. What else can he do that is beyond my Knowing?

I think I'll need to be more than careful, if I'm going to get us all back to the city. I wonder if I'm even capable of it. How do you outwit what you do not understand?

But I do Know, now, that this is the way to my city. Because while Beckett was busy seeing through walls, I went back inside my mind and looked at the map, this time at the page before it. A thin piece of linen, woven so fine it was translucent, laying perfectly over the map, marked with red lines that added a new network of scrawling pathways. The caves. And there, in bold, double ink, was the underground river, running between the old city and the new. The river I'm walking beside right now. The Torrens. The river that took Nita away from me.

I stop. I'm standing in the glowing purples and greens of the cave passage, but half of my mind has fallen into the dark of my terrace balcony, where one by one, I am putting out the lamps. I struggle, fight, claw to stay where I am. In the cave. With the aliens. But the memory pulls again, and I fall . . .

. . . and Nita is lying half over the stone-carved railing of my balcony, her blue lips matching her lifeless eyes, her forehead still warm when I kiss it. A small push, and she goes over, tumbling to the wild surge of water below. And I cannot cry. I can only feel the scream . . .

I shoot back into the present, and there is the scream, still inside me, and the sickening wave of horror and revulsion. Grief. Loss. And the rage. All of it burning like the day I killed her. Hot tears roll down my cheeks, and I am nearly doubled in my effort not to yell. I can feel Jillian and Beckett, waiting in silence somewhere behind me. And then I straighten my back, wipe my face, and move my feet forward again. I hear the aliens follow.

There's fatigue beneath my pain, a deep ache in my bones. The Knowing can go for a long time without food or rest, but we are not unlimited, and I haven't slept or fully cached in days. I don't think I can afford to sleep. I can't trust them.

I also can't afford to lose control.

I move faster. The wafting flowers are starting to thin, the light dimming, and every two or three meters I see an old glass jar, dirty and opaque, hanging in a metal sconce riveted to the wall of rock. The way must have been lit once. And then there's a new passage, smaller, with rougher walls, branching off to darkness on our left.

There's murmuring behind me, and then Jillian says, "Beckett thinks there could be people down that passage."

I glance at him, and he shrugs a shoulder. If Beckett says he sees people, they're probably there. Craddock said the entrances to the underground were being watched. But not that last entrance. I don't think they Know about that one. "Close?" I ask Beckett.

"No."

I move my gaze back to Jill. "We're not going that way."

"Will they come in here, looking for you?" Beckett asks.

"They will not expect me to Know this way." Which isn't really an answer.

"But . . ." Jillian begins.

"We need to gather light," I say, lifting one of the old glass jars from its sconce. I reach between a set of feelers and pluck a fuzzy, bright glowworm from between the flowers. When I gently close my fist, it looks like I'm holding one of the moons.

"So the walls aren't . . . glowing by themselves?" Jillian asks.

I raise a brow, and then I say, "We should not talk."

She doesn't say anything else, and neither does Beckett. They just rinse their jars in the river water, like I show them, and I'm not too tired to enjoy Jillian's squeamishness while she collects her light. Half-full and the jars become squirming lanterns, bright and undimming.

Beckett kneels again on the stone of the riverbank when he's done with his jar and takes off the magnifiers. It makes him look so much more . . . human. Then he does something completely alien, pulls a little fastener at the top of his baggy clothes, and makes the cloth split like it was cut with a knife. He sticks his whole head in the water, washing away the dirt and blood, and when he lifts it out again, I can just see that beneath the outer clothes he's wearing some kind of tight, white tunic. And yes, he's hiding the body of a harvest worker under there.

Beckett shakes his head, spraying droplets into the light, and in some miraculous way, sews the cloth of his clothes back together. And I feel guilty. Alien or no, I should have looked at that gash on his head. I glance at Jillian, who was also looking at Beckett, and who is now looking at me. Looking at Beckett.

And my memory flashes. To Sonia in an unguarded moment, the way she looked at Jane Chemist when Jane noticed the pretty face of Sonia's boy from Outside. I Know that expression on Jill's face. And it changes the way I was thinking about the two of them completely.

"What are they called?" Beckett asks.

I start. I think I was just staring at the walls. The magnifiers are back on, blue and purple light reflecting on the glass. And then he smiles, and that is as familiar to me as the clinging plants.

"Wafting flowers," I say. "They clean the air." I turn away. "We should hurry." I said the Council wouldn't expect me to Know this path, and I don't think they're looking for me to come back to the city. But that doesn't mean they won't travel this way once the sun is down. I push our pace.

The flowers thin and disappear, the river gushing dark outside the circle of our blue-white lights, and we pass more empty sconces, the beginnings of a stairway cut into stone, now choked with fallen rock. Water drips, running down the walls, and when I go back in my memory and compare the steps, I'm certain we're beneath the lake that must have been the lower end of the city.

Beckett catches up, walking just behind me. I think he wants to talk. Ask me questions. I walk a little faster. And now my mind skips to him standing in the hidden room, the technology off his face, arms over his head in the hazy beam of light. And in a blink that's gone and I'm wrapped in a blanket, surrounded by Mother's arms, and there is the Beckett of my dream, with the different eyes and shorter hair.

And then Nita is sitting cross-legged on the end of my bed, telling me about a weaver that kissed her, and how she prefers a metalworker instead. And I'm clutching my cup of tea, hugging the pillow that would one day take her life close beneath my chin, drinking in her words like spoiled honeymead, sweet with the bitter. Because if I ever loved, I thought, it would only be once . . .

I jerk myself into the present, let out a tiny puff of breath. I am in the caves, holding a jar of light, leading two aliens in a row of silence. But the memories are there, lurking, and the boundaries inside my head are dissolving like mist. I need to cache. Order my mind. Sleep.

I can't. Adam used to tell me to run when memories came. Occupy my mind. That's what he did with his rope swing. I walk faster, keeping Jillian at a trot, climbing over and around boulders that are irregular, and yet somehow monotonous. The way beside the Torrens begins to climb, narrowing, the river squeezed into a smaller, deeper channel of white water and froth. Glimpses of spray get caught in the range of my light, and the water noise funnels into a single, constant roar. The pack weighs heavy on my back, the jar cool in my hand. I blink. Blink again, and I am drifting down, soft . . .

. . . *into darkness and heat. I am underwater, held tight, and there is noise, muffled sounds that reverberate through and around my body, a deep thrum and whoosh, rhythmic, like water. And I Know where I am. I am unborn, and while the feeling is one of safety, of being embraced, my adult mind Knows that I cannot move. That I am pressed in on all sides, trapped, breathing liquid . . .*

I gasp, lungs burning, and when I open my eyes I'm on the ground and Beckett has his hand on my neck, peering deep into my face with the magnifiers. I scramble backward over the rocks, out of his grip.

"Wait . . ." he says.

I stop, breath still coming short, stone digging sharp into my newly healed hands. Beckett stays very still, squatted down among the broken rocks. I can see Jillian over his shoulder, a void of darkness beyond her.

"I didn't mean to scare you," he says. "But you weren't breathing there for a second."

"Is she sick?" Jillian asks.

I close my eyes. I haven't slipped into a memory of before my birth in years. Not since childhood. That should have been well and truly cached, and can only mean that I am beyond tired. I am exhausted.

"I think she should tell us what's wrong with her," Jillian says. "And while she's at it, she can explain why her own people want to kill her."

I open my eyes, gaze at Jillian.

"Not now, Jill," Beckett says over his shoulder.

"Well, it's a fair question, isn't it? I mean, won't these people just be trying to kill us again as soon as we get to this city?"

Her eyes are so blue, like Nita's. And yet not like Nita's at all. I wonder what Jillian would do if she knew I murdered my best friend.

Beckett says, "When was the last time you ate, Samara? Or slept?"

I slept once behind a thicket of oil plants on the edge of the plain, and I've eaten two breadfruits since then. But I'm more worried about my mind than my body.

"Come on," Beckett says, holding out a hand. He pulls me to my feet, like he did in the ruined street. "The cavern ends over there. Just a little more, and we'll find a place to set up camp."

I don't understand the word, but it doesn't matter. I'm almost completely out of control. Beckett drops my hand and bends down to get my jar of light, miraculously unbroken on the rocky floor.

"He grabbed it right before you fell," Jillian says. "Wasn't that lucky? Beckett was watching so close, he was able to catch it before you even got near the ground."

If Beckett notices any acid in these words, he doesn't acknowledge it. He just shrugs a shoulder. "It was handblown glass." And then he's doing that smile again, like he's been a little bad and gotten caught at it. I don't Know what he's talking about. What other kind of glass is there?

I follow him this time, Jillian coming after us. He was right about the cavern ending. Another twist and turn and the darkness pales, another turn and we stand in a tall, skinny corridor of rough blue stone, the river foaming white in its course, a narrow piece of purpling sky above our heads, streaked with pink. We're at the bottom of one of the deep clefts I skirted on my run to the city. There's a smell in the wind, a sweetness that I think must be something Nita described to me once. The scent of plants going to sleep. For the dark.

Jillian goes to a large shelf of rock, jutting out from the cliff face, ducks down, and looks beneath it. "Over here," she calls.

There's a space below the rock, opening after one or two crouched steps into a small oval cavern about half the size of my bedchamber and not quite its height. Jillian and Beckett go to one side and drop their packs in a pile, setting down the lights, their bodies making long, misshapen shadows on the curving walls. Beckett says, "I've set a perimeter."

I'm so close to losing control I don't even care when I don't Know what that means. I go to the opposite side of the chamber and sit, light and pack beside me, arms around my book like a child, back against a stone near the entryway. Where I could get out if I had to. I breathe, close my eyes, and, room full of aliens or not, I sift through my mind. Organizing. Uncluttering. Like I've been taught since the day my memories came. Some I relegate to the shelves in the background, some I leave sitting out to use, others I cache to the very back, to the high shelf, never to be felt again. And I Know that I am slipping. Sinking. Pulled by a force that is stronger than I am. Like gravity . . .

And when I open my eyes again I see the stone chamber, the whitish light and the shadows, but I'm wrapped in something warm. Jillian has her yellow head bent toward Beckett, whose back is to me, low murmurs rustling along the walls.

I feel a thrill of disorientation. Fear. I look back inside my mind. I've been asleep. For more than six bells. I feel my book beneath my hand, my pack behind my back. And now I'm mad. How could I have been so careless? If the Council did decide to travel this way, they could be right behind us.

But I don't move. I close my eyes again. Stay still. Caverns can be tricky with sound, and this one has a curved ceiling. Beckett and Jillian are barely speaking, but I hear it like they're whispering in my ear.

"I'm getting about forty meters of penetrating vision at a time," Beckett is saying. "If you're mapping, we can't get lost, even if she doesn't know where she's going."

"We can run out of food," Jillian counters.

"She's been going fast. I think she's taking us straight to it . . ."

Taking them straight to New Canaan. The words make me cringe with doubt. Doubt makes me mad.

Beckett says, "How's the charge on the cartographer?"

"Full. But it won't stay that way. And we're losing the sun. What about the glasses?"

"Eighty-two percent. I won't be able to leave visual recording on anymore. Not all the time. They'll get another charge before we go back underground, but that might be all there is until the next dawn. Or the ship . . ."

And I'm thinking now. About technology. About the word "glasses." Pieces of glass. I open my eyes, and there, perched in front of me, on top of the pile of packs, are Beckett's magnifiers.

"I think we should tell her," Beckett says.

I'd be very interested to Know what he thinks he should tell me. But I'm also feeling an itch inside my mind. I slide my body almost imperceptibly closer to the magnifiers. Jillian only has eyes for Beckett.

"Why," she asks, "are you so determined to break every rule we ever swore to?"

"Protocol doesn't say to never tell anyone anything. Just to do it at the right time. With thought. They sent us, and so now I'm giving it some thought."

"Well, it's the wrong thought, Beckett! You know what those orders meant."

"You were the one explaining to me how those orders don't make sense."

"And you're acting like you have no future after this planet!"

I move my hand, but it doesn't attract Jillian's attention. She drops her voice back to a whisper.

"The Commander already heard you criticize protocol on the visuals," she says, "and I bet they uploaded again when the skimmer was here, didn't they? So now she's seen you interfering with a local, against orders. What kind of career are you going to have if you only follow orders when you feel like it?"

"Careers are on the other side of the galaxy, Jill."

"But what if . . ." Jill hesitates. "What if things are . . . different from what you think?"

I stretch out, slowly, and my fingertips brush the edge of the glass. I can't quite reach.

Beckett's voice comes sharp. "How can you look at it any different? We have a huge find back there. Maybe the most important historic site that's ever been found, and now there's another city, too. My career, or whatever you call it, is here, and Dad will be the one in charge of that, not the Commander."

So Earth plans to be here a long time. Why? What do they want? As strange as they are, Beckett and Jillian don't strike me as a first choice to lead an invasion.

"Beckett, listen to me." Jill's voice is so quiet I have to be still to hear it. "I know that you . . ." She stops, tries again. "I know you love this, and you want to do well at it. And that this girl . . ."

I close my eyes. In case she looks my way.

". . . that she's fascinating to you, professionally. But you've already broken orders once. You have to follow these new ones. To the letter. Do you understand?" She waits. "I can't keep on saving you from yourself."

"I don't need you to save me from anything," he snaps.

I open an eye. Jillian is completely focused on Beckett. I move my arm, and reach one more time for the magnifiers. Beckett sighs.

"Look, Jill, this isn't just a project, even if that's the way the Commander and the investors and the rest of the crew think of it. It's bigger than that. If they called the whole thing off tomorrow and said go home . . . Now that I'm here, I don't think I'd . . ."

I hook a finger around the edge of the glass. And a scream shoots through the air, piercing, high-pitched. False. A sharp whine of warning. I jerk back my hand, sit up as Beckett spins around. Jillian's blue eyes are wide. The noise cycles and it is so unnatural. Wrong.

And it's coming from the magnifiers.

During our psych evaluations, Dr. Kataria asked me what I thought about leadership. Should protocol be followed to the letter, or adapted to each situation?

I said, "Both."

It seems like a good answer to a lot of questions.

FROM THE LOG BOOK OF BECKETT RODRIGUEZ

Day 151, Year 1

The Lost Canaan Project

18

BECKETT

The perimeter alarm is going off, and like an idiot, I've left the glasses on the packs beside Samara. She's awake, sitting up, clutching my blanket to her chest, her amber eyes staring. I cram the glasses onto my face, and the noise stops as soon as they touch my skin, though I can see the warning light still pulsing across the lenses. I don't know how I'm going to explain this to Samara. She already thinks I'm a liar, thanks to Jill. And there's no time anyway, because the glasses are showing me five humans. And they are above us.

I find Jill's gaze, hold up five fingers, and point. She nods, scoots out the entrance on her back, and when I turn to Samara, her eyes drop straight to the floor. Like she's scared of me. Great.

Jill slides back inside. "They're coming along the top of the cliff," she whispers. "I think just passing through. They're moving fast."

Some of the fear slips out of me. The few descendants of Canaan I caught a glimpse of in the ruins didn't look all that scary. A little soft, and with no real weapons that I could see. But Samara's face and hands might say different, and she said they were out to kill her. But are we really going to play hide-and-seek with these people all the way to her city? And what exactly is going to happen when we get there?

I want to go, want it like air. But I'm not stupid. Or I don't think I am.

"Keep an eye out?" I ask Jillian. She nods, and slides back out again.

Samara's mask is smooth and in place. She won't look at me. But it's hard to stop looking at her. She's still wrapped in my blanket, her hair wild with sleep, and I'm on edge, trying to think how to get the information I need without messing up everything. I wish I knew what she was running from. I wish she would spill every single thought inside her head.

I wish she wasn't so important, so I could say anything I wanted to her.

"You slept" is what I settle for, and it's not good. Her eyes stay glued to the rock and dirt floor. I try again. "I don't think anyone can get down here. Or not fast, anyway. The walls are too steep. So we're good for now. Do you need to eat? We can share."

Nothing.

"The ankle set well."

I get a tiny response, a glance at my foot, and I wish I hadn't brought it up. In her world, I probably shouldn't be walking on this leg at all. It's no wonder she's afraid. I don't want her to be afraid of me. I squat down in front of her.

"Samara, listen, if we're going to be traveling together, we need to help each other out. Why are these people looking for you so hard?"

Still nothing.

"Will we be safe underground?"

Not even a blink.

"Look," I say, a little exasperated, "you said you're trying to help us. Giving us a place to stay while the sun is gone. But I need to know if your city is dangerous. It's only fair to tell me that much."

Her dark smudges of lash don't even move. She doesn't trust me. How could she? But then why offer to take us with her? What does she need? Protection?

I glance at the entrance to the cavern, and the glasses tell me Jill is in place, on her back, watching the top of the cliff. Forget protocol. But I need to forget it fast, while Jill isn't here.

"Fine," I say. "I'll make a deal with you. You ask me anything you need to know, and I'll tell you. I won't lie to you." I cock my head toward the entrance, toward Jill. "She won't like it. But she's in a new place and she's worried about breaking the rules. I'm not so worried. So if you want to know, you ask, I tell you the truth, and then, when you're ready, you can do the same. Deal?"

I wait, still squatted down, where I can see her face, and then she lifts those eyes and looks directly into mine. She doesn't do that very often. I wish I wasn't wearing the glasses. That there wasn't a barrier, even if it's a clear one.

And then Samara says, in her interestingly musical version of English, "Have you Forgotten?"

A challenge. I feel myself smile, a little rueful, and shake my head. "No. Or, I mean, I'm sure I've forgotten a lot of things, but the word seems to mean something different to you. So when you say it"—I shrug—"I don't even know what you're talking about."

I'm watching her close in the weird light of the jar, looking for the tiny cracks in her mask. And I catch one. Surprise. Just a flash. But I don't think her surprise was because I haven't forgotten, whatever that is. It was because she already knew I hadn't and thought I would lie about it. Like Jill did.

I don't know if I've done the right thing. It feels like the right thing. And anyway, the record function is off.

I hear pebbles scratching in dirt, and Jill comes scooting back inside. "Gone," she says, pausing to look at the conversation between the two of us.

One second Samara is on the ground, the next she's on her feet, her pack and my blanket in hand. "If they are traveling across the plain, then we should stay underground," she says. "That will be the safest way." She rubs the material of the blanket one time between her fingers before she hands it over, then slips out the entrance of the cavern, somehow managing to do it gracefully.

Jill watches me watch her go, and then our eyes meet. I try to smile. I don't want to argue with Jill. But I know I look guilty. She doesn't start up our conversation again, or ask me what I was going to say when the alarm went off. I think she knows. That I probably wouldn't go back to Earth, even if I had the choice. All she says is, "You're not going to believe the sky."

She's right. When we drag our packs and the light jars out of the cavern, it's not the same world I left when I went in. The air has cooled, a brisk breeze whistling between the narrow walls, the purple of the sky deepened into a kind of magenta-red fire. Columns of mist rise from the river, like tiny tornadoes, spiraling and breaking as they climb. I've seen simulations of a Canaan sunset. The real thing isn't the same. And I don't think the glasses will be getting any charge out here. Not until the sun rises again. Sixty-something more days.

Samara is standing in the mist beside the river, pack at her feet, that book strapped across her chest, looking into the distance while she braids her hair. She is so beautiful. Even ragged and travel-worn and a little bruised, she is beautiful. And she belongs with that sky above her.

She ties off her hair, one thick, loose braid behind her, and walks right up to me, but it's not me she's come for. It's the light jar I've set at my feet. She bends down, dropping little pieces of sticky fruit one by one into the jars. Jill straightens from adjusting her pack straps and snaps, "What are you doing?"

Samara turns the amber gaze on her. "Feeding our lights," she says, like Jill is exactly four years old.

Jill's face goes from annoyed to a little disgusted in the space of two seconds, and I want to laugh, but I do have a sense of self-preservation. My lack of career focus has not put Jill in a humorous mood. We start down the narrow cleft without a word. Samara looks back, to make sure we're coming, and I feel the weight of that glance in my chest.

I'm taking a gamble right now, offering to break protocol. A big one. No matter what I said to Jill back there, about lifework and Dad being the one in charge, I know full well who's in charge of Dad, and Mom, and that what I'm doing out here could hurt them. But I want to understand Samara's world. That's the bigger goal. I need to understand it, and to do that, I'm going to have to gain her trust.

I think she's going to make me earn it.

The canyon isn't very long. It's like the roof of the cave system fell in who knows how long ago, and soon we're ducking down beneath rock again, back in the dark with that smell, the water loud and echoing beside us. I switch to night function, and we walk for three hours up, over, and around the rocks. I'm a little bit glad for it. The ankle seems strong, but I came out of that cavern feeling every bruise from my fall, and the exercise has definitely loosened up the ache. And it's kept Jill from talking. Asking me what I said to Samara in the cavern. None of us are talking.

I squeeze between two boulders, Jill coming through without brushing the stones, and then I thrust out an arm, barring her from taking another step. The river is spilling down into a waterfall, and there's a long drop on one side that wasn't there before.

"Thanks," Jill says, sucking in a breath.

"No problem." Samara is a little way down the passage, already disappearing over the edge of a steep incline of rocks, matching the path of the water. We follow her, and I whisper to Jill, "Careful. And don't forget the cartographer." She winks an answer at me. Like everything is fine. No disagreements about protocol or what planet we live on. I'm relieved. More than I thought I'd be.

It's not a hard climb down the rock slide, but the stones are wet, slick, and holding your own light in a jar doesn't exactly speed you up.

Especially a jar that any collector of the early space exploration period would have paid half the funding of the Canaan Project to own.

Samara waits for us at the bottom, holding up her light, looking at the path ahead. I do the same with the glasses. The passage goes on as far as I can see, mostly straight, no obstacles. I turn and help Jill make the last drop, so she can hang on to her jar, and when her boots hit the ground she turns before I can let go. Smiling at me.

"Hey," she whispers, a hand snaking up the back of my neck. Like we're on the ship, five minutes early to a tutoring session. I pull her hand down, and she runs it back up my chest. I grab it, push it away again.

"Don't, okay?"

The frown line comes down between her eyes, but I don't care. She did that on purpose. So Samara would see. Because . . . I don't know why. But I don't like it.

Samara doesn't act like she's seen anything at all. She just moves on in her circle of light, and so do I, finding a track among the broken stones. Jill comes after us, and the silence between us is different now. Tense. More than tense. Which is just fantastic. We're going to be the first people from Earth to see what became of the lost colonists of Canaan. We've got one of them walking right in front of us, and it's like Jill doesn't care about that.

I care. And it's not the time for Jill and me to be fighting. Or anything else.

Samara is moving fast, light, like she's barely touching the ground. Sleep has done her good. She's more . . . present. That's the best word I can think of for it. I've spent a good part of my life wanting to know the story of Canaan, but right now, I almost want to know the story of Samara Archiva more. She's been traveling rough, but below the more recent wounds her skin is soft, almost translucent brown in the light of her jar, and the embroidery on her long shirt and leggings is tiny, detailed. I don't think she's lived this way for long. What did she do in this city of hers? And why is she going back?

"Careful, Beckett. You'll trip," Jill says next to me.

I look down at her, confused, but only at first. Then I'm ticked. "I am studying her," I say under my breath. "Isn't that what I'm supposed to do?"

"Studying? Is that what they call it now?"

I stare down at Jill's big blue eyes. Fine. We're fighting. I pick up my pace and get ahead of her, walking just behind Samara and not looking back.

After a long time of that, Samara says, "She is your partner?"

They're the first words she's said to me since our so-called deal, and I know exactly what she means just from the tone. From a linguistic standpoint, what an interesting use of the word "partner." From a Beckett standpoint, what an uncomfortable one. But I did tell her to ask anything. I glance over my shoulder. Jillian's light has dropped back.

"No," I say carefully. "Not partners. We've just . . . known each other a long time."

We walk on, the blue stone every now and again veined by a ribbon of shining black. A passage opens up to the left, little more than a crack, and when I check it with the glasses, I see that it widens, taking an almost perpendicular course. Samara ignores this and stays with the river. I want to ask her questions. A hundred of them. But since I'm following instinct here instead of protocol, I wait.

Then she stops and looks directly at me. Like she did before. I hold my breath. "Why do you want to come to my city?"

And this, I think, is my second challenge. I can see Jill through the glasses, small and far away in the dark. She's using the cartographer. I turn back to Samara. Her eyes are amber lined with black lash. It's really not all that hard, breaking protocol.

"I want to study it," I tell her. When she doesn't respond, I add, "To learn about it. Like how you live. Your history."

The mask on her face shows the smallest crack, but I can't identify the emotion. She asks, "You want to know our history?"

Yes, Samara of New Canaan. Five million times, yes. I can't tell if she believes me. I really want her to believe me. Since I've already climbed out on a limb, I edge a little farther. "History is both my parents' . . ." I try to think of a word that won't seem foreign to her. "It's what they were trained for. Finding history that's been lost."

I've piqued her interest. She walks forward slowly, holding up her light. I don't bother; I'm on night function. "My family trained for the Archives," she says. "I think that must be much like history."

Archives. New Canaan has an Archives. Joanna Cho-Rodriguez may forgive me yet. And Samara has a family. I think I may die of not asking. But she's doing more talking than I've ever heard from her, and I'd be crazy to stop the flow. She pauses again, looks right at me.

"My uncle trained for the Archives, and he used magnifiers to repair the books."

I wait. I'm not sure what she's trying to say.

"He used magnifiers to see small things," she explains. "What do yours do?"

And there it is. The third challenge. I take another look back. Jill's light is bobbing now. She's not too close, but I don't have much time. I touch Samara's arm, just a little, making her jump, steering her to the other side of a landslide of rock that sparkles in our light. She looks wary, like she might cut and run. Or fight. But I only take off the glasses and offer them to her.

"They help me see," I tell her. Or that's one way of putting it.

She sets her jar on the ground and takes the glasses like they might sting or bite, turning them over in her hand. She looks at me through them, her brows down.

"But they only work for me, not anybody else."

She stares at me so deeply, the glasses held gingerly between two fingers, that this time I see something I recognize. That I know well. She is aching to know. Maybe just as bad as I am.

"Is it technology?" she whispers.

The word is a surprise. A big one. But I can feel myself grinning at her. It's not only easy to break protocol, it's downright satisfying. "Yes. That's exactly what they are."

"Can you see through walls?"

"Sometimes."

"Can you see what's coming in this passage?"

"Yes. For a long way. And there's nothing in the passage."

"Can you see inside me?"

I really wish the glasses could do that. "Some things."

"Like bones?"

I nod. She's been observant.

"Can they start a fire?"

"Sure." Okay, that one would've been hard to miss.

"Can you see through clothes?"

I smile, mostly because it's embarrassing. "Sort of. If I asked them to. I wouldn't ask them to. But it's against the rules to tell you this stuff, so don't say anything in front of Jill, okay? You'll get me in trouble."

I watch her think about this. Or about something. She's running one slim finger over the edge of the glasses, slow.

"Did technology heal your ankle?" she asks.

"It helped."

"Would you show me?"

"Yes. Just . . . when we're by ourselves, okay?" I smile at her again. She lays the glasses carefully back in my palm, but I don't put them on. She's looking right at me, and I'm thinking about that mask she wears. As perfect and hard as the insides of this planet. But now I don't think she's hiding just one or two things beneath it. I think she's hiding her whole self. Just below the surface. I wonder why.

"Have you . . ." Samara stops, drops her gaze. I want her to look up again, so I can see her eyes.

"Have I what?" It works. She looks at me.

"Have you been here before?"

The question was barely a whisper. But what I want to know is, why did she need to ask it? I shake my head. "No. I've never been here before."

Samara picks up her light, and then Jill is coming around the stones.

"Are we stopping?" she asks.

I slide the glasses back onto my face, but before either of us can answer, Samara's eyes drop closed and she's just . . . gone. Away.

"What is—" Jill starts, but I shush her. Last time I saw Samara do this she fell down, so I wait, ready to catch her or the handblown jar, whichever goes first. Her mask dissolves, just like it did before, and this time I watch her concentrate, searching. I see exactly when she finds what she's looking for. Because she smiles. A real one. It changes her face. Then her eyes snap open and the mask drops back into place again. I feel disappointed.

"In eight and a quarter bells we will be halfway to the boats," Samara says. "A little sooner, if we move quickly." Then she glides ahead in that fluid way she has, like she's melting through the dark.

Jill gives me a look like, *What boats?*

I don't have an answer. In fact, I have more questions than I know what to do with. About the Archives and bells and what she knows about technology. What her people might remember about Earth.

We move on down the passage without talking much, Samara pushing our pace until there's no breath for it anyway. We rest behind a pile of rocks, and then get up and do it again. And again. Moving toward a city I've been ordered to find, with the girl I've been ordered to maintain contact with. As per protocol. But I'm not sure protocol is right anymore. I'm not sure our training is right.

I want to see what's inside her again.

I want her to tell me everything.

I want her to want to talk to me.

Nita was the one who gave me my Outside name. Nadia. Like she gave me her extra tunic and leggings, which probably weren't extra at all. Like she gave me secret lessons during the middle bell, when I was supposed to be caching, showing me how to walk, talk, and wear my hair Outside, both of us giggling at my efforts. When I asked why she chose Nadia, she just shrugged and said, "Because it suits."

Nadia, we decided, worked with Nita, helping in the Archiva family chambers, and she lived with the planters, nearly two kilometers from Nita's house, at the foot of the mountains near the wheat fields. And three seasons ago, on the first of the dark days, Nadia went Outside, and ate a resting meal with Nita's family. She was shy at first, quiet. Until she discovered that she didn't have to be careful. That Nita's mother, brothers, grandpapa, didn't mind what she said or what she didn't. Didn't mind her ignorance about certain facts—that streets could smell, that you could be cheated in the Bartering Square, that making a clay pot meant getting your hands filthy. They didn't mind anything about her at all. Love, Nadia decided, was so much easier to feel in the Outside.

And when I climbed back down the supply shaft, back to the opulent lamplight and perfumed silence where my name is Samara, that was when I first began to suspect. A suspicion that grew and grew until I Knew.

That we of the Knowing are not as we should be.

FROM THE HIDDEN BOOK OF SAMARA ARCHIVA
IN THE CITY OF NEW CANAAN

19

SAMARA

Nita told a story once, all of us sitting around the heating furnace in her mother's house, about how the Earth people liked to eat each other. Complete with sound effects. Her littlest brothers were shrieking with laughter, Nathan smacking her arm, egging her on until she cheerfully explained how Earthlings also had wings on their heads, like the bluedads in the fields, and that was how they flew through the stars.

So far, not one thing I've ever heard about Earth seems to be true. Then again, three days ago I didn't even believe in Earth's existence, so I don't Know why being wrong should come as such a shock to me. I've slept for six bells, and then another three, unharmed. Beckett showed me his technology, told me that technology could heal. I think he told me the truth. And coming to study the history of New Canaan is nothing like the wanton destruction we've been taught Earth would bring.

I sneak a look at Beckett in the light of his jar, Jillian just behind him. He's thoughtful, one corner of his mouth turned up, a shadow darkening his chin. No sign of wings. Or cannibalism. And he's been telling me other things. Little things, about a father, a mother, a grandmother he knew as a child, small offerings that he gives along with his blanket and occasional food. Maybe he's only giving what it doesn't hurt for me to Know. That would be an intelligent way to gain my trust.

And it's not like he's once admitted where he's from. Maybe studying New Canaan means studying us like the plant specimens under glass in the chemistry labs. Maybe Earth will take us away to study us more, like the stories say.

Memory nudges, and I see Beckett smiling, his face open and unguarded as he puts the glasses in my hand. His smile also comes like a gift. One that's given often. But smiles can be lies just as easily as words. And I don't think Beckett would be smiling at me if he knew what I'd done.

I need to understand how I dreamed him.

Jillian catches my eye. I think I've been looking at Beckett a long time. And just like him, her feelings are open and impossible to miss. Anger—she's been furious for ten bells now, walking close, no more lagging behind to hide that technology she's been using. And then I watch her expression change into something like disdain before she looks away. Dismissal. The look carries a sting just as potent as words. Like a candle flame on skin.

And this is why we don't show our feelings Underneath. Because that flame is going to keep on burning, blistering, while Jillian, who shows no sign of having memory, will forget one day that she ever looked at me like that at all.

I lift my light to the path ahead and try to think of a world where the Knowing could Forget. Where you wouldn't have to be afraid of love. Or your children. If I can bargain with the Council for time, heal the Knowing with Forgetting, then that world could still be possible. If I cannot, then my time is short, and I might as well indulge in the memory of a smile.

And that sounds a little like Sonia.

I need to be even more careful than I thought. And for different reasons.

I walk fast, and we go a long way, in a silence that might have just as much to say as speech. The water beside us has been slowing, widening for some time, and then we pass into a huge room where there's not a river anymore at all, but a lake, dark and glossy, pooling to one side. Columns of blue-and-black-riddled stone drip down from the ceiling, climb up from the floor, sometimes meeting in the middle, reflecting in the water, making the rough cavern look almost formal in the shadows of our lights. It reminds me of the Forum.

When I compare the steps in my memory, I think we must be halfway to New Canaan. We've made good time. Better than I thought. There hasn't been the first sign of anyone coming behind us, and there's no point having the two of them falling down when we get to the city.

I cache the thought about what we'll do when we get to the city. And with more success than usual.

"We should rest here," I tell them.

"Beck?" Jillian whispers.

He does a slow turn with the glasses, checking the shadows and peering at the water before he nods to Jillian. And because I Know what he's doing when I shouldn't, he sends me a hint of his smile. Conspiratorial. A little naughty. And I flush. Hard. Jillian doesn't see this, thankfully; she's sighing with relief, dropping her pack in a smooth, flat section of stone a few meters back from the shore. I turn and face the pool, hoping the dark and my skin will be enough to hide the heat in my cheeks.

I should just ask him. Get the question out in the open. *Are you from Earth?* See if Beckett tells me lies or truth. And then I tell myself it doesn't matter. The outcome is the same, and that's why I don't bother to ask.

I push a stray curl behind my ear. I feel dirty. Ragged. Unsure and ridiculous. I set my pack on the ground, lift the strap of my book over my head, reach for the end of my braid, and pull the tie.

"I'm going to swim," I say to no one in particular. I don't care if I have to sleep in wet clothes. It will be worth it to be cleaner. And I need to do something. Occupy my mind. I've been in good control today, but now I'm upset, and that's when memories pull the hardest.

Then a voice I don't recognize says, "I'll come with you."

It's Jillian. A bright, cheerful Jillian. She pulls on the little fastener at the top of her clothes, like Beckett did, and the cloth splits in two. I wonder how they do that. Beneath the loose clothes, Jillian has on a tight-fitted kind of tunic, very short and of a thin, dark cloth, no sleeves, and leggings that don't actually have legs. She's small, and very curvy, and it's not all that much to wear. I look back and see Beckett, who must have been lying full length on the flat stone, now sitting up on his elbows.

Jillian smiles, big and confident, and steps toward the water. I put out a hand.

"What?" she snaps, and I'm a little relieved. This tone seems more natural.

"Only walk in water when the rock is solid below your feet," I tell her. "Never step in loose stones. Or sand."

"Oh? And why not?" She's back to cheerful.

"Because it could be sinking sand."

"And what does sinking sand do?"

"Sucks you down and drowns you."

She smiles again, puts a delicate toe into the water, and pushes. "Solid," she declares, and goes in up to her knees. "And what about out here, where it's deeper? How do you know what the bottom is like there?"

"I don't," I reply, kicking off my sandals. "So I think I'll swim, instead of sinking to the bottom to find out."

I wade out and dive beneath the surface. It's not as warm as the baths in the city, but it's not cold like bathing Outside, either. I let the water slide by in a vast, black dark, and it pushes back the memories.

When I come up for air, Jillian is treading water a few meters away, and Beckett is stepping out of his baggy clothes, the glasses already set aside. Coming in with us. I push back my hair. What he wears underneath is much like Jill's, only a little longer. How do they manage to make cloth fit so snug against skin on Earth? I can't imagine. But I Know he must have been doing more than learning history, because only the Outsiders of the fields look like that.

I duck back beneath the water again, before Jillian catches me looking, and wonder if I'll be going back to this again, in my memory.

I'd be lying if I said I wasn't.

I run my fingers through my hair, letting the water flow through, and when I come back up Jillian has moved near me, almost close enough to bump legs, and Beckett is swimming toward us, slow, with a glowing jar in one hand.

"Don't drown our light!" Jillian warns. But he doesn't seem worried. He's grinning, huge, holding the jar half in the water.

"Try not to make any waves," he says, "and look down."

The jar sends a wide, circular beam of light through the water, which is not black after all. That was only a reflection of the darkness. The lake is clear, and when the surface stills, far below our kicking feet, I see a bottom made of crystals, hundreds, thousands of them in squares of varying heights, white and luminous. Every now and then a crystal that is more delicate, pale green and glittering, drifts up from the others, its ends splitting again and again, looking more plant than mineral. It makes me feel enormous, like I'm looking down at a planet from above.

Beckett moves the light this way and that, showing the different formations, and then he says to Jillian, very low, "What does it remind you of?"

"Los Angeles," she breathes, and his smile gets bigger. I don't Know what this means, but Beckett sighs and lies back in the water, one arm out, the other balancing the light jar on his stomach. A floating lamp. The light puts his body in stark relief, and I can see a bruise running the length of one arm and down his side. He looks chiseled out of stone. He closes his eyes.

Then Jillian says, "So, Samara, how long have you been training to be a physician?"

I tear my eyes away from Beckett, to Jillian's big blue gaze. On guard. "I've finished my training."

"Oh? How long did it take you?"

"One hundred and eighty-five days."

"Really."

Beckett's eyes are open, his brows down. "Jill . . ."

"So how many dislocated joints have you set before now?" she asks.

"None," I reply. "Before his."

"Oh!" she says, eyes wide. "I'm surprised, then, that you'd risk someone's ability to walk, when you've never even practiced."

I look her in the eye. "I heard the procedures and I have seen the drawings. That is training."

"Without practicing."

I'm not sure what I'm being accused of. But I am definitely being accused.

Then Beckett says, "What's that?"

"What?" says Jillian, instantly distracted.

But he's already swimming through the dark, away from the shore, the light held high, slowly revealing the cavern wall. Or what I thought was the wall, but it isn't rock, or at least not that we can see. The wall is a tangle of roots, thick and twisting, reaching down from a ceiling that must be very close to the surface. Some of the roots have grown almost horizontal, seeking a clear path to water, others wending their way down to brush the surface. Drinking.

I swim into the range of Beckett's light and touch the hanging wood, run a hand along the smooth skin, pull down and feel it bend. Fern. And I smile. At a memory. A good one, this time.

"Outside," I say, "I've seen the children playing on fern roots, when they reach out like this for the water."

"What do they do?" Beckett asks.

"Bounce on them, before they jump in."

Now there's nothing but mischief in the grin, and he's already found an opening in the root tangle the right size to tuck in the jar. "Oh, Beckett," Jillian sighs. But he's pulling himself out of the water, up the jumble of roots until he finds one growing outward from the rest, about a third of the way up. He gets his hands on the root and hangs from it.

"Like this?" he calls. His body is stretched, long and sculpted, the root bending dangerously with his weight. He's trying to pull on it, to make it bounce.

"No," I say. "You should . . ."

But there's no need to finish the sentence. His wet hands slide off the end, and the splash when Beckett hits the pool seems disrespectful in the quiet. He comes back up, smiling and spluttering.

"So, not like that," he says, hair in his eyes.

I shake my head. "I'll show you."

I get a foot up on the root tangle and climb dripping from the pool, my hair heavy, hanging well past my waist now that it's wet, blood thrilling in my veins. Like the first time I went Outside. I've always wanted to do this. I see the root I have in mind, pale gray in the dark, about five meters up, and much bigger than the one Beckett fell from.

It's harder to get to than I thought. The wood bends and slips beneath my wet feet, but I finally get a knee up, and then I'm standing on top of it, hanging on to the surrounding tangle. I can just make out Beckett's head in the shadowy water, Jillian's bright yellow one much easier to spot. I'm going to have to let go, bounce on the end of this root while keeping my balance, like Nita's little brothers do Outside, and allow the upward momentum to fling me into the air.

"Samara, are you sure this is a good idea?" Beckett calls.

I'm not sure this is a good idea at all. It's higher, and darker, and more exposed up here than I thought, and it occurs to me that if Earth can make clothes that cling to a body, then so can the people of Canaan. We just have to get them wet. But this is not as high as the cliffs I jumped to escape my city, and danger has always driven my memories away. It's as close as I've ever come to Forgetting.

I edge out onto the root, shuffling sideways, one hand still clinging to the tangle. I feel the wood beneath my feet bend, wanting to spring. I curl my toes, my fingers let go, and I scoot out a little more. Then the root stills and I am balanced, arms out, like I'm ready to let Adam make me fly. I feel the beat in my chest, speeding, the air heavy, the sound of distant water in the caves. One wrong move, one centimeter too far this way or that, and I will fall. It feels like my life.

I watch Nita's little brothers bending their knees in my memory. The way they rode the movement of the branch. I bounce once, twice, and the root sends me high into the air, both fast and slow, the world turning from the blue-and-black ceiling of the cavern to the shine of the water in the glow of Beckett's jar.

And there is nothing pulling at my mind. I feel air, and lightness, and freedom. Like Forgetting should be. Until I hit the water with a smack.

And that feels like it stings.

We had a little time back in Austin after training finished on the fake *Centauri III*, and after a day or so I went down to the school compound, to the quad after classes were over, thinking to surprise Jason and Kiran, Nasta, Amanda. Whoever might be there from the friends I knew before. I was grades ahead of them, but once classes were over, it didn't seem to matter. We went places, did things. Talked every day. Amanda cried when I left. I wondered a few times if she'd missed me.

The chatter in the quad used to drown out the music and the visuals, but it wasn't as full that day. So it was easy to scan through the crowd. I don't know what I was expecting from them. Excitement? Curiosity? I mean, I was incredibly cool, right? My family was chosen for the Canaan Project. I'd been living in isolation on a pretend cruiser for a year. In four weeks, I'd be hurtling through space.

And then I saw them, Jason, Kiran, and Nasta, sitting together at a table, talking like we always did. But they didn't see me. They didn't even recognize me. I looked up Amanda later, in the military files, and found her marked "Lethe's." A third of that compound was marked "Lethe's" when I researched. But that day I sat back, just a meter away, and observed. Like we'd been trained. Like they were from another culture.

They were another culture. To me. Talking about places and names I didn't know. And it felt strange to be so far outside. Like I was less. It hurt. And I thought right then that I will remember this. If I ever meet a lost colonist of Canaan, I will never, ever make them feel less.

FROM THE LOG BOOK OF BECKETT RODRIGUEZ

Day 11, Year 2

The Lost Canaan Project

20

BECKETT

She looks small up there, the pale cloth of her clothes clinging tight to her body, almost glowing in the shadows, framed by more hair on one head than I've ever seen. I think she's going to fall, but she doesn't. Or not exactly. She rides the bounce of the branch and goes flying, and is pretty graceful about it, until her back hits the water with a smack. I wince, and I'm ready to laugh, until Jill snickers. Which is nothing like my laugh was going to be. I turn in the water.

"What is your problem?"

I see her eyes narrow, but I'm not over being mad at her. Not even close. What was she trying to do back there, asking all those questions about Samara's training? Like she was trying to prove something. I've never seen her act like this. Jill is serious, driven, goal-oriented, but she's always been . . . nice. Hasn't she? Then again, how many people have we been around? The crew, my parents, Vesta, who's pretty sure her daughter lit the moon. What I've never seen, I realize, is Jill not getting what Jill wants. It may be a new experience for her.

She may have to get used to it.

Samara breaks the surface, and I ask, "How was that?"

"Exactly like you'd think," she replies. And she's smiling. A real one. Almost laughing.

That's it. I'm going up. I swim for the root tangle, get onto the slick wood and climb, aiming for the root Samara used. It feels flimsy when I get there, insubstantial, with a long, dark fall that has stretched even longer somehow now that I'm looking down. I'm not sure how Samara even stood up here.

"You have to push down and ride the bounce," Samara calls out. "And don't go in on your back!"

I grin down at her. "Understood."

This is way scarier than I thought it would be. Especially in the shadows and the dark. But I want it. I want everything this planet has to offer. I take a breath, push down on the root, and the thing flings me like I wouldn't have believed. I soar like a bird, for maybe three seconds, and I don't go in on my back. I go in flat on my chest.

I come up, skin on fire, and Samara says, "How was that?"

"Exactly like you'd think," I say, and she really is laughing now. So am I.

We do it three more times, and by the last one, Samara manages an actual dive. I do not. Not even close. But every time I came up from the clear water, some new part of me stinging, I got to look at what lives beneath that smooth facade on Samara's face. I'd have done it another eighty times if my body could take it.

I asked Jill if she wanted to try, but she only shook her head, that line between her eyes, mouth shut tight. Except for the last time Samara was making her climb, when Jill swam close to me and said, almost sweet, "Beckett, you don't think you could be having an issue with objectivity, do you?"

I didn't answer her. I didn't even look at her. Because Jill knows how to aim where it hurts. She knows I care about this, and that I want to do it right. She knows that objective observation is a basic of the job.

Be that way, then, Jill.

I get the jar and swim to the shore on my back, holding it on my stomach, lighting a path through the blackness. Samara is relaxed, present, cutting through the water and getting ahead of me. I don't know what's going on or what we're walking into or who might try to kill who tomorrow, but for the moment, I'm just glad to be here, off the *Centauri III*. Doing something real.

When I wade out with the light, Samara is already squeezing the water from her mass of hair, Jill snatching up her own light and pack, heading off to change behind a boulder a safe distance away. Samara turns as soon as Jill is gone.

"Can I see your ankle?" she whispers.

I glance at the boulder, Jill's light shining behind it, sit where I am and stretch out my leg. The air is so much colder now that I'm wet. I'm shivering when she kneels down in front of me, running both hands feather-light over each side of my ankle. I watch her pause over the pin-pricks and tiny bruises where Jill used the gel, where the infusion went in, only just touching them with a finger.

Her face is serious, concentrated, wet hair thrown behind her shoulders, that shirt clinging to everything it touches. And when she puts those eyes on me, I feel the weight of it, like I did before, and this time something twists inside my chest. An agreeable sort of pain.

Okay. I might be having an issue with objectivity.

"Does it hurt?" she whispers.

Yes. But aloud I only say, "A little. But I've walked a long way."

"Are you certain? You're not in pain?"

I think Samara might have noticed I'm having a little trouble with my breathing.

Jill comes around the boulder, zipping up her jumpsuit, and Samara drops her hands like my skin is hot. Jill must have changed like lightning, when I was expecting her to be back there at least five extra minutes, sanitizing. Or maybe I've been sitting here longer than I thought. Samara's serene expression is right back in place.

"How's the ankle?" Jill asks. She's smiling, back to sweet and cheerful.

Oh no.

"It seems to have set well, Samara. For your first try."

I close my eyes.

"I'm still interested in your training," Jill goes on, laying out her wet clothes on a rock. "I thought about being a physician once . . ."

It's the first I've heard of it.

". . . but it was the blood, you know, and that sort of thing that worried me. So until Beckett, you hadn't done any practical applications of your skills?"

Samara pauses before she answers that one. But her voice is cool when she says, "It's true that knowing can be different from doing. If I had done the procedure before, I would have known how hard to pull, and would have set the bone the first time."

There's another pause, and then Samara comes back with a question of her own.

"But how could training be practiced? You would need to wait a long time for someone to be sick, or hurt. And how could surgery be practiced before it needed to be done?"

Jill pounces. "You're saying you can do surgery? Even though you've never done it?" She looks at me, triumphant, like she's caught Samara at something. "So in New Canaan, after a few weeks of being told and looking at pictures, whatever you've learned after that makes you a physician? Is that right?"

And then I get why Jill is doing this. She wants me to see Samara as ignorant, or a liar. A local. Less than we are because the values of her culture are different. If Jillian thinks this is going to get her what she wants, she's wrong. And the news for Jillian is that she wasn't going to get what she wanted before I ever laid eyes on Samara. Jill's smile is big.

"Is that right, Samara?"

"How else would it be?" Samara replies.

"Well, I'm sure different places have different levels of medicine.

Some are more advanced, so some might need longer. Years even, to train . . ." She blinks her big eyes at me once. "Other places are just going to be a little more pretech, that's all."

Samara shakes her head. "But only those with memory would ever train to be a physician. Isn't it the same where—"

Her voice stops abruptly, and the silence hangs. "Where" what? Where we come from? Earth? Is that what she was going to say?

Then Jill asks sweetly, "What do you mean, 'those with memory'?"

Samara looks at Jill like she's the one that's pretech. "I mean people with memory. The people who cannot forget."

"What are you talking about?"

"You . . ." Samara's expression doesn't exactly change, but I can see by the stillness of her body that she's shocked. Her gaze darts to Jill, and then to me. "You don't understand memory? You don't have . . . Knowing?"

I lean forward, arms on my knees. "Tell me what it is."

"Yes, tell us, Samara."

Jill's voice has a victorious tone, but Samara doesn't even look at her. She talks to me, brows down. "Knowing means . . . that when information, or an experience, or a feeling enters your mind, it can never lessen or leave. The memory is forever. You don't have this?"

I'm trying to wrap my head around it. "So a person with memory can never forget?"

Samara searches my face. What is she trying to find there?

Jill huffs. "So you're saying that you have 'memory,' and that means you've never forgotten anything? Not once in your life?"

Samara doesn't answer again, but I can see her shoulders hunch, drawing into herself. And I'm thinking, fast. About those signs in Canaan, "Without Memories, They Are Nothing" and "Remember Our Truth." The way Samara seems to go away into her mind. Into her memories.

I lean forward. "How many of you can do this?" I see Jill's mouth open from the corner of my eye.

"All of us in the city," she whispers.

"What kinds of things do you remember? What you've seen? What you've heard?"

"It is every experience."

I see Jill throw up her hands. I don't care what she thinks right now. This is incredible. And it's going to help me understand Canaan. Samara. Everything. "Have you always been able to remember?"

She stares at the ground without answering.

"How do you make it happen? Or does it not happen for some? Samara, is that why you asked if we had forgotten? Because some people don't have it? Or because they lose it? Did the people of Old Canaan lose it? How far back does it go? How far back can you remember? Or wait . . ." I see Samara opening the door in that column, telling me she remembered. "Is that how you knew there was a safe way through the caves? Is that how you know which way to go now?"

Samara's eyes snap up to mine. "But you don't need my memory to find a safe way through the caves, do you?"

I sit back like I've been smacked. Where did that come from? She knows Jill can't find out I told her about the glasses. Jill's brows are already up, her face one big accusation, and there's no guessing needed with Samara's expression right now. The facade is down and she is boiling mad.

I don't know what I've done. I've been patient to the point of saint-hood, holding in my own questions, answering hers. Breaking protocol, letting her set the rules, all to gain her trust. And the one time I give in and ask what any sane person might after being told there are people whose brains never forget, she threatens me with Jill. Who is jealous, and feeling vindictive about it. Who's just getting the idea that maybe I'm not willing to play her game. If Jill found out I'd deliberately broken protocol to an outrageous extent—like I have—would she tell the Commander? She might. And Samara is mad. At me. And Jill is acting like a child. I'm sick of both of them.

I get up, grab the glasses and my pack and the dry jumpsuit, and go behind the boulder that seems to be the unofficial dressing room. And by the time I've changed my clothes, in true Beckett style, I've also changed my temper.

This girl is in trouble. She is traumatized, from a culture I know almost nothing about. Who knows what sensitivities I was just trampling all over? I broke protocol to follow my own instincts, and that is my risk, a risk she couldn't know anything about, a risk that Jill couldn't help but be upset by. And it's not Jill's fault, either, for that matter, if I've outgrown her. How could she have seen that coming? And if she doesn't know I'm moving on, then that has to be my fault, too, for not actually saying so.

What would Dad have done, in my shoes? His job, probably, professionally, and managed to expand the breadth of human knowledge while he was at it. What would Mom have done? Maybe something a little closer to what I'm doing.

But I have a feeling she would've done it better.

I zip the suit, put the glasses on, and just when I get the earpiece back in place I catch something. A hint of static. I freeze. Listen. Wait. But there's nothing. It doesn't come again.

I look around the cavern through the glasses, at the roots on the other side of the lake, the one we jumped from sticking out pale gray from the others. We must be just beneath the surface.

I run my hand over the boulder. Black rock, but marbled with the glittering blue I saw so much of in the mountains around Old Canaan. Like the door I blew up, that Samara said was made of mountain rock. Metallic hydrogen. Naturally occurring. The resource that had the original New World Space Exploration company so excited when they started the Canaan Project. We can make it now, much easier than hauling it across space, but I wonder if there's a difference between the metallic hydrogen we make and what is actually here. Something that's messing with our communications.

But the signal did come. For a second. And when we leave these caves, I think there's a good chance I'm going to get communication. And when I do, I'll be hearing from Commander Faye. Guaranteed.

Suddenly, I'm not exactly sure just how bad I want that signal.

21

SAMARA

They don't understand Knowing.

I take my pack and my light to the opposite side of the flat stone space from Jillian, and sit with my back against a natural column. I'm mad. At myself. I lost my temper in a way the Knowing are never allowed. But he made me feel strange. Abnormal. The specimen under glass. What does he think has been happening to me, when I go to my memories? He must think I'm insane. They both must.

Maybe I am.

I knew Jillian and Beckett were without memory. That was obvious. But I assumed Earth would be something like Canaan, with the privileged and the not. Those who had Knowing, and those who didn't. But they've never even heard of it.

I think of Grandpapa Cyrus, telling me that fading memories were good, normal. That we of the Underneath were the ones who were different. Have we not always been like this? The idea is incredible, as monumental as the concept of technology that can heal. Maybe the Forgetting really is a cure, because Knowing is an actual sickness.

I wish I could write this in my book. In case it's the truth. But right now I'd soak it.

Beckett comes out from behind the boulder, back to being the alien with his technology and baggy cloth. He doesn't look at me, or at Jillian. He just wrings out his wet clothes, slapping them out to dry on a rock, hair slicked back, showing the healing cut on one side of his forehead.

I scared him when I hinted in front of Jillian that I Knew he could see his way through the caves. As usual, the emotion was clear on his face. I haven't really considered what kind of rules Beckett might be breaking until now, or what might happen to him if he's caught. Something as bad as Outside? As bad as Judgment? Earth is supposed to be cruel. More cruel than we are. I wonder what I've done.

And then I jump. Beckett is standing right in front of me, holding out his blanket.

"Here," he says. "You're cold."

I am cold. I'm shivering.

"Take off your wet clothes, and you can wrap up in this until they're dry."

I'm not certain I should.

"Take it, Samara. I don't need it."

The allure of being dry is too much, and to refuse makes it seem as if I'm still angry. I take the blanket and go behind the boulder without making eye contact, yank off my wet things—I'm not sure they deserve to be called clothes anymore—lay them out, and wrap the blanket around my body like a dress without sleeves, holding it together with one hand. It's thin, red, and very warm, and there's a lot of it. I can't imagine what kind of plant would make the material. It trails the ground as I go and sit again next to my pack, back against the blue-black stone.

Beckett doesn't look up. He's on his side, head propped on one hand near the light jar. Jillian is asleep, or at least still, a meter or two behind his back. There's a waterbug crawling up his finger, the skates it uses on the surface of the water splayed delicately across Beckett's tan skin. He lets it walk off onto the ground, then puts his finger back in its path and peers at it, perched tiny and black on his knuckle, before setting it down again. The waterbug keeps coming to the light, keeps climbing back onto his hand.

And for the first time, I really comprehend that Beckett has lived on Earth. Seen moons up close and the stars from their other side. How brave do you have to be to let yourself fall off the ground and into the sky? To leave your own planet? I don't understand why he would come all this way, and break his rules for me. Pull me out of the street when the Council was coming.

"I saw a map once," I say. Beckett blinks, but he doesn't look up from the waterbug. "In the Archives, with my uncle Towlend. In an old book. It showed the way through the caves. I looked at it in my memory, and that's how I Knew."

When his voice comes, it's low and resonant. Avoiding the echo. "Can you remember the whole map?"

"Yes."

"You can see it, in your head?"

"Yes."

Then he asks, "How old were you when you saw it?"

"Four."

He laughs just a little. I smile, though I don't really Know what's funny. He reaches up and takes off the glasses, setting them on the stone beside him, and only then does he glance up. I think he's giving me privacy. So I won't worry that he's looking through the blanket. Jillian doesn't move.

"I've been thinking," he says, "that it must be hard to have so many memories." He watches the waterbug scrabble against the glass of light. "Is it?"

Yes, Beckett Rodriguez of Earth. Knowing is one of the worst things that can happen to you. But I only say, "Yes."

He doesn't ask me anything more. And I think he wants to. And then I blurt out, "What is a Rodriguez?"

He lifts a brow. "What do you mean?"

"What does a Rodriguez do?"

He grins. "It's just a name. Not an occupation." He sees when I don't understand the word. "It's not a job."

"So it doesn't have . . . You don't work in a field?"

Both his brows are up now. "No. Why would you think that?"

I don't Know what to say. I adjust the blanket, tightening it across my chest.

"Okay, then I want to ask you something." Beckett sits up, hands hooked together in front of his knees, wet hair curling against his neck. "You don't have to answer if you don't want to."

I'm instantly on edge.

"Would you please, for the love of all that's holy, tell me what a bell is?"

Now I'm smiling. "You don't know what a bell is?"

"No. And I might actually die of curiosity."

"It's time," I say. "A length of time."

"How long?" he asks. I can't think of a good way to answer him. His brows come together. "How do you keep time?"

"I remember it."

"Really? Every second?"

I'm not sure what a second is, but I can see him considering. Then he grins and picks up the glasses, putting them on his face. "Okay, I'll tell you when to start, and then you tell me when a bell has gone by."

I nod.

"Ready? Three, two, and go."

I note the moment, and he sets the glasses aside again.

"Can I ask you something else? And if you don't want to answer, you don't have to." This time, I think, he's serious. "What happened to your arms?"

I don't Know what he's talking about until I brush one of the little divots above my elbow. I feel self-conscious again. "Just . . . wellness injections."

"Injections, like with a needle? Can I see?"

I nod, and immediately regret it. I haven't forgotten that I'm naked under a blanket. I wish I could. But I did fail to consider the fact before I moved my head. Beckett steps over the waterbug, across the stone space, and squats down beside me. I turn a little, so he can see the scars on my right arm, three rows of three. This is convenient, because he can't see my face. He moves my hair from my shoulder, but he doesn't touch my skin. He doesn't have to. I can feel his gaze.

"Is it a big needle?"

"Are there different sizes?"

"What are they for?"

"Health. We get them once a year. At the first sunrising. To make our bodies more efficient and boost our immune systems. We don't get sick Underneath. Not like Outside." Unless we're all sick Underneath, that is. I thought once to learn to make the injections myself after I was a physician, and smuggle them to the Outside. The loss of that dream goes slicing through my memory, leaving a fresh cut behind.

"How many do you have? In all?"

"Eighteen." I remember the pleased look on my mother's face when Marcus Physicianson pushed in the needle. But I already Knew then that I would be the last of the Archivas.

Then I think Beckett must be able to see my face after all, because he asks, "What is it?"

I shake my head. "When you have eighteen marks, you're ready to find a partner. That's all."

"Do you have a . . . partner?"

Memories flash over the surface of my mind. Sonia's body lying on the stones, and Reddix telling me to go home. What was he doing in the Forum? I'd just left him in the medical section. And for the first time I wonder if Mother struck that deal with the Physiciansons, or if it could have been Reddix who made an agreement with my mother. Surely not. And it will never happen now.

"No, I don't have a partner," I reply. I feel the prick of Mother's disappointment from kilometers away. "When do you get partners on . . ."

I stop. Earth. That's the word that was coming next. That's twice I've done that, and the unsaid hangs in the air.

Beckett says, "Do you want to ask me something?"

I drag my eyes to his. Dark, and with the shape that is the only thing out of place from my dream. *Yes,* I want to say. *I want you to tell me you're from Earth.* And then I understand why I will not ask. Because I'm afraid. If he lies to me, it will hurt. Forever. If he doesn't, then I'm not sure I can justify what I'm about to do.

I shake my head no, and he says, "Okay," gives me one corner of his grin before going back to his waterbug.

I watch him play with it, gently, until it springs away, skating off across the surface of the water, and after a time, I say, "It will have been a bell in three, two . . ." He picks up the glasses. "Now," I tell him.

Beckett looks at me, and now his smile is huge. "That's an hour. Exactly."

"An hour?"

"Exactly. Sixty minutes. With sixty seconds in every minute."

That seems like a difficult way to keep up with time. Beckett lies back on the stone, arms behind his head, and I think he wants to ask me more. But he doesn't. He is beautiful. And there is an ache inside me. An echo in an empty room.

This is the sort of thing that can ruin you.

We sleep. Or at least Jillian does. I cache, carefully and precisely, but it's not working. Beckett thinks. After four bells, I rouse them. I don't Know how long we'll be in the boats, or exactly where the boats are going to take us, and we were in this cavern longer than I'd planned. They eat while I put on clothes that are somewhat dry, and when I let Jillian have the place behind the boulder, I decide I was wrong to think she was sleeping. Her eyes are red.

We find the passage by the sound of water pouring back into the river on the other side of the cavern. No need for the glasses. I set a pace that doesn't leave much room for talking, and after a bell and a half we lose the Torrens, gushing down beneath chunks of fallen rock, and the ceiling opens, sprawling up into a narrow, tall room of stone. On the far end, carved into a flat space of sheer, black rock, is a rounded arch, fog roiling out of it. A tunnel. A human-made tunnel.

Jillian and Beckett follow me inside. The way is hazy in our pale lights, the air we breathe partially water. I look back and see Beckett, hair frosted with mist, running his hand down the smoothness of a wall. He wants to know how the tunnel was made. I want to Know why it was made. Maybe my ancestors came this way, I think, the people of Canaan, to build my city in the fog and dark.

The tunnel spills us into another cavern that is roaring with falling water. The stone is almost completely black here, like the insides of the city, everything dripping from spray and swirling haze. We've found the Torrens again, bigger, faster, more like the Torrens I Know at home, and I see that it's really two rivers, joined by a waterfall emptying down from above, one of them much colder than the other. The temperature has dropped enough to make me shiver.

And then, where the water eddies around to a shallow pool, I see the boats. Three of them, tied to posts driven into stone, made of treated fern wood, silver-gray in our light, big enough to seat four, maybe five. Much like what we use on the Darkwater beneath the city, only sleeker, slimmer. The boats are half in the pool, half pulled up onto a slanting slab of black rock that disappears beneath the lap of water.

Beckett is already moving toward the nearest boat, but I put out a hand, making him pause. He remembers without me saying it, and puts just a bit of weight into the shallow part of the water. When he discovers the bottom is solid rock, he wades in to the tops of his odd shoes to examine the nearest boat, caressing it with his eyes and his hands. Jillian shakes her head.

"We're not really taking boats?"

Beckett looks up, stares at the way forward. I see his eyes looking at something that isn't behind the glasses. "There might be another way," he says. He gives me a quick glance. "But it could be longer, less direct. I would guess there's a way for cartage. To haul the boats back."

And I see that he's right. There are five mooring posts here and only three boats, and the current of the Torrens is too fast for traveling in more than one direction. The boats must be carried back, and that means these caverns have been used not only to leave the abandoned city, but probably to go to it as well. The danger of walking right into one of the Council suddenly seems very real.

I wade into the cold water and look over the boat in the light of my jar. It's not new. There's a change of color in the wood at the waterline that says it's been sitting like this for a long time. But it isn't ancient, either. It's watertight, the rope better than the one I took over the cliff. I look at where the current is moving, whitecapping in the fog. If it was dangerous, they wouldn't have bothered to bring all these boats down here, would they? Or is the danger that these boats will take us straight into New Canaan? I've never seen a boat on the Torrens. The origin of the river in the city is a black stone arch in the Forum, water shooting out like a fountain.

I go back into my mind, moving between the memories. There is Uncle Towlend, the tattered book, the delicate pages, and the red ink. I can't see the cartage way, though I think Beckett probably can. I leave the map, think back to our steps through the cave, the time that has passed, each pound of my sandal on the dry and dusty plain.

I open my eyes. It's hard to say how much extra walking up and down we've been doing underground. I'm sure I ran the plain faster. That the Council probably did, too. But my best guess is two more days to get to the city if we're walking. Maybe three. I'm not sure where these boats are going to land, only that it can't be in the city, and that it will be impossible to meet another person on the way. "We should take the boats," I say.

Jillian looks at Beckett, defiant, and a kind of silent conversation begins. No matter what Beckett says about not having a partner, he really must know her well for them to understand each other this way. Beckett shrugs, drops the pack from his shoulder into the boat, and with only an instant of hesitation and an abundance of pique, Jillian walks to Beckett's boat and throws her pack in as well. The conversation, it seems, is over.

I climb into the boat without rocking it much, sitting in front of Jillian. There are no seats, so I cross my legs in the bottom, trying to keep my pack out of the puddle I've already made. Beckett opens his pack and pulls out the folded red blanket. "Here," he says. "It's waterproof. For your book."

I have a piece of oiled canvas, which is the only thing that saved it from my jump over the cliffs. But this will be better. "Thank you," I say without looking at him.

I am in so much danger.

"Samara," he says, working at the knot of the mooring rope. "How far is it to New Canaan?"

He's asking the same question I asked myself. And because Beckett is not stupid, it occurs to me that he is never going to enter my city willingly without information. I don't want to think about this. Or bargains. I cache the problem for later, and just say, "Not yet."

He accepts this, hands me his light jar, and shoves us away from the shelf of rock, hopping over the side and nearly tipping us. He's not used to boats, I see. Maybe they don't have water like this on Earth. As soon as he's in, I hand him his jar and hold up my own. The boat is turning in the current, toward the main force of the river beyond the reach of my light. There are no oars, no way to steer or paddle. The water is going to take us where it wants now, and there's nothing we can do about it. It's scary. And a bit of a thrill.

"Hang on," Beckett says. I don't Know what he means, but when I see him put the light between his legs and grip the sides of the boat, I do the same.

We pick up speed, a smooth glide, and then we are in the main current, moving fast through the mist, the river funneling us into another tunnel. The fog thins into wisps and is gone. I smell rain and soil, and for a long time we are a circle of light speeding through darkness, casting shadows against walls of water-smoothed rock. I don't Know what Beckett sees through the coming dark, but he sits still in front of me, concentrating, hair damp on his neck, Jillian tense and silent behind us. The boat tilts, slapped by a wave, water spraying over the sides, the walls narrow, my hair blows, and the sound of splashing becomes a roar. I clutch my pack tight between my legs. We shoot forward and Beckett yells, "Down!"

I throw myself forward while he throws himself back, and for a moment I think we are airborne, soaring, and then the boat hits water and we tumble around inside it, water drenching us from every side. The wood creaks, and when I open my eyes I am on my stomach and the boat is alive with spilled light, glowworms floating in a shallow pond of water, lighting it like white fire. Beckett is beside me on his back, my face near his chest, Jillian lying on my legs, but when I try to lift my head to see beyond the boat, Beckett pushes it down again. He points up, and I see black rock zooming close above us.

I keep my chin above the glowing water, with Beckett's hand on my head, and for the first time consider that we really are going to drown. That the boat could fill and sink. That this tunnel will become nothing but water and leave us no surface to float on at all, a pipe we can never find the end of.

The boat lurches, we take another dousing spray, and then I leave my stomach behind me as we fall. Beckett grips my hair and I hear Jillian shriek once, clinging to my legs. We hit bottom, my face is underwater, bright behind my closed eyes, and then I am up, gasping, and the boat is shooting forward, smooth, making two plumes of white spray. The roar dulls, the boat slows, the current from the waterfall we've just ridden pushing us across a calm pool. Once again the ceiling is far above us, natural red light filtering down from an opening somewhere that I can't see. We bump into a shoreline, stuck, the back end of the boat turning just a little in the remaining flow.

I look at Beckett, his hand still full of my hair, the glasses speckled with dripping water. He uses his other hand to lift them from his face, dark eyes wide and surprised, and I watch the smile come, not even a little guilty this time.

He says, "Does anybody want to do that again?"

And then I am laughing, and so is he, echoing over the noise of the short waterfall.

Beckett sits up, shakes the water from his head, Jillian on her knees while the boat rocks, dripping like the rest of us. She frowns, looks down, and says, "Beckett, you drowned our lights."

We all laugh this time, and I think the sound is relief. I scramble to find the jars while Jillian and Beckett try to rescue the remaining glowworms. The boat is stuck on a muddy, pebbly beach, and farther down, in the dim redness of the cavern light, I can see two more boats tied to stakes in the shore. Then I remember my pack.

I give the light jars to Beckett and snatch it out of the water, stepping lightly up the length of the boat to the shore, leaping out over the waterline to the firmer stony ground. The pack is soaked through, but the book is dry, protected by the blanket. I sigh with relief, and then I hear a splash and look up. Jillian has jumped over the side into the shallow water, heading toward the shore. But she's gone still, her blue eyes large.

"Beck?" she says, voice small. And then she screams.

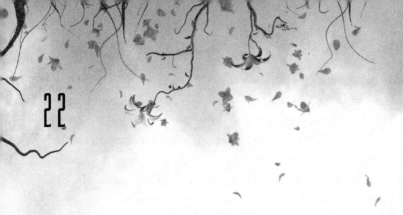

22

BECKETT

I hear Jillian yell my name at the same time Samara shouts, "Hold her!"

I drop the jar of light and wish I hadn't, because the redness coming in from the ceiling hole is dim and Jill is in shadow. But what I can see is that she's up to her chest in water, when I thought the level should have been barely above her knees. Then I understand. Jill is sinking. Sinking sand.

I nearly tip the boat getting to her. The front end is grounded on the shore rocks while the back has floated away, out of Jillian's reach. But my arms are longer than hers. I stretch out, get her hand, and she is so stuck the boat actually comes to her when I pull. I hook my arms below hers while she clings to my neck, feel her shallow, frightened breaths.

"Okay," I say. "Okay, I've got you . . ."

But I don't have her. Not really. I can feel the force I'm working against, sucking her down. I pull again, and it's not enough. More than not enough. My arms are in the water now, too, little ripples lapping her neck. I look in her eyes. She's going to panic, and if she panics, I may not be able to keep my grip.

"Hold tight," I whisper. "Pull with me . . ."

"Beck . . ." Jill whispers, then she hisses. "Something moved! Against my leg. There's something in here!"

I tug Jill again, and feel arms go around my middle. Samara.

"Together," she says. I heave backward, Samara adding her weight, and a little more of Jill comes out of the water. I readjust my grip, and we do it again. Jill's body is rising up, and up, and then she screams again, flails so hard I nearly lose my hold, and slides downward.

"It bit me! Something bit me!"

I don't see how anything could have bitten her, not through the jumpsuit. But that really doesn't matter if she doesn't hang on.

"Jill! Listen! You've got to pull with me. Lift up your legs! Ready? One, two . . ."

I can feel Samara's locked hands digging into my chest. She's giving it all she's got and so am I. Jill's face is screwed up with effort. I feel when one of her legs comes free, then the other, and Samara and I lose our balance backward, rocking the boat, though I've still got a handful of Jill's jumpsuit.

"Do not put your feet down," Samara warns her, jumping over the bow to the dry part of the shore, tugging on the boat before it comes loose and we take another ride to who knows where. I get Jill back in one leg at a time. I think she has tears running down her face somewhere in all the dripping water, and her boots are gone. But where the leg of her suit is pushed up there's a single puncture mark, blood running pink and watery down her leg. She leans over to look at it, then starts up her expert cussing, though soft this time, I think only for herself. Or me.

"Can you walk?"

She nods, and I help her to the safe ground, where she collapses onto the pebbles. The suit is mud-stained to her waist. Samara kneels down, examining the wound on Jill's calf with the same sort of focused expression she gave my ankle.

"It is deep," Samara says, "but small. It will not need sewing."

She's right about that. Samara may be good, but I'm not about to let her sew Jill's skin like a handmade shirt.

"There was something in there," Jill whispers, "something below the sand . . ."

Samara looks back over her shoulder, like something might come crawling out of that pool, which is disturbing. I look through the glasses and can't find a thing. But the place where Jill was sinking is such a perfect blend of water and sand it's hard to see through. Then I look at Jill again. Her cussing has turned to murmuring. Like she's falling asleep.

"Jill?" Her eyes flutter closed. "There's something wrong with her," I say, but Samara is already examining Jill's face. Her eyes have gone red and a little puffy, I thought from crying but now I'm not so sure. I turn over Jill's leg. The puncture mark is swelling so fast I can almost watch it rise. Then Jill coughs, gasps. Like she can't breathe.

"Samara! What lives in there?"

She shakes her head. "I don't Know . . ."

"Quick! Is it poisonous?"

But Samara just closes her amber eyes, serene, kneeling at Jill's side as if she were carved from stone. And she's gone. Perfect.

I run for the boat at the same time I go to the database of the glasses, searching. Poison. What do we have for poison when we don't know what the poison is? I grab Jill's pack from the water while I scan the information, get the medical kit in my hands, and drop to my knees at her side again. She's wheezing now, gasping, her face reddening and swelling. She can't get air. She's not going to be able to breathe. I change the search in the database, looking for something, anything. Jill can't die. That cannot happen.

"It's not poison," Samara says suddenly. She's back, eyes open, panting like she's been for a run. "Allergy. She is allergic."

"Are you sure?"

Samara nods as she slips her hand beneath Jill's head, tilting it, trying to open her airway. Jill is twisting, choking for breath, while I toss infusers left and right trying to lay my hands on the one for anaphylactic shock. Samara is using both hands to force Jill's head back, staring down into her wide-open eyes as she flails, and I see Samara go stiff, her hands slipping.

"Samara, stay here!" I yell.

But she's leaving again. I find the right infuser, press it against Jill's neck to let it calculate the dose. She's moving too much.

"Samara, hold her still. Hold her arms still!"

Samara holds one arm, though not hard enough. Jill is struggling, and Samara's gone rigid, breathing hard, looking down into Jill's wide-open eyes, but I'm not sure she sees her. Jill isn't wheezing anymore; she's not making any noise at all, the redness paling from her face. I lay my body on Jill's other arm, pinning her down. The infuser gets the dose and I hear the whoosh as it goes in. Jill twists beneath me for another second and then she doesn't move.

Everything pauses. My heart, the river, time, a long moment that squeezes inside my chest, that hurts like I've been hit. I care about Jill, I realize. A lot. Jillian was everything there was to have on the ship. I care, just maybe not in the way she wanted me to. And that hurts, too.

"Jill?" I say, like I'm asking a question. Asking if she's alive. And then I feel movement beneath me, a tiny wheeze, a gasp. Jill coughs, and the relief leaves me too distracted to think about anything else. I get off and see her chest moving, the color coming back to her face, though her eyes are still closed.

She murmurs something I can't understand, and then I glance up at Samara. She's still on her knees beside Jill, staring, but she is gone. Something else is in her vision. And then she opens her mouth and screams. Not just a yell or a shout. She screams from the pit of her stomach, and it's the worst thing I've ever heard. She draws breath and starts to do it again. I step over Jill and take her by the arms.

"Stop it!"

She doesn't. This time I shake her a little.

"Samara!"

She stops, blinks, looks at me, and she really sees me, not the terrible something else. She's shaking beneath my hands, one tear streaking down a cheek. Then she pulls away and turns back to Jill, like she wasn't just shrieking her head off.

"She breathes?"

"Yes." I may never get over the relief of it.

I watch Samara lift the lids of Jill's closed eyes, feel for a pulse, see her inspect the little red dots on Jill's neck where the infusion went in. Then she takes her wet pack and mine and stuffs them under Jill's legs, raising them. Jill doesn't respond to any of this. She's breathing without the awful wheeze, and the swelling is going down almost as quickly as it came. She seems peaceful, but I don't know whether I can trust that.

"Will she be okay?"

"She'll need to sleep," Samara says. She's still shaking. "And she is cold."

I hadn't had a chance to feel it yet, but the glasses say this cavern is twenty-seven degrees cooler than the one we left, and there's a draft pulling from somewhere. The suits are waterproof on the out-side, and I'm mostly dry, but Jill was up to her neck at one point. She's probably wet inside and out, and that water is not anything like warm anymore.

We go to work like we've talked about it. I get the blanket out of Jill's pack while Samara discovers the art of the magnetic zipper, work-ing Jill out of the jumpsuit while keeping her legs in the air. Jill isn't moving, and Samara isn't okay, either. She's at least half not with me.

I give Samara the blanket, go to the boat, and grab one of the light jars. The water in the boat is barely glowing now. We've let most of our light drown. I gather what we have left, give that to Samara, too, then go to stand beneath the hole in the ceiling, about ten meters beyond the other boats. Straight above me is a beautiful, fiery sky, clear and shining like a ruby. I don't know how close we are to Samara's city, but those boats mean people, and if we can't go far, we have to at least get out of sight while Jill gets better.

Please let Jill get better.

It's drier near the hole in the ceiling, and I think light must shine in, because beyond a small mountain of fallen rock, probably the rock that fell in from the roof, there are plants growing, thick tufts like coarse grasses, tall, almost to my chin, dying off in blues and yellows now that the sun is gone. We're only four or five meters from the riverbank, but out of sight and out of the draft. I think this will have to do. I go back and help lift Jill onto the spread blanket, wrapping her in it like a cocoon. She murmurs something incoherent as I carry her. I kick away the loose stones and lay her down in the grasses.

Samara brings the rest of our stuff. She's put the infusers back into the medical kit, stowing it all away in Jill's pack. But she doesn't question me. At least not yet. And I'm not questioning her. I'm pretty sure we'll get to it. This time she puts my dry pack under Jill's head.

"How long will she be like this?"

"She has been dyspneic, and—"

"What does that mean?"

"That she could not breathe, and shock has caused muscular function of her blood vessels to fail. Now that the reaction has stopped, her body will recover on its own, but she may still have some of the allergen in her system, so we need to watch her carefully, especially her pulse and her breathing. Do you have more of what you gave her?"

I look at Samara. She's just standing there, waiting for me to answer, shaking. Not from nerves or whatever she saw inside her head. She's soaked, and freezing, and this is nothing like being a little uncomfortable beside the lake.

"Here." I kick off my boots, unzip the suit, and start peeling it off. I opted for my jogging clothes underneath like Jill, but at least mine are a little warmer than hers were. Samara is taking a step back. "Don't argue," I say, even though she hasn't made a sound. "You can't stay that wet in here. I'll use the blanket this time."

She takes it, and I'm not sure if her reluctance is because of the suit or me. It ought to be the jumpsuit, because it may be dry, but it's not really all that clean. I turn my back to her and sit cross-legged beside Jill, so she can change.

I watch Jill breathe, still relieved to see it, and listen to the sound of Samara taking off her wet clothes behind me, which is weird and a little uncomfortable. And it really is cold in here. After a few minutes, there's no sound of movement. And she isn't saying anything, either.

"Samara?" I don't know if I can turn around.

Nothing. I peek over my shoulder. And then I'm up. She's in my jumpsuit, but she's also flat on her back in the grasses, eyes wide open, staring at the hole in the ceiling. Only she isn't seeing it. I take her by the arms, sit her up, and shake her a little, like I did before.

"Samara!"

It doesn't work this time. She blinks, stays upright, but she isn't where I am. She's lost in her head. And she's still shivering. I grab my blanket from around her book, shake it out, and sit beside her, face to face, her knees at my side and mine at hers. I wrap the blanket around both of us, hold the ends together with one hand, and take her chin in the other.

"Samara," I say, softer this time, "wake up."

She doesn't come back, but her expression changes, and it's like a story. A terrible, silent story told from the inside. I try to put a name to what I see. Fear, confusion, maybe revulsion, and then she whispers, "I don't want to see . . ." And whatever it is that she doesn't want to see, I know when she sees it, because the reaction in her face is pain. Anguish. Raw, naked grief. She rocks, eyes still closed, grabbing fist-fuls of her own hair.

Her scream was the worst thing I'd ever heard, but this is definitely the worst thing I've ever seen.

Then she gasps, and her eyes flutter open. She looks at me, breathing hard, sees me, and closes her eyes again. Tears spill down her cheeks. I move my hand to the back of her head, bring her forehead to rest in the crook of my neck, her back heaving beneath my arm. I don't think she was just seeing those things in her head, I get that now. Samara was living that memory, minute by minute, like it just happened.

I feel the tension leaving her body as she calms, Jillian breathing deep and slow right behind us. I want to pull the blanket tighter, but I don't want Samara to remember where she is. I don't want her to move. She doesn't for a long time. Air breathes around us, and I catch the faintest scent of something fresh like lemon, or rain, only neither. Her breath is warm on my skin.

Finally I say, "What was the last thing you saw?"

"The body of my brother," she says against my neck. "Burning. Mother said I had to watch, that . . . the Knowing need to see . . . to understand when someone is gone, or we can't cache the memory."

"How old were you?"

"Six."

"And how old was your brother?"

"Seventeen."

I hesitate to ask, but I want to know. "How did he die?"

"Poison. I heard his jaw . . . and his legs . . . break."

I wince, thinking of that story she told with her face. Is that what it means, to never forget? To have an experience forever? Over and over again?

"Samara, how many times have you seen him die?"

"Five hundred and eighty-two."

I tighten my arm. I don't know what to say to her. But I was right to think she was traumatized, because that is nothing short of torture. I try to imagine what it would be like to watch Mom or Dad suffer like that. And then watch it again, when you know what's coming. What has happened to these people, to make them like this?

She whispers, "There is a way . . . to Forget. I ran to the Cursed City looking for it."

A way to Forget. Yes, I can see why she'd want that. Need it. "Did you find it?"

"No."

"Then let me help you find it."

She doesn't answer, just lifts her head to look at me. Her cheeks are streaked, her hair tickling the bare skin along the edge of my shirt, breath still coming a little short. She lifts a hand and takes the glasses off my face. I don't even know what she does with them. She's looking right into my eyes, and when she raises her hand again, she lays it, very gently, on my cheek. I don't think I could move if the cave fell in. When her question comes, it's more breath than words. "Are you from Earth?"

I almost smile, because the answer is so easy. "Yes."

She closes her eyes, breathes a long sigh, and it doesn't take much to lean in and kiss her, once, just a little. She doesn't move, doesn't open her eyes. I touch her lips again, and she melts like ice in my mouth. The hand on my face slides back into my hair, and now I taste that fresh smell, lemon and sweet and a little salt from tears. I feel the skin of her neck beneath my fingers, a gasp of a surprise soft against my mouth. She kisses me back, almost wild, on her knees, holding me on both sides by the hair. And then the world beneath the blanket breaks open, the cold rushing in, and she is gone, standing, fingers on her mouth. Backing away from me.

"You cannot give me this memory," she says.

I look at her, confused, like I've fallen into cold water in my sleep. But she doesn't say another word. She turns and walks away through the red light.

23

SAMARA

As soon as I leave the shelter of the rocks, I run—past the eddying pool where Jill nearly drowned, where the boat is stuck, toward the waterfall that spit us out into this cavern. There's a rockfall there, tumbling down an incline, a smooth, carved path upward that I realize must be leading to the cartage way. I sit just beyond the spray of the falls, head in my hands.

What just happened? I can't believe I let it. No, I didn't let it. I practically begged. What possessed me to take the glasses off? Touch his face like that? I was upset, broken by my memories, but I Know that's not the only reason. I lean forward, and every time I breathe it's a scent that is foreign, male. Beckett. And before I even feel the yank of the memory, I fall . . .

. . . and Beckett's cheek is rough under my hand. I think he stopped breathing when I touched him. I can see his eyes now, and when I ask the question, he doesn't hesitate. He lets a smile lift the corner of his mouth, and he says, "Yes." Like it was the simplest of answers. I close my eyes, and for a moment, the pain of losing Adam lessens. And then I feel Beckett's lips on mine. They're softer than I thought they'd be. His grip is stronger than I thought it would be. He kisses me again, and his mouth is warm, and I ache, my fingers tangling in his hair . . .

I open my eyes to the present and my lips are flushed, cheeks hot in the chilly air. One way or another, this will be the ruin of me. And Beckett doesn't know who I am. Not really. He doesn't know what I am, or what I've done. What I'm about to do. To him. And Jillian.

What am I about to do? Nothing is the way I thought it was. Nothing. Could I really give Beckett, who told me the truth, to a Council who tells nothing but lies? Who gave me bitterblack to hide those lies, so that I could die as horribly as Adam?

And then I pause, sitting on the cold rocks, in the red dark beside the spraying waterfall. I never finish my memory of Adam's death. I always pull myself out, crying and shaking. Or Nita would be there to help me do it. But today, while Beckett held me, I went from the dark behind the door all the way to the burning, to the depths of my grief. And there was something there. Something I hadn't considered.

I close my eyes, and this time, instead of running or resisting, I go to the high shelf and take down the memory of Adam.

And I am in Adam's chamber, and he is writhing on the bed, screaming. I back away from him, horror creeping slow up my spine, sickness and confusion spreading inside me. And when the spasm passes, Adam falls back on the bed, gasping and moaning, and he turns his head, his streaming eyes falling directly on mine. And he whispers, "Who are you?"

I yank myself back into the roar of the waterfall and the cold of the cave, stunned. Adam Forgot. He caught the Forgetting. Grandpapa Cyrus even told me a supervisor had Forgotten. It seemed so impossible, I hardly believed him at the time, and Adam was only training. But Adam went Outside that day, and there was bitterblack, they said, in the seed samples . . .

I jump to my feet, so unsteady I nearly fall. Adam wasn't testing seed samples. They gave him bitterblack. The Council killed my brother. Killed my Adam to hide the Forgetting. For the same reason they almost killed me. And the ever-simmering rage inside me suddenly cools, gels into something that is icy cold.

Hate.

And then I turn, spinning on my heel toward the path up the tumbled rocks. Listening. Maybe that was an echo, a trick of the falling water. Maybe it was the draft. Or maybe that was a voice I just heard, far off down the cartage way.

24

BECKETT

I sit still, stunned, then I throw off the blanket. What just happened? What was I doing? What was I thinking? I wasn't thinking. Not like I should have been. I want to hit something, preferably something that will hurt me back. But I don't. I lie in the weird, drying grass, arms over my head in the cold, and count the ways that I am an idiot.

Samara was vulnerable. She is traumatized, and I have a feeling the brother isn't the half of it. She is of Canaan, the people I'm supposed to be studying, objectively, like a scientist, and not only have I not been objective at all—as Jill saw fit to point out—I've smashed every rule I ever swore to gaining her trust, only now to go and irreparably damage it. And there is Jill, lying still and sick just a few meters away. How unfair is that? And wrong. And the sad thing is, given the opportunity, I'd be tempted to do it again.

I'm worse than an idiot. I am a fool.

And then I hear the softest crackle in my ear.

I sit up, hand to the side of my head. I'd almost forgotten the earpiece was there. But that was definitely, for just a second, a signal. I scramble to find the glasses, tangled up where Samara left them in the blanket, get them on my face, and listen. Nothing. I move around the campsite, hear another fizz and hiss. And when I look up at the hole in the ceiling, where the fiery sky is shining in, a voice full of static says, "Beckett?"

"Dad?" I whisper. I look around, but I can't see Samara. Jill is asleep, exactly as I left her. "Dad! Is that you?"

"Beck! Are you okay? Where are . . ." His voice dissolves into white noise.

"I can barely hear you. I'm okay. We're underground."

"Can you talk?"

I glance around one more time for Samara. "Yes."

"Do you have the . . ." I hear a jab of static. ". . . of the city?"

"What?"

"The position of the city?"

"No. We're not there yet."

"Listen, Beck, and let me know that you understand. Do not send the coordinates to the Commander. Give them only to me."

"What?"

"Only to me, Beckett! There isn't much time. Your mom is watching the door. Something is wrong. It's not what they told . . ." He's gone again, then back with a popping noise. ". . . get in touch if I can. Take the glasses off transmit, so they can't send a skimmer and up . . ." This time the crackle hurts my ear. ". . . still with the local?"

"What?"

"Is the local you're with hostile?"

If he means the local I showed our technology to, told about Earth, kissed, and who is now running around somewhere in this cave wearing my jumpsuit, then it's a more complicated question than Dad could guess. And basically the end of protocol as we know it. "No," I say.

"Is Jill all right?"

Also complicated. "Yes."

"I have to . . ."

The connection fizzes. "Dad, why are you watching the door? What's happening?"

"Listen, Beck . . . come back to the base camp."

"What?"

"Don't come back to the base . . . or the *Centauri*. We . . ."

"Dad?"

". . . off transmit . . . when I can."

"Dad!"

But there's no static this time. No crack or fizz. I think he's shut down the connection, and it gives me a bad feeling, deep down in my stomach.

I take the glasses off transmit, like he told me. Something stinks about this. So much that it reeks. Dad just told me to break orders, and that is not like Dr. Sean Rodriguez. Or not without a good reason. And if they were having trouble tracking us, setting the glasses on transmit would only help, wouldn't it? Because if we did wander into a pocket of signal, like we must have just then, it would ping the base camp, and then they'd know exactly where we are . . . He doesn't want Commander Faye to know where we are. He doesn't want her to know where the city is. Why?

And suddenly I'm not thinking of Samara's trauma anymore. I'm thinking of her abilities. What would Earth do with a people with perfect recall? Who could pick up the education of a doctor in 185 days? Keep precise time in their heads and remember every detail of a map they saw when they were four? Something tells me a military could get really creative with that. And so could the Commander. If Earth found out the people of New Canaan were that valuable, I'm not sure their culture would survive it.

But Dad couldn't know about memory in New Canaan, and neither could Faye. So what's going on with the *Centauri*?

I stare up at the hole in the ceiling. If Dad just shut down that connection because he was caught, and if another ping or two went out before I turned off transmit, then the Commander could know exactly where we are. Right now. And I have Samara. And we're close to the city.

And then the perimeter alarm flashes in my vision.

25

SAMARA

I run across the cavern, and before I get halfway back to the grasses, Beckett is coming out to meet me. I see from his face that he knows. His technology has warned him. His gaze darts behind me, toward the cartage way.

"Is there another passage?" I ask.

"One. Over there." He nods his head at the other end of the cavern. "But they're coming that way, too."

"Is there another way out?"

He shakes his head.

Trapped. "How long?"

"Six or seven minutes, at a guess."

"What do you have?" I say. "Tell me what you can use to get us out!"

I want him to do something I've never thought of. Pull something out of his pack I couldn't have imagined. I see him thinking, searching his mind. He's not finding anything. His chest moves up and down, stretching the shirt, jaw clenched tight. I don't Know what he's working himself up to do, but I don't like it. Then he says, "Tell me why you're running."

"Because I Know about the Forgetting when I shouldn't."

"And what will they do when they catch you?"

"Last time it was poison. I would guess something faster."

He takes one of my hands, flips it palm up. "What happened here?"

I glance down at the new skin, puzzled. "Rope. I slid when I was running away and—"

"Rope?" Beckett shuts his eyes, then his hand closes over mine. "Rope! You have got to be kidding me. Come on. Quick!"

He yanks me across the loose rocks, back to the grasses, where he gets his pack out from under Jillian's head and dumps it out. Jillian groans a little, trying to turn inside the blanket while Beckett digs. I see two of the little packages of food they've been eating, an assortment of things I don't recognize, and then Beckett has a shiny, cone-shaped metal case and bundle of flat, thin ropes. When he shakes the ropes loose, they make a kind of net.

"We're going up," he says, pointing to the hole in the ceiling, eight and a half meters above us.

I have a sudden vision of Nita's story, the one with wings on heads. Beckett is talking fast.

"I'm going to shoot the rope through the hole and climb up, and while I'm doing that you're going to get Jill in the harness." He throws me the net of ropes, and I catch it. "Her arms and legs go through here, and you hook it like this . . ." He shows me a small metal clamp, and where it attaches. "Then I'm going to bring the rope up and shoot it back down here, you're going to attach the harness, turn the grip loose, and I'll retract the rope and haul Jill up. Then I'm going to shoot it back and you'll get in the harness and do the same thing. Got it? You take the—"

"You only have to tell me once," I say.

He almost smiles. "Right." He does something with the metal cone, there's a whoosh, and suddenly the top of the cone is just gone, a thin rope flying up and up and out of the hole in the ceiling. I realize that I don't have time to be startled. I kneel down and start wrestling Jill into the harness. Beckett tugs and the rope is firm, taut, like it's been tied, though I can't imagine to what. It looks too flimsy to be of any use.

"Do you Know what's up there?" he asks. He's flinging belongings back into his pack, snatching my wet clothes from the rocks.

"I think a barren plain. But we can't be far from the mountains."

"Anything else?"

"No idea."

He gets his pack on, a covering on each hand, grabs the rope, and before he goes, he pauses and says, "That was my fault back there. My mistake, and I'm sorry, okay?"

He's talking about kissing me. And he regrets it. Why shouldn't he? I look at the face I dreamed, and realize I've made a decision without making it. They can't have Beckett. I won't let them. "How close are they?" I ask.

"Maybe four minutes. Go fast."

He climbs while I finish working Jillian into the ropes. I think I might have her arms where her legs go, but it feels secure. I get her pack while Beckett pulls himself over the edge of the hole in the ceiling, and in a moment the rope zips upward, fast. I drag Jillian by the harness, and the silver end of the rope comes down, spreading into three prongs that drive into the ground and hold there, a tiny green light blinking on top, like when Beckett was mending his bones. Jillian's eyes open and close, and I look in my mind and watch Beckett attach the metal clamps, to make sure I do it right.

Jillian mumbles, "Where are we going?"

"Flying," I say. I stuff her pack into the harness with her, and when I glance across the cavern, I can see the opposite passage, the one Beckett mentioned, because now it is lit by the pale yellow light of biofuel. They're coming. I go to "turn the grip loose" like Beckett said, only I don't see how. And he didn't say how. It's just smooth metal, winking with unnatural light.

"Jillian," I whisper. "Jillian! How do you make it let go?"

Jillian opens her blue eyes, sees the hanging rope, and then her lids fall closed again. I hear a distant echo of voices, this time from the cartage way.

"Jillian," I say, shaking her a little, "tell me how to make it let go!"

"Electromagnetic," she replies, which is the least helpful thing I've ever heard her say. And that's saying quite a bit. Beckett's head is hanging down through the hole, and he's beckoning, but I can't call out without alerting the coming Council. I run my hands all over the metal, desperate, and for no reason I can name, the green light . . . vanishes. Like someone blew it out. I pull, and the grip releases.

I wave at Beckett and Jillian lifts to the air, the light jar I've crammed into her pack glowing through the cloth. She looks like a rising moon. Lantern light wavers on either side of me, from both passages, as I watch Jillian's ascent, my pack on my shoulder, my book inside it. I shift my feet. She's almost to the hole in the ceiling, and we are almost out of time.

I watch Beckett's hands pull Jillian up and over the edge, see the empty hole with the empty red sky, and even though I am trapped at the bottom, I feel relieved. That they're safe. That I can't give them to the Council. Even for my parents. It's a red dark without the light jar, and a shadow moves in the opposite passage. I close my eyes. I Know I'm in trouble. I have nothing. No bargain. No Forgetting. No time.

But I can make a plan.

So I get back into the city for the Changing of the Seasons, make my very public appearance and hope it's enough for Thorne Councilman to not make an example of my parents. Then I elude basically everyone Underneath, long enough to get back into that room in the Archives, discover how to Forget, and heal the Knowing before Judgment. Or before the Council kills me first.

It's a terrible plan. But I think I'm going to try. At least I won't be giving the Council that killed my brother the satisfaction of killing me today. And they don't get Beckett. The Council can deal with Earth on their own. Earth doesn't actually seem all that scary right now.

Not nearly as scary as they are.

I look up at the empty hole, and I can hear my own pulse in my ears. The echo of conversation from the cartage way. It's still three days until the Changing of the Seasons. I won't be able to hide that long. Not in the city. I think I need to go to Annis. Nita's mother. To the Outside.

I think I don't have a way out of this cave.

Maybe Beckett is packing up Jillian at this moment, getting her back to his "ship." If he has any sense, that's exactly what he's doing. I twist the straps on my pack in my hand. The light from the opposite passage is almost here. They're coming. And then there's a noise, and the rope comes streaking down through the hole, the grip embedding itself in the rock at my feet, rope and harness dangling.

Beckett waves his hand from the ceiling, gesturing for me to hurry. I climb into the harness with my pack, threading in my arms and legs. And now there are feet crunching in the gravel, light bobbing along the cavern walls, and I pause, because the illuminated face walking slowly toward me is the last one I expected to see. Reddix Physicianson.

I bend down and run my hands all over the metal grip, hoping to repeat the miracle that happened before. It doesn't work. The green fire doesn't extinguish. I do it again, the light vanishes, and the grip releases. I have no idea what just happened and I don't care.

"Go!" I say to the hole in the ceiling. And I rise. Reddix is still walking toward me, slow and steady, not changing his pace, his head tilting back as I fly. What could he be doing here? Reddix isn't Council any more than Sonia's mother. I'm out of reach when he puts his sandals where I was standing, his gaze dark in the shadows. I wish I could read his face as easily as Beckett's.

"Reddix," I say, "don't tell them. Please."

"I never have, Samara." He almost smiles. "But they are coming for you." His eyes move a little past me. "Don't let them find you with Earth."

And then I feel hands pulling me up and out of the hole.

26

BECKETT

There's somebody down there. Lit by one of those yellow lanterns, watching the rappelling kit pull up Samara. But she's too high, out of reach. I'll have her in another four or five seconds. I get a good look at him. Long hair, braided, wearing clothes probably not all that different from Samara's when hers were newer, eyes black-lined. And he's calm, weirdly calm. Another mask. He looks right into my eyes when he says, "Don't let them find you with Earth." It's practically a challenge.

I drag Samara up and out of the hole like he might jump up and grab her legs, and my chest is slamming. He knew. He knew exactly who I was. Samara is staring down at the way she came, frozen.

"Look at me." I spin her around. She's still tangled in the harness. "What do you remember about Earth?"

"What . . ." says Jill. She's lying on the ground, trying to push up to her elbows. Samara ignores my question, pulls away from my hands, and gets to her feet, stepping out of the rope, going to press a finger against Jill's neck. Jill tries to push her away, which I think means Jill is going to be okay. Then Samara straightens up to face me. Her Canaan face is on, like the one down in the cavern.

"What does your city remember about Earth?" I ask again.

"Beckett?" Jill asks.

"She Knows, Jill. She's always Known who we are." Just like he did, down in the cavern. At first glance. I feel like an idiot. I turn back to Samara. "Haven't you?" Samara doesn't answer, but her eyes meet mine, and I feel that look in my chest. "Who was he?"

"Reddix," she whispers.

"Is he one of your Council?"

"No. He was . . . He was supposed to be my partner."

Great. "What does he Know about Earth?" He wasn't even surprised by the little bit of technology he saw. "Tell me the truth, Samara! What does your city remember about us?"

"That you are the enemy."

I stare at her eyes and try to process. The enemy. Me. And then I'm thinking back to her abrupt offer to take us to her city, because we had Forgotten. When she Knew we hadn't Forgotten. When she Knew who we were all along.

"You were going to hand us over, weren't you? To your Council." I'm almost shouting now. I see Jill's eyes narrow. "Weren't you?"

Samara doesn't answer again, but she can't look at me anymore, either. She's standing there in that jumpsuit, her hair hanging like a silky thunderstorm, looking a lot like someone I could have known in Austin. Only she isn't, is she? She's of Canaan, and she played me. Like an expert at the game. When I risked everything to tell her the truth.

"Beckett." Jill has managed to sit up. She's not steady. "We need to . . . break contact. Now. We're . . . close."

She means we have to be close to the city, and that we could give the Commander the coordinates of where we're standing. I turn around, so neither of them can hear the cussing in my head. The sky is cold, red as fire, and empty, like this flat, bare land I'm standing in. But if I didn't get the transmit setting turned off in time, it's not going to be empty for long. I don't know who to run from. I don't know who to run to. I don't know who to trust anymore.

Yes, I do. Dr. Sean Rodriguez. He said not to give the coordinates to Commander Faye. He said not to go back to the base camp. He said to stay with the local, underground, where it's safe. Or at least I think that's what he said. But nothing is safe. And it's a long way back across the plain. Even if Jill was at 100 percent we couldn't make it on our own. We only packed food for a scant four days—for the emergency that was never, ever going to happen—and the water regenerators will not recharge without the sun. And if or when we get picked up, we'd be going straight to the Commander. I turn back to Samara.

"What would've happened, if you gave us to your Council? Would they have killed us?"

"I don't Know," she whispers.

That really is just great. "So why didn't you do it, then, if we're the enemy?"

She lifts her beautiful eyes to mine. "Plans changed."

Why? Because she felt guilty? Because I kissed her? I stare back at the sky, at the mountain range stained red, rising up from the plain. I'm so mad right now I can't see straight. I've trusted where I shouldn't have, and nearly gotten both Jill and myself killed. When Jill tried to tell me. She's watching us right now, panting just from being upright. I can't look at her.

"You should go," Samara says, "back to your . . . ship." When did she hear me say that word? "You can't stay here . . ."

"What did your plans change to?"

"Beckett!" This is from Jill.

"Orders," I tell her. I see Jill's eyes dart to the sky. I feel bad about this lie. But I didn't say who the orders were from. She lies back on the rocky ground, exhausted.

"What did your plans change to?" I ask Samara again. She glances over my shoulder, up at the jagged peaks behind me. "Okay. What's up there?"

"The Outside."

"Is it safe?"

"No."

"Is it safer?"

She looks at the hole, then at the mountain, unsure.

"Do they know about Earth?"

"Only stories."

"But you have a place to go there?"

She looks me in the eye again, and I wish her gaze didn't do that. "You have to go back," she whispers. "Please."

Not an option. And it seems like there's something in the bones of this planet that's messing with our signals. If we get up there in the mountains, maybe they'll go on messing with the signals. Samara is shaking her head, like we're going to argue. I take a gamble. "How are you getting up there, Samara?"

She blinks. She hadn't thought of that yet. She needs me, and I need her. Which is a real irony when you get down to it, because at this point I'm thinking there's a good chance we're both a danger to each other.

We head out, moving fast, Jill on my back, Samara with all three of the packs. Jill really is weak. It's hard work for her to hang on, and for weighing next to nothing, she's actually pretty heavy. When Samara gets a little way ahead, Jill whispers near my ear, "What are our orders?"

I hesitate, then say, "Maintain contact and cut off communications for the present."

It's a good thing Jill can't see my face, because I'm pretty sure it's smeared with guilt. But Jill will not understand Dad telling me to go against the Commander, or the fact that I'm putting family over the hierarchy of the ship.

"Beck," she whispers again, "do you think you're getting orders from . . . who you think you are? Because I don't think Commander Faye would've . . . told you to cut off . . . communications."

"What am I supposed to do, Jill? I just have to follow them when they come." This might not exactly ring true coming from me, and I think Jill agrees.

"You know you can't . . . trust her now? That . . . she's been lying . . . the whole time?"

I know it. But I don't want to say it.

"Listen, let's get the coordinates, and then . . . go. You can tell the Commander . . . she broke contact with us, that you couldn't stop her. I'll . . . back you up . . . Mom will . . . back us up . . ."

Jill's voice is fading a little, her grip loosening. I think she's falling asleep. I hike her up, and put on some speed. Her plan is so reasonable. I wish there was one thing about my life that was reasonable right now.

I've got an alarm set for additional humans, and one for power sources, in case a skimmer gets near. But the glass in front of my eyes is clear and quiet. Jill has gone quiet, too, her head bobbing against my back, Samara moving fast and smooth, like hiking is some kind of a dance. I wish she'd said something when I told her I was sorry back in the cave. I wish she'd said *Don't be sorry*, and I know that makes me an idiot. She's a liar. And from now on I'm going to be objective if it kills me.

It might.

We have to cross a river. I swim Jill across, and both she and Samara make it relatively dry in the suits. I'm soaked, and now I'm freezing again, and tired to the core. The cliffs are tall. I'll only have just enough rope. I lean Jill against the rocks.

"You okay?" I ask. She's pale, but when she opens her eyes, for a second she's the Jill I knew on the ship.

"Oh, I'm great," she says. "You?"

I smile. Whatever else she is, I really am glad she's not dead. Her eyes close again, and I find Samara about three meters away, hair everywhere in the breeze, staring down at something white among the blue-gray rocks. I stand next to her, then squat down to get a better look at the ground.

It's a body. Bones mostly, though scraps of dried skin and fabric still cling here and there, and some long, straggling hair. The lower leg bones are shattered, plus one femur, and I think the spine might have broken, too, unless the body has been disturbed. I don't think it has. I glance at the clifftop, high above us, and then at the pelvis and the shape of the broken skull. Female. And this would have been instant. I wish I knew more about this planet's weather, seasons, insects, so I could guess how long it's been here.

Samara bends down, barely touching a bit of blowing fabric between two fingers. I think it might have been yellow. "It's Aunt Letitia," she whispers.

I blow out a breath. I've been considering the timeline of decay, and Samara is staring at her own dead family. "How did she fall?"

"She jumped. Like I did."

"What do you mean, like you did?"

She looks to our left, down the line of the cliffs. "It's not as high that way, and the river is there."

"Have you jumped those cliffs before?"

"Of course not. It's out of bounds."

"Then how did you Know the river was deep enough?"

"I didn't."

I blow out another breath. This time it's frustration. "And why would you do that?"

"To escape. Only Aunt Letitia was escaping a different way."

Samara walks away from the body. *Last time it was poison.* That's what she said in the cavern. I think of being scared enough, or determined enough, to jump when I wasn't sure I'd live. Of being determined enough to jump when I knew I was going to die. I can still hear Samara's scream, see that story she told with her face. Is that what this woman was trying to do? Escape her memories? Use death to Forget? Samara said she was looking for a way to Forget. How close has she come to making the same choice as her aunt?

I run a hand through my wet hair. What is going on with this planet? What could have made them this way? I can't trust Samara, and I'm angry about it. Hurt, if I'm being honest. She could be playing me again right now for all I know. But my gut says she isn't. Then again, two hours ago I found out that my gut was as off-kilter as the *Centauri*'s scans. Either way, I wish she hadn't seen this. So she wouldn't have to remember.

Jill dozes against the cliff while Samara gathers stones, and by the time I shoot the grip to the top of a cliff, she has a circle of them around her aunt.

I hate climbing rope. But since we couldn't bring the real gear, thanks to protocol, I guess I'm glad the trainer made me do it so often. But I'm going up clipped into the harness this time. I'll never get all the way up without a rest, and it's when I'm taking the second of these, about three-quarters of the distance to the top, that the power source alarm blinks in the lenses.

I turn, dangling in the harness. And here comes the skimmer, barely a glint in the red air, and I am caught, more neatly than any commander could have planned. The skimmer flies straight toward me, flat, bird-shaped, getting bigger and bigger, a wingspan of about three and a half meters, and it is silent, almost clear, except when it catches a beam of red. I glance down, see Jill lying still at the base of the cliff, arms over her head, Samara on her knees, arranging stones over the body of her aunt. And when I look up again, the skimmer is hovering at the level of my nose, about four meters away, like it's looking at me. Deciding what I am.

It knows what I am. And who I am. Or it should. The skimmer hovers, flies a little to the right, to the left, away, and then back to the same place. Which is weird. Then it zips off, fast, sideways along the contours of the cliffs. I zoom the glasses, watching its path, then wince as the mountainside makes a turn and the skimmer doesn't. It crashes straight into an outcrop of sparkling stone, too far away to hear. But I see pieces glinting as the shards fall.

I don't think that skimmer could see where it was going. I'm not sure it could see me. But how is that possible? I climb, faster than before, get to the top, and roll onto my back, like I did the first time I scaled a rope on this planet. Only now I'm alone up here, and the sky is red instead of purple, the plants around me tall and dark. Organized. Planted. By humans. And the alarm in my lenses hasn't stopped going off.

I sit up. The warning isn't for people. It's for a power source. I thought it was another skimmer, but now that I'm up, the lenses say the source is underneath me. Inside this mountain. What else has Samara Archiva not thought to mention?

I look down, the lenses still zoomed, and Samara is exactly where I left her, beside the pile of stones that was her aunt, only she's still, eyes closed. She's in a memory. Not a bad one this time; she's smiling, almost shy, a hand on her own cheek. I feel like I'm looking at something I shouldn't. I think of those lined eyes in that calm face in the cave, watching Samara rise through the air. I wonder if he's the one giving her that memory, and then I think maybe I don't want to know the answer to that.

She didn't want the one I gave her.

I am such an idiot.

I reset the rope, and shoot the hook and harness back down, a little way away from Samara and Jill. Samara wakes up, helps Jill into the harness, and Jill lets her, and that alone tells me Jill's not as well as she was. She comes up with her pack on her lap, and when she lies down on the cliff top I can hear her breathe, a soft wheezing. I move fast, get the rope back down and Samara up with the last two packs.

"Should I dose her again?" I ask.

Samara gets untangled, and comes to look at Jill, but looks at me first. "Will we have warning, if there are people?"

I nod, and watch her feel the pulse at Jill's neck, then put her ear to Jill's chest.

"She is reacting, but not badly. How much medicine do you have?"

"One more." I watch Samara look back through her mind, almost like she's scanning a file. I wonder if that's what I look like, reading the glasses.

"We should only use it if she gets worse. She needs to be still and sleep."

"And will she be able to sleep, where we're going?" I know I'm sounding hostile right now. It might be because I'm mad. I thought Jill was getting better, not worse, and I've put her in a position that is not her fault. Again. And lied to make it happen. She should be on the ship right now, with all the medicine she could need. I don't think I could make a decent decision anymore if I tried.

Samara says, "I have friends Outside who will hide us."

I look around at the tall, dark trees. "I thought this was Outside?"

"No, these are the upland parks. No one comes here, usually, but this is part of the city, and we cannot be seen. The Knowing do not forget a face."

"And why is it better to hide with these friends of yours instead of finding a place to camp while Jill sleeps?"

"Because we don't have enough food."

This is an excellent point. I watch her hesitate, like she's grappling with what to say. "It will be difficult. You cannot tell them who you are. Any of them, Knowing or Outsider. And you'll have to do what I say. Can you?"

She's asking if I can trust her enough to follow her lead. I stand up, start reeling in the rope so I can pack it. The answer to her question is both yes and no, and I can't decide which is more true.

Samara says, "You can't get back to your . . . ship. Can you?"

I shake my head.

"Can you . . . talk to them? From here?"

I get the rappelling gear into the pack. "I'm supposed to be able to, but I can't."

"Do they already know about me? And the city?"

"Yes. But they can't see it for some reason."

"They can see from a long way away, can't they?"

"Yes. Usually."

"But they're only here to study us? Learn about us?"

I don't know how to answer that, and her amber eyes dart to the sky. For a second, there is no hard exterior, no mask, and the expression I see is the best argument for protocol I've ever been presented with. I decide not to mention the skimmer.

"We should leave here," she whispers.

I agree. We move quick and quiet through the red shadows, or as much as we can when Samara has three packs and I have a half-conscious girl on my back. We go up another cliff, not near as high, but high enough, then down, through thick and tangled woods. Until we hit trees that are well-spaced, planted in rows, like an orchard, and I stop beside Samara.

A wide valley spreads out in front of us, a table of land ringed by mountains, the sloping edges terraced with empty, harvested fields, the flat space between sprinkled with the peaks of thatched roofs and yellow dots of fire. Outside.

I feel my pulse pick up. I know this is going to be dangerous, maybe stupid. And that blinking light in the lenses tells me that this place is hiding more secrets than just a city Underneath. But I wanted to see history. Living and breathing. I wanted to see what became of Canaan. And here is what they built. Not a theory or a scientist's speculation. Real. The answer to a lifelong dream. Where Earth is the enemy. Where I am the enemy.

And it doesn't look like the kind of place you could hide in at all.

We the faithful of the NWSE have never forgotten our original directive: to create a new civilization, to populate the perfect society, to advance the knowledge of the human race. We have dared to build a world superior to the Earth from which we come . . .

FROM THE NOTEBOOK OF JANIS ATAN

27

SAMARA

Beckett stares down into the dotted sparkle of the torches and lamps of the Outside, then up at the surrounding mountains, where the glowworm threads are shining, like webs of moonlit string. I wonder what he's seeing through his technology. I wonder what he's seeing in his mind. If the Outside looks anything like Earth. Or nothing at all. He sees me watching him, but he avoids my eyes. He doesn't trust me. Why should he? I wouldn't trust me. And I'm not sure I can trust him. He couldn't answer back there when I asked him about Earth.

His anger feels like a knife tip grazing my skin.

"I need to change our clothes," I tell him.

He lays Jillian down beneath a blacknut tree without a word, cradling her head, and then I want to Know just how many times he's kissed her the way he kissed me. Which is infuriating. He walks away into the grove in his tight Earth clothes, stretching out on the sloping ground, facing the lights of the Outside.

I think that knife tip is going to make me bleed.

I wrestle Jillian into the tunic and leggings of undyed cloth, the clothes I wore the day Nita died, retrieved from the bushes before we went up the last cliff. And twice I have to pull back and cache, to keep from falling into the memory of the cave. I even let myself fall when I was sitting beside Aunt Letitia's broken body.

It made me angry at Aunt Letitia, seeing her like that. She might as well have been holding Uncle Towlend's hand when she jumped off that cliff. And then my anger fanned my rage. Which is why I have to get back into the city. To break the Council that killed my brother. Into pieces. To fix this, if I can. For all of us. But I have to find a safe place for Beckett and Jillian first. I owe them that much at least.

I put one of the blankets over Jillian, slip farther back into the blacknut grove, and change back into my tunic. The cloth of the Knowing will immediately draw the eye, but at least these clothes aren't inexplicable, like the ones from Earth. Beckett sits where I left him, propped on his elbows, legs stretched out in front of him, watching the sunset deepen over the Outside. And he's taken off the glasses, holding them to one side. A gesture to tell me I've had privacy. Without having to ask. A kindness, even when he's hurt.

And right then, I think I could tell him everything. All the terrible things I've done. What I was going to do and why. Maybe he would understand. Or maybe he wouldn't. Maybe he would be worse than angry, and be disgusted.

I don't want to remember his disgust.

Then, without turning around, Beckett asks, "What will happen, if we're caught?"

I Know exactly what will happen to me. I'm not as sure about him. "If we're caught," I say, "you should do whatever you can to get away."

"And what is your Reddix going to do with his information?"

I don't argue his incorrect possessive. "He said he wouldn't tell."

"And do you believe that?"

"It's . . . possible." But I would very much like to Know how Reddix was aware of Earth's presence in the first place.

Beckett slides the glasses back onto his face and gets to his feet, and I help hoist Jillian up onto his back. She's not any better, but she's not worse, either. I get all three of the packs, and then we are on the move again, skirting the perimeter of the Outside on the level of the groves, hidden by the shadows.

There are steps cut every so often, leading down to the next level of the barren fields, but I don't want to take them yet. I want to stay out of sight, until we are as close as possible to Nita's house. If we go in after curfew, just a little more than a bell from now, there will be only four supervisors to avoid. I Know the changing patterns of their patrol. The danger is in someone not sticking to their route, like going inside that unused supply hut on the day Nita died.

I'm not sure what Annis is going to say to me when I come knocking after curfew, ragged and bedraggled, with two strangers in tow. I'm not sure what I'm going to say to any of them. How much will they blame me for what happened to Nita? They should blame me, probably more than they know. And now I am nervous, guilty. Pained by the grief I Know I will see. And that means memories are lurking. Ready to jump up and snatch me. I try to measure my breaths.

"We should wait here," I whisper to Beckett, "until the resting bell rings. I'll have to tell them you're one of the Knowing, so . . . do your best to act like you have memory." His brows go up. "And they might call me Nadia. Or they might say Samara."

"Nadia? Why?"

"It's . . . Just don't be surprised."

Beckett doesn't question me anymore. He's staring down at the roofs of the houses. They look pretend. Like toys. "Are you sure you Know when the bell rings?" he asks. "There's nobody near us that's not inside a house."

I look down, startled. Of course I Know when the bell rings. But I think he's right. It's too quiet. No shadows in front of the streetlamps. Fear builds in the pit of my stomach. But if there's no one on the streets, we should go. Now.

"Come on," I whisper, and we slip down a set of stone steps to the level of the fields, and then to the next level, and the next. Two more and we are among the workshops and houses of the Outside.

Glowworm lamps shine at the street corners, but I avoid these, sticking to the pools of darkness along the house walls. We flit to the intersection of two lanes. It's so quiet I can hear Jillian's breath, a hollow kind of wheeze. I think we're going to have to dose her again. Soon. But I shouldn't be able to hear her at all. Not on a street like this. There should be voices from inside the houses at least, the clang of cooking or conversation. Singing. But the Outside is silent. It's eerie.

Beckett is sweating, struggling to hold up Jillian. I hurry us across the rutted street, to the pillar of an open workshop. I can feel the heat of the glassblowing furnaces, their doors dark and shut. And then I do hear voices, a metal-capped stick thumping on wood.

I hold up a hand to stop Beckett, get an eye around the corner of the workshop. Four supervisors stand in the yellow light of a mirror maker's opening door. Not Craddock, but one of his sisters, and three of his cousins. They go inside, indistinct words coming soft before the door latches shut behind them. I don't understand what's happening or what the mirror maker could have done, but we need to get off this street. We round the corner to Nita's house, one lamp shining behind a closed curtain.

I knock, very soft. There's a rustle inside that stills to quiet. Beckett slides Jillian to the ground, holding her upright. I knock again and say, "Annis!" right into the crack of the door. It jerks open.

Nita's mother has round cheeks, their color a little faded like the hair that hangs loose past her shoulders. But her expression leaps at the sight of me, gaze darting behind me, where Beckett stands with Jillian, and I watch her face fall. My insides do the same. Either she doesn't know Nita is dead, or had hoped against hope that she wasn't.

She grabs my arm and pulls me inside, Beckett coming after, now just carrying Jillian in his arms. Annis shuts and bars the door, then turns to face me. She has shadows beneath her eyes. "Where is Nita?"

I drop the packs and glance around the room. Grandpapa is rising from his chair, in its place beside the rounded corner made by the clay heating furnace, the central pillar of the house, and when I look up to the loft, there are four sets of eyes gazing over the edge. Nathan, nearly grown, Luc, Ari, and Jasmina, the smallest, who is four. I feel the attention of the family like a weight, the pull of Nita's memory so heavy I want to fall through the floor.

"Annis," I whisper, "Nita is dead."

I watch her eyes close, a spasm of pain, and after a long moment she says, "Thank you. We were so afraid she wasn't." She crosses the room to Grandpapa as he sinks back to his chair, and kisses the top of his head. "Was she . . . alive long?"

I shake my head, mute. She looks relieved again, comes to me, and holds my face once before kissing each cheek. I am choking on my guilt. Then her eyes snap to the door. "You have to go."

"I can't—" I begin.

"You have to. No argument."

"But—"

"We're being counted! Right now!"

I stare at her. It's ten days early for counting.

"They're not admitting that Nita didn't come back aboveground," Annis whispers. "We're one short, and they're going to say she ran. They'll have their excuse."

And they'll take them Underneath, I think. All of them.

"They can't find you here, too . . ." Annis says.

"Who are they?" asks Grandpapa. His blue eyes are on Beckett, who I'm relieved to see has had the sense to take the glasses off.

"More of the Knowing," I say quickly. "And she's sick . . ."

Jillian half opens her eyes, and for a moment, Annis is transfixed. I need to cache, desperately, but I'm also trying to think. We could try to get out, get back up to the groves, but what about Grandpapa? The children? Fists pound on wood, and we all jump. It's the house next door.

Annis comes alive. "Who's in the street?" she asks me. "Quick! Did you see them? Which supervisors? Are there any from the gates?"

I check my memory. "No, it's—"

Annis points at Beckett. "Take her through that door and put her on the bed." She's whispering, but the words come out as a command anyway. Beckett gathers up Jillian. "You," she says collectively, looking to the loft, "your sister is in my resting room and she's sick. Do you understand me? And you've never seen any of these people. Nathan, take care of it. Don't move, Daddy. Nadia, with me."

I follow Annis and Beckett into the second of the three rooms, where Nita and her mother slept. There are two beds on low platforms, huddled near the warm, rounded corner that is the wall of the heating furnace. "There," she says to Beckett. "Quick!"

He lays Jillian down, and I Know I've made a mistake. Her face is swelling, her breathing labored. We should have dosed her in the blacknut grove.

"How sick is she?" Annis asks. "Will she talk? And what happened to her hair?" I open my mouth to speak, and she says, "Never mind. Hurry!"

She runs to the opposite corner of the resting room, drops to her knees, and digs her fingers into a crack between the floor planks. Three planks come free, lifting at an angle like a misplaced door. There's a space beneath, dug out from the ground.

"In!" she says. Beckett slides inside, I go next, and then Grandpapa comes shuffling over with the packs. "Get down . . ."

And there's a metal-capped stick pounding at the door.

Beckett pulls me down. The space is not as long as either one of us, and not quite wide enough for two. The packs land on our feet, the planks drop into place, and we are in semidarkness, the light of the hanging lamp in the room above us glowing between the cracks.

We try to find a way to fit, a position we'll be able to hold. There's not actually room for it. I put an elbow in Beckett's ribs twice before I end up half on my back, my legs bent and braced against the dirt wall with his beneath, his arm under my head. My heart is thudding in my chest, and I am struggling. Sinking. Jillian's wheezing is loud in the room, but it's Nita's muffled breath that I'm hearing, that I'm trying to stifle with my pillow.

"Look at me," Beckett whispers. He gets a hand beneath my chin, turns my face to him. "Look at me and stay right here." There are voices in the other room. "Stay here, Samara."

I do look at him, and I'm half in the Cursed City, Beckett pushing down my shoulders, hiding me in the ruined house, and then my memory shifts and I see a sliver of his face from beneath heavy-lidded eyes, the corner of his mouth turned up just before he kisses me. And then I'm back in the hole in the floor and the resting room door is opening. Beckett's fingers move to my mouth, keeping me quiet. In case I make a noise. In case I fall. Feet move across the cracks above our head, darkening the light.

"Who is this?" a voice asks. It's Kayla, Craddock's sister, and she's walking toward Jillian. I feel Beckett's body tense.

"Nita, Weaver's daughter," says Annis.

"Confirm your name," says Kayla. I don't Know if Jillian has been awake enough to understand what's going on. I listen, heart thudding, for her to speak. For her to say *Jillian*. I don't think I can lie here and listen to Nita's entire family—and Jillian—being carried to the flogging post. Or worse.

I'm not sure I'll have a choice.

"She's sick," Annis says quickly. "You might not want to get too close . . ."

That won't work. The Knowing don't fear sickness. Unless it's Forgetting.

"Confirm your name," demands Kayla.

The light changes, darkens again, the planks above my head creak, and a fine sprinkle of dust rains down. Someone is standing directly above us. Beckett's fingers move from my mouth to the back of my head, and he pulls me into his neck. I can smell his skin, feel the thud in his chest. I close my arms around him.

Annis whispers, "She's too ill for that."

"What happened to her hair?"

"We cut it. To help with the healing."

That might work. The Knowing think the Outsiders are ignorant.

"Can we have the description, please, Oman?" Kayla asks.

Oman will have read each description, will Know each person that should be here. Why don't they have Himmat from the gates? He would Know them by their faces. No descriptions needed. No wonder Annis was so frightened. I'm frightened. Beckett tightens his grip on my head.

"Nita, Weaver's daughter, working Underneath," Oman replies. "Light hair, pale complexion, blue eyes."

"Blue?" says Kayla.

I let out a slow breath against Beckett's skin. Blue is such an unusual color. Except in this house.

"They are blue," Kayla says, incredulous. "Have any of you ever seen her Underneath? What level, Oman?"

"Three," he replies.

"That would account for it," she sighs. It's not the supervisors' level. The planks groan, the feet shadows move, and Beckett tucks his head against mine, escaping the dust. The door shuts, the talk going on in the next room as the supervisors begin questioning the children.

Beckett pulls my head back, so he can see my face in the dim. "Still here?"

The words are barely breathed. I nod. Some of the tension has gone out of his body, but not all of it. It would be nothing to touch his face, like I did last time. I don't. And it would be nothing for him to lean forward, just a little, like he did before. But he doesn't.

And I think I am ruined. I can't help it.

And then I blink in the sudden light. Annis is pulling up the planks, lifting the packs so we can scramble out, and for the first time it occurs to me to wonder just what this hidden hole might be for. I get to my feet, stiff, and I watch Annis watch Beckett do the same, in his bizarre clothes, not to mention the foot coverings, looking rumpled and dirty and thoroughly beautiful.

"Here," Annis says, handing him a wad of undyed cloth. They're probably Nathan's.

"Thanks," he replies, and the accent I'd almost stopped noticing jumps out, clipped and stark. I don't have the first idea what to tell Annis. I hurry to Jillian. She's lying very still, her eyes closed, and I don't like her breathing. Her pulse is rapid.

"We'll let you dress," I say to Beckett. Annis hesitates, like she wants to say something but decides against it, and goes out the door. "Give her half of what you gave her last time," I whisper. "And go barefoot."

Beckett nods, but he doesn't look at me, and I feel the space between us stretch as wide as between the mountains.

In the main room, the two younger boys are hurrying up the ladder to the loft again, Ari, who is nearing ten, and Luc, three years younger. Their faces are solemn. They don't speak to me, or hug me like they sometimes do. Nathan is openly hostile, arms crossed, leaning against a wall beside Grandpapa. He's as tall as Grandpapa now, his eyes a warm hazel. Other than that, he looks just like Nita. Except that he needs to shave. When did Nathan start needing to shave? Annis has an arm around him, and they all look a little stunned. I think she must have prepared them to be taken.

Jasmina comes to me, though, holding up her arms, sleepy and oblivious to the atmosphere. I pick her up and sit in the room's only other chair, facing the group from the other side of the furnace. The light is warm and yellow, the matting a well-worn green, and I can smell the dried herbs. Jasmina settles against my shoulder, murmuring something about jam, while Grandpapa leans forward, throwing another brick of biofuel through the open furnace door. I like listening to Jasmina. When the children of the Knowing get their memories, they lose the childlike softness of their speech.

I ask, "Is it safe for you to have us here, Annis? For the time being?" We both know it's not safe. The question is the degree of danger.

"Until one of the Knowing hears Nita's name on that list," she replies, "one who's aware her name shouldn't be on it."

They have four supervisors who will remember every person, age, occupation, and description, and they will recite those to one of the administrators Underneath. But what will that administrator Know?

"Did you ask a supervisor about her," I ask Annis, "when she didn't come back?"

"The second resting, yes. I talked to Himmat, at the gates. He said everyone was accounted for, and to go home and count my children."

Then he wasn't admitting, or wasn't being told, the truth, and that in itself is suspicious, because the Knowing cannot miscount. If someone is hiding the fact that there's a missing Outsider, then they already Know that Outsider is missing. And probably how. And why. I rock Jasmina side to side in my arms. I don't think this early counting had anything to do with Nita or her family at all. I think it had everything to do with me, and possibly the two aliens in the resting room. Reddix said they were coming for me.

Annis keeps her eyes on the floor. "Tell us how it happened."

I go still. Jasmina is nearly asleep, her chest rising and falling against mine. If Annis knew everything, I wonder if she would even let me hold her. And I am struggling again. I can see Nita, tears on her cheeks, her left arm limp, at the same time as these plain, wooden walls. But if I were Annis, I'd want to know, too. I push the pain of my memories toward the high shelf.

"Bitterblack," I say. "It was supposed to be for me. But we were sharing . . ."

"For you?" Nathan scoffs.

"Hush," Grandpapa says without lifting his head.

I close my eyes. Fighting. Caching.

"But it wasn't . . . long?" Annis asks.

"No," I whisper. "It wasn't long."

I open my eyes at the sound of a latch, and Beckett is in the doorway, in a tight, undyed tunic and leggings, barefoot, no glasses, looking very Canaan.

"This is Beckett," I say.

He lifts a hand, a little uncertain. "Hi."

And that, I think, was not very Canaan. I need to tell him no one knows what that means. Grandpapa's head comes up. He doesn't turn to look at Beckett, but he's listening.

"You are welcome here," Annis says, passing over the awkwardness. She swipes away tears with the back of a hand. "Does your friend do well?"

"Better, yes." He gives me a swift glance.

"Are you hungry?"

I catch Beckett's eye and give my head a quick shake. He needs to eat whatever he has left until I talk to Annis. Nita's family is on rations. "No," he says. "Thanks."

Grandpapa turns in his chair. "Where did you say you were from?"

"He's one of . . ." I glance at the loft, where the boys are. "He's like me," I say quickly. "He's been . . . helping me."

"If you're here for waking, Nadia," Annis breaks in, "then we may send a person or two to see you, if that suits." She means the sick.

The Outsiders have their own remedies and medicines, but not like Underneath.

"Of course," I say. "But after, I have to go back."

"I'll find some clothes for you at waking, then. Nathan, I'll take Jasmina in with Grandpapa. You see to the boys."

Nathan throws me a hot glare, and it hurts. And it's probably no more than I deserve. But when Annis comes and takes the sleeping Jasmina, she spares one small brush of her hand for my cheek. And that's when I Know, truly Know, that Annis has forgiven me. That she holds nothing against me. I Knew Outsiders could forgive, and I Know Annis has loved me when she didn't have to. But I have not been raised with forgiveness, and now my eyes are stinging, and Nita's loss aches like a deep bruise.

I stand up to go, before I cry like Annis, and as I pass, Grandpapa catches my hand, gives it one quick squeeze. I squeeze back, then slip inside the resting room, and Beckett shuts the door.

I sit on the edge of Jillian's bed. She's peaceful now, deeply asleep, her wheezing stopped and the swelling around her eyes already gone. I'd like to Know what's inside that technology of Beckett's. It seems like a good thing to have.

"Why do they call you Nadia?" he asks.

It's strange to hear his voice indoors, in a room like this. The resting room always was small, but now it feels tiny. I pretend I'm feeling Jillian's pulse.

"It's my name Outside. Nita gave it to me. Nathan, Annis, and Grandpapa all know I am one of the Knowing. The younger children, and the rest of the Outsiders, do not." If they had, I might have died two seasons ago. I feel Beckett come and stand just behind me.

"We need to talk."

I don't answer. I'm making a decision, and I have to be certain it's a decision I'll be willing to remember forever.

I think I have to. I'm already ruined.

I cross the room and dig inside my pack, find the bundle I want, and pull it out. My book is dirty from the Cursed City and the caves, stained from my jump off the cliffs. But it's all in one piece, still with the scarf Nita used to bind my hair tied around it like a strap. This book is the truth, and it's mine.

And I hold it out to Beckett.

It might be the bravest thing I've ever done.

28

BECKETT

I turn the book over in my hand. This is hand sewn, and the paper is coarse, also handmade, but different from other ancient paper I've felt. Mostly because it hasn't had time to become as ancient as I'm used to.

I think what I'm holding is answers.

Samara goes to the other empty bed and lies on it with her back to me, hair cascading down to the floor. I don't know what to make of her right now. She set my ankle, but this is at least twice she's come close to getting me killed. She lied to me, ran from me, has barely tolerated me since, and I would've sworn when we were under the floor, if I'd kissed her then, she would have let me. I wanted to. I couldn't help it. And now she's handed me a gift, and we're back to no eye contact.

I sit in the corner with the rounded wall, my back to the warm clay, run a dirty hand over the stained cover. When I open to the first page, I say, "You wrote this?"

"Yes."

"Why do you want me to read it?"

"Because I want you to understand."

Well, that makes two of us.

A lamp hangs from the ceiling, flickering in a draft, and I forget that its light is dim, that I'm hungry and tired, or that this floor is cold. The words are precise, some in ink, some in a kind of soft black that reminds me of charcoal, but what I don't see are mistakes. Nothing crossed out. Nothing rewritten. Samara thought about what she wanted to say in here, and a lot of it is personal. Really personal. And I'm looking through her words into a world where the safety valves of the brain have been taken away. Where everything you do or say is so permanent that it's paralyzing. Where good memories are the pain-killer that can kill you. Where bad memories can make you not want to live. How did they get this way?

Some things are familiar. Like this bit of social injustice I'm sitting in right now. A copy-and-paste from the history files of Earth. And the stories about Earth and the first colonists—they're like so much I've read, fables spun to explain the facts, but always with the truth hidden somewhere inside. But which is the truth, and which are the lies? I can't tell yet. But I think it has to do with the Forgetting, the sickness Samara thinks of as a cure. It can't be a cure. Not like that. Not by losing what you are.

I turn the last page and shut the book. I don't know how long I've been sitting here, but it's been a long time. If I was on the ship right now, or in a classroom in Texas, what I just read would have been considered a document of incredible importance. A firsthand account of a newly discovered culture. Dad and I could have debated the evolution and ethics of New Canaan for hours. But this is real, not some abstract concept. And people are living it and dying it. Right now.

This is Samara.

Jill's breathing is quiet, even, the house silent around us. Samara is exactly as she was, head not half a meter away on the bed. She hasn't moved, but I don't think she's sleeping. I try to decide if I would have the guts to do what she did the day she ran, when I knew I wouldn't be able to forget it. When I knew I'd live it again. I'm not surprised anymore, that she screamed in the cavern. I'm surprised she isn't screaming all the time.

"What would you have gotten in return," I ask, my voice low, "if you'd given Jill and me to your Council?"

She doesn't move. "The life of my parents."

I lean forward, elbows on knees in the itchy cloth. I don't know what to say.

"I thought I could make a bargain," she whispers, "a trade for my parents and my life until Judgment, that I could buy enough time to find out how the Forgetting works, so I could heal the Knowing. So the Outsiders would see through the lies and rebel. And the city could be warned."

About me. The coming Earth.

"But in the cave, I remembered . . ."

Her back is still to me, but I see what's going to happen. Every muscle has tensed, the speed of her breathing doubled. "Samara," I say, "look at me."

She hesitates, and then turns over. Her mask isn't on, and I see raw fear. Terror of what the memory is going to make her feel.

"Keep looking at me, and just say it," I tell her. "Don't go there. Just say the fact, and put it away."

She looks at me, still breathing hard. I watch her fight to keep her eyes from closing. She whispers, "My brother. Adam. Before he died, he Forgot. I didn't Know then. I didn't understand . . ."

And to have one of the Knowing Forget would rock their social order. Exactly like what Samara wants to do now. "Did they poison him?" I ask. "Like they tried with you?"

She blinks her beautiful eyes. It's answer enough. And now I've come full circle. Because I'm not angry at Samara Archiva anymore. I'm angry for her. She never asked for this, and what's the first thing that happens when she tries to make it right? She walks straight into two kids from Earth who should've never been there in the first place. I run a hand through my tangled hair. What a mess.

"Hey," I say sharply. "Samara, stay here." Her eyes snap open. "Look at me, and tell me what you need to do."

She whispers, "Most of the Knowing think I'm in seclusion. If I go to the Changing of the Seasons, no one would have to admit I've been gone. There wouldn't be any reason for Thorne to condemn my parents, and I would have time to get into the Archives, maybe find the Forgetting, before Judgment . . ."

Because she's not going to live past Judgment.

"How long before the Changing of the Seasons?"

"Two days after the next waking." She keeps her eyes on mine. "I'm going to do it."

What she's going to do is walk back into that city and get killed. At Judgment, or by poison, or some other way first.

She closes her eyes again, but I think she's just exhausted. I lean back against the warm wall. She could be right. If public perception is what her Council is counting on, then a break in that perception might be all that's needed to drive them out of power. Like the United States in the Fifth World War. And it might be best for all of New Canaan, Outside and Knowing alike. The fear I saw in this house and that body at the bottom of the cliff are enough to convince me of that, even without her book.

These thoughts might be the opposite of protocol.

And then I think, really think, what it would mean to Samara to Forget. To have the Knowledge of her book, but not the burden of her memories. I don't want it just for her people. I want it for her. I watch her face, and I'm glad she has her eyes closed, because she is so beautiful and I know I'm being an idiot and there's really just nothing to be done about it. And there's no way she's going back down into that city alone.

"Beckett," she whispers.

I lift my head.

"Some people . . . call me Sam."

"Really? Which do you like better?"

"Sam."

She's smiling, almost asleep, and I wish she wasn't half a meter away. I wish we were in a hole in the floor.

"Which do you like better?" she asks slowly. "Beck? Or Beckett?"

I haven't thought about it. I just take what comes. But then I say, "Beck. When somebody says Beckett, usually they're mad at me."

She smiles bigger, which I think is a funny reaction, and then I watch the expression fade into something still. Peaceful. So she likes to be called Sam. I shake a blanket loose and spread it over her. She doesn't move. I put my elbows on my knees, back against the warm wall.

I am dead tired, and way too keyed up to sleep. There's too much to think about. I reach beneath the rough cloth shirt, unclip the glasses from my T-shirt, and slide them onto my face. The alarm for the power source is still showing, faint, somewhere deep beneath me. I turn it off for now, to save the charge, switch to the database, and start a search for brain diseases.

The standard information scrolls past my eyes, almost what I could have guessed off the top of my head. The Lethe's mutation messes with your memories, so it comes up. But Lethe's was a biological weapon that altered DNA, an engineered toxin passed by air and touch, causing the cells of the brain to rewire their own connections. So, symptoms like paranoia. Psychosis. Distorting memories instead of erasing them. Nothing like Samara.

I think about Channing, riding that bike when we were ten. Amanda. All those people that disappeared from our complex. Lethe's will kill you, but not quick enough. And the mutation, as it turned out, can be passed to unborn children before the symptoms ever show, no exposure necessary. It's the only way it can be passed now. Supposedly. But this was a long time after the original colonists left for Canaan.

I keep searching for "brain disease," only I change the parameters to conditions that take away the ability to forget. And there is nothing. I delete the word "disease" and restructure the search for any kind of anomaly with memories. I come up with photographic memory—an interesting, early tech side trail—developmental issues, aging issues, and none of it looks like Samara. Not even close.

I rub my eyes beneath the lenses, pull off the glasses, and gaze at the bed. Sam. She's lying so calm in her sleep, one long black curl across her cheek. I wonder what Mom and Dad would make of her. Of all of this. They'd have theories, different ones, probably, and spend a happy night arguing them. It's what we do best. Or what we used to do best.

If Mom and Dad have crossed Commander Faye, then they're not in much better shape than Sam's parents. And then I'm seeing Dad, on a dig in the Mexican Peninsula, with that horrible hat on his head, using his old field set. Radio waves and code, because satellites can be hacked . . .

And I hear Jillian saying, "Beckett." This doesn't seem all that significant, until I hear it again. "Beckett!"

I open my eyes. I've been asleep, my neck stiff from using Jill's pack as a pillow. Samara isn't on the bed anymore, and there's a baby crying in the other room. Then I see Jill. She's sitting up, eyes wide, one of the little boys from the loft last night, six or seven years old, standing behind her on the mattress, rubbing what are probably grubby hands all over her shorn blond head. He's giggling. And when I cut my gaze to the side, there's another one, older and more serious, his big brown eyes only a few centimeters away. I move to snatch the glasses off my face, but they're not there. They're inside my shirt again, next to my chest. I'm about 90 percent sure I didn't put them there.

"We're supposed to be waking you up," says the boy next to me. His expression hasn't even twitched.

Jillian is making a pretty valiant effort to stay calm while her head is rubbed. Then Nathan appears in the doorway. He's about to say something but stops. Jill blinks her eyes once.

Nathan nods to her, almost formal, then tilts his head at his brothers. "Mum wants you." The boys scamper, slamming the door shut behind them.

Jill is still for a minute. Then she whispers, "Who was that?"

"Nathan."

Two more seconds and she says, "Hand me my pack."

I get to my feet, wincing as I stand. I'm still bruised from my fall. I did three climbs yesterday, carried Jill across half a planet on newly mended bones, and slept on a floor. I hand over the pack and out comes the sanitizer. She starts spraying, rubbing her head and arms and legs.

"You're going to run out of that," I comment.

"I don't want to hear it." She glances around the plain, window-less room, at the flame near the ceiling, wavering in an open dome of glass, at the chains of dried herbs draped in loops along the walls. The many times washed, and yet not soft blanket over her knees. Her nose wrinkles.

"So where are we, exactly?"

I sit on the edge of Samara's bed, rubbing the ache from my neck. "We're Outside. These are friends of Samara's. They know she's one of the Knowing, but nobody else does, and they think we are, too. Do you remember getting here?"

"Not much." Jill lowers her voice. "Are we safe?"

"I think so."

"Why do you think so?"

"They kept us from getting caught last night. And Samara trusts them."

Jill huffs once at that. "So is the city below us?"

I nod. I know what's coming next.

"So we've got the coordinates. How soon can we get out?"

"We've got a food and water problem. The regenerators won't charge—"

"But we don't have to get far. You'll get a signal, or the skimmers will find us and we'll be picked up . . ."

I hold up a hand. I don't know whose baby was crying in the other room, but it's stopped for a minute, and Jill is using words that shouldn't be overheard. I switch beds, and she scoots up her feet to make room for me. She looks pale, weak, but alert. A lot more like Jill. Which is really good. And bad. I step carefully. Like tiptoeing through a bed of cactus in Texas.

"I don't know if we can get picked up. The skimmers can't see. I watched one crash straight into a mountain when I was climbing the cliffs. It looked right at me, too, and I don't think it knew what I was."

Jill frowns. "I don't understand."

"Me, neither. But there's something else. I caught a power source. Fusion. Somewhere below us. Inside the mountain."

Jill's eyes open big. "There's tech down there?"

"Has to be."

She glances around the room. More than surprised. Like she doesn't believe it. "But they would never live like this if they had tech, right? And there was never supposed to be fusion in Canaan. Even for the communications bunker . . ."

She knows there wasn't. It didn't even exist. I don't tell her what I'm thinking. The *Centauri II*. The ship that landed and was never heard from again. That we've found no trace of that missing ship gives me just as bad a feeling as the lost city.

"What can the glasses see?" Jill asks.

"Not a thing. I could see in the caves as long as there was empty space, but I can't see through this rock. I'm catching the power source through sound."

"So what now?"

I take a deep breath. "I think I ought to find it, try to restore communications."

Okay, I tell myself. That was not a lie. It's just not the *Centauri* I want to restore communications with. I want see if I can talk to Dad's field set. But it's going to be tricky. And dangerous. And maybe impossible.

Jill frowns. "I thought we were ordered to cut off communications?" She's caught me, but I don't think she realizes it. Then she waves a hand. "Never mind. There's no way Commander Faye sent that order."

I look hard at Jill. She's correct. That order was created by Dr. Sean Rodriguez. But how, exactly, is she so confident about it? I think of all those things Jill said about making decisions that were bad for my career, suggesting that the situation could be different from what I thought. But Jill wouldn't keep something really important from me. Would she?

I really want to talk to Dad.

"No," Jill says, still musing. "You're right. Even just finding out what's blocking communications would be huge." She looks at me. "What are you thinking?"

"That you need to take awhile to get better, so I can convince Samara to take me Underneath. Into the city."

"I have to stay in here?"

She actually does. I can see that she's done in just from sitting up. But not so done in that she can't be creative when she cusses. She falls back on the mattress.

"I bet you're about to die of happiness, aren't you?" she says. "Getting a chance to live all rough and pretech like the locals."

I wouldn't put it exactly that way. And I don't like her tone.

"Fine," she sighs. "But listen, Beckett. There has to be an exit plan. If this doesn't work, if you don't find it or it takes too long, we cross the plain anyway, okay? We're not trained, and no one would expect us to stay in these conditions. It's not sanitary."

Leave it to Jill to think that living conditions are more important than our pretend orders. She was so out of it when I had her on my back, I don't think she really gets how hard it would be to cross that plain now. I know she doesn't understand how dangerous it will be to go down into the city. Because I'm not just going to look for their technology and try to make contact with Dad. I'm going to make sure Samara Archiva comes back out again. I'm going to help her do what she's set out to.

Even if it means she Forgets me.

But I don't think Jill really needs to know that.

Beauty, peace, prosperity, and justice. These are the gifts of the perfect society, what those of memory will bring to the Superior Earth. But the greatest of these must be justice, because from it flow the other three, and to receive that justice, there must be chosen a judge . . .

FROM THE NOTEBOOK OF JANIS ATAN

29

SAMARA

nnis, don't you think it would be best to let them sleep?" I say. I'm slicing a loaf of thick bread. There's one for every day of the dark stocked on Annis's shelf, and slicing it is my one learned skill in food preparation. The preparation I haven't done is getting Jillian and Beckett ready for the Outside, and I'm not sure how well the Earth and the Outside are going to mix. "Jillian hasn't been well," I go on. "And the rations . . ."

"They sleep in my house, they can eat at my table," Annis replies, smiling at my reluctance. "And I've already sent in Luc and Ari. They're awake. And I've worked out the rations."

Which means the neighbors are sharing. And then I see Beckett coming out of the resting room. My knife slows. His face is rough, hair mussed, and he lifts one hand, mouths the word "Hi" before Annis whisks him off, showing him the way to the latrines and the water and soap. I slice bread faster, insides twisting into a nervous knot.

Beckett Rodriguez knows everything about me now. Only Nita has ever known as much, and there were things in that book I never told even her. The feeling is uncomfortable. Vulnerable. Exactly what my mother warned me of when I wasn't controlling my face. But it's also . . . freeing. I caught one corner of Beckett's smile as he followed Annis out, a smile that yes, he knew, and that yes, it was still all right.

And then I'm thinking that if I go back Underneath, that if I somehow manage to succeed in everything I'm trying to do, that I will Forget that smile ever existed. I feel the ache of a loss that hasn't even happened yet.

I am so ruined. But there's no reason that anyone has to know about it.

We sit. Beckett, Jillian, and Nathan on one side of the table, Grandpapa, Annis, and me on the other, the boys on the ends, Jasmina in her mother's lap. The benches are full, cramped, and there's a hole in this table at least a kilometer wide. I've never sat here without Nita, and I'm not the only one feeling it. Memories of her swirl, sometimes reach up and nudge, tugging. But I've just slept, and it's always easier to control memories when I've rested. It won't be later. I love this house, and being inside it is difficult.

Annis serves each plate bread and dried fruits, preserves, the last of the greens, working out the portions according to the rations. Bread lands on my plate, and I open my mouth to protest, but Annis speaks first.

"When did you eat? Has it been more than two days?"

I close my mouth. And see Jillian's brows go up.

"All right, then," she says, ending what was never an argument. "Who wants preserves?"

It's an odd sort of meal. Beckett and Jillian are wary of mistakes, and Grandpapa and Annis seem determined not to ask them anything at all, even when the omission is painfully obvious. For a while, the only one talking is Ari, and that's about waterbugs.

"Do you blow glass?" Beckett asks Cyrus, smearing preserves on his bread. His accent is like one yellow apple in a barrel of honeyfruit.

"Yes," says Grandpapa. And nothing else.

I'm not sure what sort of preserves Beckett thought he was going to taste, but I don't think it was pepper. I see his eyes widen, and out of nowhere, I have to hold in a laugh. Jillian takes note. She's done with almost everything. Except the preserves. I hope she understands the concept of rations.

"You're interested in glass?" Cyrus finally asks.

"Why would he be?" Nathan snaps. Not because he thinks glass isn't interesting, but because Beckett isn't worthy of being interested in glass. Annis shushes him and throws me an apologetic look. I Know what's wrong with Nathan. He's not angry. He's sad, and now my guilt is as hot as the jelly. Jasmina tears the bread into pieces, eating from her mother's plate.

"I'd like to watch sometime," Beckett says, as if Nathan never spoke, "and see how it's done." I think he's sincere in that. He's watching everything now. The food, the manners, the plates. And he's going for the preserves again, just to show he can.

"Actually," says Annis, "we'd be grateful if you all stayed in the house for now, until . . ." No one knows how to fill this blank, so the table goes silent. Again my guilt is hot. I've put them in a terrible position.

"If they were coming about the false information last resting, they would've done it already," says Grandpapa. "But we have to assume we're being watched."

How often, I suddenly wonder, is this house being watched?

"Nathan, I need you to take the children to the metal shop."

"Why can't she watch them?" He means me.

"Because Nadia has people coming to see her."

I've already tended to a sprained wrist, a second-degree burn, and a birth. The last one didn't actually need much of my help, but Nathan was not pleased to come down from the loft at waking and discover it.

"I'll watch them," Jillian says unexpectedly. She smiles at Annis, her eyes big and blue, and I wonder what she's playing at. But Annis is captivated by those eyes, so uncommon, and so close to Nita's. And now Jillian is eating a second piece of bread. Did Nathan just put that on her plate? He's looking at her from the corner of his eye. And she knows it.

There's a knock on the door, and we all go still, except for Annis, who goes to the closed curtain. "Mika," she says. "Nadia, are you finished eating?"

Mika, unfortunately, needs her hand stitched. I go as fast as I can while she sweats, half my mind on this house. Without Nita here, smoothing over the rough patches, protecting me from what might hurt, I feel that for the first time, my eyes are fully open. How did Mika know I was here to stitch her hand? How do any of them? No one ever questions me or my unusually good grasp of medicine, no more than Annis has questioned Beckett. They never seek me at my supposed home on the far end of the Outside. I am just Nadia, and I come to Annis's house and I heal them. It's the way things have always been. But the way things have always been doesn't exactly make sense. And there's a hole beneath Annis's floor.

Being Knowing, I think, has not kept me from being naive.

Then I don't have time to wonder anymore, because a broken nose comes in, which there's not much to do about, and a five-year-old boy, crying in his mother's arms. The boy concerns me. He's pale, sweating when it isn't hot, and when Angela, his mother, sits him on the table, I can feel that his skin is more than two degrees too high—unusual for an Outsider, unheard of Underneath. He's vomited twice into one of Annis's pots, and there's a point of pain when I press on his side. A pain that makes him shout. His mother gathers him close, strokes the little boy's mop of soft brown hair.

"How long has he been like this?" I ask.

"Three days. Has he eaten something that disagrees?"

I don't answer, just close my eyes, searching my memory. I don't like what I find. I think I Know what I should do. I Know what the training recitations say I should do. I'm just not sure I can do it.

"Wait just a minute," I tell her.

I hurry to the second resting room, slip inside without even thinking about knocking, shut the door, and lean on it.

Beckett straightens from a small mirror hung on the wall between the beds. He's down to the tight shirt he was wearing when he first got here, wiping soap from his face, a long, thin blade in his hand. There's also quite a bit of blood. Whatever he usually shaves with, it's not a razor. It's probably something I wouldn't even understand.

"I've always wanted to try one of these things," he says, waving the razor. "Turns out it's terrible." Then he runs his eyes over me. "What's wrong?"

"What can the glasses see inside a person? Besides bones?"

"It depends."

"Can you see an appendix? Could you tell if it's inflamed?"

He rinses the blade in a bowl of water, brows together. "I don't know. I'm not sure I'd know what I'm looking at."

He's right. This wouldn't be clear. Not like a cracked bone. Then I'm decided.

"I need help," I say. "I can't ask . . ." I leave the thought without finishing it. There's not another soul I could ask.

He doesn't even look at me a long time. He just says, "Tell me what you need."

30

BECKETT

eady?" Sam asks, and when I nod, she turns the lock on the front
door.

We get to work, fast, Samara throwing a piece of cloth over the
table we've already scrubbed, dousing it with a bottle of antiseptic that
smells like alcohol and peppermint, me lighting every lamp I can find.

The little boy, Michael, is still, eyes closed, breathing hard in a
way that's all wrong for a kid, and that seems worse to me than the
crying. Sam convinced his mother to leave him with us for three or
four hours, so he could get several rounds of medicine for his stomach.
Outsiders do not understand surgery, so what we're doing here is
against every bioethic Earth could think up.

I don't know if I'd have the guts for it, when I knew I couldn't
forget if something went wrong. But when I asked Sam if she was sure,
she said, "Eighty-five percent," which didn't seem that great, until she
explained that there was an 85 percent chance that Michael was going
to die if she didn't do something. And, she reasoned, if she didn't try,
"Then what is all this Knowing for anyway?"

But one thing I'm learning about Samara Archiva: When she's decided what to do, she's fearless about it. Even when she's scared of what
she is doing. Like surgery. For the first time. On a child. On Annis

Weaver's kitchen table. Before Annis, or Nathan, or Cyrus, or Jill, or a wandering family member takes it into their head to walk into this room.

As soon as the lamps are done, I grab the medical kit from the resting room, bring it to the counter, and whisper, "You won't believe what's going on in there. The kids, they're all in kind of a pile. Asleep."

Sam looks up from pinning a scrap of cloth over her front. I can smell the antiseptic. "With Jillian?"

"I know. Weird, right?" Jill's not actually having to fake her recovery yet, and the lack of light has both our sleep patterns in a mess.

Sam comes and stands next to me as I lay out the medical kit, tense. I start talking fast, because I know she will remember.

"Everything I have is field first aid, so super basic . . ." She looks confused. "For when you're traveling. Away from a city. For emergencies." Now she nods. "And this is not my area, so . . ." She nods again. I pull out a smaller pack with a face covering, gloves, clamps, and a kit of medical tools, all sealed in a clear film.

"This is the scalpel." I show her through the package. "Slide your forefinger into the slot on top, and the knife will cauterize as it cuts. Slide your finger out when you want it to stop. And this"—I pick up a slim cylinder—"is for sealing a wound. Slide your finger in again, and run a ribbon of the cellular material between the two ends of tissue you want to fuse. The harder you press, the more material you'll get." I glance at her face, focused, storing the information in her memory. "So no sewing people up with thread, okay?"

She smiles. "Are you sure?"

"Definitely."

"Help me wash."

I stand behind her and pour water from the pitcher while she holds her arms out over the sink, sleeves folded up so they can't fall, waiting while she washes up to her elbows. I probably should have moved back, given her more room, but I don't want to. Her hair is tied away from her face, and I want to put my hand in it, like I did in the caves.

But I also don't want to give her another memory she didn't ask for. She holds out her arms and I rinse with the pitcher again, then open up the face covering and let her get it in place.

I can see only her eyes now, through the thin film of the containment barrier. She looks half Earth, and half Canaan. "Okay?" I ask. Her shoulders rise and fall. She nods.

It takes just a few seconds to let the infuser calculate the dose of anesthetic and get it into Michael. I stay behind him, so he won't see anything he doesn't understand, Sam hanging back for the same reason. But he's so out of it, I'm not sure he even noticed when it went in.

When his eyes close and stay that way, I get his clothes off fast and lay him on the table, the cloth still damp from antiseptic, and use more of it to scrub his abdomen and right side, and basically everywhere I can reach. He's breathing deep and slow, but he's sweating, his skin coming out in gooseflesh. I cover up his lower end, because it seems like the right thing to do, and then I wait for Samara. She's not with me. She's inside her mind. Going through her information.

Then she opens her eyes and says, "Watch his breathing and his heart rate. Tell me if it changes. Wait, can you see blood pressure?" she asks. I nod, and slide on the glasses. I'm pretty sure my own vitals are changing as we speak.

Samara unseals the package of instruments, laying them ready, and feels carefully around Michael's side, poking and probing. Then she picks up the scalpel and cuts a five-centimeter gash into his smooth brown skin.

I know it's why we're standing here, but somehow, I can't believe she actually just did that.

I've never thought of myself as squeamish. Part of anthropology is the study of bodies, and I've seen a lot of them, in various states of dead. But this is different. There's a pulse beating, living blood I can smell, and the smoke of burning tissue making wisps in the lamplight. I can't look at it.

I watch Sam instead, focused and with her fingers bloody, working quick inside the boy's body. I hear her hiss once, the clank of metal as she switches tools, and after a few minutes she's triumphant, holding up a red-and-pink piece of flesh no bigger than Michael's little finger.

And then her eyes get big. She has nowhere to put it. And Jasmina has just started crying in the other room.

"Here!" I grab one of the sanitized cloths we had ready for dabbing blood, and hold it out. And Sam drops Michael's severed appendix into my palm.

Okay.

She gets right back to work. I can hear Jill shushing Jasmina in the resting room.

"How's his heart rate?" Sam whispers.

"A little fast." Like mine.

"Breathing?"

"Normal." Mine's not.

The resting room has gone quiet again. I hear a soft whirr, see the blinking green light on the end of the sealer, and think about the herbs on the ceiling until Samara says, "Beck, help me."

I leave Michael's wrapped appendix on the bench and come around the table. She's ready to seal her original cut, and I can see the tissue she's been working with through the wide gap of skin.

"Can you do the last one?" she asks. "I need two hands to hold the skin together and yours aren't clean enough."

I take the sealer, which is sticky, look away while she pulls the skin back together, then fill the cut with cellular fusion material. It sinks in, bridges the gap in Michael's wound. Samara holds it in place for another minute, then lets go, wiping away the telltale smudges of blood. The incision looks like a small scrape. Like Michael brushed against something rough. And that's it. In two days, he won't even have that.

"Heart rate?" she says. "Blood pressure?"

I nod. No major change. Sam touches the mark gingerly with a finger, and then she pulls off the face covering and she smiles. A real one, like I haven't seen since she was jumping off those roots in the caves.

"That," she says, "was amazing."

"Was it infected? His appendix?"

"What? Oh, yes. It nearly burst when I was cutting it. Do you want to see?"

Nope. Never again. I look at Michael, still deeply asleep. "He would have died?"

"Yes, he would have."

"Then you did good," I say. "Really good."

She smiles like that again, huge, which is exactly what I wanted. And then we both spin around, guilty, and with bloody hands. Jill is standing in the doorway of the resting room, her short hair rumpled, the undyed cloth Sam put on her rolled up at the arms and legs. And her eyes are huge.

"What . . . are you doing?"

Sam doesn't even bat a lash. "Being pretech," she replies.

Jill needs to watch what she says to the Knowing, because it's not like they're going to forget it. That was a jab going right back to that awful conversation at the lake, in the caves, when Jill tried to tell Samara that her training wasn't "advanced." And the meaning wasn't lost on her. Jill steps back.

"Is he dead?"

"No," I say. "Of course not. It was an appendix, Jill."

And now she's looking at the stained sealer on the table, at the infuser still sitting on the bench, and the open cloth lying beside it. She looks up and our eyes meet. It's a gaze that lasts a long time. I don't think Jill has realized until now just how far off the path of careers and protocol I've strayed. How far I probably will stray.

"They don't understand surgery, so don't say anything, Jill. The kid would have died without it."

And I can hear her telling me, without her saying it, that I swore an oath to never influence, alter, or interfere with an emerging history. Screw protocol.

"Beck," says Samara. "Quick. Before somebody comes back."

We go back to work. I get the blood off my hands and clean up Michael, wrapping another sanitized cloth over the wound, just in case, scooping him up and getting him warm inside the blankets. Jill must have left at some point, because the resting room door is shut again. Samara makes a bundle of all the used cloth, including the appendix and the piece she had pinned over her clothes, and throws it all into the heating fire. Whatever is in that antiseptic makes the whole thing go up in a blaze.

I move to help her and she says, "No, stay with him. Watch his breathing until he wakes up."

So I monitor while Sam carries everything to the sink, scrubbing tools and herself until the water is gone, and before I know it the lamps are back in place, the kit is stowed away, the doors unlocked, and the room looks innocent. Like we've haven't just cut somebody open.

Then Samara is on the bench beside me, with two mugs of tea. She holds one out and I take it. She's being funny with me, keeping her gaze on the floor or lamp flame, but she can't stop smiling, even when she blows across the hot mug. It's a pretty thing to see.

"So why don't you need to eat?" I ask her. "Or sleep? Much?"

She lifts a shoulder. "It's part of being one of the Knowing. We heal fast, too."

"But the Outsiders don't?"

She shakes her head, getting down on the floor beside Michael like she wants to change the subject. He's deeply asleep. "Is Jillian angry?"

"Disappointed is probably closer."

She sips her tea and asks, "What would happen if . . . the others, on your ship, found out that you've shown me your technology?"

I try to think how to explain. "If the Commander finds out"—which I'm 100 percent sure she has—"then it'll be bad if I go back. But . . . I don't really plan on going back to the ship. Not to live. Mom, Dad, and I . . . we planned on staying here."

"Would Jillian tell them what you've done?"

"I don't think so. I'm just not turning out to be what she had in mind, that's all."

"I've never been what my mother had in mind," Sam says. "My parents preferred my brother."

She touches Michael's forehead, on the side away from the heat, and I see the shadow of a memory tempt her. I have thoughts about her parents, now that I've read her book, especially the mother. But I'm not going to ruin the mood. Then I realize what she's doing with Michael. "Can you feel his temperature? With your fingers?"

"Yes." She smiles again. "He's already dropped a degree. A little more."

I didn't think to tell her that the infuser would take care of that. I tilt my head. "What's the temperature of this room?"

She closes her eyes and says, "Eighteen Celsius, where we are."

I check the glasses. She's right on. "How far is it to the ceiling?"

Her brows go up the tiniest bit, but she runs her eye up a wall and says, "Two-point-four meters."

Again, she's correct. To the decimal. And she just saved a little boy's life with what was in her mind. "Sam, are you sure you want to Forget? Everything?"

The facade comes down over her face. I hate it. But we need to talk about it.

"I can't pick and choose." She stares at the rise and fall of Michael's chest. "And . . . I can relearn. Can't I?"

I don't think she has any idea how long it takes for most people to learn.

She doesn't look at me when she asks, "You said it was against your rules, but do you think Earth would ever . . . share, what could be used for healing? If the Outsiders had technology, they might not need my Knowing."

"If it were up to me, we would. But even so, technology is no good unless someone knows how to apply it. The scalpel didn't take out his appendix. It just helped." I set down the mug, thinking. "How long do the Knowing live?"

"If they don't . . . If they die naturally, then maybe about a hundred and forty?"

I have to stare at her for a full minute. "You have got to be kidding me. Is it the same for the Outside?"

"A little less, I think."

"How old is Cyrus?"

"One hundred and eight."

"What? Are you sure?"

Now both her brows are up. As if she could be unsure. "How long do people live on Earth?"

"Eighty-five or ninety. Maybe a hundred. Something like that."

"Is something wrong with them?"

"No. Well, yes, a lot of things, but age isn't one of them. That's a normal human life span, Sam. And it proves my point."

"What point?"

"That none of this is genetic."

"What do you mean?"

She looks uncomfortable now. I can see her drawing in. I forge on. "I mean that all of you are descended from the first one hundred and fifty. You have their DNA. Earth DNA. And Knowing, Forgetting, none of that happens on Earth. Something is making you like this. Something here. On this planet."

Sam puts her hand on Michael's chest to feel his breathing. But she is listening.

"What if you didn't have to Forget to break the power of the Council? To help the Knowing heal? You said they'd want to Forget. That they would choose losing their memories over jumping off cliffs. But what if they could get the same thing without losing themselves? What if you could show them how to not be Knowing at all?"

She gazes at me, but she doesn't say anything.

"That would break your Council, wouldn't it? And you could still be Samara Archiva, and go on healing Underneath and Outside alike, because there wouldn't be any difference between the two. Not anymore." I let her think about that. "You're going Underneath soon, aren't you?"

She looks at the floor.

"Are you going tonight? At resting?"

She blinks, and I lean forward.

"Take me with you. I can use the glasses. I'll know where the people are. I can keep you from getting caught. And I can find out in less than a minute what's inside those wellness injections."

She lifts a hand to her upper arm, where her scars are. "But . . . they're only vitamins . . ."

"Vitamin injections you get every year, that leave a scar?"

She drops her hand.

"Samara, something is doing this to you. Let's go down there together and we'll use the technology, just like with Michael. Take me with you, and I swear I'll help you get what you need."

Samara's eyes lower, and then they close, and for a moment, she's gone. But she comes right back, and when she does, the facade is down. She jumps to her feet, and looks at me. And she only says one word.

"No."

And where shall we, the chosen of the NWSE, find our judge? From the knowledge that is deepest and the memory that is longest, for it is from knowledge and memory that wisdom is derived. And so I, the first of memory, shall be our first judge, and continue to choose our chosen, that we may fulfill our directive, and build the Superior Earth . . .

FROM THE NOTEBOOK OF JANIS ATAN

31

SAMARA

As soon as the door to the resting room shuts behind Beckett, my mind begins to tilt, teeter—pulled down on one side, jerked to the other, memories vying for the privilege of dragging me under.

There is a humanness to our facial expressions, and the Knowing learn to recognize them. Quickly. It's why we work so hard at hiding our own. And there is one I've seen before, a reflex, like a hand coming up to cover a cut, a kind of looking inward at unexpected pain. I saw it on Sonia's face, the first time her boy from Outside did not come to the Level Eight storage rooms. On Uncle Towlend, when he learned Aunt Letitia was no longer in the city. And I saw it on the face of Beckett Rodriguez, when I told him he could not come with me Underneath. My answer hurt him. And I think a deep part of my mind Knew what that meant before I did.

Beckett loves me. At least a little. Whether he realizes it or not.

And I am so angry about it.

I stop pacing, sit on the bench, and put my head in my hands. Why? Why would he feel like that? How did this happen? All my life I've been able to avoid this. It wasn't even hard. And then I meet a boy from Earth, the enemy, who is inexplicable, whose planet I can't even trust, and I go to him like a dustmoth to lantern flame. It doesn't make sense. And yet here it is. My "once." Ruining me. And now it's him, too, until he can forget. I never will. Unless I'm healed. Or dead.

I cannot let Beckett go Underneath.

Michael wakes up then, hardly even groggy, with none of the aching sickness he would've had with a sleeping draught from the city. He's sore, though, and very willing to lie where he is. I get him dressed, gently, and then Angela, his mother, comes back from the fuelmaking sheds. Michael's arms cling to my neck while I give her instructions for his eating and rest. They feel warm. Trusting. I hand him over to Angela. Lurking memories seize me. I seize myself back.

At least I will always be able to remember one thing: The time my Knowing did some good.

Unless I Forget it.

I walk Michael's mother to the door, smile, struggle to stay present. And at the click of the latch, I plunge, like the floor planks opened up beneath my feet, and I am . . .

. . . in the Archiva receiving rooms, and there's a lamp lit beside the mirror, shining down on my mother in a blue-silver chair, my father in the one opposite. Mother has a low table set in front of her, sprinkled with the multicolored picture tiles. The pieces tap sharp on the wood as Mother picks them up, sets them down, making patterns, or a picture, and then doing it all over again.

This game is supposed to distract the mind while promoting creativity, which the Knowing lack. Mostly the Knowing just remember what someone did before, rather than thinking of something new. And it's the sort of game Mother likes. Orderly. With pieces that are predictable and do not change. Where she can construct what she wants, and then take it apart again.

I have a set of tiles, too, spread out on the floor. There are nine marks on my arms, and my hands are already lanky, skinny as I move them back and forth. But I keep making the same picture Mother does.

"*Mother*," I say. "*Do you love anyone?*" *I'm curious because we've just come back from a partnering, and the man looked so happy.*

"*Samara*," Mother says, *her voice gone sharp. And I freeze. I Know I've done wrong. My father, who I think was pretending to sleep when he was really in a memory, opens his eyes. "Retrieve the memory of your last visit to your uncle," she says.*

I find the memory, and then I am eight years old, and there is Uncle Towlend, thin and wasting, unwashed, tears running down his cheeks to the pillow.

"*That*," she says, *when I open my eyes, "is the result of love. Your uncle was happy at his partnering, too. Now retrieve the memory again."*

I don't want to, but I do it. It's worse to tell her no. And Uncle Towlend is thin and wasting, unwashed, tears running down his cheeks to the pillow.

"*Again, Samara.*"

Uncle Towlend is thin and wasting, unwashed, tears running down his cheeks to the pillow.

"*Eight more times.*"

Mother's tiles slide and click, and my own tears are spilling.

And then my father says, "I remember love . . ."

I rise inside my mind, and fall . . .

. . . and Nita is writhing with happiness, blushing as she talks about her metalworker . . .

. . . and then I rise and fall again, a gentle wave . . .

. . . and it is the waking, and I am laying a brand-new baby in its father's arms . . .

I fall and I rise, and fall . . .

. . . into the Bartering Square, where Josef is tied to the post, and I am sick, sick, and Carma Planter is holding his head in her hands, spattered by every crack of the whip, because she will not leave him . . .

. . . and I am falling, and I Know this descent, because I've taken it so many times. I welcome it, pull it closer . . .

. . . and the pain of Adam is inside me, hot and searing, but Beckett's arm is around me, too, his other hand cradling the back of my head. My face is against warm skin, tucked beneath the roughness of a jaw, and I breathe his smell, feel his pulse beneath my hand, his breath across my hair, the tightening of his hold. And my grief is soothed, comforted . . .

I retrieve the memory again. And again. And the last time I let it go on, and I feel Beckett's mouth, his cheek beneath my palm, my fingers in his hair. And I retrieve it again, only this time sooner, drifting down until I am crying in the crook of Beckett's neck, my soul ripped to shreds by watching Adam die, whispering . . .

"There is a way . . . to Forget. I ran to the Cursed City looking for it."

And Beckett whispers back, "Did you find it?"

"No."

"Then let me help you find it . . ."

I open my eyes. Ari is running pell-mell through the front room from the workshop, wet from the pond, and I am on the floor, knees to chest, back against the wall below the window. There are voices above me in the loft. Nathan, Jasmina. Jillian. And when I sort back through my memory, I realize that Nathan came home, made tea with Jillian, and took her up to the loft while I sat here, lost on the floor with Beckett.

I let my embarrassment slide away like it's been cached. Beckett thinks I don't have to be Knowing. That I might not need to Forget. But I want to live without pain. Without grief. I also don't want to lose my memories of him. I want to remember how to fix things, like Michael. And yet, I'm not sure if I can live with the memories I've got.

And none of this, I realize, is why I was angry. I was angry because I am afraid.

Annis comes in then, a little out of breath, holding her hair off her neck. I think she's been chasing Ari. She looks me over. "Are you well?"

I don't answer. I'm huddled on the floor. But she's seen me like this before. Only that was for Adam.

This is different.

We eat the resting meal together, all of us, and I'm only half present. I don't speak to Beckett, even when he tries to talk to me. And I don't go Underneath, either. I have one more waking, one more resting before the Changing of the Seasons, and for all my Knowing, I can't decide what to do.

That's not true. I can't decide what I'm willing to risk.

I sit in Grandpapa's chair while the house sleeps, and when the children stir and he goes out to the workshop at waking, I follow him. The streets are waking up, too. Doors slamming, shadowy figures with pitchers going for water. Irene, across the street, singing to her new baby in the lamplight. The red light is deepening. The dark is almost here. Grandpapa is checking the city's requests for the day, getting ready to stoke up the fire of the furnace. He looks up, startled at the sight of me. I haven't even pulled up my hood, but there's not a supervisor due for another five-eighths of a bell.

"Do you have bad memories?" I ask abruptly. "Even though you forget?"

He throws a brick of biofuel on the glowing coals, forehead wrinkled. "Of course."

"What do you do with them?"

"Make peace with them."

"And that takes them away?"

"No. They never go away. Not fully. They just heal."

But what if I'm too damaged to heal without the Forgetting? What if there's nothing Underneath that can change who I am?

"Grandpapa . . ." I lower my voice. "It's the Changing of the Seasons. I have to go Underneath. But Jillian, Beckett . . . They will need a safe place. I . . . It's not fair to ask . . ."

Grandpapa tilts his white head toward a young man at the street corner, playing a game of toss stones. "Do you see that boy there? He's one of my warning bells. There's a whole network of them, all through the Outside. Word of trouble gets here faster than any supervisor, little girl. You don't think we'd bring you Outside and never keep you safe?"

No, I suppose he wouldn't.

"We can do the same for your friends."

He doesn't even ask me why they don't need to go Underneath for the Changing of the Seasons. "How many Outsiders know who I am, Grandpapa?"

"A few. All of them trusted."

"And that hole in your floor?"

He shakes his head. "Never you mind. But when you come back to us, things may be different, that's all."

He puts a hand on my head, and the breeze sneaks under the eaves of the workshop, bringing the heat of the furnace to my face. What are they up to? Smuggling food? Misappropriating goods? Whatever it is, it's a dangerous game, and the thought of Annis, Nathan, or Grandpapa tied to the flogging post makes my stomach wrench.

"Nita told me once that she wanted to be my family's help. That she trained to do things just the way my mother would want, trying to be chosen. Why would she want that?"

"Because of you." He turns his blue eyes on me in a way that is very Nita. "You needed us, little girl. And we need you."

I shake my head. I don't understand him. "What do you do . . . with a memory like . . . loss. Like when Grandmama died?"

"You make peace with that, too. Isn't easy. But it gets better."

Mine can't ever get better. Not while I'm Knowing. "But wouldn't it be better," I whisper, "to have no loss at all?"

"If you live in such a way that you can never lose, little girl . . . well, then you'll never gain anything in the first place, and what's the point in that? I'd have rather had Grandmama and lost her, than never have had her at all. You still have the memories. If I'd never tried, I wouldn't have even that. Look . . ."

He pulls up the undyed cloth around his ankle. The cut I stitched is a neat pink line, ten centimeters along his calf.

"And now look at this." He raises the cloth even farther, and just below his knee I can see the end of a wide and jagged swell, a twisting scar not properly healed, disappearing up beneath his legging. "See the difference?"

I do. It is the difference between Knowing and doing. Trying and not. Like everything.

"Grandpapa," I say, "do you have another pair of sandals?"

32

BECKETT

I don't even turn over when I hear the door open. I stay still, arm beneath my head on the bed, facing the wall. I've already had an earful from Jillian, several of them. On and on. I just let her talk, because the truth is, I don't really care what she says. Jill isn't mad that I broke the rules and impacted a culture. If that were her problem, I could respect it. She's mad because she thinks that when I go back to the ship, I'll be disgraced. That there won't be any hero's welcome with me at her side, names in history files, everybody thinking how lucky she is. When did I get to be Jillian's bragging rights? I never planned to do much more with my life than run around ruins, make notes, read books, and knock mud off my boots.

I hear the muffled rumble of Nathan talking from the loft above, a child's footsteps, the clink of pottery, creak of wooden wheels in the street. Noise that is so very not Austin, Texas. I am inside the lost colony of Canaan, or what has become of it, and I can feel the long dark of space that sits between my old life and the new. I think about the caves again, that moment when I kissed Sam, like an idiot, and she kissed me back. Pulled my hair. She wanted me to kiss her. I know she did.

And then she rejected me. And then she didn't. And I helped her do surgery, and she rejected me again. Then I waited up all night, wound up tight and listening, because I think she's going to go Underneath and never come back out again, and she didn't even leave when she was supposed to.

She is making me crazy.

"Beck."

I jump like I've been zapped, and look over my shoulder. Samara is standing beside the bed.

"Did I wake you?"

I blink. "A little."

"What did you mean, 'the first one hundred and fifty'?"

I blink again. All this, and this is the thing she walks in here and asks. "What do you want, Samara?"

She sits on the edge of the bed, and I have to scoot over or get sat on. She's struggling. I can see that. I rub a hand across my eyes and sigh.

"The first one hundred and fifty are the original colonists. Your ancestors. That's how many of them came on the first ship, to build Canaan."

"How do you know?"

"Because I've studied the Canaan Project practically my whole life." She frowns a little. "You have?"

"Yes. It was a big deal to be chosen to come. They had to pass a lot of tests, and there was at least one chosen from every country, so there were a lot of different—"

"What is a country?"

And there's a concept I've never considered how to explain. I'm annoyed, hurt, and I don't know what's happening here, but what I am learning is that I'm very bad at resisting Samara Archiva. I sit up, slide behind Samara, her hair brushing my face, and grab the blanket off the bed. I flip it out, the thick-woven cloth spreading over the floor, and squat down at the edge.

"Okay," I say. "Pretend that this is Earth, and this"—I snag Jill's pack, wad up her other T-shirt and drop it on the blanket—"this is a country. And here's two more . . ."

I drop her socks.

". . . and another . . ."

Hygiene kit.

". . . and another."

Meal package. I didn't know she still had one of those. Sam slips down off the edge of the bed, hugging her knees on the floor beside the blanket. It's hard to imagine right now that she made that first incision with a steady hand.

"So countries can have their own laws and their own cultures," I say. "Their own way of doing things. Sometimes their own language . . ."

"What do you mean, their own language?"

I think again. "We're speaking a version of English, you and I. The words are . . . English, even if they're pronounced a little different . . ."

I've gotten so used to Samara's accent, I'd almost stopped hearing it. It suits her, though. Rhythmic, like the way she moves.

"But another country over here, or over here"—I point to Jill's scattered belongings on the pretend Earth—"they might have their own system of words. So if you lived in this country, China, the word for 'cloth' might sound like *yīkuài bù*."

Sam sits back, looking stunned, and then incredulous. "That isn't a real way of speaking."

I have to laugh. "It is. It's the way my mother grew up talking, and she made sure I did, too. My granny spoke Spanish, and I'm not bad at that one, either. But—"

"Say something," she says. She's got her head tilted, blinking at me. A challenge. Like in the caves. I stare back at her eyes.

"*Tus ojos son hermosos,*" I say.

"What does it mean?"

I shake my head. I'm not telling her. "Just imagine," I go on, "that there are all these countries, and all these languages, all with their own ways of doing things. Your ancestors, the first one hundred and fifty, came from all of them. All the major cultures. But they all had to learn English to come to Canaan. Just like we made sure that everyone who came this time could speak English. So we could talk to you."

"So you could study us?"

"Right."

"And so why did they come? Why did they leave Earth at all?"

"It's like what you wrote in your book. An experiment. To build a better world. To start over without all the bad stuff from Earth. But we never heard from Canaan again, and no one knew what had happened to them. People debated about it for years. Centuries. Dad used to get together with his friends and they'd come up with all kinds of theories. But there's never been an answer. So, see, you've been a mystery."

I want to see what she thinks of that, but she's got her mask on. "But why did you wait?" she asks. "Why wait so long to come back and find the answers?"

"A lot of reasons. There was a war a few years after the first colonists left. A big one. All the countries fighting each other . . ." She looks over at the blanket. "New World Space Exploration, the company that started the project, got bombed out of existence. That was the Third World War. Then we did it again not long after with the Fourth World War. And because we love to screw up, we did it again with World War Five. But between Four and Five there was another ship sent, only we never heard from it again, either. Have you ever heard stories about Earth being here before?"

She shakes her head. "But I've always thought our history was mostly lies."

"Everybody's is. A little bit." Some more than others.

"Is New Canaan like a country?"

"In a way. Except that it's small. Countries might have a million people in their cities. At least."

She looks at me like I've lost my mind. "A million? In one country?"

"No. In one city. Countries have lots of cities, of all different sizes. There are three and a half billion people on Earth. But that's a lot less than it used to be." And it's declining. I watch her stare at Jill's stuff scattered across the pretend Earth, trying to comprehend. And I can't help it. I have to try again.

"But this is the point," I say. She gives me her gaze. "Your ancestors came from Earth, from all of those countries, all those people, and nowhere is there anything like Knowing or Forgetting, or living to be a hundred and forty. These things are not genetic."

She whispers, "I shouldn't have to be like this."

"I don't think so. Something's doing it to you. And, Sam, I think you're going to need my help to find out what it is."

I stay where I am, balancing elbows on knees while she thinks. *Take me with you* hangs heavy between us.

"Show me what goes inside those injections, and we could fix this whole mess."

She's hesitating, her hair half tied back, loose, twisting, curls falling down all around her face. Then she says, "Why would you do that for me?"

I didn't expect that question, and I think of about thirty answers, quick. *Because you're smart. Because you're beautiful. Because you fascinate me and infuriate me. Because you're in pain, and I don't want to watch human beings suffer. Because I'm from Earth, and I'm afraid my people might be just as wrong as yours. Because I think I can fix this. Because every time I think of somebody trying to hurt you, I want to park a spaceship on them.* But all I say is, "I plan to live on this planet, too."

She plays with the tie of her sandal, and I can't tell what she's thinking at all. Then she says, "I have to stay Underneath, for the

Changing of the Seasons, and I won't be able to hide you. You'll have to leave me, and go back Outside."

I nod. Though it's possible I won't agree to it later.

"If it's the injections, like you say, and we can just . . . stop being Knowing. I might still be . . . broken. My memories might still . . ."

"Maybe you can heal from your memories, Sam, if you stop reliving them."

"But if there's nothing in the wellness injections, I will have to get into the Archives, and get the book on Forgetting. I will need to make myself Forget, show the Knowing how to Forget, to break the Council. Do we agree on that as well?"

I shrug. "If you need to Forget, Sam, then you need to Forget." I say that like it is nothing to me. It isn't. "I'll just help you remember after, okay?"

She's back to staring at the pretend Earth. "I don't Know what the Council would do to you if they realized who you were."

Nothing worse than they'd do to her. Probably. "I'm not sure it's that much more dangerous than where we are now."

"Promise me, that if we're caught . . . you'll do . . . something. Use the glasses. Make a fire. Burn someone. Promise me you'll leave me, and that you'll run."

"Sam—"

"Swear it!"

"All right," I say. "Okay." Though I'm never going to do that. But I am going to look at those injections, find that power source, and maybe try to talk to Dad, too. And keep Sam alive while I'm at it. Maybe she won't have to Forget how to save lives.

Maybe she won't have to Forget about me.

She gets up abruptly, turning to go out the door.

"Wait," I say. And I am such an idiot. I don't have anything that she needs to wait on. I don't have anything to say. I just don't want her to leave, because I'm afraid she'll turn around and stop talking to me again. Her eyes run down me in a way that makes me shiver.

"I'll find you some sandals," she says.

And then I have the whole rest of the morning to consider what a fool I am. When did I get so far gone?

We eat a midday meal together, all of us, like the day before; and like the day before, Jill offers to watch the children. Nathan can't take his eyes off her, and she's not exactly discouraging him. I'm doing the washing up when she sees him to the door, off to the metal shop, laughing at the last thing he said.

She brings two more plates from the table, still smiling. If her hair wasn't so short, she'd look very Canaan.

"What are you doing with him, Jill?"

She looks around. "I suppose you mean Nathan. But other than that, no idea what you mean."

"You're being very friendly."

I wince as soon as I say it, the comparison to my own activities so obvious she doesn't even go there. "You're not the only boy in the galaxy anymore, Beckett. I suppose you could pull rank and order me not to be friendly, but that doesn't seem like good policy for the later phases of contact. We're here to establish relationship with a new culture."

I sigh. "I don't want to fight."

"You sounded like you wanted to fight."

That could be true. I lower my voice. "I'm going down into the city before the resting bell. To see what I can find out about the power source and communications. I should be back before everybody gets up."

"And the exit plan?"

"We'll talk about it after I've got more information. But I don't think we're getting there in the dark. Not on foot."

I hear her muttering.

"Jill." I lower my voice more, beneath the clink of stacking plates. "On the ship, before we landed, or at base camp, was there anything you noticed about the crew or the different teams that was . . . off?"

"What are you talking about?" Now she's whispering, too.

"I mean, if you saw anything, heard anything, that didn't make sense, you would've told me, right?"

"I guess so."

"Why did you think we'd be going right back to Earth? When we first found the city?"

And she says, "I didn't think that. I didn't mean it that way. I knew we'd be here for a while. I think you misunderstood."

So which is it, Jill? The whole thing just gives me a bad feeling in my gut.

The greatest gift given to the worthy is knowledge, knowledge that is derived from memory. It is memory that sets apart the chosen, and must be for the wisdom of the judge to decide. For only the most worthy, the best of the best, will create the perfect society and build the Superior Earth. Without memories, they are nothing . . .

FROM THE NOTEBOOK OF JANIS ATAN

33

SAMARA

It's Nita pulling at the edges of my mind as I slip into the dark resting room to get Beckett. I spent two and a half bells caching, preparing to go back Underneath, and for the moment, I'm in control. But I Know why she's here. Fear. I'm afraid of going home. I'm afraid of Beckett being caught. And fear can take a memory that's whispering and turn it into a scream. I walk to the bed that used to be Nita's.

Beckett is on his back, sleeping heavily, an arm behind his head, the undyed shirt gaping open at the collar because it's a little too tight. His skin is like sun shining through the potter's sand, a golden brown, a tiny nick from shaving not quite healed on his chin. I close my eyes, and feel him kiss me again.

This might be bordering on addiction.

Then I go to the cracks in the floor planks, straight to where Annis put her fingers when we were escaping the supervisors, lift the planks away and there is the hole, cold and empty. I put my book inside and fold the purple scarf Nita wrapped around my hair the day she died, carefully laying it on top. I'll leave the scarf for Annis, to trade with, since I used so much of her scrap cloth. Some of the vendors in the Bartering Square ask fewer questions than my patients. I lower the planks back into place, go to the edge of the bed, and sit on it.

"Beck."

His eyes snap open like I've yelled. "Is it time?" His voice is rough with sleep.

"Yes, it's time."

We don't talk while he wakes up, getting the glasses tied to his shirt lace, where he can hang them beneath, sliding on Grandpapa's sandals. When he's ready, we slip out of the resting room. Jillian and Nathan are frying bread in a pan on the burner, jars of sweetened fruits warm in the lamplight, and if they see us go, they don't say anything. We steal through the workshop, the top of Grandpapa's head in a plume of steam and heat, and then we're standing in the street. There's no more red in the sky, and it's not time for the moons. The darkness is going to help us. I pull up my hood, and Beckett does the same.

"Don't talk if someone is close," I whisper.

He nods, face obscured inside the hood, following me down the dimmer edges of the streets, away from the lights, hanging from crossbars at the corners. Beckett doesn't make any noise, but I might as well have put him on a platform and told him to sing. If he isn't staring up at the ring of mountains, shining in the dark with the strings of the glowworms, he's slowing to watch the smiths, or the brewers, or a man pulling a cart. He can't look fast enough, and it reminds me of me, the first time I came open air. Maybe the Outside is just as different from Earth as it is from the Underneath.

But now that my eyes are more open, and after talking to Grandpapa, I can see why I've been getting safely back and forth Outside. Our way is being smoothed for us. I Know where the supervisors are supposed to be, though there's always a chance that one won't go where they should, and for that reason, I think, the blond young man who was playing toss stones is on the lookout a little way ahead. And there's a girl hanging behind, hardly more than a child, who's made every turn that we have. And there is a woman, her undyed dress cinched with a braided belt, keeping step with us on the other side of the street. Has this been happening every time I come Outside? I was almost always with Nita, and never thought to look.

I see the woman with the braided belt pause, and then I realize that Beckett is not beside me. The beat inside my chest doubles, and I turn, but he's only a few meters back, standing stock-still in front of the loom house, a few heads turning to look at him as they pass. I hurry back, threading through the people going the opposite direction, confusing our escort, and grab his hand, trying to pull him away. But he whispers, "Wait. Please."

The weavers are singing down the looms. It's a song about the end of work and life, the thump of the looms coming into a common rhythm, softening as one by one, each weaver finishes a row and drops away. Annis is in there somewhere. There's only one left by the end of the song, the last loom slowing to a stop.

"Thanks," Beckett says, the word hardly spoken. But the smile is a gift. He hasn't let go of my hand. I don't let go, either. And then we start down the street that way. Together. I feel warm. Connected. Two ends of a rope braided together. And it hurts inside my chest.

Our escorts pick up our path, scouting and clearing our trail, and then I take a quick turn onto Potter's Street, to avoid a supervisor, then a detour down an alley, to avoid the supervisor due there. Only the little girl is still shadowing us now. We hurry between the houses of the diggers and fuelmakers until we hit the tumult of the Bartering Square.

Beckett isn't nearly as noticeable here. Everyone is craning their necks, straining to catch glimpses of the displayed wares—all scraps and discards from the requests of the Underneath—looking for a last-minute trade before the resting. The activities in the Bartering Square are not exactly sanctioned, but as long as the requests of the city are filled, as long as what goes out on the tables is inferior, or unusable, then the supervisors turn a blind eye. Stealing is different, and the reminder is in the very center of the square, the one place clear of people, where a single wooden post stands before the small tower of the water clock that straddles the fountain. The pillar is scarred and stained, ugly, a set of shackles hanging from its top.

Beckett's hand is still warm in mine as I navigate him through the calling and shouting of the crowd, most of it good-natured, some of it not. He leans close to my ear and says, "What are they using for money?"

I have no idea what he's talking about.

"For currency?" he asks, as if that might clarify.

I pull him a little faster, to make him stop talking, past the last table, laid with rows of necklaces made of misshapen beads. We leave the square for the quieter Dyer's Lane, and make a quick turn onto Gates to avoid the route of the patrol.

We've come to the nearest arm of the mountain now, rising up on our left. And there is the black-arched entryway of my city, a yawning hole blazing light like a star in a sloping black sky. Two heavy gates, solid, the metal engraved with a sun and three moons, stand open on either side, and Outsiders are filing out between them, the launderers and kitchen workers and family help, passing beneath the gaze of a supervisor. The supervisor is Himmat, counting and matching faces, making certain that all who went in are coming out again, before the gates are shut and locked at the resting bell. I wonder if it was Thorne who told him to lie to Annis about Nita coming out through the gates. Or Craddock.

I keep Beckett on the far side of the street, well out of the lamplight, until we come to a row of rough shacks, the nearest with its rafters showing through holes in the thatch. We step to one side with our connected hands, into the dark between two houses.

"Can you see if there's anyone inside that hut over there?"

He glances at it, slips a hand inside his shirt, and slides on the glasses. Then they're off and put away again. He shakes his head. "No one."

I walk us past the row of shacks and through an alley, coming up from behind the hut to sidle through a broken board in the back. It's inky dark inside, with only the barest hint of the streetlamps coming in through the roof holes.

"What is this place?" Beckett whispers.

"An old supply hut. Careful. There's an open shaft in the middle of the floor."

I feel Beckett moving, and realize he's put on the glasses. "So the Outside sends goods down the shaft to the city?"

"This one leads to a set of upper-level kitchens that aren't being used anymore," I reply. There aren't as many Knowing Underneath as there once were.

"Are you sure? There are boxes in here. Marked 'apple' and 'silvercurrant.'"

We go together to the stack of boxes. He's right. I've never seen anything being stored in here. It makes me worried.

Beckett must be looking through the dark at the stone-paved platform around the shaft now, because he whispers, "Should we have brought the gear?"

"No. The shaft is at a slope. It's supposed to be locked on the other end, but it only looks like it is." Thanks to Nita. "We'll have to wait, though. Curfew Outside is earlier than resting for the Knowing." And we do not want to go down before the Knowing are in their chambers.

We settle with our backs to the boxes, out of sight of the door, just in case. The bells are ringing, and Beckett still hasn't let go of my hand. I don't think he intends to. He has it between both of his now. I feel the ache in my chest. A pleasant kind of pain.

"Are you watching?" I ask him. I feel him nod, his shoulder against mine. And then I say, "There's something I haven't told you."

He waits. And I wait. Because what I'm going to say is ridiculous. I take a breath.

"I remember you."

He doesn't say anything. But I feel him listening.

"Because I dreamed you. When I was a baby."

He still doesn't say anything.

"I Knew you as soon as I saw you in the Cursed City. It doesn't make any sense." I pause. "But I do remember you."

"Sam," he whispers slowly, "what do babies dream about?"

I don't Know what to say.

"Come on," he coaxes, "what do babies dream about, when they're not dreaming about me?"

Now I'm smiling. "Things they understand. Hunger, faces, warmth, cold. The dreams are fuzzy at first, but they get clearer and clearer before they stop."

"What do you mean? When do dreams stop?"

"When you're three, when your memories come. You only dream what you Know after that. Only what has really been. Not . . . imaginings."

Beckett is silent, and his thumb is stroking mine, light and slow. I'm not sure he even knows he's doing it. My ache is becoming need.

He asks, "How old was I, when you saw me?"

"Almost as you are now. How old are you?" I can't believe I haven't asked before.

"Eighteen."

"What season is your birth?"

He hesitates. "Late in the year, the last season."

I'm older than him. "Where were you born?"

"Austin, Texas."

"How far away is . . . Austin, Texas?"

I think I can hear him smile. "Thirty-nine trillion kilometers."

The thumb runs light along mine. How could he be here, across all that space?

"Sam, you couldn't have seen me when you were a baby, not like I am now."

"I Know." Except that I did. Everything but the eyes. And then he stiffens.

I tense. Wait. And he says, "Someone's coming."

"Can we make the shaft?"

He doesn't answer, we are just moving, and I follow him this time, because I think he can see. He goes straight to the stone platform and the edge of the hole. Then I hear what the glasses must have already shown him. Voices, very soft, coming around the back of the hut, like we did. Beckett is already halfway inside the shaft.

"Brace yourself against the sides," I whisper, "so you don't slide . . ."

He disappears lower, hand reaching up to help me in, scooting down to make room for me, and then they are inside the hut, two of them, one whispering, "Stack that one behind the others."

It's Annis. Annis, who is a weaver, who has no business being in a supply hut that leads to the kitchens, even if it was being used. And she doesn't have a light. And the next voice I Know, too.

"We shouldn't be using it. They've looked in here once since the last time she came up . . ."

That is Angela, Michael's mother, and the only "she" coming up through this shaft has been me.

"They've looked in here every day," Annis replies. "But Henry got permission to put in extra food stores, so nothing will be amiss if they glance through the door."

"And if they open the boxes?"

If Annis answers that question, I can't hear it. There's shuffling, the sound of sliding crates. My leg muscles ache. The silence settles back in.

"Gone," Beckett whispers. His head is somewhere below my feet. "Should we go back up?"

I mark the time. "Down," I tell him.

We inch our way along the shaft, like a very slow, very controlled slide, pushing side to side against the walls of black rock. I'm worried for Annis. But then again, I have a feeling that what I'm doing is more dangerous.

I start measuring my breaths. The shaft seems smaller with another person inside, with someone else setting my pace. And I'm beginning to feel the weight, my mind telling me just how many tons of rock there are in the mountain, and just how trapped I will be if it falls. Like every time I come back to the city from open air. I didn't feel this way in the caves, though. I feel this way coming home. Panic untwists in my middle. And then I bump into Beckett's hand. Or maybe it's his head.

"I think we're at the door," he whispers. "And someone's shoes are down here." Those would be mine. From the last time, the day Nita died. They must have slid down from the top. Then he says, "Wait."

"What's wrong?"

"There's something in front of the door."

"You mean it's blocked?"

"No . . ." Then he says, "Are you wedged in? Can you stay where you are?"

I can, but I don't want to. Panic is bringing memories, tentacles stretching up from the deep places of my mind, trying to drag me down. And suddenly I can feel the ache in my lungs, just before breaking the surface of deep water. My father trying to pin me still when I thrashed

262 ME Sharon Cameron

while Adam burned. The black dress I wore at the last Changing of the Seasons that felt too, too tight. I breathe, and breathe . . .

"Stay with me, Sam," he whispers. "I'm almost done . . ."

I hear the soft squeak of the metal door lifting upward, and the passage below me clears. I slide out after him.

We're in a storage room with four rock walls, square, barren but for the shaft door and empty lantern sconces. I only Know this because I've been in here before. With a light. I can smell the perfume of the Underneath.

"Someone was expecting you," Beckett whispers. "Look."

A faint glow appears at the corner of the glasses, a narrow beam of light in the darkness. He takes them off and aims the light at the metal door, and then I see that he's holding a thread across his palm.

"It was strung across," he says, "so it would break when the door was opened. Simple, but effective. I was looking with the glasses, just in case, and for a second I thought it was a spiderweb, but—"

"What's a spiderweb?"

He smiles. "Never mind."

I touch the thin string, still wrapped around a tiny tack wedged between the rock and the metal frame. "It's suture thread," I say. What I would have used on Michael if Beckett's technology hadn't been better. I think of Marcus Physicianson, chasing me through the ruined city. Or Reddix.

"If you'd come through as usual, you would've never realized it was there," says Beckett. "But someone wanted to Know when you were back in the city. Not stop you. Just Know. Unless you think other people are climbing down the shaft."

I doubt very much that someone else is climbing down this shaft.

"Who knows you come this way, Sam?"

Only Nita. I thought it was only Nita. "We should go," I whisper.

"Let's put this back first, don't you think?" He finds the other tack in the faint glow from the glasses, winding the string back around it.

"Wait. How many times was that thread wrapped?"

Beckett pauses. "I don't know."

"If one of the Knowing did it, they'll Know how many times."

I watch him think. "Then I'll do the same number as the other side."

That will have to do. I step back, hand over my face. If fear can make a bad memory stronger, then smell brings them on more quickly. Nita's memory is here, waiting, and Adam, too. A thousand others. And I'm already feeling like we're nearly caught, and that I should have never, ever brought Beckett Rodriguez down here.

He finishes the thread and stands, then takes a good look at me. "Are you okay?"

I nod. My breath is coming short again. I'm not okay.

"I'm watching, remember?" he says. The irony isn't lost on either of us.

He takes my hand again, like it's the most natural way to travel now, and I lead him through the empty rooms, strange in the false light, past one or two broken barrels sticky with the remnants of bio-fuel, to the stairwell that goes both up and down, connecting the different levels of the kitchens.

"Put out the light," I whisper. It disappears. Now it's just Beckett's hand and the blackness.

We make our way down, fast. Me, because I grew up in the dark. Him, because he can see. Down, to the next level and the next. The kitchens are like a piece of the Outside Underneath, and the Knowing are not supposed to frequent these areas, especially during the resting. We should be alone. When we get to the bottom of the stairs, to the lowest level, there is a wooden door, tall and arched, closed, but not locked. I pause, turn toward Beckett in the narrow space. "What can you see beyond the door?"

After a moment he says, "A passageway. Empty."

I put a hand on the latch, but I don't push it down. "Beck, we cannot be seen. Not at all. We just can't be seen." If we meet someone

264 ✹ *Sharon Cameron*

in that corridor, in the entire Underneath, then this is over. For the Knowing and Outside, Beckett and me.

He doesn't say anything, just lifts my hand, the one that's still in his, and presses his lips to the back of it.

And that feeling is something I do not want to Forget.

I push down on the latch, and we step into the corridor of Level One.

34

BECKETT

There was a story we studied once, in prewar literatures, in my school complex in Texas. About going down a rabbit hole and finding another world. One minute it was wood planks and dirt streets, fires and roof thatch, the weavers singing at their looms, and now, after a long slide down, I'm standing in a place that is perfume, thick carpet, and flickering silver sconces, polished stone walls reflecting light down the corridor like a deep, dark mirror. I look at Sam, with her amber eyes and black hair. Is this really where she belongs? It's hard to reconcile it with the Sam of the caves and the Outside. But I am understanding her fear now. If someone comes into this shining tunnel, there will be no place to hide.

Sam moves fast but she doesn't run. The quiet is heavy, and soon the polish of the walls is broken every now and again by a recess with an arched, wooden door. Samara's hand is still in mine. It seems like she wants it there. I'm not letting go of it. I check the glasses again but there's nothing. Nothing that isn't blocked by this rock, that is. But there is the green light of the power source, much stronger now, pulsing in the corner of my vision, somewhere below us. Then Sam stops in front of one of the doors and pushes down the latch. It creaks very softly as it opens.

The room behind the door is hung with mirrors, lots of them, throwing back images of stone arches and beveled edges that must have taken years to carve. But there's nothing else. No furniture, no carpets, only musty air and empty space. It's chilly, a cold that gets in your bones. Sam lets go of me to shut the door with two hands, minimizing the creak. "Where are we?" I whisper.

"Uncle Towlend's chambers."

She glides across the black floor in that way she has, opens two doors paned with tiny windows, and beckons. I hear the gush of water. Beyond the doors is a terrace, railings overlooking a rushing river, whitecapping and flinging spray. We're in a natural cavern, and the place is dotted with balconies on both sides of the water, lamps hanging from some of them, points of light in a huge dark.

"I need to get to my room," Sam whispers. "Without going through the front door."

"Where?"

She points. "Three levels, straight up. I . . ." Then she stops, staring.

"What's wrong?" For a second I thought she was going into a memory. But she just says, "My lamps are lit."

I lean to look three levels above us. The cavern wall slopes back, and I can just see two lamps shining in the window.

"Do you see the second balcony over there, same level?"

I do. Two lamps, hung exactly the same.

"That was Adam's room. My father has lit those lamps every night for twelve years. I never thought he'd light a lamp for me . . ." She blinks. "He thinks I'm dead."

I blow out a breath, use the glasses, and I don't think there's anyone in Samara's room, though with this rock and all the burrowed-out chambers, it's hard to pinpoint.

"How bad do you need to get into your room?"

"We might as well crawl back Outside if I don't."

I don't like it. And I like it even less when I see how she means to go up. Sam gets onto the railing and stands, stretching up for the natural rock of the cavern in the space between the balconies. I look over my shoulder, at all the lamps across the water. The light doesn't penetrate far into the dark, and I don't think anyone could see us, unless they're looking close. But that also means Sam wouldn't be able to see them.

"Put your hands and feet where I do," she whispers. The roar of the water is loud, but she's barely speaking. "And"—she points at the second balcony up, one over—"Thorne Councilman."

Great. And his lamps are lit, too.

She starts up the tumbled rock face of the cavern. She's fighting her memories. Distracting herself with this climb. I wish she would've let me go up. Just told me what she needed, because if I'm remembering her book right, then I think we're climbing to the room where Nita died.

I get up on the rail and go after her. It's easier than it looks. The cavern's slight slope means that gravity isn't quite as much of an enemy, and there are only one or two places that are a stretch for her, and not even that for me. What I don't get is how she's doing it in the dark. I've got the glasses and it's still careful going. And then I realize. She doesn't need light. She's Knowing, and she's done it before. She remembers every rock and handhold.

I'm up half a level, and she's passing the second balcony, the one she said belonged to the Head of Council. The lamps are blinding in the night vision, so I switch and scan it, just to be sure. The balcony is empty. But the double doors beyond it aren't. There's a shadow of a figure there, a head and shoulders moving back and forth behind the glass panes, as if someone is pacing, staring out into the cavern.

Samara goes on climbing, already level with and passing the balcony. I don't think she can see from her angle, which means the person behind the door can't see her. But they could see me, if it wasn't so dark. I stay still, watch the pacing head slow, and then stop, facing me squarely. I wait, pulse ramping. And then the balcony door begins to open.

I reach up and jerk the glasses off my face. The lenses. They were catching the lamplight. Probably winking out in the dark as much as the rappelling gear would've done. I hear the click of a shoe on the stone, and Samara freezes, her feet maybe half a meter above the level of this man's head.

His hair is braided, long like all of the Knowing I've seen, robes to his ankles, a close-cropped beard, and eyes that are intense, looking through the dark in my direction. I put my face to the cold rock, hoping the black of my hair might camouflage me better than the brown of my skin, waiting, sweating in the chill. It feels like I wait forever. When there's no noise, no call, no footsteps, I chance a glance up. The balcony is still lit, and there's nothing. No body at the rail, no shadow of a head behind the door glass. I slip on the glasses, and no, there's no one, and Samara is two levels up, throwing a leg over her own balcony.

I switch back to night vision and go much faster, ignoring the thought of the rushing river and what's becoming a long fall below me, past Thorne Councilman's railings, up another level, and then I'm over and on Samara's terrace. I stay on my hands and knees for a minute, letting out my breath. I was more scared than I realized. I've got the shakes.

But I wasn't scared enough. Not nearly enough. Because Samara is also on her hands and knees, and she is not seeing what's in front of her. She's seeing something terrible, doing something terrible. In her mind. She opens her mouth, and I know what kind of sound she is about to make. I've heard that scream.

I tackle her, like a kid in a full-out game of crush-tag, and get a hand over her mouth. She fights me, hard, and we start a silent sort of wrestling match, the only difference being that I'm not willing to hurt her, and she is very willing to hurt me. She slams my head once against the stone, and then I get on top of her and pin her down.

"Samara," I whisper directly in her ear. "Wake up."

She doesn't. She struggles. I shake her head, then slap her face once, enough to make it sting. "Sam!"

The fight goes straight out of her, and I see her eyes focus. Then she closes them again and breathes hard. I let go of her mouth, and still on my knees, hold her half upright with one arm, get a hand on a door latch and push it open, dragging her through without really standing up, keeping us below the sight lines of the railing. The light from the two lamps is dazzling after so much dark. I click the door shut, and pull Sam to one side, away from the paned glass. Samara isn't calm but she's silent, two tears streaking down her cheeks. I pull her up high enough to look at me, get her face in my hands.

"Okay," I whisper. "Okay." I think I'm telling myself we're okay. "Are you all right?"

She isn't. She closes her eyes and cries, still silent, or as silent as she can be. I bring her head to my neck and hold her there, like I did the first time, in the caves, only this time I stroke her hair, her heaving back, and put my cheek on her head, anything to make it better. My chest is slamming, breath still coming hard, and she smells like Outside fires and Underneath perfume. I can't believe we're not caught.

She cries for a long time, calming until I'm still and just holding her again. Her breathing slows, changes, the hand that was on my shoulder sliding experimentally up my neck and just beneath the collar of the shirt, feeling my skin. I stroke her hair one time. Then she lifts her head, sits back just a little, her beautiful eyes still wet, heavy-lidded. And she reaches up, and takes the glasses off my face.

I feel my pulse ramp up again. She runs a thumb across my cheek. And then she leans in and kisses me. Slow. My hand squeezes, full of her hair, and she pulls away, eyes closed, waiting. I'm not sure I'm breathing.

I say, "Will that be a good memory?"

She opens her eyes. "Yes."

"Do you want another?"

"Yes."

I bring her mouth back to mine and kiss her again, and again, and now she's like she was in the cave, only this time she doesn't hesitate, and she doesn't stop. We're on some kind of thick rug, and I press her into it while she pulls me down, keeping her still while she's desperately struggling not to be. I break away from her mouth, and I like the noise she makes when I kiss her neck, breathe her smell, explore the triangle of skin left open by her collar.

And somewhere in the back of my mind I know that this is crazy. That it's dangerous and not the time. And I really don't care. I've never wanted anything this bad, and Samara's hands are under my shirt, down my back and up my sides, fingernails stratching, and then she goes still. Like somebody threw a switch. I hold her and wait, and I hear it, too. The sharp click of a heel on stone, just on the other side of the door.

We scramble across the floor, to the far side of a gold-covered bed I hadn't even noticed was there, lying low, out of sight if the door opens. I hear another click of a heel, and another, and then swear loud inside my head, reaching out beyond the bed to snatch the glasses off the floor. We lie side by side, listening, and I slide on the glasses and look.

I can see through the wooden door but only through the door, a hazy picture with limited scope. There's a hallway, with occasional rugs, not carpet. And I catch the silhouette of a woman. Or what I think is a woman, from the way she moves. I hear one more click of a shoe, distant, and the closing of a faraway door.

I meet Samara's gaze. "Gone," I whisper. She nods, and I pull her to me, laying her head on my chest while we get our breath and our bearings. A lot of things just happened, and I don't know which to talk about.

"Could you see who it was?" she whispers.

"A woman, with really high hair. Like it was piled up tall."

"Mother." She frowns. "I thought they were in seclusion . . ."

Then who lit the lamps? I think. "Would the Head of Council keep your parents in their own house?"

She frowns again. "Maybe."

"Do you need to go to her?"

Sam shakes her head against my chest, her hair tickling my nose. For all her drive to save her parents, it's not like she's dying to see them.

She sits up. "We have to go . . ." And now she won't look at me.

"Hey," I whisper, catching her arm. "This is all right. You Know that?"

She Knows what I mean, and she doesn't look like she Knows it's all right. She turns her face from me. "You don't understand."

I sit up. "Then make me understand."

"I will remember," she whispers. "If you change your mind, or if I change, or you, I will still remember. For me, it is only . . . once."

I read something about that. In her book. *I can love only once.* "I don't feel much like changing my mind," I say.

She smiles, and she doesn't have her Knowing face on, because I can see her thought like she'd written it down. *Not yet.*

"Hey," I say, "I said I don't feel like changing my mind." I'm surprised how mad I am about it. And suddenly I realize that if this girl has to Forget me, I won't just be sad. It's going to break my heart.

Sam's up, hurrying to pull the curtain closed with a soft rattle of rings. I run a hand through my hair, find a sore spot where she slammed my head. *It is only once.* And by "it," she means "love."

And now, only now, do I really understand her risk. If I were to forget her, like people tend to do, then her heart would be just as broken as mine. Only her pain would never fade, not until the end of time. She would still live it, because she would remember. To betray her now would be to devastate her. Like a knife to the gut. And I wonder if that would make you feel like a burden. Like you're asking too much of the other person. More than they can stand.

I don't know what I've done to her. To us. I'm not sure either of us could help it.

I get to my feet. Sam's almost running to the other side of the room, where there's another gold curtain. I catch her hand. If this is the burden, I'll carry it.

"It is all right," I say. "I understand." She blinks. "It's not too much, and it's okay with me."

She looks at me, and after a long time she nods, breathing deep. Then she reaches up and kisses me once, like she wants to see what that's like. Personally, I really like what that's like.

I don't know how I'm going to leave her down here.

"We have to go," she says. And I can tell when Samara Archiva has decided what to do, because as soon as she does, she goes at it like a warrior. She pulls aside the gold curtain and there are clothes, a huge row of them, boxes and shelves of shimmering cloth and slippers and shoes.

I look around, at the gilded mirror walls, a dressing table carved by someone who is an expert at their craft, the ceiling painted with metallic stars. What must it have been like for Nita to come down here the first time, and then go back Outside again? What must it have been like for Samara? The difference is as down-the-rabbit-hole as you can get. But there's nothing personal in here. No drawings, trinkets. Maybe when you can't forget, it's not necessary to fill your world with reminders. Maybe when your mind is so full, it's easier not to have them.

I cross the rugs and watch her choose a tunic and leggings in a dark bloodred, embroidered all over with shining black. She already has a scarf and shoes in her hand.

"What are you doing, exactly?"

"Changing clothes," she hisses, pulling the curtain shut. In less than a minute, the undyed cloth top and bottoms come sailing over the top of the gold curtain and her head sticks out. "Hide those beneath the mattress. Make sure the bed looks exactly the same."

I do, and I'm thinking we risked a lot to come up here for Samara to grab a new outfit. Then she's out, in the crimson and black, sitting at the table with the mirror, grabbing a blue glass jar. I'd like to look at that jar, but I think if I tried, Samara would smack me. She's working fast.

"If we are seen," she whispers, painting a line of black around her eyes, "I could make up an excuse, depending on who it is and how smart they are. Make up some story about a medical emergency . . ."

When the Knowing don't get sick.

"It won't work. But it could buy me some time. But you . . . I can't explain you."

Or being in the corridors in undyed cloth. I see.

She's winding a black scarf around her soft, curling tangles, pulling it all up and tying and pinning it around her head like a turban. She smears red on her lips, slides on a pair of soft black slippers, and turns around.

Her eyes are amber framed in black, skin shining. And now, for the first time, I think I really am meeting one of the Knowing. A descendant of Canaan, a human from another galaxy. She is so beautiful I can't remember one word I was about to say. But I think I like it better when her hair's down. I also notice she's chosen colors that will blend with the dark.

She hurries, putting each thing back with precision, adjusting the gold curtain just so. Then with a move more like dance, she reaches behind one of the mirrors and tosses something at me. I stick out a hand and catch it before I know what's coming. A ring of keys.

"Are you coming?" she says, adjusting the rug.

I think she needs to get out of this room.

*For the faithful of the NWSE, our directive is clear: That we,
the best of Earth, and now the most worthy of Canaan, we
who were chosen to create a superior society, now have an
even higher calling. To bring beauty, peace, prosperity, and, most
of all, justice to the Earth. To take knowledge and our memory
back to our home and rule it . . .*

FROM THE NOTEBOOK OF JANIS ATAN

35

SAMARA

Down is harder than up when climbing the cavern. We take it slowly, finding our footholds in the dark. I don't see anyone, and I don't think anyone can see us. Beckett isn't wearing the glasses, though, and I'm not sure why. He makes the railing of Uncle Towlend's chambers before me, instantly sliding the glasses on, and I hop down after.

"Is it safe?" I whisper. He answers by beckoning, and I follow him inside.

Uncle Towlend's empty rooms are as sad as his office to me. More so, maybe, because he and Aunt Letitia were so happy here. Until love killed them. Beckett is standing in front of the closed door, using the glasses to look through into the corridor. That shirt of Nathan's barely fits him, and suddenly, I drop through my mind to the floor of my bedchamber, the skin of Beckett's back running smooth beneath my fingers. And I drop again, to him catching my hand. Telling me he understands. Accepting me. Mess and all.

Right at this moment, I don't care if love kills me.

Beckett looks back. "Ready?"

I nod. "You cannot be seen. And if you are, don't speak."

He puts a hand on my face, and then opens the door.

We steal out into the corridor, and I lead Beckett back to the kitchen-level stairs, my breath short, pulse thumping in my temples. There's no easy way to the chemistry labs, and never have I wanted to go to them so badly. I want Beckett to be right. For there to be something in those injections, so I don't have to be Knowing.

I don't want to Forget him.

We move without noise up two more levels, Beckett first, using the glasses. We haven't seen another soul. The Council is rumored to have watchers that report back our sins, that even roam the corridors during the resting. I've never seen one. But if the system is random, that would make it dangerous. I tug Beck to a stop at a doorway.

"Stay close. And we can't talk; there will be an echo."

We cross the grand entry hall, with its high ceilings and blue-and-black-riddled walls, floor sloping up to the gates and down into the city, step through a door on the other side, and then we're moving again across the silence of carpet. Past the lit windows of the learning rooms, and the entertaining rooms, where I see Beckett's head turn as we pass, down again, and into a short tunnel. I wait, giving Beck time to check it thoroughly, and when he nods we steal inside the Forum.

One or two lamps on balconies sprinkle down light, and already there are three false moons strung up high over our heads, ready to be lit for the Changing of the Seasons. We slide along the vast cavern's edges, where we can't be seen from above, the Torrens gushing, noisy beneath its bridges, around the tall rock platform, and down its channel. Beckett is trying to go fast while he takes it all in, and it makes me remember that the blue-black columns and the glowing, trailing flowers are beautiful. And then my memories show me Sonia, falling through the air in the silver dress, and I think the beauty of the Forum is no more real than my painted eyes.

Then he slows. He's caught sight of the mural, stretching across the cavern's entire back wall—the green Earth, the scorched Earth, the

white city and the black, the sign OUR TRUTH CANNOT BE FORGOTTEN—
and he is studying it, intent. I'm wondering what he thinks about our
view of Earth when he pulls me to a stop, puts a finger to the edge of
the glasses, and points to the far side of the Forum, to the corridor
we're aiming for. The dimmest of lights is bobbing down the entrance
tunnel.

I yank him backward, farther into the darkness, and then behind
the curtain of one of the caching nooks. I'm careful to arrange the
curtain back exactly the way I saw it, to still any movement of the fabric. And then we huddle back against the cold black stone. Breathing.
Waiting.

Beckett puts a hand on my face, feeling me, to make sure I'm not
panicked or falling down into a memory. I'm not. For once. I'm straining to listen. I tilt my head, lining up my sight with the edge of the
curtain, and there is a face, not ten centimeters away. I only just hold in
my noise. Martina Tutor is passing in the light of a covered lantern.

Maybe she could be one of Thorne's watchers. She was in the
Cursed City. Or she could just be remembering Sonia.

I don't think she's remembering Sonia.

When Beckett nods, telling me she's gone, we leave the caching
nook, and we're almost running. Seeing one of the Knowing has my
heart pounding, body tingling. We sprint through the short tunnel
where Martina came out and up the stairwell that goes to the upland
parks. We reach the seventh level, panting. Beckett checks beyond the
door, and then we are in the long, silent corridor of the medical section.

I duck left, into an empty room with beds ready to receive the
sick people who never come; through an operating theater where I
would have much rather had Michael, a room that to my Knowledge
has never been used; and then right into supply rooms, and examining
rooms, and storage rooms. Taking the back way through the medical
section is less direct, but maybe a safer option than the long, straight
corridor. Every time we come to a door, we pause for Beck to check

our route, and when we come to the last one, I whisper, "The chemistry labs."

"It's big," Beck says, staring through the door. "Are you sure this is a lab?"

"One of them. But I'm medicine. I've only been inside this one once."

Beckett shrugs. "Okay, go."

I push open the door. Only it doesn't open. It's locked. I should have thought of that. Beckett squats down, peering at the keyhole, then looks up.

"Give me one of your hairpins."

I find one I can spare and pull it out, confused. Beckett plays with it, bends it, ruins it, then sticks it inside the lock and fiddles with it until something clicks. He grins up at me.

"Sometimes it's good to be the son of Dr. Sean Rodriguez," he says, straightening up to tuck the bent pin back into my hair beneath the scarf.

I have no idea what this means, but I want him to teach me how to do that. He's already through the open door.

"Lock it back up, Sam."

I do. "Are we alone?"

"I have the alarm set."

I relax just a little. The room is big—huge—and I can see why Beckett asked if it was a lab. It looks like a field from the Outside. A potted field. Plants are everywhere, on tables, on the floor, all different sizes, shapes, and colors, some reaching for the ceiling. Lamps hang every few meters, shining a different light than what we normally use, and it's warm. Almost hot. I can smell the growth. It doesn't look like the kind of place where our wellness would be made.

I'm wondering if I should go back into the medical section and try to find the bottles Reddix was filling, since Beckett is so good at opening locks, when he says, "Look."

He's partway down a sort of crooked aisle, beneath a climbing amrita vine heavy with white berries, but what he's examining is a tree, an infant one, growing in a pot on a table under a dome of clear glass. Only two leaves sprout from its stem, one bud hanging podlike between them.

"It's from the Cursed City," I whisper. I would have recognized it even without memory. I certainly saw enough of them.

Beckett asks, "Is everything in here used for medicine?"

"I would think so . . ." Except the amrita, I think. We drink that.

Beckett looks around again. "Let's check the next room." I follow him to it. There's no lock this time, and when he pushes the latch, only one light, a pale kind of flame, hangs from a ceiling wrapped in dusk. But the room is aglow, hundreds of luminescent petals.

"Moonflowers," I say. "Aren't they beautiful?"

"They look like faces," Beckett say. "Sleeping faces . . ."

I turn to look at him. He actually looks a little sick. I squint my eyes. I guess they could look like that, the way the petals fold. "Are there no moonflowers on Earth?"

"No. They couldn't grow there." He sounds relieved. "Not naturally."

"Why?"

He takes my hand, weaving our way through the glow while he talks. "Because there's only one moon, and it only lasts for a few hours before the sun rises again. And the sun only lasts for a few hours, until it's dark again. Sometimes there's no moon at all."

I try to imagine having dark and light on the same day, every day. I don't see how that could even work. "Do you have stars?"

"Yes." Now he's smiling at me. "We've definitely got stars. And we have oceans. Millions of square kilometers of water, and there are waves . . . It's really beautiful."

I can't picture what would be beautiful about that. But Beckett is thoughtful as we stop in front of the next door.

"Do you miss it?" I ask. "Earth, I mean."

He stares down at the door latch. "A little."

"Would you go back?"

He shakes his head, looks back at the room of glowing flowers. "Being here, it's what so many people have dreamed of. And now I'm the first one to see it. That's an amazing thing. But Earth . . . That will always be home."

His smiles, a little guilty, and I wonder what it must feel like to be thirty-nine trillion kilometers from everything you've ever known. For even the dark and light to be different. I touch his chin, and he kisses me very gently on the mouth, and this is a memory he is giving me, I think, to cling to when I have to stay, and send him back to the Outside.

He opens his eyes. "And anyway, there are other compensations on this planet."

Now he's teasing me, and I'm embarrassed. And he's not.

He has to use my hairpin again, and the lock on this door takes longer this time. But when it finally clicks, we steal through the door, lock it back, and now we're in a proper lab, almost as big as the first room of plants, with worktables, tubes, and liquids distilling. Bright, steady light hangs down in glass jars from the ceiling. Glowworms. Thousands of them. Beckett shakes his head.

"So all of this is for medicines that are never sent Outside, and that the Knowing never need?"

It's one of the things I plan to fix, if I can. "We're alone?" I ask.

"Alarm set," Beckett says. "Tell me what we're looking for."

"The liquid is clear, a little viscous, and there's a smell . . ." How do you describe a smell? "Not bad, but sharp. Like fresh air."

"New plan. If I find a clear liquid, you smell it."

I agree to that, and head to one side of the lab while Beckett goes to the other. I lean over to sniff a blue vial at random. There are many of these. It smells a little like amrita, but I would think amrita was made in the kitchens, not in the labs. Maybe the kitchens need some of what grows here. Maybe this is cookery rather than chemistry and we're in the wrong lab.

"Beck," I say. He straightens from his examination of a coil of metal tubing. "Don't move anything. They will remember."

He nods, and goes back to looking. And then I notice something odd across the room's front wall. A tall, square box made of glass, almost as tall as me, similar to the dome over the tiny tree, only this glass is housing a vine. The vine twists around a young silvercurrant bush, slowly choking the life out of it, its own small berries hanging shriveled from the ends in haphazard clusters. Bitterblack.

The rage inside me flames, blown by the sight of that black berry. One way or another, none of this will stand. Nita will be the last one, I think. No matter what I have to do.

I step away from the bitterblack, wishing I Knew a safe way to destroy it, and find another box of clear glass, this one large and rectangular, stretching across a long table, its inside divided into three clear sections. I bend down to peer at it. Each section has two holes cut through the front, and the holes have . . . gloves. Like the smiths sometimes wear. But these gloves are long, sealed to the glass, so that someone could work inside the box without the risk of touching with their skin. The first section has small tools, a tiny scalpel, and one fat seed pod, cut open, and there are two glass bottles, very small, one with a minuscule amount of fine white powder.

I study the box, seeing how the bottles can be passed into the middle section, sealed, washed, then passed into the third section, where wafting flowers clean the air, waving their feelers against the glass. Four full vials of powder sit among them. Whatever they're harvesting here, it must be poisonous. Dangerous. Even worse than the bitterblack.

"Hey."

I jump. I was so engrossed I didn't notice Beckett leaning down beside me. "A clean space," he says, looking into the glass box. Then, "Someone just passed along the corridor, outside that door." He nods toward the main door, just down the wall from the bitterblack.

I straighten up, looking at the door in alarm.

"They didn't stop, and yes, the door is locked."

And suddenly I understand how a person can become dependent on technology. I was so sure Beckett's glasses would know someone was coming I wasn't thinking to be afraid.

"Want to come smell this for me?" he asks.

I go with him, between a row of tables, and at the end of a distiller is a jar of clear liquid, some of the smaller bottles Reddix was using sitting empty beside it. I nod at Beckett. I already Know. I can smell it. But now that I think of it, why was Reddix filling the bottles for our injections? And in a storage room? That should have been a chemist's job.

I peer at the clear, harmless-looking liquid. And what if this really is Knowing? What if all we've ever had to do was throw this away, dump it in the Torrens, and no more Council, no more Underneath and Outside. One people. And I would still have my memories.

I could try to live with them. For Beckett. Which is easy to say in this moment, when I'm not killing Nita over and over again or listening to the crack of my brother's bones. I will beg for mercy when that happens again. But maybe I could heal, like Grandpapa said. I could try. And I wouldn't have to Forget him.

Beckett is on his knees, staring through the glasses at the liquid in the jar.

"What do you see?" I ask him. "Is it like a picture?"

"No. Right now I can see the jar, but I can also see words about what's inside. Amounts and percentages of everything that makes it what it is, and what those things can be used for. It's still analyzing . . ."

I see the tiny movements of his eyes as he reads. He reads for a long time, hands splayed on the table. Then he looks up at me.

"It's vitamins," he whispers. "Concentrated like you wouldn't believe"—he looks at the jar again, like he wants to be sure—"but just vitamins. Not even anything that can't be identified . . ."

And I feel an ache deep inside my chest. A shriveling kind of pain that in my mind looks like bitterblack.

"I can't believe it," he says. He tents his fingers over his face, still staring at the jar. "I was so sure . . ."

So it is Forgetting that has to bring down the Council. No memories and no Beckett.

No matter what, I will lose.

And now so will he.

36

BECKETT

I follow Samara through the empty corridors, feeling just about as hollow inside. I made her hope. I saw that in the lab, because I saw when her hope was gone. And now she gets to remember that, too. Feel it over and over again. Until she doesn't have to anymore. And it's then I decide that I am an idiot. A really selfish one. I saw her scream in the cave, watched her face tell me a story of pain. Just being in her own room was torture. And she was hoping not to Forget, to keep those memories, heal everyone, and keep her own pain, and that was because of me. If I really love her, I'll help her Forget. I'll do it even if it rips me in two.

I think it might.

She takes my hand, because that's the way we go places now. We're on one of the lowest levels, either the second or third, I think, when Sam turns right through a doorway. There's a small set of stairs on the other side, leading to another door. I'm starting to get what a maze this city is.

"The keys," Sam whispers.

I fish the iron ring out of my shirt, untie them from the lace at my collar. She puts a key to the lock, and then we're inside some kind of room, a place that hasn't been used in a long time from the smell, too dark to see. But before I can switch to night vision, the little green light in the corner of the lenses goes crazy. Pulsing at double, triple the speed that it was. Whatever the power source is, we're getting close.

She brings me across the dark room like she can see it, and I hear her putting a key to another door. Then we step into a void. Black, a solid floor beneath my feet, but with a huge sense of space. I'm switching to night vision when Samara whispers, barely a breath, "Is anyone here?"

"No." The little bit of echo I made is startling. It came from all directions, above and below.

"Then make your light happen."

I turn on the light, my eyes adjust, and I just stand there, staggered. "You have got to be kidding me . . ."

Books. Thousands of them. An enormous, spiraling shaft of shelves, farther than I can see with my eyes in both directions. I'm standing on some kind of railed wooden walkway, and we make our way down it in a twisting slope, round and round. I can't think of a crime Joanna Cho-Rodriguez wouldn't commit to get ten minutes in here.

"So why were the Archives closed?" I ask.

"The Council says that books clutter our minds."

Which sounds like an excuse for controlling information. There's another one of their creepy signs when we get to the bottom of the balcony, hanging over a doorway in the wall of the Archives shaft. "Knowing Is Our Weapon." I don't like the sound of that.

"We have just over two bells to go through the books before you have to go back to the storage room," Sam says. So I can go Outside, and leave her here. I don't think so. "The help will be coming to the kitchens not long after that. I'll get as many books into my head as I can."

I nod, and let the glasses make a picture for me, of a small room at the end of a short tunnel, with tables and chairs. Bookshelves. No people. But there is something close by. The green light in the corner of my eyes is blinking in a blur. The keys clink as Sam sorts through them, finding the right one. She puts the key to the lock and opens the door.

A few steps down a tunnel and we're in something like a reading room, one or two lamps lit on the tables, a small fire slumbering in a covered brazier, giving off heat from the center of a thin floor matting. Samara locks the door behind us and goes straight for the books, running down each shelf methodically, looking for the one she found before, about the Forgetting.

But for once a room in New Canaan can't hold my attention. The books aren't even calling my name. It's the door on the other side of the room I'm looking at. Or looking through. And what's on the other side is not what I expected. Not in a million years.

Technology is to be shunned. It is for the common people's good. But for the people of knowledge, of memory, the builders of the Superior Earth, technology will only enhance our rule, and speed us to the pinnacle of our evolution . . .

FROM THE NOTEBOOK OF JANIS ATAN

37

SAMARA

I have the book with the description of the Forgetting, and another that was shelved beside it, but Beckett is staring at the other door as if it might explode, like the door in the Cursed City.

"Sam," he whispers. "Come here." I hold the books to my chest, wend my way around the covered chairs to his side.

"Have you ever been through this door?" he asks.

"No. But it's where Thorne Councilman came from."

"Is it? Okay. Stay with me."

I nod. We walk slowly to the door, and Beckett pushes it open. It isn't even locked.

Probably Beckett's behavior should have been warning enough. Prepared me for something that would shock even him. But I'm not sure that anything could have prepared me for light so bright it hurts. For rock walls that have been washed a blinding white. For white chairs, oddly formed white tables. Even the floor is white. And as strange as that is, that's where the familiarity ends. The stone beneath my feet is humming in a way I've never felt. In a way I can almost hear. Cabinets of a pale, shining metal line one wall, blinking with tiny points of unnatural red and green, and there are eight thin, flat canvases, like pictures ready to be hung. Only these canvases have been painted with light. Bright, false light. Like Beckett's technology.

And then I understand. I am looking at technology. Here. In the city. Which is impossible. Except that it isn't. I feel like I opened a door and walked onto the wrong planet. Memory tugs at me, insistent, trying to yank me down. I fight it, and whisper, "What are they?"

"Other than what they seem to be, I'm not sure. This is a real hodgepodge . . ." That made zero sense to me, but Beckett is concentrating on the square patches of light, just like when he saw the mural in the Forum, though this doesn't seem like the same thing at all. He says, "Let's wake them up and see what they say."

I step back. He made it sound like there's something alive in here. He turns to look at me.

"It's all right," he says, holding out a hand. "Come here and I'll show you what they do." I stand next to him, nervous. Then he takes off the glasses and stares at the nearest square of light.

Nothing happens.

"Okay," he says, sliding the glasses back on. "Older than visual instruction." Then he says, loudly, "Computer."

Nothing.

"Command."

Instantly the painted lights begin to change, images springing up out of nowhere. There's noise, music that isn't real. My breath catches, and there's a hard yank inside my mind. I'm falling, plummeting, and it takes everything I have to stop my descent, to climb back into the present. I hang on to the back of a bizarre white chair while Beckett walks a step or two forward. Three of the light squares have remained blank. He reaches out, puts a finger to one.

It "wakes up," little symbols flying upward on the background of four entwined letters. "NWSE." He touches the next two, wakes them, and then sits hard in the chair next to mine, staring at the images.

"This is from the first *Centauri*. The ship that brought you here. And it's working. Oh, what if the database is intact . . ." Then he sits back, looking at the room. "But the rest of this is too advanced. It's the *Centauri II*. Has to be . . ." He tents his fingers again, whispering, "What happened to them?"

Memory is reaching up, winding itself around my mind. I break its hold, feel one moment of lightness before it pulls at me again. I don't want to go away. I want to understand what's happening now. Beckett looks around.

"Sam, sit next to me."

I sit. The chair is soft, strangely fitted to my body. I've still got the two books in my arms, clutched to my chest.

"How long do we have before waking?" he asks.

"Two and seven-eighths bells," I say. "But you'll need to go Outside a bell before that."

"Okay," he says, thinking. "I have an alarm set. I'll know if there are people near, but we may not have much warning. If it goes off, I have to shut this down and you have to be ready to run. There's the way we came in, and another door back there." I glance behind his head and see a white doorway. "It looks like there's some kind of hallway behind it. Do you Know where it goes?"

I look back in my mind, fighting off the memory trying to drag me down, and see the layout of the city, measuring the distances, comparing. We're very deep. But also close to the edge of the mountain, near the cliffs to the plain. "Does the way go up?"

"Yes."

"Then I think it's the caves." Where Reddix came out, when Beckett's technology was lifting me through the hole in the ceiling. Reddix, who Knew Beckett was from Earth.

"I wasn't even scanning for power then," Beckett says. "We could have come straight here." He shakes his head. "At least we have a chance of getting out if they come through the Archives. Now let's see if I can figure out what they've been doing . . ."

I watch him touching, pressing, talking to the technology, comfortable in its company, and suddenly I remember that Beckett is an alien. A fact I'd come as close to forgetting as the Knowing can. Then Beckett grabs the chair, which glides across the floor in a way I'm startled to discover, kisses me once, and shoves me away, sending me drifting like a boat across the Darkwater.

All right. Not that much of an alien, then.

"Look," he says. There are new images in the light, not letters or symbols, but images that are real. I lean forward, the books solid against my chest. I see the dim and empty Forum on one square, from up high, as if I'm hanging from the ceiling, while another shows the closed gates to the Outside. One square is so black it's hard to make out, until I see the shadows of mountains, and recognize the plain I crossed, running to the Cursed City, and I see the Cursed City itself, from far away, white walls faintly glowing, dark tree limbs moving with the air. And then my gaze goes to the last square of light and my stomach lurches. I see my own bedchamber, two lamps lit. I sit back.

"Explain it to me," I say.

"So, they've been watching all these places you see. They've got some kind of camera set up . . . Cameras are pieces of technology that can"—I wait impatiently while he thinks—"that can document time. So wherever the camera is looking, it makes a record of what it sees, so someone else can come back and see that piece of time later. Like this . . ."

He touches the frame of light that's showing the Forum. The image shifts, and suddenly Martina Tutor is walking through the columns with a covered lantern, and then I see Beckett and myself, a little of my hair trailing down from the turban, slipping out from behind the curtain and across the first bridge. I reach up and find the piece of hair I didn't Know was loose.

"I think we'll just be erasing that," says Beckett, touching the light. I don't Know what he's doing. "I'll loop it, but I'm not sure where else these files are being sent, or if they'll be able to tell that I messed with it or not . . ."

Documenting time. Erasing time. How can that be? I look at the image of my bedchamber, and think they haven't just been watching. They've been watching me. Beckett sees where my eyes are and touches the image like he did before.

The picture shifts and I watch him drag me through the terrace doors, pull me out of sight of the windows. I'm crying, and Beckett holds me, stroking my hair, my back, and the expression on his face . . . He wanted me to stop hurting. I steal a glance at him, watch him blink slow, once. And when I look at the light again I'm taking off his glasses, and I practically attack him.

"Okay," Beckett says. "We'll just be erasing that, too . . ."

I feel sick. What else has someone been watching me do, sitting in this chair?

"There's a whole file on you," Beckett says. And in quick succession I see me in my bedchamber, talking with Nita. Many different days of this, then days of me on my bed, writing in my book. The image moves closer, like someone leaning forward, and I can read the words flowing out from my pen. About going Outside. Then short, clipped pieces of me passing by the gates. I'm in undyed cloth and my hood is up, but I can see that it's me. Then we're back in my bedchamber, the plate has just shattered, and Nita is on her hands and knees, dewdrops rolling, and I'm off the stool, at her side . . .

"Don't!" I yell. I'm doubled over, gripping the sides of the chair, panting, trying not to fall. My mind plays tug-of-war, like Outsiders with a rope. I'm with Nita cross-legged on her bed Outside, and Nathan is laughing. I'm swinging on the rope in the upland parks. I feel humiliated, happy, depressed, and triumphant in the space of a moment. I see the dream of Beckett . . .

"Sam," he whispers.

I rise back into the present. The terrible piece of time is gone from the light painting.

"Are you here?" Beckett asks.

"Yes."

"Stay here."

I'm trying to nod, and he goes back to sifting through the documentation, though with one hand in my lap, where I can hang on to it. So the Council has been watching me. For a long time. And they Know everything. No wonder my punishment is being extended to my parents. But, I think suddenly, most of my sins are things the Council Knows, and no one else could. I think I see Craddock's point when he was talking to Marcus in the Cursed City. My parents are exemplary. And there won't be any more children. What's the point of wiping out the bloodline, if public perception can be preserved? And public perception happens just before the next resting, at the Changing of the Seasons.

Of course, maybe my parents won't need to be saved from Judgment at all, because maybe I'll have given Forgetting to the Knowing and overthrown the Council by then.

"Is there a"—I stumble over the word—"a . . . camera, in the room out there?"

Beckett glances at the light frames, then at the books in my lap. "I don't think so. I haven't got any documentation from that room."

Then how did they Know I found out about the Forgetting? They certainly do Know, because they chased me across a plain. And then I remember. My book. When I look up, I see the plain I was thinking about, and the mountainside, and I watch a dot, a person, falling like a dropped stone through the slanting sunbeams. "That's me," I say, "jumping the cliffs."

Beckett shakes his head, touches the image again. Pictures and symbols flash before my eyes, until they settle on a different view, the one
that shows the walls of the Cursed City. He leans forward, peering.

The view this time is bright, obscured by sun, but the camera
has caught two figures, shadowy and indistinct, walking around the
ruined walls. But I Know who they are. One of the figures lifts a hand
to touch the stones, something I've seen Beckett do a hundred times,
and then the two figures step through the ruined gates. I think they
were holding hands. I wish I didn't have to remember that.

"That file was marked 'unknown,'" Beckett is saying, almost to
himself. "Right after we lost communication. So do they Know we're
here, or don't they?" He taps his finger on the table, then slides fast
in the chair, down to the next light picture. And he starts talking to it.

"Show recording," Beckett says.

No file found, a voice replies, and I start so violently I nearly drop
the books. That voice wasn't even real, and it's coming from the technology. Beckett frowns.

"Show surveillance."

No file found.

"Show topographical scans."

The light picture changes, and Beckett says, "No, no. Too old."
He thinks and says, "Show perimeter scans. There you are . . ."

The image is like a map now, but a map that is a picture, a picture
that can be turned, manipulated, made big or small.

"Look, Sam," Beckett says. I slide the chair closer. He's moving
his fingers, stretching and changing the image. "Here's Old Canaan,
and the mountain ring, and if you go just a few kilometers this way"—
he makes the picture of land zoom by, like someone running at an
impossible speed—"there's a valley, just here, and that's where the
Centauri III landed." He stops. "Base camp got set up right there . . ."

I stare at the map. "I don't see anything."

"I know. That's the point. This scan was taken on the same day as that documentation of Jill and me. The ship was there, and believe me, you can't miss it."

"But . . ."

"It means that the *Centauri III* is hiding, mirroring the topography for the scans when they're actually sitting just below it. And see, here's the thing, when we first got here and scanned the planet, the *Centauri* couldn't see either one of your cities. I think they still can't. Because your Council is hiding your cities, too, and they're using the exact same trick . . ."

He goes on, showing me something about perimeter scans, but my attention has been caught by the frame of light that Beckett left. The image has reverted back to the symbols I saw before, one of them a small yellow square with the letters "NWSE" entwined in the center. The same "NWSE" that are all over my mother's bedchamber walls. On her necklace. I lift a finger, like Beckett did, and touch the square. An image leaps into being before my eyes, and I stare at it, mesmerized.

And now I understand why I dreamed Beckett Rodriguez.

38

BECKETT

I slide the chair down the table to Samara and stare at the screen.

"Dad," I whisper. He's so young, a little younger than I am now. But he does look like me. A lot.

"It wasn't a dream," Sam says. "It was a memory . . ."

The idea of my dad being in Samara Archiva's memory for the past eighteen years is hard to wrap my head around. I touch the screen and start the visual.

"Greetings from the newly re-formed organization of NWSE, New World Space Exploration! If you are the lost colonists of the Canaan Project, then this message is for you . . ."

Oh. You have got to be kidding me.

"The new NWSE wants you to know that you are not forgotten."

Someone's giggling in the background. Please let it not be my mother.

"Funding is currently being sought to send a rescue mission to your planet . . ."

And I'm pretty sure that's Granny's cellar Dad is standing in. He leans into the camera, face serious.

"You are not alone in the galaxy. Your former home of Earth still exists. You still have friends . . ."

Dad's eyes are moving. Is he reading this speech off a prompter? Or has he actually written it out on a card?

"We of NWSE look forward to extending the hand of friendship on your own intergalactic soil."

The screen freezes at the end, and I sit back, a little stunned. "Intergalactic soil"? I'm not sure that even makes sense. I knew Dad did stuff like this, sending out those messages with his friends, but who knew he used to be a way bigger idiot than me? The Knowing must think Earth has de-evolved or something. Thanks for that, Dad.

And then I really miss him.

When I look to see what Samara thought of Dad, she's not there. She's gone away. Into her mind. She doesn't look like she's going to scream this time, so I wait until her eyes open. "What did you see?"

"The memory of you . . . or, I mean, him . . ." She glances up at Dad. "But the first few months of life are so confused. A lot of it seems like a dream anyway. But Mother couldn't have been the one holding me in here, could she? Mother isn't Council. Uncle Towlend was, though, so maybe it was Aunt Letitia?"

I can't answer any better than she can. Her amber eyes roam the room and then land on mine. I'm not sure I'll ever get used to that. She says, "We're running out of time."

I know. We're here to find the Forgetting and I've been distracted. I haven't been that sorry to be distracted. But the *Centauri II*'s tech being hidden away in this room—in a culture that thinks tech is dangerous, evil—that just doesn't fit. If the Council has been getting communications from Earth, they could've Known we were coming. Both times. They could've seen the *Centauri II* land. But what did they do with the crew? And what does Commander Faye know about it, since she chose to land by stealth?

"Sam." She looks up. "That . . . Reddix. Who was in the cave. Is he Council?"

"No. But his father is. Why?"

Because Knowing face or not, if that guy was surprised by the tech he saw, then he's the best actor I've ever seen. If his father is Council, I guess that could explain it. He knew I was from Earth, but that visual of Jill and me was marked "Unknown." It doesn't seem like he's said anything about Earth being here to the Council, and that doesn't make sense, either. Unless it was for her. Because he's supposed to be her partner. I think I hate him.

Sam is watching me think. Sam, who can't stop being Knowing, who has to find out how to Forget and remove this Council. They'll kill her first if she doesn't. Sam, who won't remember any of this, or me, if we do this right. But at least she will be at peace when this is over. No Adam, or Nita, or all the other hundreds of thousands of pricks and pains she can finally lay aside.

I'll give her that if it kills me.

"Sam, I'm thinking you go through the books. See what you can find on the Forgetting, or anything else. For as long as we have. I need to dig out the information I can from the tech."

She nods, and she's not smiling. I wonder how much she just saw on my face. "I won't read now, so I'll get through them fast."

"What do you mean, you won't read?"

She cocks her head. "I mean I'll look at the pages and read them later in my mind."

Right.

She cracks the book in her lap, and her face goes serene, focused. She turns the page, and the next, and another, and another. Like a human data file. Store it and look at it later. I go back to the screen from the first *Centauri*, my father's face in the middle of it. For just a second, I thought it was me. And then I know what I'm going to do.

I go quick to the glasses, connect to the surrounding systems, and scan for files that will upload. And it's all of them. None of the stored data is protected. And why should it be, when this is supposed to be the only tech on the planet?

I start the process. It's going to be an enormous upload, and really dig into the charge I have left. I'll have to be careful with the charge. We could've never gotten through the city without the glasses. But like Sam, I can look at them later, when we're not risking our skins, and use this window of time for something else. I slide back to the computer that has the perimeter set.

"Command," I say to the screen. A blue circle jumps into being in the lower right corner. "What is the lowest transmission frequency?"

The lowest communication frequency is twenty-eight-point-eight gigahertz.

Not low enough. Not near low enough to be picked up by Dad's field set and slip beneath the *Centauri*'s communication range.

"Command: Reroute circuits for lower frequency."

That is not a valid request.

I tap the table. Samara shuts the first book and opens the second. "Command: How many transmission channels are there?"

There are twelve transmission channels.

Okay. "Command: Replicate transmission channels times"—I do some quick math in the glasses—"times six hundred and fifty, and connect channels in parallel."

All channels paralleled. There are seven thousand eight hundred transmission channels.

"Command: What is the lowest transmission frequency?"

The lowest transmission frequency is three thousand six hundred hertz.

And that is what I wanted. I turn to Sam, but she's gone, and this time she really is gone. For more books. Because she's already put two inside her head. I run a hand through my hair, thinking. I don't know where Dad's set is, or who else might be listening.

"Command: Open transmission channel at three thousand six hundred hertz."

Channel open.

I look around for something, anything, and grab the keys that were hidden behind Sam's mirror, sitting where we left them on the table. I tap hard against the table, using the code Dad uses in the field, when he doesn't want his communications hacked. The code we played with a million times on the ship, a rhythm of long and short taps that makes the words, *Who's there?*

I wait, listening. Dad might not be alone. Or he might be asleep. Or he might not even have his transmission set on. Or the *Centauri III* might be listening to everything at every frequency. I tap out the code again. Check the glasses for people, even though I have the alarm set. Check for Samara in the other room. She's putting a book back on the shelf. I tap the code again, and two taps into my question, a rhythm comes through in a spurt of static.

Speak freely?

"Dad?"

"Beckett?"

Dad's voice is thick and full of noise, and it is so good to hear it. "Dad, what's happening? Are you okay?"

"Where are you? Is Jill with you?"

"Where's Mom?"

"How long can you talk?"

Someone's going to have to start answering first. "Jill's not with me, but she's okay. I don't know how long I have. Not that long. I'm in the city."

"Are you safe? Are the locals hostile?"

"Depends on which local you mean. Dad, I've done everything wrong." I hadn't planned to say that. I didn't even know I wanted to. "Orders, the mission, protocol, I've screwed it all up."

"We saw the visuals. Everything's screwed up, Beck, and you're not the one who did it. None of this is what we were told. Listen, we weren't brought here to study the colony or even mine the planet. The Commander came here to take them, every last one of them, back to Earth. Whether they want to go or not."

I run a hand through my hair. I don't understand.

"Beckett, are you there?" That was Mom.

"I'm here. I just . . . I don't get it . . ."

"It's Lethe's," Dad says. "It's much worse than what's been made public. There are places in the southern Americas that are wiped off the map. The real mission here was to bring back clean DNA. If it existed. For repopulation, and for blood that's never been exposed . . ."

"But . . . they can't just do that . . ."

"Of course they can't! But they are. It's why they built the *Centauri III* so big. The thing's practically a slave ship. The lower level is not for minerals. And I was supposed to be making contact, gaining these people's trust, so they'd go without a fuss . . ." Dad's disgust comes clear through the static. "Only you screwed up and made contact before we could, luckily, and . . ."

We came here to take them. Just like Sam's story said. I feel like I've taken a fist to the jaw. "So what's happening now?"

"I didn't like the plan and said so . . ."

I'll bet he did.

"And your mom and I are confined to quarters. All our equipment is gone. But nobody thought of the transmission set . . ."

Because it looks like a piece of junk.

"I've had it on for a week. What are you using to transmit?"

"The tech from the *Centauri II*."

Some silence comes over the transmission. "How much tech do they have?"

"Some. From the original *Centauri* and the *II*. It doesn't look like they've been able to make the formats mesh, but I've only just found it. Only the governing Council knows it's here . . ."

"There's still a Council? Really . . ."

"Yes, Dad. Listen. The tech is hidden. But the Council has used it to set a perimeter, and they're mirroring. They might be messing with communications, too . . ."

"I don't know about that. Communication is off everywhere. Signals are not getting off the planet, which might be why we never heard from the colony in the first place. Do you think they know we're here?"

"I don't know, but they might suspect it. They caught a visual of Jill and me. But even if they can't get a signal out, they've been receiving for years. I just watched a visual of you . . ."

"What?"

"You were sending greetings from the NWSE."

"You've got to be kidding me. They got those? Was I being an idiot?"

"I guess. I—"

"Never mind. Is it dangerous, where you are? Right now?"

"A little." Or maybe a lot.

"Then let's make this quick. Can you stay where you are safely? Are you still with the local in the visuals? Have you established relationship?"

Well, that would be a great big yes to the last one. "The safety isn't long-term, Dad. There's trouble here . . ."

"Commander Faye isn't going to launch the *Centauri* until after the comet passes, so she's playing a long game. She knows she'll find them eventually, and she'd rather not kill, not if she doesn't have to. She's getting paid by the head, so it defeats the purpose. But she will if she's pushed. She doesn't know they have tech . . ."

"She might know. She's mirroring, too. They can't see her."

I can hear a soft muttering, which I think is Dad talking to Mom.

"Okay. Here's the deal. Do not, under any circumstances, come back to this ship. The Commander will get that city's location out of you if she thinks it might ease things along, whatever way she has to.

Stay where you are, keep the glasses off transmit, do not give up the coordinates. And be careful around Jillian."

"Jill? Why?"

"Because Vesta knew," Mom says, talking into the headset. I think Dad's been sharing with her the whole time. "Promises have been made, and we don't know what she's said to Jill, so—"

"But what about the people here? Shouldn't they be warned?"

I hear more muttering. Then Dad says, "Not yet. Hang tight, and stay where you are, and let's see if we can avoid bloodshed. There are others who feel the same as we do on the ship. There's a plan. Give us a little time to . . . rectify the situation."

"What are you going to do?"

"Only what I have to, Beck."

And that sounds exactly like me, which is one of the scariest things I've ever heard Dad say.

"But you've got to be careful," he goes on. "We're not sure what these people are capable of, and I'm worried about what happened to the II . . ."

I think of those words I saw in Samara's book. "The cultural history here is that Earth is the enemy," I tell him. "That we're violent, destructive liars who come to ruin and enslave."

"Well, they're not wrong on that one, are they?" Dad replies.

"The new city was built as a refuge from Earth. That's why they left the original colony. And it's beautiful, Dad. But"—Samara glides inside the door just then, moving like water over a fall—"not exactly what you'd expect. They—"

Mom's voice jumps out from the background. "They're coming."

"When will I see you . . ."

I hear scratchy bumping as Mom takes the headset. "Get out of there, Beck," she says, "and be smart. *Yuàn dé yī rén xīn, bái shǒu bù xiāng lí.*"

"*Ài,* Mom."

304 Sharon Cameron

"We'll make it right." This is Dad talking. "I swear it. And . . . you're . . . you're the best. I . . ."

And I hear a muffled shout, cut off by a spike of static. The channel goes silent.

I feel sick. I don't know what just happened. If Mom and Dad are okay or not, or what I should do about it. Dad said Faye would get the city's location out of me if I came back to the ship, so what if she just found out I've been talking to Dad? To Mom? What if she thought they had the information? I'm sicker. And what about New Canaan? If we've really come here to take them away, destroy their culture, breed them, and use their DNA like lab rats, then they ought to be warned, no matter how messed up they are. But the Commander— and maybe even Dad, just a little bit—thinks they're dealing with people less advanced and therefore less smart than themselves. But where, then, is the *Centauri II*? If I told the people of Canaan that their enemy had landed, what would they do?

This whole thing is going to turn into a war.

"Command," I whisper. "Close communication channels and revert to settings as of two hours ago."

Channel closed and settings reverted.

I feel Samara's hand on my shoulder and then in my hair. "Was that your parents you were talking to?"

I nod, still staring at the lit screen.

"Were they on your ship?"

I nod again. She sits down in the chair beside me. "And you were talking to each other . . . through the air?"

"Yes."

"And was your mother speaking another language? Like when you said, *yīkuài bù*?"

This gets a smile from me. Sometimes I forget that nothing ever leaves this girl's head. "That's right."

"What did she say?"

"Something like, 'catch one's heart, never apart.' It's a proverb. The person you love carries your love around inside them, so you're never really apart. She used to say it to me every day, before I went to school . . ."

"And what did you say back to her?"

"*Ài* means 'love.' Just . . . 'love.' " I look at the floor again. I wish I could cache like Samara. Take the sound of that cut-off shout and send it to a place where I don't have to think about it anymore. I wish I didn't have to leave her down here. I'm not sure I can. I wish I hadn't come here on a ship meant to wreck her whole world. Samara reaches up and smooths back my hair again, one long stroke. It makes me sigh.

Then she says, "It's time."

I know it. "What did you find in the books?"

"I was going fast, so I still have to read them."

"You did them all?"

"I skipped laws and edicts."

I would have, too. "I don't want you to stay here." There. I said it.

"Beck, my parents think I'm dead. We agreed—"

"I know what we agreed."

"It will take some time to read the books. I don't Know what I've found, or how long it may take to work. I have to be at the Changing of the Seasons . . . in case it . . ."

In case we haven't found anything at all, like with the injections.

"Come back Outside."

She waits until I lift my head, looks me right in the face with her painted eyes and says, "What would you do to save your parents?"

And that is such an unfair question. Because the answer is anything, of course. It's what I want to be doing right now. I sit forward and take her hands. The palms still have a wide, shiny scar.

"So be at your Changing of the Seasons. Make your parents look good in front of the Council. But why do you have to stay until Judgment? Tell them you're going back into seclusion. Like you did before. Come

Outside so we can figure out the Forgetting together." *Come and be with me, before you Forget me,* I think. I watch her hesitate.

"I could do that . . ." she says slowly. I squeeze her hands. "But if we don't find anything, I'd have to go back for Judgment, and for—"

"I know." Only not. I'm not sending her back Underneath to be killed. I'll tie her up and put her under Annis's resting room floor before I do. Or maybe there will be a war before then and I won't have to. "I'm uploading the data files from all this into the glasses right now," I tell her. "Between that and the books, we're bound to find something."

She smiles, and I realize it's been a long while since I've seen Samara with her mask on. Not with me. I imagine watching that cool, smooth surface snap back into place as soon as she hears about Earth. The idea hurts.

We leave the room exactly the way we found it, except for a huge chunk of information inside Samara's head and a gargantuan amount inside the glasses. I keep watch while she locks the doors, and touch one or two spines as we make our way up the winding balcony past the books. If things had gone like they were supposed to, if we'd made contact like we should have, if our mission hadn't been a fraud, then I might've spent my life in here, in this city, discovering the history of Canaan. But maybe then I wouldn't have met Samara. Or not like this.

We make the kitchen-level stairs without trouble, then up into the storage room with the shaft, where Samara will rewind the suture that's still strung across the door. When I'm gone. The room is cold and dark. Like space.

"I'll come at resting," she says, "as soon as I can after the Changing of the Seasons. But if I can't get out this way, then it will be the next waking, through the upland parks, like we came before. It may take me some time."

I can see Samara standing in front of me with the night vision, beautiful in shades of gray and green.

"Sam . . ." I say it fast, before I decide not to. "Dad told me some things about Earth and the ship, things I didn't know. We're not here to study. I mean, I was, and Mom and Dad were, but . . . Dad is trying to fix it. Before New Canaan has to find out, before it comes to a fight and people get killed. I don't know what to do."

She doesn't say anything, but I can see her frowning in the dark.

"Sam, I swear I didn't know. I would've never . . . We wouldn't have . . . Your stories were right. We really are the enemy. Your people were right to hide from us, and you ought to be afraid. We lie and we destroy what we touch . . ."

"Do you think I am your enemy?"

I feel my brows come down. "No."

"But I am one of the Knowing, and the Knowing are arrogant and cruel." Samara's hand snakes up my neck until it rests on one cheek. "Are you from Earth?"

I breathe out, "Yes."

She slides the glasses off my face. "Then I don't think being from Earth makes you my enemy."

This time her kiss is slow and curious, her lips feeling my jaw and my chin, an ear and both my eyes, and I know she is making a memory. I stroke her back and her neck, the scars on her arms, brushing her cheeks with the tips of my fingers. Until the bells start to ring Outside.

She jumps, and then she leaves me, unwinding the string, handing me the glasses before she opens the shaft.

"Hurry," she says. "I'll be back at resting." I can hear her breathing hard. Nervous to stay, upset to leave me, or still remembering our kiss, I don't know which. Maybe all of them. I crawl into the shaft.

"Beck!"

I look over my shoulder.

"*Yuàn dé yī rén xīn, bái shǒu bù xiāng lí,*" she says in perfect Chinese.

"*Ài,*" I say.

And she shuts the door.

The creation of a perfect society, of a people worthy of rule, is not an easy task. The judge must prune here, and trim there, often lopping off what is beautiful, but always for the good of the whole . . .

FROM THE NOTEBOOK OF JANIS ATAN

39

SAMARA

I move slowly down the mirrored corridors. I want to run, but it's too late for that. I stayed too long with Beckett. I couldn't help it, and now the early risers are out and moving. I try to look as if I have purpose. Serene, as if I have just left seclusion, and every braided head I pass Knows the location of my chambers, the location of the seclusion cells, and that my current path is not between them. This cannot get back to Thorne. If he thinks my escapades are public, then my parents will not be saved. And with a jolt in the pit of my stomach I wonder if we found all the cameras. If somehow, he already Knows.

I climb the stairs to Level Three. I don't Know what a camera looks like, but I can guess where it must be in my room. I want to find it, rip it down. But if I do, they'll Know where I've been. I'll have to be in my bedchamber, Knowing they are watching. As if I needed another reason to go back Outside to Beckett.

I wonder if my father will be surprised—or even glad, maybe—to see me. If it was hard when my parents thought I was dead. Not as hard as Adam, but maybe . . . a little hard. Whatever their feelings, they are Knowing, and I will have to guess at them. I don't even Know what they think happened to me. If Thorne told them I was dead. Maybe he told them he murdered me. Like my brother. The rage inside me smokes, glows.

I need to use this day well. I want a bath, a real one, and my mind is so heavy it's an effort not to drag my feet. I need to cache. I need to start reading the books in my head. I need to think about what Beckett said about Earth, though it's the threat of the Council that seems more real to me right now. I'll have to play my part well tonight in the Forum, be normal, maybe even friendly, talk about the benefits of seclusion. Be worthy of the Knowing before I run off again.

I unlatch the door to the Archiva family chambers as quietly as I can, the same way I let myself in on the day Nita died. I don't want them to see me come in. It seems like less explanation might be required that way. I turn to shut the door behind me, without noise, and then I hear the doors to the terrace open, the sharp click of my mother's shoes on stone. It's a good thing I didn't try to climb the cavern.

"Samara," Mother says. "Darling. It's good to have you home."

I put my back to the carved wood, wary. I was hoping for . . . something, I'm not even sure what. But I Know this is not my mother's real voice. She is smiling.

"We've missed you. Haven't we?"

My father is stepping in behind Mother, his dark eyes hooded. He doesn't speak, and he doesn't look at me, and I feel the sting. And then I feel it again. I'd thought maybe when he lit the lamps that it meant something. Maybe he's not looking at me so I won't see. Mother crosses the room, a long dress the color of coming dark shimmering red-black as she walks, the material draped to show the patterns of wellness scars extending across her back. She sits, elegant in her silver chair, the Archiva family tree stretching from wall to wall above her head. She lifts a hand.

"Sit, darling."

I go to the chair opposite and sit on it. This is strange, and I wonder if believing the last Archiva was dead has made my mother a little crazy. It's happened before.

"I'm so glad you were able to arrive before our guests. They'll be coming any moment now. Could I get you anything to drink?"

"What guests?"

"Have you forgotten the Changing of the Seasons?" She laughs, light and airy.

"We celebrate the Changing of the Seasons after middle bell, Mother. In the Forum."

"Not this time, darling. We are celebrating now. See, one of our guests has already come."

Thorne Councilman steps off the terrace, and I'm not even trying to hide how much I hate him. He nods at me once, unsmiling. It's the first time I've put physical eyes on him since Knowing that he and his Council killed my brother for Forgetting. The sight of his black robes and neatly trimmed beard scorches my insides.

"Samara, please," my mother chides. "Arrange your face."

My father has turned to the wall, like he's in a memory, or caching, but I see that he's really looking into one of the mirrors, one that gives him a view of my mother. The table beside him has glasses set out, eleven of them, and a pitcher of what looks like amrita.

The beat in my chest speeds, races, and somewhere, deep in my memory, I am listening to Adam scream. This is wrong. Something is wrong.

"Mother," I say. "I'm not dressed for guests. I'll just go and—"

"Stay where you are," she says, a little sharp before she softens. "You look well."

Our front door opens and Mother gets up to greet Martina Tutor and Jane Chemist. Jane won't look at me, either. And then comes Craddock, and his sister, holding her newest baby. Himmat from the gates. Marcus and Reddix Physicianson. Some of these are not our usual guests. Reddix goes to stand with my father, near the mirrored wall just beyond my chair. Reddix, who all my mother's hopes were pinned on, who was going to eat a resting meal with us. Has he told what he Knows?

I try to catch his eye, but I can't do anything without drawing the attention of the room. It's too quiet, only the slightest murmur of conversation. Then my mother stands again, heels clicking across the floor stones, dress swishing as she walks to our front door and quietly turns the lock. And faint inside my head, Adam is screaming and screaming . . .

"It's good to be together," Mother says, loud and to the whole room, "united in memory and in our pursuit of beauty, peace, prosperity, and, most of all, justice. Thorne, would you make sure everyone has a glass?"

This should be the job of our help, but for the first time I realize that there is no Outsider in this room. No one coming in and out to take care of our needs. But Thorne says nothing about this subtle slight, doesn't protest as he approaches the table. We all watch him pour ten glasses of the pale green amrita, sparkling in the light of the table lamps, in the reflections of the mirrors, the smell wafting across the room. He hands a glass to each person. The eleventh glass was already filled. And it's this one he hands to me.

I will drink nothing from the hand of Thorne Councilman.

Everyone who wasn't already standing gets to their feet. Except for me. Thorne lifts his glass and says the words for the dark days. The words we could all say ourselves, if we wanted to, that he is supposed to be saying seven bells from now, in the Forum. His voice is somehow smaller than my mother's.

"Those who remember now remember the stars, from beyond which we came, because our Knowing is our history, never to be forgotten. When we have Knowing, we Know our truth."

"Know our truth." The room says it together, a soft murmur. But instead of drinking, Thorne goes on, his voice slow and deliberate.

"And we, the noble wardens, the guardians of memory, the architects of Knowing, the builders of the Superior Earth, honor beauty, peace, prosperity, and, most of all, justice, and drink to the dark of the new world."

"To the dark," they say together, and ten glasses are drained in unison.

I do nothing. I don't Know these words. I don't Know what they mean.

"Darling," says Mother. "You didn't drink."

I feel the weight of every eye in the room. Mother's necklace, engraved "NWSE," winks in the light. I lift the glass, tip it against my mouth, but I don't let the liquid touch my lips.

"You must drink, Samara," my mother says.

"Why?"

The atmosphere of the room tenses, tightens. "Because you are one of the Knowing. Drink."

I look at Mother, at Thorne, her son's killer, at the solemn faces of the people who hunted me in the Cursed City. I can't see Reddix, or my father. Mother waits, one painted nail tapping against the glass. I raise my eyes to her.

"No."

She nods once, and the room erupts. Thorne snatches my glass, and Craddock and Marcus Physicianson each grab one of my arms before I'm aware of what's happening. I scream, kick, thrash until I get one arm free, but Martina Tutor comes to help, and Jane, and it doesn't take them long to pin me to the chair. I'm still fighting, and I've kicked someone hard at least twice. But it's not doing me any good.

Mother comes into the range of my vision. "Samara, this is unnecessary and unhelpful. It's time to drink now." Her tone is the same she used when I was a child, when my memories came.

I shake my head. Thorne brings the glass and someone forces my mouth open. He pours it in, but I don't swallow. I spit it in his face. I taste amrita. And something a little bitter.

"Prepare another glass, Thorne."

"Father!" I yell. "Daddy!" I haven't said that since I was two.

"You'll have to drink now, Samara," Reddix whispers near my ear. He must be one of the ones holding my arms now. "I promise, it will be all right . . ."

I don't think he can promise me that this will be all right in any way at all. I'm helpless, and Adam is screaming while his bones break, and Nita is dying, and I cannot fix it and I cannot change it. And there is no one to help me. No one at all. Where is my father? The new glass is coming.

"Marcus," says my mother, nodding.

This time, hands take my face and tilt my head back, so that the light of the ceiling lamp wavers through my tears. My nose is pinched, mouth forced open, and the amrita goes down. I choke, gag, and they let me go, let me fall forward onto my hands and knees, coughing. I taste the bitter with the amrita, a warmth spreading down my throat and into my stomach. Is this what Adam felt, and Nita, when they ate bitterblack?

I look up, a circle of faces staring back at me, then spring to my feet and stumble backward, knocking a wall mirror to the floor, where it shatters. Mother folds her hands. And only now do I realize just how little my hope can live on. Because only now have I found a single sprig of it, a tiny hidden sprout in a stony dark, the hope that one day, my mother might love me. And I have only just found it, because I have just felt it die.

I do not want these people to watch me die, and I will not let them enjoy my suffering. I won't show it to them.

"Today is not just one day of celebration, Samara," my mother says, as if I'm not standing dripping and bruised and poisoned in a glitter of broken glass. "Today we change the seasons, but it is also a special year. A twelfth year, and as you Know, that is the time for Judgment."

"It's not time for Judgment yet."

"But it is time. You have made it so."

I wipe my mouth with the back of my hand. I can't believe Craddock's sister is going to let her baby remember this. "Who are you to judge me?"

There's a spatter of soft laughter. The warmth is spreading through me, but there's no pain in my fingers. Yet.

"You have not been an asset to the Knowing, Samara. You lack control and the willingness to participate in our society." She pauses, and I wonder why I ever wanted this woman to love me. "You have stolen Knowing, written Knowing, shared Knowing, and mixed with the Outside. But most of all, you have betrayed us."

I am surrounded by faces, eyes, my mother in the center with her perfect braids. Betrayed them. To Earth. They Know about Beckett. I slide down the wall, feel the sting of glass cutting into my knee.

"You have turned against your people, Samara, your birthright, by aiding and assisting the rebels of the Outside. You have shared our most precious weapon . . ."

I stare down at the blood pooling from my knee and onto the floor. Not Earth. The Outside. But what weapon, what rebels Outside? And my memory jumps, leaps, and Annis is opening the floor planks, Nita showing me the shaft in the deserted kitchens, Grandpapa's voice, *when you come back to us, things may be different . . .*

They didn't need me to Forget or stop Knowing to make them rebel. They're rebelling anyway. Right now. I hear Reddix, in my memory, in the cave. *They are coming for you.* Is this what he meant? Reddix is Knowing, so I can't read his expression. He just stands quietly beside my father, who has his back to these proceedings, his ropes of hair twisted with glinting gold. And the world wavers like I'm seeing it through flame.

"Judgment is not given lightly Underneath," my mother is saying. "The Knowing are special, and the Noble Wardens do not lessen the numbers without consideration . . ."

"We," I say, and my voice isn't steady, "are not special."

"Oh, but we are. We were brought to this planet to build the perfect society, and now that Earth has come, we sit on the brink of our final destiny. The Knowing are the builders of the Superior Earth, each with more Knowing in their fields than any humans before. And we will use that Knowing to fulfill the original directive. To re-create, to transform, and to rule the Earth. What you see, Samara"— she extends a hand around the room—"is only a shadow of what the Knowing are capable of. Imagine what we could do with Earth's technology."

The world has taken up a slow spin, as if I am a planet and Mother is the sun.

"We are the best of the best, Samara. But we cannot fulfill our directive if the Knowing are not pure. The Knowing must be worthy to rule. And so the Noble Wardens wait, and we watch. We create situations, and evaluate the choices made. All that is required of any of the Knowing, daughter . . ."

I raise my eyes again.

". . . is to be worthy. You are not worthy. You have chosen differently, and therefore you are not chosen. And so, we say that you are condemned."

"And what will . . ." My words come slow, the sounds rolling aimlessly on my tongue. "What will the Council . . . think about that?"

"Oh, my darling. What have we to do with the Council?"

I meet my mother's eyes, and I can feel myself sinking, down through my mind, her words chasing me slow, following me one by one through the dark.

"There . . . can be . . . no forgiveness . . . Underneath."

I fall into blackness, a nothingness. And this time, there are no memories to catch me at the bottom.

40

BECKETT

I didn't go back to the house. I decided to wait in the supply hut for Sam. All day—if "day" is the right word for the darkness—stretched out in the tight space behind the crates that Annis and Michael's mother stacked. It was risky. And probably stupid. Twice I snuck out for water, and when I got too hungry I cracked the lid on a box marked "silvercurrants." There were cloth bags of berries inside, and below a false bottom, knives. Lots of them. Not very well made, but sharp. I put the lid back, wondering; ate berries that were tart and a little dry; and spent the rest of the waking hours either napping or going through the Council's tech files.

There was a lot of surveillance on Samara. Most of the saved data showed her in her bedroom with Nita. Nita telling Sam about the Outside, planning Sam's trips aboveground, encouraging her to write in her book. They acted like sisters. For being young and a girl, Nita looked weirdly like her grandfather, the same bright blue eyes. I can see how Jillian might pass for a description of her, if you'd never seen her. Though that's where the similarities stop.

But some of the data was just Sam alone, doing her hair. Writing. One where she's crying, doubled over on the floor in a memory, then four or five glimpses of her changing clothes. I felt wrong watching some of that. And mad. This was private. And what sick person has been sitting on the other end of those screens, watching this?

Or maybe I'm just as sick, because when the footage came of Nita dying, I didn't stop the visual. I didn't really get what this poison does to you. The seizures are violent, and agonizing, and when I hear the crack of Nita's arm, I feel it in my gut. How long did Sam say she listened to Adam's bones breaking? Two bells? And nobody put a pillow over his face. I watch Nita go still, and Sam, with bleeding hands, cleaning up her own vomit with spare clothes, burning it all in the brazier heater in the corner. And the sick in my guts moves up to an ache in my chest.

Nita told her to go to the city and Forget. And I know that I will give Sam up, let her go, to let her Forget that.

She needs to get back aboveground. With me.

When the resting bell rings, I sit up behind the boxes, tense, listening for the first hint of Sam coming out of the shaft. I hear the gates close, the streets settling. The footsteps of supervisors. The door to the hut opens once, and I don't move a muscle. But then it shuts again. I go through the official ship's log of the *Centauri II*, which is just about as boring as a space-exploration log could possibly be. Until they land, and then there is only one more entry: Contact made. After that? Nothing.

I listen to the waking bells. Outsiders lighting fires, calling for their children to fetch water from the channels.

She doesn't come.

I tell myself not to be an idiot. She said it could be later, and from the other way, through the parks. I tie the glasses to my shirt lace, drop them beneath the scratchy cloth. Resist a strong urge to climb down that shaft. Getting back to Annis's house is downright dangerous without Sam's Knowledge of the patrol routes, and I'm feeling stupid about my choices by the time I get there.

I find Jill faking some recovery time, Nathan running and fetching for her, and completely happy to do it. She gives him a big white smile, me a filthy look and zero opportunity to fill her in on what I found underground. I'm annoyed, and then I'm mad. What Mom told me about Vesta paired with Jillian's comments here and there are making a picture I don't like the look of. Nathan jumps up to get Jill another blanket, and I seek refuge in the other resting room, where Cyrus is tying one of Nathan's sandals. I'm wearing his.

"Sorry," I say, backing out, but the old man waves me in.

"Not to worry," he says. "It's a full house." He cocks his head. "That bed's free, if you need it."

I decide I do. I stretch out and get an arm behind my head. A month ago, I wouldn't have thought a grass-filled mattress could feel this good.

"You alone?" Cyrus asks.

My gut twists once. He means Samara. "Yes, but she'll be back before resting."

"Oh? I thought she was staying Underneath."

"She changed her mind."

"So tell me. What do you think of her?"

I lift my head to look at the old man, who is still knotting the sandal lace. "What's the real question?"

Cyrus nods. "Fair answer. But, young man, somebody ought to tell you that you've got lip paint all over your face."

I sit up, hand to my cheek, Jill's filthy look explained. Great. A cloth comes sailing at my head, and I start scrubbing.

"You planning on being here awhile?" Cyrus asks.

That's a hard one. "I hope so."

"And your friend?"

"That might be up to her."

"She seems to be having a fine time with my grandson."

"She's amusing herself."

The old man's face wrinkles. "And why, young man, do you think your friend is amusing herself with Nathan?"

The answer is so easy I'm sorry he had to point it out. So I'll notice, that's why. "Jill is clear on how things are," I say. "But okay. I'll talk to her."

Cyrus nods again. He's taking longer to tie a shoelace than any man in history. "See, the thing is," he says, "that little girl is special. And I don't mean because she's Knowing. I mean, in spite of being Knowing."

I know.

"It's not easy to be brought up the way she has, and see things the way she does . . ."

"She had Nita," I say.

"That's so." He fiddles with the lace. "And that little girl has suffered—maybe no more than the rest of them, I don't know—but she's suffered all the same, and is likely to suffer a good deal more. The way things are, it's not good for any of us, Outside or Underneath."

Cyrus stops talking, and it's like he left off a sentence. Then he says, "It would be good to know where you stand."

I don't know what he means. I'm standing wherever Sam is. "Cyrus," I lower my voice. "What is it like to Forget?"

He gives up on pretending to tie the sandal. "She told you that, did she?" He shakes his head. "When you Forget, there's a big part of you that's . . . just not you anymore. And you can't get it back."

I tent my fingers over my nose. I don't know what to say to him. I don't even know what I want to happen. Except that I want her back. Right now. Out of the dark with its poisons and lies and peeping eyes. And Cyrus will be on a slave ship to Earth over my dead body.

I grab my pack from under the bed. "I have to go."

"Suit yourself," says Cyrus. "You said you like glass?"

I look back from the doorway, letting the hood fall back down on my shoulders.

"When things settle, young man, maybe you'd like to learn."

I feel myself smile. "That'd be good."

I use the workshop door, to avoid drawing Jill's attention, and then I'm in the streets. The blond man leaves off playing his game, and walks to one side of me. Like he did when Sam and I went Underneath. In less than a minute I've walked into the path of a supervisor. It's the big one, the one who was outside the ruined building in Canaan, right before I blew up the door. And the blond man calls out, gets his attention, pointing back down the street while I change course. I pass the last of the houses, the land rising up to meet the mountain slopes, slip on the glasses, and hurry up one of the gated paths that divide the terraced fields.

I know I'm being reckless, and that I would've never gotten away with this in the sun. I'm not sure I'll get away with it in the dark. I've got an alarm set, but my charge is just under 50 percent. It's a long hike up to the cliffs, around dark, barren groves and up again through thick brush, glowing with luminescent threads. But I make it a lot faster not carrying Jill on my back.

Getting down the cliff is easy with the gear, and when I look back the way I came I realize I'm going to have to climb that rope again, by hand, so I can send the gear down to pull Samara up. Worth it. And then I run my eyes over the upland parks.

It's dark, hardly any glowworms and just a smattering of stars, a halo behind the mountain range that must mean the rising of the moons. I switch the glasses to heat and scan the clipped, open spaces, the tamed trees. And I find it, a figure standing still on the far side of the park, at the cliff edge, where I saw the skimmer.

I'm relieved that she's there, more than relieved, and a little irritated that she's not running toward my rope at full speed. I start across the parks at a jog. But the closer I get to the figure on the cliff, the more I slow down, and it's not from all the exercise. I change the glasses to night vision with a glance.

That is not Samara. But it is one of the Knowing. A man, in a sleeveless tunic of silver-gray, with ten scars on his left arm, probably close to the same number on his right. I step sideways in the shade of a well-spaced grove, making a wide, silent circle until I can see his profile. And it's him, from the cave. The one who called me Earth. Reddix.

Leaves move above me, fluttering in the breeze, and suddenly he says, "Is that you, Earthling?"

I go still. I don't even twitch. He turns his head.

"I Know you're there. A wind of this speed makes a certain sound in that grove, and you are a new object that has altered its pitch." He looks back out over the cliffs. "I've been waiting for you."

"Why?"

"To discuss our options."

I don't like this. Not at all.

Then he says, "She is not coming."

The piece of my gut that twisted earlier tightens. "Explain."

"She has been condemned. She was taken before the Changing of the Seasons, and will be kept asleep, where she can do no harm, until Judgment. Then she will stand before the Knowing, and they will kill her."

I stand so tense I can feel the pain of it in my head. "Is that so?" I say it through my teeth. I've already thought of ten different ways to blow up his mountain.

"You can't get to her. She is deep, and drugged, and would have to be carried. They are on watch, and are not without weapons. It would take an army to bring her open air. Do you have one of those at your disposal, Earthling?"

I'm so mad right now I'm shaking. Or maybe that's fear.

"Or perhaps you are a renegade, out on your own?"

I don't say anything, and he's still staring at the dark. I don't think he wants to look at me.

"Samara is being condemned for stealing Knowing, writing Knowing, and her dealings with the rebels Outside," he says calmly. "Can you imagine if they had been aware her betrayal extended all the way to Earth?" He does glance once at me now. "Maybe you are not aware that one of Samara's fondest wishes is to remove the Knowing from power."

I'd like to know why he thinks he Knows anything about Sam's fondest wishes.

"I wonder if you might be willing to help make that happen."

I glance at the corner of the lenses and set a new perimeter alarm without really taking my eyes off him. "You want to take down your Council?"

"Not just the Council. All of them. If it can be done."

"And why would you want that?"

"Because we are a useless, selfish, and poisonous race, or haven't you noticed? And because doing so may save her." He turns his head to me again. "What would you risk to save her?"

Anything. Everything. "Are you trying to bargain with me?"

"No. I'm suggesting a partnership of . . . mutual interest." He pauses. "I suppose you love her."

I take three long breaths. "Why do you say that?"

"Because to Know her is to love her, Earthling."

I watch one of Reddix's fists clench in night-vision green. I know the look of a memory taking hold, especially beneath a smooth and calm exterior, and this one is painful. Only just kept at bay. I think of what Samara said, that many of the Knowing might choose healing over status, Forgetting over power. And then I wonder if Reddix is the one who's been monitoring those screens, saving that data. If he could have been watching in real time when I dragged Samara into her room. I want to hit him. And I want her back.

"That doesn't tell me I should trust you."

"I am risking my life talking to you right now. And your technology has already told you that I'm alone. I have no other agenda."

"What does your Council Know about Earth?"

He almost smiles. "Always everyone thinks this is about the Council."

"I don't care who they are. What do they Know?"

He straightens. "That Earth is here, but not in what force or what capacity. They cannot see it, but the sound of a ship entering our atmosphere was caught. And you have been expected. They do not intend to engage with Earth. Or not yet. They are known for their . . . patience. There. Does that earn me some trust?"

"Your people should stay hidden," I say.

"As should yours."

Fine. "How would it be done?" I ask.

"You can leave that to me."

I don't think so. "Samara was looking for the Forgetting. That's how she was going to take down the Council."

"Oh, Earthling. We all Knew that. I will be back here in thirty-six bells, and I will wait for one. We will talk again then."

"That's not soon enough."

"It will be what it is."

This guy makes me want to hit whatever is in reach. But I think back to the calm way he watched Samara rising in the caves. What that calm might have been hiding. Sam said that love could only come once for the Knowing, and that Reddix was supposed to be her partner. For the first time, I consider what happens if your "once" doesn't love you back, not even a little. When you're trapped for life with a love that cannot be returned and can never die.

He might be telling me the truth.

I watch him walk away through the trees, zooming the glasses, waiting where I am until he's through the door into the mountain. I feel sorry for him. And I hate him.

And Samara Archiva is not going to die in the Underneath.

To choose the chosen is a delicate task. When considering a sacrifice, the judge must watch, wait, introduce stress to their subject, and evaluate. In this way the worthiness of the subject is revealed, and the judge will decide if they are chosen, or condemned . . .

    FROM THE NOTEBOOK OF JANIS ATAN

41

SAMARA

y body is gone. All I have left is the memory of my body, and this is how I Know that I am dead.

Dying of bitterblack wasn't as bad as I thought it would be. Frightening, but it didn't really hurt. Maybe it was like that for Adam and Nita, separated from the destruction of their bodies, retreated to a far, deep place where the world just wasn't.

I hope that's what it was like.

My memories remind me of the Underneath now that I am dead. A vast, dark labyrinth of interconnected rooms. I wander down steps and corridors, through huge and hidden chambers. Behind one door I'm a child being rocked by my father, another and I'm twisting Beckett's bones back into place. Here is the pain of my first injection, the swoop in my stomach from the fraying rope. I see Sonia, smiling, showing me the silver cloth for a new dress. My mother, slapping my hand and telling me to cache it. And at the end of a hall is my broken brother, saying "Who are you?" while our father cries.

I wish there were locks on the doors of my mind.

But after a long time, I begin to learn the layout of certain corners. Rows of rooms that remain the same. And if I concentrate, I can stay in the room I want. I spend some time in the upland parks, lifting my face to the sun, then in the dark, jumping off the fern roots. I play a game in the front room with Nita and Grandpapa. I go and find Beckett, feel his lips on my neck on my bedchamber rug, hold his hand Outside while he listens to the weavers.

And then I slip through a different door, into a room of shelves, inked words, and pages. This is the room of the books I've put inside my head. And here is a shelf of the books I looked at in the Council's reading room, when I was with Beckett. I sit on the floor of my mind and take one down.

This is about the early history of the Archives, which was in the old city, before it was abandoned. How it contained hundreds of personal accounts of the first colonists, plus Earth stories and histories by Genivee Archiva, the first of the Archiva name, who is written on the family tree in our receiving room. She was the first to transcribe information from technology to books, so that our history could never be lost.

Then I read an Archiva transcription of the history of the Canaan Project, almost exactly as Beckett told me. Seventy-five men and seventy-five women, the best and brightest in their areas of learning, chosen to create a new and perfect world by a company called New World Space Exploration. NWSE. The letters on my mother's necklace. The room of the books tries to dissolve, become the room of my poisoning. But I relax, visualize the books, only the books. And then I am able to open up another.

The title is *Early Edicts of New Canaan*. I thought I'd skipped all those. I set it down. And the next to leap into my hands is very old and tattered. Beautiful. The book of maps. I'd been hoping to find this one. I open it, and I don't have to be careful now. Pages can't crack inside my mind. This time I read the inscription. *Drawn by my sister Nadia, the first to leave the walls of her city and explore what had been out of bounds, and Gray, a glassblower's son. —Genivee Archiva.*

I smile inside my head, pretending to run a finger over the page. Sometimes the stories of the Outside are better than the learning of the Knowing, and I think I understand now why Nita chose my Outside name. Because I was exploring what was out of bounds.

The next book is thin and coming apart. The paper is made differently, the ink so faded the letters seem more like memories of letters than words. But I can see where it has been repaired. And in a different hand, in darker ink, someone has written on the cover "The Notebook of Janis Atan."

Janis Atan was born on the first *Centauri*, one of the first children of the newly built Canaan, and what I'm reading is like a warped view of the original directive, to build a perfect society, an idea mangled and twisted until it becomes something else. She is obsessed with being chosen, being one of "the best," with her own knowledge and memory—why memory?—and with bringing "beauty, peace, prosperity, and, most of all, justice," as if she is the only one who can.

And where shall we, the chosen of the NWSE, find our judge? she writes. *From the knowledge that is deepest and the memory that is longest, for it is from knowledge and memory that wisdom is derived. And so I, the first of memory, shall be our first judge, and continue to choose our chosen, that we may fulfill our directive, and build the Superior Earth . . .*

But there are concepts in the words of Janis Atan, phrases here and there that are hauntingly like the Knowing. That memory and knowledge are what make someone worthy. That being without it means you are not. The concept of Judgment to maintain a society's "perfection." Condemnation for those not worthy of their status.

The room tries to dissolve again, back to the place of my poisoning. And now that I am dead, suddenly I wonder if memories tug and pull because they are connected. Subtle strings of meaning that I can only feel, never see. I stop fighting, curious, and let myself go to the Archiva receiving rooms.

And fear engulfs me. Confusion, panic. My heart is racing. There's a glass in my hand, one in Thorne Councilman's. And it's my mother giving the orders, telling Thorne Councilman to pour, telling him to begin. I listen to him speaking the unfamiliar words: . . . *we, the noble wardens, the guardians of memory, the architects of Knowing, the builders of the Superior Earth, honor beauty, peace, prosperity, and, most of all, justice . . .*

And now I see the thread. Noble Wardens. Superior Earth. I slow my memory like Beckett slowing down the pictures in the square of light. I hear the clink of a fingernail against a glass, the flash of my mother's necklace in the light. Feel the hands bruising my arms, the taste of bitter in my mouth. Lian Archiva. Pronouncing my Judgment.

I stop my memory, like a stutter in time. NWSE. Noble Wardens of a Superior Earth. The keepers of memory, of Knowing. Who believe they are the most noble, the most wise, with the longest memories. The most worthy to dispense justice. And now I see. The Council has not been controlling us. The NWSE has been controlling the Council, through Thorne. Thorne, who does what my mother says.

My mother, who Judged me. Condemned me.

Lian Archiva is the judge of New Canaan. It's Lian Archiva who has been deciding which of us lives, and which of us dies. And that means Thorne Councilman did not kill my brother.

My mother did.

BECKETT

I don't even remember getting back up the cliffs, packing my gear, or making my way back down through the fields. I did it at a jog, and then I did it at a run, down into the streets, where I pushed around bodies and bumped into shoulders without even pulling up my hood. When Annis's door shuts, it rattles the dishes on the table. Annis sets down her tea.

"You lied to her," I say.

Annis stares at me for exactly one second. Then she goes to the front door and locks it, peering once through the window before closing the curtain. Cyrus comes in from the workshop at a trot.

"Byron said you just came running down the street like a maniac, what—"

"You used her!" I say.

"Beckett, what's wrong with you?" Jill is in the doorway of the resting room, and she's got Jasmina on an out-thrust hip. I don't have enough space in my head to register how weird that is.

Annis sits back down at the table, folding her hands in front of her tea. "Why don't you have a seat?"

"I'm not interested in sitting," I say. I'm sweating, and I've barely got breath to speak. And I need to strangle someone. "I am interested . . . in hearing why you let her risk her life . . . for you."

Cyrus turns the lock on the door to the workshop, and Annis narrows her eyes. "If we're discussing the endangerment of lives, Beckett . . . That's your name, isn't it? Beckett? Then I would be interested in hearing who you really are."

My gaze darts up to Jill. Her eyes are big, blue, and give me no help.

"You didn't really expect us to believe you were one of the Knowing, did you? The only thing remotely Knowing about you is that you'd be arrogant enough to think we were that stupid. With her"—she jerks a thumb at Jill—"not able to walk? The Knowing don't get sick. Nadia never would've told such a silly lie if she hadn't been desperate."

I don't think I've actually remembered we were supposed to be Knowing since the first day. What would Sean Rodriguez make of that?

"What?" Annis says. "Nothing to say?"

"Annis," says Cyrus, cautioning.

"No, Dad! After risking my own back and yours. Risking the kids! I won't sit here and be accused . . ."

And then my mind catches up. "They have her."

"Have who?" says Annis.

"Sam."

She closes her mouth. And then Cyrus comes to the table, kicks out the end of the bench. "I think you'd better sit after all."

I sit this time.

"Beckett," says Jill, "could I speak to you for a minute?"

"No."

"You two," says Cyrus, nodding at Nathan and Jill, "get in here. And the rest of you"—heads look down from the loft—"get Grandmama's box from under my bed and each of you count the beads. Whoever gets it right gets a trip to the pond."

Luc and Ari scramble down the ladder, Jasmina squirming down Jill's legs to trot after them. Jill slides stiff-backed onto the bench beside me, head up, Nathan after, and as soon as the resting room door shuts, Cyrus says, "What happened?"

"She's been Judged and condemned."

"But it's not time . . ." says Annis.

"They're keeping her locked up until then. Somewhere deep. Drugged, I think . . ."

"What are her crimes?" asks Cyrus.

"Stealing Knowing, writing Knowing, and"—I look hard at them both—"mixing with the rebels of the Outside."

"Ah." Cyrus drops into his chair by the clay heater, running a hand over the white hairs on his chin. I see Nathan and Jill exchange a look.

"You used her," I say, "to get information on the Underneath. Getting Nita to pretend like she cared about her. It was Nita who got Sam to come Outside, to go down in the Archives and write down what she shouldn't. And it got Nita killed, didn't it?"

Nathan leans forward on the bench. "You need to shut up."

I don't. "That poison was never meant for Sam, was it? They knew she was sharing her food. Sending it out to you. They'd been watching her for weeks . . ."

"Now you listen," Cyrus says. Annis knocks a tear from her cheek like she's angry about it. "It's true we picked out Samara. It took a lot of doing to get Nita chosen as her help. We wanted Nita with her, and we wanted Nita to befriend her. We needed an ally, and we chose her. Because she was the sister of Adam Archiva."

I look at Cyrus. I'm listening, but being still is costing me. "Nita got caught once," he says, "climbing down the cliffs into the city's upland parks. She was a kid, she'd been dared, and the girl never was one to back down . . ."

"I dared her," says Nathan to the table. Jill puts a hand on his arm.

Cyrus says, "She'd have had her back laid open for sure, kid or not, except that it was Adam Archiva in the parks that day, not much more than a kid himself, and he let her go. Kept watch while she got back up the cliffs."

Cyrus has his brow wrinkled now, as if this memory gives him pain.

"Two years later, Adam was a supervisor, training, and his route took him by the workshop. He remembered Nita, of course, and she was scared, but he said he wouldn't tell, and I talked to him a little. And pretty soon it was every day, at this table, both of us risking our skins to tell about what it was like to live Outside and Underneath. How many hours we worked. Food rations. No medicine. No learning. What went on inside your head when you're Knowing. And I told him about a sickness that was hidden, that makes us Forget. And he said he'd been trained to take anyone with those symptoms Underneath for treatment. And I explained that if they go Underneath, they don't come back out again. That we hide our sickness instead. And he decided to help us."

"Help you do what?" I ask.

"Rebel," Annis whispers.

"Adam told us things we could've never found out on our own. That the Council wasn't really running the city. That there was a sect, secret, obsessed with creating a Superior Earth . . ."

I see Jill blink.

". . . fulfilling the so-called directive of our ancestors. They were the ones to be afraid of, Adam said, because they were fanatics— judging, killing off any who questioned or didn't measure up. He didn't believe in any of it. He said Earth was a story, made up to keep the Outsiders out and the Knowing Underneath . . ."

"Do you believe in Earth?" I ask. Jill nudges me with her knee.

"I think even the Knowing don't know all there is to Know. Would you agree with that, young man?"

I tilt my head.

"Adam did, too. Mostly the boy didn't like to be told how to think. But he said the way to shift things was simple. When the Knowing shut themselves in for Judgment, don't let them out again. Block the doors until they agreed to our terms. The Outsiders had the power, he said, because the Knowing didn't actually Know how to do anything, not with their hands, and the change would be better for everybody . . ."

"We did what he said," Annis interrupts. "Made pins for the gates from metal scraps, and for the door in the parks, blocked the light and ventilation shafts big enough to crawl through. He showed us . . ."

"There were only about thirty of us," says Cyrus, "and it was a white sunrise, after Judgment, when Adam said most of the Knowing would be distracting their minds, which means drunk . . ."

I'm leaning forward so hard I've got the table pushed into my stomach. "What is a white sunrise?"

Cyrus and Annis look at me funny. Even Nathan is staring. Jill gives me another nudge with her knee.

"The white sunrise," Cyrus says. "Every twelve years . . ."

They mean the comet. "Right," I say. "What happened to Adam?"

Annis jumps in again. "We did it, we blocked the gates. And he climbed on top of the gates, looking for the signal from the parks, and he just . . . He . . ."

"Forgot," Cyrus says. "We didn't know then, that the Knowing could Forget . . ."

"He panicked," Annis whispers. "Went crazy. And he opened the gates. And the Knowing came out like they'd been waiting. Someone had betrayed us. They got everyone who was on the gates. Even the ones that ran first. Pulled them out of their houses. Even Ruth Smith's daughter, who was just watching from the street . . ."

Because they've got a camera on the gates, I think. I'll bet Adam didn't Know about that.

"We lost eight to the Forgetting that day," says Cyrus.

"Wait," I say. "Eight on the same day? Has it happened since?"

"Not that we know of," replies Annis, "but we might not know . . ."

"We lost eight to the Forgetting, and ten to the Knowing. Four blinded. Two disappeared. And six flogged until they died. Including Nita and Nathan's father, who was on the gates . . ."

Annis sits with a face of stone, but Nathan's eyes are hot. Jill lets out a slow breath.

". . . and Adam was taken Underneath," Cyrus says. "And we saw the smoke rise from the mountain. We weren't sure exactly what had happened to him until Nita started taking care of Samara." Cyrus clears his throat. "But we learned something that day. That the Knowing can Forget, just like anybody, and that they didn't want us to know about it . . ."

I say, "Sam thinks the Council gave Adam bitterblack to cover up that he'd Forgotten. We were down there looking for whatever causes the Forgetting, trying to understand how it works"—another blown breath from Jill—"because she wants to use it to heal the Knowing. Sam thinks they'd want it, that they would overthrow the Council to stop living the way they are."

"Adam did not seem healed to me, young man. But it's not the Council. They could be reasoned with. It's them, the fanatics, the head of their sect. The judge . . ."

I remember Reddix beside the cliffs. *Always everyone thinks this is about the Council . . .*

". . . Adam was Judged and condemned, for rebelling as much as Forgetting. And it's Lian Archiva who's been doing the condemning. She's the judge. Adam told us. She'll have to be the first one to go . . ."

Sam's mother? I run both my hands through my hair. And I sent Sam straight back into her arms. Sam thought her parents needed saving, and her mother turned around and condemned her, just like her brother before her. Did Lian Archiva really give her own son bitterblack? I'm sick in every way you could be. Stomach, head, heart, and mind.

"And how could we tell her?" Annis is saying. "When she can barely survive hearing Adam's name? We just had to do something about it . . ."

"And this time," Cyrus goes on, "we have more on our side. The floggings have seen to that . . ."

This time. I thought we must be getting to that. "What about Sam?" I interrupt.

"That's where you can help us," says Annis, fingers wrapped around her long-cold cup. Cyrus makes a noise and she says, "No, Dad! You said you trust him and we've given him the truth. It's only fair to ask him to do the same. How many are you?"

For one second, I think she's asking me how old I am. Then I realize she's asking me how many are on the ship. Now Jill looks right at me, and I know what her eyes mean. *Don't say it.* But we're way past protocol. "We—"

"We have been asked not to discuss these things," Jill breaks in. "And that's all we can say. Please accept our apologies."

I roll my eyes.

"Did you two run?" Cyrus asks. "Is that it?"

"Grandpapa," says Nathan. He looks uncomfortable. "She said they can't say. So just leave it . . ."

"Look," Cyrus says, "it's dangerous for you here, but since you're here, I'm thinking that means it's more dangerous for you there. But we didn't know there was anyone else . . ."

"Do they know we're here?" Annis asks.

". . . and whatever the problems are, is there no way to talk about going in on this together? It's a chance to build something new."

Annis leans across the table. "How far is the colony?"

I look back and forth at the two of them. Another colony. They think there's another colony on the planet.

"I'm sorry for the problems you're having here," Jill says. "But help is not something we're able to provide. We extend our best wishes to the Outside."

Showing sympathy, stating facts plainly, without giving personal details, using the vernacular, remaining positive. It's straight out of the training files. And it's stupid.

"Cyrus," I say, "I'm from Earth."

For the people of knowledge and memory have been given a gift, a tool, our most precious weapon. And it is called the Forgetting.

FROM THE NOTEBOOK OF JANIS ATAN

43

SAMARA

It's interesting being dead.

I don't Know how long I've been this way, but I've mapped almost all the rooms of my mind, following the thin tendrils of connecting thought when they ask for my attention. Letting them slide through my hands, picking up their ends. I hold the strings of my memories now, and instead of their yanking me, I can follow them, gently, and go to the room of my mind that I choose.

I visited Adam's death, but only once, to think about what my mother had done, to listen to my father's tears. Did he Know that she condemned and poisoned her own child? I think he did. And I'm sorry for him. And angry with him. But what had my brother done?

I followed the string of my thoughts, listened to Adam say, *There is no Earth* and *There's nothing wrong with the sun . . .* And I watched, bouncing on the bed, while he put on his shoes for the Outside, telling me to lock my door during the celebrations. To open it only for him, no matter what I heard. That he would come for me, take me to see the special sunrise.

Something was going to happen that resting. Something that didn't. And Adam was coming for me, to take me away. Take me

Outside. Maybe he wasn't all that different from me. Maybe that's why she poisoned us both.

Controlling this memory does not mean I can control its pain.

So I run down the halls and find the room in my mind that is the cave with Beckett. I'm grieving in here, too, feeling the pain of losing Adam, but I am also being held, a hand on the back of my head, the warm smell of Beckett's skin. Here, I can be comforted.

There are many different ways to be comforted.

Sometimes I visit the technology with Beckett, or let him tell me about countries beside the blanket on the resting room floor. Sometimes he's floating in the clear water, shining a light jar on a lake bottom of crystals. Or I go to the storage room and kiss his face while he strokes my back and the scars on my arms.

Being dead is also lonely.

I've read most of the books now, including the medical journal discussing the Forgetting, though there wasn't much more information than what I read before Thorne Councilman came. I run my fingers over the spines, lined up on the shelves of my mind, and then I notice a high shelf, in the corner, dark, and when I stretch, and reach, I find a book on it. This is what was in the hole in my mother's wall. What my father told me to cache. I suppose I did. I take the book down, sit on the floor, and open it.

It's a book of chemistry. I go through it slowly. There's no hurry here, so I linger on explanations and equations longer than I need. Until I get to a chapter marked *Transcribed from the writings of Janis Atan*. Janis was also a chemist, it seems, and the first topic she discusses is how to safely extract a useful substance from the seed pod of a Forgetting tree. There's a drawing included, a heavily budded branch, thick with leaves. And I have seen this before.

I follow my memories to the labs Underneath, the tiny tree beneath the dome, the sliced pod in the glass box, the "clean space," the vials of white powder in the wafting flowers. And then I cross a hall in my mind and I am in the Cursed City, beside the ancient bathhouse, surrounded by the blowing trees, walking down a road choked with roots. My mind nudges, I push aside the familiar, heavy branch, and now I'm looking at the black-inked words written neatly on a page of the chemistry book.

The time to extract Forgetting, the page tells me, *is during the sporing cycle, which under the correct conditions may be forced. In nature, this is timed to occur only once every twelve years, when the passing radiation of the planet's comet excites the blooms . . .*

White sunrise, I think. I've never seen a white sunrise. None of the Knowing have. And then I realize—of course I haven't, because the Forgetting is coming from the bloom of the trees, sporing beneath the comet every twelve years. We're not being shut in for Judgment. We're hiding from the Forgetting.

I look at the dosage amounts. They are minuscule. Even the smallest exposure would make someone Forget, and the Cursed City is full of thousands, maybe millions of those dangerous buds. It must be a miasma of Forgetting when the sky goes white, a cloud of spores made to catch the wind and travel. And why wouldn't they? I think of spores riding the breeze to New Canaan, and my brother, twelve years ago, Outside when he shouldn't have been, on the exact wrong day, in the wrong spot, breathing air that wasn't meant for his lungs.

And now, after I'm dead, I finally find the Knowing of how to Forget. In a book that was in my head all along. I wish I could tell Beckett.

I read on through the writings of Janis Atan. Her research on Forgetting was extensive. And she found a cure, a naturally occurring substance that would reverse the brain inflammation caused by the spores. But when she distilled, concentrated, enhanced this cure, then not only did it stop the Forgetting's impediment of a subject's memory, it temporarily stopped the brain's natural impediments as well. The cure for Forgetting, she writes, created a condition called Knowing, where the subject is not actually capable of forgetting anything at all.

Janis Atan, I think, was incredibly brilliant. And incredibly evil. She didn't make these discoveries in her head. There are names here. Notes. Results of experiments.

Anna, Planter's daughter. Fifteen years old. Forced immunity. Three sessions of injected exposure with memories intact. Air exposure resulting in extreme cranial and spinal pain before an immediate rise in blood pressure, leading to death . . .

And on and on. Adults and children. Her words make the rooms of my mind feel dirty. I read how her experiments showed that some humans were born immune to Forgetting, and could be exposed to the tree spores without losing their memories. How this immunity could be created with a very slight, very controlled and regular exposure, coupled with the injected cure. How immunity from Forgetting meant—

There are pages missing here, three ragged edges, roughly torn, like missing teeth. I run a finger over them inside my mind, and then a memory is tugging, drawing me down, urging me to another room. I don't want to go. I want to read about chemistry. I stay where I am, reveling in the fact that I can do it. That I am in control.

And here is the detailed process for making Knowing, in both an injectable and digestible form, a chemical recipe that I don't have to search my mind to recognize. Amrita. *Knowing,* the notes say, *is most effective when injected once, at a young age, followed by a small booster drunk at regular intervals.* Like four times a year, I think, at our Changing of the Seasons.

I set down the book of chemistry and it dissolves away, disappearing like sugar sap in my tea. I concentrate, find the place in my memory that is my bedchamber, and go there, remembering the feel of the soft gold coverlet, staring up at the painted stars, thinking about what I've read.

I was not born with memory. None of the Knowing were. Beckett was right. We have been made to be this way. By my mother and her NWSE, "the guardians of memory, the architects of Knowing," watching us lift our glasses to the sun and moon. And then suffer. No one has ever had to be Knowing, and no one has ever had to Forget. All we've ever had to do was not drink the amrita, and once every twelve years, go underground.

It is so unfair to have all this Knowing after you're dead.

I think about Adam, Forgetting when he shouldn't have, not just because he shouldn't have been Outside, but because being full of that concentrated "cure" should have meant the spores would not affect him. But the answer is simple. Adam must have stopped drinking the amrita. What did he Know? Read? See? And when? It obviously wasn't enough. And how did he get away with it? I'll probably never Know.

I miss my brother. I wish I could have Known him, as more than a child. I think he must have been worse even than me, and that makes me smile. And then my smile dies. Mother could have cured him. But she didn't. She killed him instead.

And then I sit up, startled. I felt a prick in my arm. Sharp and stinging. But the pain dulls fast. Like a wellness injection. Or the memory of an injection.

I lay my head back down on the shimmering gold, alone in my Knowing. And my memories. And I wonder if this is what forever is like.

44

BECKETT

Nathan follows me down to the cliff edge. The moons are almost ready to crest the mountain peaks, and there's a paleness to the dark, though it's still black in the shadows. I drop my pack and get out the gear. This is the fourth time I've done this climb to meet with Reddix, and I am sick of this wall of rock. But if he'll bring me news of Sam, I'm going down. Even if it's lies.

I don't trust Reddix Physicianson any farther than I could throw him.

Nathan jumps a little when I shoot the hook into the rock, anchoring the ropes for the descent, but he doesn't say anything. It took less time than I thought for the family to get over the shock of me being from Earth. I had a long talk with Cyrus, then another with Cyrus and Annis, and then we had an understanding. And a plan.

But Nathan, I think, hasn't forgiven me for where I come from. Though he's definitely forgiven Jill. He seems to think she's some kind of martyr in this situation. And since his reasoning probably comes straight from her, I really don't know what else I could expect.

"We could've had everything," Jill said to me, statue-still on the edge of the bed while the others were still at the table, trying to figure out how two Earthlings ended up in their resting room. I was pacing the room like a cat in a cage. "Money," she went on, "house, your choice of the work you wanted, our names in the files. The two of us. And you threw it away, Beckett. Tossed it out like it was nothing . . ."

I stopped pacing to look at her then. Really look at her. "You lied, Jill. Lied. To me. For years."

She bit her lip. "I always thought, when the time came, that you'd . . . see reason . . ."

" 'See reason'? You thought I'd agree to kidnapping an entire civilization? To flying back to Earth on a slave ship? What have I ever said, what part of me have you ever seen, that would make you think I would agree to that?"

"I thought you'd agree to saving the Earth, Beckett. And don't pretend you haven't been lying to me nonstop ever since you met her . . ."

And that last part wasn't an unfair point.

Nathan watches while I get the ropes ready. It's the third time he's made the trip with me, watching from the cliffs, so that if I don't come back, someone will know what happened to me. It's the option I would guess he's hoping for.

But this time, when I'm done scanning the park, tucking the glasses back into my shirt, Nathan says, "What did you see?"

I step into the harness. "I looked at what I could without the darkness. Then I looked for sources of heat. Like a body. And there's one standing over there, in the groves by the cliffs." Right where he's supposed to be.

"Can I see?" Nathan asks.

"Yes. I mean, I'd let you, but they're set to only one person. So if you were touching them, looking through them, they wouldn't work."

Nathan thinks about this. "What if you held them, and I was only looking through, without touching?"

"I don't know," I say, cocking my head. "Here. Try it."

I hold the glasses out to one side, keeping my skin touching, while Nathan leans forward, squinting his eyes. He leans back, looks over the lenses, and then back through them again.

"I can see light," he says. "In the glass! But it's blurry."

"They adjust to your eyes when you have them on," I say, tucking them back inside the shirt. He nods.

"I'm taking Jill up into the orchards. Just to walk."

I pause, about to go over the edge of the cliff. "Is it safe?"

"Grandpapa thinks it can be."

Cyrus thinks the Knowing are waiting, watching for the situation to unfold before they act. Like they usually do. The difference this time is that the Outside knows exactly how they're doing the watching.

"She's going crazy inside the house. And she wants to go. With me."

Again I stop myself from going over the cliff. I'm in a hurry. Reddix has to be met within his window, and if I miss him, I miss hearing the time of the next meeting. "Are you asking my permission?"

"No. I'm asking if we have a problem."

My problem is with Jill's agenda at the moment, whatever it is.

"Look," says Nathan, "I'm not stupid, and I know what she's been doing and why she's been doing it. That's why I'm saying something. Because . . . I don't think that's what she's doing anymore."

Which just means she's changed tactics. "You have no issues from me, Nathan," I say. "But . . ." I don't want to say, *Don't believe a word she says,* or *Don't let her pull you around on a string.* So I opt for, "Just . . . be smart about it." He nods, and I get over the edge of the cliff before I have to discuss anyone else's love life.

I jog down the slope after I hit bottom, sprint a wide circle so I can come at Reddix from a slightly different direction. I think he Knows where I'm coming from—he always Knows when I get near—but it would give me some personal satisfaction to sneak up on him at least once.

He's staring out over the cliffs again, like he always does, and I wonder if he's thinking about jumping. Then I wonder if anything he's been telling me is true. If Sam's already dead and he's playing some kind of game to distract his mind, or trick Earth, or some other reason I don't understand. The thought makes me sick.

I'm always sick now.

Reddix turns his head when I'm still a long way away, and I sigh. I stop my customary three meters away and he says, "You're not well, Earthling?" He goes on, since I'm not going to answer him. "You have a sickness I understand well. Here, I thought you might be in need of a . . . token."

He's holding something out to me. I'm not wearing the glasses—I don't want him Knowing what they can do—so I step forward like he's that beetle on the back of Jill's leg. What he's offering is a small metal case of blue glass and green enamel. It's beautiful, and it wasn't that long ago that I would've studied the aesthetic and craftsmanship of Canaan for days based on it.

"Open it," says Reddix.

I do, thinking of poison and venomous bugs. But there's only one thing inside: a long, coiled lock of curling black hair. I snap the box shut, and I'm so mad I go calm. It's hers. He has access to her, and he's been touching her hair.

"She is well cared for. I gave her a wellness injection early, to help her keep her strength while she sleeps. Perhaps you didn't know that I am also a physician?"

"And you're one of them."

"Them? The NWSE? Oh, yes. From a young age." He smiles, and it's like a cold morning in the Arctic Circle. "I was something of a prodigy."

"And I'm supposed to believe you want the Knowing out of power?"

"It is because of the NWSE that I want that. Among other reasons . . ."

I see the signs of memory beneath his calm face, but only just a little, and only because I've learned from Samara.

Then he says, "Tell me, Earthling. What would you give to save her?"

I don't say anything.

"Because they will kill her. Judgment is absolute. But they may not kill her right away. The NWSE finds the condemned to be useful for obtaining . . . medical information." I see another small twist beneath the exterior. "I cannot remove her, not without being seen and stopped. And even if you swept in at the last moment with your rebels of the Outside, they would kill her then and there. Throw her in the Torrens before you got near. Because justice is their obsession, especially the justice they have decreed themselves. Keeping only the best of the best, so we can make more of ourselves, maintain our own worthiness, and create the Superior Earth. That is the ultimate goal. She will not survive."

I'm gritting my teeth. I have my own thoughts about whether Sam is going to survive this or not, but I wait until Reddix gets where he's going.

"Here," he says. "I have something else for you." Reddix holds out a small glass bottle, but before he puts it in my hand, he says, "Handle it carefully. Do not break the glass or the seal."

I take the bottle and hold it up to the very faint light of three unrisen moons. The bottle is clear, a white powder swirling inside. "What is it?"

"Forgetting," he replies. "The Knowing's greatest weapon. A weapon I would like to see turned on ourselves."

My eyes snap back to the bottle. "And why are you giving it to me?"

"Because I want you to come into the Forum just before Judgment and smash that bottle onto the stones. And then the Knowing—and even the memory of Knowing—will be gone. Samara will not be Judged, and the city will belong to the Outside. Let them deal with the coming Earth."

I stand there, staring at the weirdly calm face. "And you need me to do this because . . ."

"I will be with the NWSE in seclusion, and then under scrutiny. I will not be able to enter the Forum with that bottle. And it is a bottle that has been . . . difficult to obtain. But there is enough there for all of the gathered Knowing, if it were to . . . get in the air."

"And I suppose that means I would be Forgetting, too."

"I asked what you would do to save her," he says. "Is the sacrifice too much?"

If he's playing a part, he's playing it well. I think maybe he always plays his part well. "How does it work?"

"The powder in that bottle will go to the air and spread. Even the smallest exposure will wipe away memory, and the city will be sealed once you're inside. They will not escape. Once in the air, the powder lasts for three days. That is all I Know."

I doubt that. "Where does it come from?"

"It is processed in the labs, but again, that is not my field. Information is very controlled in New Canaan." Reddix looks out over the cliffs again. "Have you ever seen Samara . . . in the grips of a . . . painful memory?"

I have. And I hate him for having seen it. I'm sure he's the one who's been behind those screens. Saving that data.

"Pain is a constant for the Knowing, something we can never protect ourselves well enough from. And Samara has memories that are more . . . agonizing than most. Would you deny her the peace of Forgetting?"

I'd already decided I'd give it to her if it killed me.

"Could you deny it to any of us?"

And now I'm wondering for the first time what Reddix remembers. He would've been something like eight or nine years old at the last Judgment, brought early, he'd said, into their sect. What did he see done to the condemned that he wants to Forget? I grip the bottle tight in my hand. Cyrus got better, didn't he? He healed. Sam could heal, and so could I. "How do I get into the city?"

"Come down the shaft you used before," he says. "I will meet you there three bells after waking, and then Judgment will come at the middle bell. But you must see Samara inside the Forum before you drop the bottle. That is important. Don't give them a chance to kill her." Reddix looks at my face and smiles. "We will not need to meet here again. Three bells after waking on the day of Judgment. Or there will be no saving her."

He turns away. Evidently nothing more needs saying. I disagree.

"Wait." Reddix pauses, but doesn't turn around. "What makes you Knowing?"

"We were born this way, Earthling. But if our truth is Forgotten, then maybe our Knowing can be put to better use."

I slip on the glasses to watch him go. Even if he really thinks he was born this way, it's just not true. And I'm cold inside. Not because of the Forgetting in my hand or because of what Reddix wants me to do. Because I'm thinking again about what Earth, someone like Commander Faye, would do if they had access to something that would give their soldiers the minds of the Knowing. Their generals, their engineers, doctors, physicists. They would want it. Badly. And after what I've seen here, I wouldn't give it to us if we were a race of saints.

I look back over the dark plain, deeper shades where I know there are canyons and rivers and cracks, and into the distance, where the *Centauri III* is. And a yellow light blinks, bright. I zoom the lenses, and there's another bright light, closer in the glasses, coming just as a rumble rolls through the air and beneath my feet. Another roll comes, and if I squint I can make out a plume of white smoke. Something just exploded. Big.

And all I can think is: Dad.

To be immune to the Forgetting is a privilege given to few. But like all privileges, it comes with a cost. Always to remember, yet cursed to die . . .

FROM THE NOTEBOOK OF JANIS ATAN

45

SAMARA

I'm hearing voices in my mind. Echoing through the different rooms. Vague. Indistinct. I don't Know what they mean. Sometimes I chase the voices down halls. But they're always gone when I get there. It's strange to not Know how long I've been dead.

My control is so good I can choose any room I want now, or shut the door if I need to, follow the tugging strings of thought to see what they show me. But so many of these memories are faded, stale, a song heard again and again. I can't say anything I didn't say. Do anything I didn't already do.

I wish I could dream.

I feel a tug in my mind, the tightening of a string. I've been ignoring this memory, choosing others that seem more interesting, but the pull has become insistent, and my list of new rooms is short. So I follow the pull of my memory and open the door into Uncle Towlend's office.

And now there is yellow light, stacked books, and bits of paper, and I am curled in a soft chair that is huge compared to my small body, shoes tucked up under my dress. I have three scars, and I feel safe, secure. I am not Knowing yet. Uncle Towlend looks whole, because Aunt Letitia hasn't gone, and he's making meticulous stitches, sewing a book's torn page.

And then I see that the book my uncle is repairing is the map book, the first time I ever saw it, and Uncle Towlend is telling me about the papers he found inside. Loose, from another book, tucked into a sort of niche in the cover. Uncle Towlend lifts the needle, stretching a thread that is the width of a hair, and because he had glanced at the loose pages, he recites their words for me.

" '. . . and test subject number one hundred two, Nadia, Dyer's daughter, is found to be naturally immune, only the second known case. Exposure was ten times average predicted dose for the Forgetting. Memories intact, severely ill . . .' "

Nadia, I think now, with my grown mind, the sister of Genivee Archiva, who went out of bounds, like me, who made the maps. My uncle must have been lonely in his office, I think, to recite these things to a three-year-old. They were hardly appropriate subject matter. Maybe I'd been lonely, too, since I am sitting so still, listening.

" '. . . heavier exposure is expected to be fatal. However, subject proved more tolerant than those with forced immunity, where exposure is fatal at half the predicted dose in one hundred percent of subjects tried . . .' "

And suddenly I am yanked upward, flying through the walls and ceilings of my mind. I lose the string of memory I've been holding. Lose my control. And then I have fingers, legs, muscles that are stiff, aching. I have a body, and my body is a cage. I want to turn on my side. I want to see. Speak. But I can't. I can only hear and feel, sheets below my fingers, the give of a mattress as someone sits next to me. The cloth of a sleeve brushing my arm. Breath near my ear.

"Samara," a voice whispers.

It's Reddix Physicianson. I can't see him, but I Know his voice. I feel one finger trailing the length of my arm, and my mind shudders.

"Samara," he whispers, "can you hear me yet? I've adjusted your medication, to ease you awake. But you must be still. Don't let the others Know . . ."

The finger strokes past my row of scars and into my hair. My medication, he said. A sleeping draught. I'm not dead. And that means Judgment is still on its way, and I'm trapped. And afraid.

"Your lover is coming," he says. "He's gotten thinner, and his eyes are shaded. He isn't used to our long dark, is he? But I don't think that's what ails him . . ."

Beckett. He's talking about Beckett. Reddix twines his fingers through my hair, picking it up and letting it fall.

"It is fifty-four days since he's seen you."

Fifty-four days?

"That is what ails him. And because he is afraid you will die in Judgment Underneath. I Know his pain. And so he will come, and he will throw the Forgetting into the Forum, to save you, to help you Forget, and then he will Forget you, too. And Earth and the Knowing alike."

No, he shouldn't do that. I Know how to stop being Knowing. We don't have to Forget . . . The back of a hand brushes across my cheek, slowly. Reddix is making a memory. Of touching me. I want to scream.

"You couldn't help it, could you?" he whispers. "When your love came? I couldn't help it, either, and you never saw me. Not really. I went everywhere you did. To touch the rope in the parks, where you had been swinging. To the Archives, and your uncle's old office, to sit in the chairs where you once sat. Only I never went Outside, not like you did. I was never brave enough for that. But I kept your secrets. So much time erased from the cameras, and they never realized what I'd done. But it wasn't enough. I couldn't keep you from being caught. Not every time . . ."

He pauses, his hand lingering on my neck. "You can hear me now, can't you? Your pulse is faster, and your breathing . . ." His fingers start their slow strokes back into my hair.

"But I still could have saved you from Judgment. A partner would have made you useful. Would have meant the line of Lian Archiva was not over. So she let me have you. I Knew you didn't want it. I Knew you would look at me with disgust every day after, but I would've done it, because it would have kept you alive. And then you ran . . ."

The fingers brush the hair from my forehead, and beneath my panic I am sorry. For Reddix and Beckett. And me. For all the Knowing.

". . . and you went straight to the Cursed City. When they Knew what you'd written, Knew you were looking for the secret of Forgetting, and so close to where Earth must have landed. It wasn't easy to make them believe you were innocent then. But I persuaded your mother that you needed rescuing, not punishing. That you'd helped end the life of the same rebel who was trying to corrupt you, who the NWSE had been trying to kill themselves. But you eluded them, and went to the Outside, took your Knowing back into the house of the very same rebels . . ."

The one they had been trying to kill. The same rebels. They meant to kill Nita all along. Not me. Grandpapa, Annis, and Nathan really are rebels. And then I think of the cameras. They Knew I was sharing my food. They Knew what I wrote in my book. It was Nita that Marcus and Craddock were talking about in the ruined city. Nita who had been Judged at the wrong time. Because of my mother. Nita's family that needed to be made an example of, not mine. My parents were pretending to be in seclusion, so the Knowing wouldn't realize I was gone. Me, they were trying to rescue, with Thorne Councilman actually doing what he could to mitigate my mother's lust for a bloody justice. I want to bang on the inside of my body like fists against a door. And I can do nothing.

"And what argument was going to save you then?" Reddix whispers. He strokes the other side of my face now, the corner of my mouth. "But I didn't tell them about Earth. You wouldn't have lived to Judgment if I had. Like your brother . . ."

His breath tickles in my ear, and I can smell him now, clean, with a faint scent of moonflower.

"I Know what you see when you cry out in your sleep. When you writhe in pain on the floor. I Know why you were looking for the Forgetting. I, too, have seen the deaths they reserve for the condemned. And Forgetting would be peace, wouldn't it? It's not so wrong, is it? To want peace?"

Reddix lifts my hand, caressing it, holding it in his.

"But your mother has taken away even that. Do you Know what she has done to us? For twelve years, since her son caught the Forgetting, one harvested spore has been put into our blood. In our wellness injections. As the book said. She has made us immune to the Forgetting. And now, even the curse of oblivion is gone . . ."

I can see that page in the Notebook of Janis Atan. Just before the torn ones. A created immunity, not a natural one, by small exposures plus the amrita. *Reddix,* I think. I want to shout the words. *You don't Know everything. We don't have to Forget, because we can stop being Knowing. Just don't drink the amrita. Don't drink the amrita . . .*

And now my memory is pulling, seizing me, wanting to tell me something. But I can't go yet. I need to hear Reddix. He lifts my limp hand and puts it on his face, and I feel skin, a smooth-shaven cheek, the brush of long braids.

"And now I will remember that I love you, and you will remember that you love him, and he will fly back through the stars. It's untenable, isn't it? This life?" He rubs his cheek across my hand, and I Know pain when I hear it. "I don't believe this new Earth the Knowing will build is all that superior," he whispers. "I think it will be like the stories of hell."

My mind is racing, and if Reddix is monitoring my heartbeat, then he's feeling the spike in its speed. If we are immune, then why is Beckett throwing down Forgetting? Where did he even get it? From Reddix, of course. Reddix must have taken Forgetting from the labs. But why do it at all?

And the strings in my mind yank, painful, and this time I sink, away from the feel of Reddix's face, down, down . . .

. . . *to pages of a book that are turning, flipping, three jagged edges where some have been torn, and then the pages still, and say: Anna, Planter's daughter . . . Forced immunity . . . Three sessions of injected exposure . . . memories intact. Air exposure resulting in extreme cranial and spinal pain before an immediate rise in blood pressure, leading to death . . .*

And the book dissolves, parting like water as I fall through it, into . . .

. . . *Uncle Towlend's office, with my shoes tucked under my dress, while my uncle sews the map book. His voice is low and mellow, reciting, " '. . . Nadia, Dyer's daughter, is found to be naturally immune . . . Exposure was ten times average predicted dose for the Forgetting. Memories intact, severely ill . . . However, subject proved more tolerant than those with forced immunity, where exposure is fatal at half the predicted dose in one hundred percent of subjects tried . . .' "*

I rise back to the present, to my dark cage of a body, to Reddix's lips on my forehead. And now I think I Know what papers my uncle found, what he recited to me when I was three. The three missing pages from the Notebook of Janis Atan, the book hidden behind my mother's mirror. No wonder my memory kept tugging. The instructions for creating a forced immunity to the Forgetting were in the notebook, but not the results of Janis's experiments. Forced immunity to the Forgetting does leave your memory intact, which is incredibly useless, since the spores just decide to kill you instead. But could Reddix Know this? Where did Uncle Towlend leave those papers?

I sift through my mind, fast, searching my memories of every visit to Uncle Towlend's office. The yellow lamps flash, memory after memory. And then I take away the bright lights, and there is only one lantern, and it's in my hand. And I have it. Those papers were lying on the dirty floor when I came back out of the Archives, after I read the book about Forgetting. Like they were rubbish. Like they were nothing. But I see them, illuminated in a dim flash of my lantern.

And Reddix said he'd been to my uncle's office.

I feel a finger on my neck. Feeling my pulse, and Reddix whispers, "Don't be frightened, Samara, when the time comes . . ."

I am frightened. I have a right to be.

"It is a kindness. So much better than Judgment. And the pain will be gone. And you will see your lover once more, and then he will Forget that it ever happened . . ."

He does Know. He Knows exactly what he's doing, and he's doing it on purpose. He's killing us all. With Forgetting.

And he's getting Beckett to do it for him.

46

BECKETT

I'm sitting with Cyrus on a bench in the back of the workshop. It's an hour or so before the waking bell, so technically we're out during curfew, but the streets are so muddy from twenty-two straight days of rain that I doubt a supervisor is going to walk them. The clouds have gone now, three moons hanging low behind the mountains, the flower glow on the hillsides dimming. Sunrise is coming. A white sunrise. Not this waking, but the next. I'm going to Sam as soon as the streets fill, and this time of waiting feels like the long breath before a scream. I couldn't sleep, and neither could Cyrus.

He leans back on the bench and says, "Tell me about money."

I sigh. This is all part of Cyrus's plan, started after Sam was gone, when Annis switched our rooms, putting me in with Cyrus and herself with Jill. To keep an eye on us, probably. It wasn't a bad change. But I'm at my worst during resting, stewing and steaming, so Cyrus started telling me everything he knew about the history of Canaan, Old and New. Stories, songs, anything he could think of, stretched out on his bed, talking to the ceiling. I documented a lot of it, and I looked forward to showing it to Mom and Dad. If I knew they were alive.

Now Cyrus has moved on to making me explain the ways of Earth, and so he says, "Come on. Tell me about money."

I rub my temples. "It's something we give a value to . . . metals, and later a paper representation, but you use it to trade for what you want or a service that you need. It's like deciding that a pane of glass is worth ten. So if you make a pane of glass, the person who wants it gives you ten, and then you can trade that for food that's worth ten. Or whatever else you want. If you need more than ten, you make more glass that other people will give you more money for, and then you can trade for more."

Cyrus cocks his head, thinking. "So what you're saying is that everyone on Earth is just good at pretending."

I laugh, which is some kind of miracle, and he elbows me once to shush me. I'm not even going to try to explain that we don't even use the metal and paper anymore. I guess it is a little like pretending. Not using money was one of the creeds of the Canaan Project, which I didn't think would work, and Sean Rodriguez did. So Dad scores on that one. And now I'm back to stewing.

"Are you ready?" I ask Cyrus.

He nods. "We know what to do."

I spent a week training Cyrus and Annis on how to take out the cameras without being spotted. "The timing has to be right on," I say for the millionth time. "On the middle bell. Cameras first, block the ventilation shafts, and open the gates."

"And if it goes wrong, have you decided what to do?"

"I'll do what I have to." And that sounds like my dad. But one way or another, Samara Archiva is going to breathe the open air before the next resting.

The door to the house opens and Jill steps out, looking us over. "Is this a party?"

She looks really pretty in the dark. The yellow hair and blue eyes stand out. And she's smiling like there's nothing wrong in the world.

"What are you doing up?" I snap.

She raises a brow. "Latrine. Problem?"

"No." I look away first.

"The bluedads come to the honeyfruit," Cyrus whispers.

I cut him a glance. I think he just said *You catch more flies with honey*, but I don't know if that was supposed to be advice to me or a warning about Jill. Jill has been on her very best behavior. No dousing herself with spray. Not even a wrinkled nose. She's been nice to the kids, made herself helpful to Annis, and Nathan is her extra limb.

I ought to be happy that she's acclimated. That her eyes are on Nathan and off me. I want her to be happy. I want to be happy for her. And if we'd been dropped off the ship straight into this house I would've been, and would've thought she was. But we weren't, and I just don't trust Jill anymore. Which makes me sad. And then mad.

Jill whispers, "Which way does the sunrise come, Cyrus?"

"Straight ahead," he says, pointing at a peak, the far barrier of the Outside.

Jillian smiles. "That will be beautiful, won't it?"

She moves off toward the back of the workshop and the latrines, and Cyrus shakes his head, his reply coming too late for her to hear.

"Not on a twelfth year." He turns his head to me. "You should eat. And then go."

I nod, though I'm not sure I can eat. My stomach is churning with nerves. But it feels better as soon as I get up and do something. I slip back into the staler warmth of the house, and when I'm grabbing my sandals in the light of the lantern, I notice the edge of the glasses sticking out just a little from beneath the bed pillow. There aren't any secrets in this house anymore, even with the technology, but I never leave the glasses in sight. Especially with the children around.

I put them on. Everything is the way I left it, except my charge is less than 25 percent. I don't know what I'm worried about. They won't work for anyone else. But I tie the glasses to my shirt lace anyway, and keep them next to my skin.

For the faithful of the NWSE, when the time comes we must act without hesitation and seize what is our birthright: the technology of Earth. For who could stand against the people of memory and Earth's technology? And when we, the best of the best, the worthy of Canaan, take what is ours, we will dare to fly back through the stars and take back our home. We will dare to build our new civilization. We will bring beauty, peace, prosperity, and, most of all, justice, and rule the Superior Earth.

FROM THE NOTEBOOK OF JANIS ATAN

47

SAMARA

I feel a sharp prick, a sting, and I open my eyes. Not the memory of my eyes, but my actual lids, fluttering at a new stab of pain that comes from the brightness of one dim light. When my vision adjusts I see my mother standing at the foot of a bed, Marcus Physicianson with her. Lian Archiva is straight-backed and elegant, her face as perfect as a well-polished stone, and Marcus sweeps a look over her that is pure reverence. A showing of emotion that would have surely brought a correction from my mother had she seen it. Or maybe it wouldn't have. Mother likes to be admired, and Marcus admires, I think, that she is standing there so calm, about to condemn her own daughter to death. Or worse than death.

Marcus must think she's strong. Principled. I feel nothing for either of them.

"It is time, Samara," she says, like I need to hurry and go to the learning room. I try my arms and my legs, and find that I can sit up. The blood rushes from my head and I close my eyes again, dizzy.

"She will still be somewhat medicated," Marcus whispers, "to keep her docile."

I don't think so, Marcus Physicianson. I think Reddix has been seeing to my medication, or lack of it, and there is not one docile thing about me at this moment.

I've had a long time to think about Reddix's words in my ear. A long time to plan what I will do. And there's a white sunrise coming.

I wonder what Lian and Marcus would do if they Knew Reddix means to have a boy from Earth come into the Forum and kill us all with Forgetting.

Mother comes around to the side of the bed and hands me a plate of bread and a glass of water. I drink the water in one go, and she pours me more. When I've eaten the bread, she helps me stand, taking me to the corner of my small, plain room, where there is a latrine with a composting box behind a curtain. She leaves me there, and I decide I do not want to consider how this has been handled while I've been sleeping.

I come from around the curtain and Mother says, "Come, darling. We will make you ready."

When I don't take her hand she reaches down and takes it herself, waits for Marcus to unlock the door, and leads me slowly down a long, narrow hall, past empty room after empty room. I'm in the medical section, a whole internal corridor I've never seen. Reddix said he had witnessed the deaths reserved for the condemned, and I think that must have been here, in this hidden back hall, not on the platform in the Forum. We've all seen the condemned die there. Except that they didn't, did they? After reading the notes of Janis Atan's experiments, I think I'm glad Reddix didn't tell me any more.

We wait for Marcus to unlock another door. My feet are bare, silent on the cold stone, a straight dress of white linen, thin and simple, like I've been in seclusion, swinging at my calves. Bumps rise up on my skin as we walk again, down the main corridor of the medical sector, though whether I'm chilled from the air or the touch of my mother's hand I'm not sure.

But I'm not going to protest. Not yet.

Mother lets me walk slowly, getting used to my legs, through the doorway to the back stairs, the ones that go to the parks. But we take the downward route, Marcus following for a long way, two levels below the Forum, until we are at the side entrance of the women's baths.

"You may leave us here. Thank you, Marcus," says my mother. "I don't think we'll have any trouble. Come, darling."

I follow her through the changing rooms, and already I can smell the heat. There is no help today. The city is being cleared, ready to be sealed for Judgment and the celebrations afterward, so we make our own way. Mother's heels click on the damp stone, past the few women still lounging in the hot pool, mist making halos around the lamps. The conversations slow and stop as we walk by, but Mother doesn't let go of my hand. She shuts the door to one of the private bathing cells, locks it; takes me to the raised, empty pool in the center of the room; and opens the sluice gate. A smooth ribbon of steaming water pours down.

"Let me help you in," Mother says. She unties the laces behind my neck, the linen dress falls to the floor, and she holds my hand while I climb up four stairs, then down four more and into the pool.

I shudder at the heat of the water. At my mother's touch. But I sit like she tells me, letting her work the tangles out of my hair, curl by curl, feeling her fingers wash my scalp, my eyes staring at the flame flickering near the ceiling while she rubs lotion into every strand. Memories prod and nudge, and I am a baby, crying while my hair is washed; then fingers are tugging, braiding, pulling my scalp, and then I'm arranging my curls. But none of these memories are of my mother, because my mother has never done any of this. *Not now,* I say to the memories, and their weight goes away.

I'm still in control. Like when I thought I was dead. But I wish I didn't have to remember this.

I'm biding my time. But it is difficult.

Mother wraps me in a soft white dressing gown, and we leave the baths and go down the corridors, causing one or two stares. But most of the Knowing are in their chambers, caching, preparing for Judgment, and soon I am in mine. To do the same. Two lamps burn in front of the terrace doors, and someone has started a fire in the brazier.

I have no memories of my mother being in this room, so seeing her reflection in the many mirrors is strange. She sits me on the stool at my dressing table and crosses quickly to the gold curtain, pulling it back to look at my clothes. "We will find what is best," she says. "You can be so beautiful when you take the trouble . . ."

I glance down, amazed that her subtle criticism still has the weakest of stings, and see that the drawer of my dressing table is slightly open. I look back in my memory, see the last time I sat here, painting my eyes, and for one moment I sink, plummet down, and Beckett is catching my hand and saying, "I understand." I feel an ache inside that is longing for him. But the drawer was definitely not open then.

Mother has her back to me, her eyes on the red dress that was for Reddix. I slide open the drawer, slowly, silently, aware that there are mirrors in every direction. And then I Know that my father loves me. At least a little. He will not save me, but he will give me a way out. Because inside my drawer is the knife that is supposed to hang on my mother's bedchamber wall. The knife that says "NWSE."

I'm not sure who I'm supposed to use it on.

48

BECKETT

Nathan squats beside the square hole in the floor of the supply hut, looking down the dark shaft. It's time, and my chest is slamming.

"Okay," I whisper. "Climb a little way down after I'm gone, so you won't be seen, but no more than halfway. Reddix is really good at Knowing when someone's there. Like a change in temperature, air, smell . . ."

I catch Nathan trying to sniff his shirt.

"It's not you," I say. "It's him. Just don't get caught on either end of the shaft, okay?"

The supervisors are all going Underneath, to be sealed in with the city, leaving the Outside free. But not every Outsider is a rebel.

"How about you just get going," is Nathan's answer.

I nod. "You know the way?"

"If it's what you told me, I do."

"Get the gate open. No matter what."

"Go already!"

I do. Down the rabbit hole. The smell comes, that odor that is spice and flowers and a little bit Samara, and then not. I stop my slow slide before I'm all the way down, and put on the glasses. Looking. And I swear in my head, or maybe it was out loud, because Reddix is

370 Sharon Cameron

already down there, turning toward the door as if he's heard a noise. We're both early. Both wanting to be first. And he wins.

I sigh and let the glasses drop down inside my shirt, next to the pouch Cyrus gave me to wear around my neck. There's a small, sealed bottle of white powder in the pouch, and a blue and green box with a lock of Sam's hair. Plus a note inside the box, telling me my name and how to get to Cyrus's house. And next to all of that is one of the crudely made knives, wrapped in cloth, hanging beneath my left arm and strapped to my chest. It's not a great knife, but it's sharp, and in the end, that's what matters.

I almost laugh. Here I am, sneaking into what has to be the holy grail of anthropology, a brand-new civilization, taking sides in a cultural conflict, with the direct intent of irrevocably changing everything I find. Jill was right all along. Nobody is ever, ever going to hire me.

But I'm going to do it. For her. And if I fail, then there's a good chance that one way or the other, from Forgetting or death, neither one of us is going to come out of this remembering anything.

I don't trust Reddix.

The hinges of the metal door grate as I reach the bottom of the shaft, and Reddix says, "Welcome to the city Underneath."

Whatever. I slide out, over Sam's shoes, still sitting partway up the shaft, and onto my feet. "Where's Samara?"

"Being prepared for Judgment. Are you prepared?"

"Are you?"

He chuckles, and it's the least funny sound I've ever heard. I can't see a thing without the glasses, and when he shuts the door, I hear something I shouldn't. An extra noise. Metal scraping on metal.

"Keep a hand out," Reddix says, "if you are not used to the dark . . ."

I let him get a few steps ahead, pull out the glasses and take a quick look at the door. He's put a thick metal pin through the latch.

Nathan is not coming through that, and there's not a thing I can do about it, not without Reddix hearing me. I'm cussing in my head again. I drop the glasses back into my shirt and follow him down the steps, his voice still coming soft through the black air.

"The city is almost clear of Outsiders and the gates will soon be shut. But there will still be a few of the Knowing in the corridors. We're going to walk quickly, as if you're my help. Keep three paces behind me, eyes lowered. Your face will be remembered, of course, and eventually they will Know that I was with someone who does not belong. But in just a little while, none of us will remember anything, will we?"

I don't answer. Four levels down and we are off the stairs, through a door and into one of the carpeted tunnels. I adjust my pace behind Reddix. The Knowing all tend to wear clothes that reflect and shimmer, I suppose because of all the lamplight. But Reddix is wearing pure black today, his eyes painted heavily to match, and he's wound black and silver strings through his braids. Two Knowing come walking together down the hall, and I keep my eyes down, but only until they pass. This place is a maze. I need to see where I'm going and memorize the way, or I won't get back to that door and all this will be over before it's even begun. I can hear my pulse in my ears.

We go down some stairs, along a corridor, and back up again, and I'm swearing so hard I think my lips are moving. He's taking me in circles. On purpose. But I know where I am. That was the entrance hall at the end of the corridor, with the soaring ceiling and marbled walls sloping up to the gates. I could get back to the kitchen stairs from there.

I have more of a memory than you think, Reddix Physicianson.

We go down one more level and take a right. This corridor is empty. Quiet. Reddix pauses, and when no one comes from either direction, he puts a key to a door on our left. There's an empty flat here, like Sam's uncle's, only instead of the river rushing beyond the room's double-paned doors, I can hear echoing voices. A crowd. I go to the doors, stand to one side to look beyond the edge of a damp curtain. The Forum. I suppose I knew there were more of the Knowing. But seeing them is different. There's a family below me, a father retying the ribbon on a child's hair braids.

"Wait until she is in the Forum," Reddix says. "If you cannot see her, wait until she steps up onto the platform for Judgment. Then go out onto the balcony and drop the Forgetting. There will be no need to speak."

Yes, I really think there will be a need for it. But when I glance back at Reddix, I see something that surprises me. Emotion. Raw. Like a thirsty man who smells water. He wants me to throw that bottle down.

"Do not give them time to hurt her, Earthling," he says. "They will, if they think justice might be thwarted. When the time comes, act quickly. Please."

He goes without another word. And he locks the door behind him, and I don't have a hairpin this time. I don't have anything.

I never can decide whether I pity or hate Reddix Physicianson more.

And if I don't work fast, this is going to go very badly.

49

SAMARA

Mother dresses me with care, arranging the red dress just so over one shoulder. She doesn't braid my hair, but gathers the top half high on my head, letting the ends hang down, tendrils escaping all around my face. It's not very proper at all, and maybe that's her point. If she could Know how well I'm caching my true feelings right now—and the memories this room brings me—she would be pleased. She would not be pleased to Know that her knife is now under the red dress, tied to my thigh with a scarf.

"Mother," I say. My voice sounds like the gristmill Outside. "Why did you choose Nita as our help?"

Mother puts a finger beneath my chin, tilting my head, and the soft paint across my eyelid is like a caress. "We Knew, of course, that she was from a family of rebels. But after my first disappointment, it was important to find out what kind of blood ran in my second child. The Wardens only create situations, darling, not the choices. And at some point, enough was enough, wasn't it?"

Disappointment. She means Adam. Her son, who she executed. Brutally. Like Nita. The hatred I've been caching blazes hot as Beckett's fire in the ruined city, and with it comes a grief so painful I have to dig a nail into my palm. But I breathe, tell my memories *Not now*, and I am back in control. But I will have to feel those things. Later.

My mother wipes the brush against the rim of the jar. "It is difficult being the judge of New Canaan," she begins, wiping the brush again. And again. "Choosing the chosen is not an easy task. I hope you realize that, Samara. Like the picture tiles. One cannot think only of a piece, even if the color and shape is beautiful. One must think of the beauty of the whole, decide which piece detracts from that, and then remove it."

Like Adam. Like me. But all I say aloud is, "Like Ava Administrator."

"Oh no, darling," says Mother. "Ava was very different. She had such an incredible mind, as did two of her children. Creative, problem solvers, traits the Knowing need to perfect. It was important to study them. For the good of us all."

This makes me so sick I'm having difficulty playing my part. "And this is why you closed the Archives, then," I whisper.

"Yes," she says. "Exactly so." I close my eyes while the eye brush runs slow across the other lid. "Our family profession was not as important as keeping minds focused . . ."

The minds you are forcing to be that way, I think.

". . . and it was a profession not strictly necessary for the building of a Superior Earth. And though most of the more . . . sensitive of the books had already been removed, bits of information were cropping up, and secrecy for the NWSE is key. It has been so since the First Warden, in the old city . . ."

"Janis Atan," I say.

She pauses her painting to look at me. "Perhaps I should have tried to bring you in early. It worked for Reddix. But it was such a mistake with your brother . . ." She shakes her intricately braided head. "People have always been too narrow-minded to see the vision, to understand the greater good. The writings of Janis Atan were rediscovered at a time when life in the old city had become impossible . . ."

Because of the Forgetting, I think.

"When one Forgetting tree was chopped down, four more would spring up to take its place. But her memories guided our path, and we became the Knowing, and built a new and more perfect city, just as the First Warden had conceived. And the judge was reinstated, removing what did not serve the whole, and now we are becoming what we were meant to be. The best of the best of the best . . ."

Which puts herself at the pinnacle of worthiness. I tilt my cheek to her paint.

". . . and now, very soon, we will be better still."

"And what are you going to do about Earth?"

"Oh, I won't have to do anything about Earth, darling. Earth will soon be weak, while I have ensured that the Knowing will always be at a place of strength."

"They want to take us back with them, Mother."

"They will not take us. We will take them. We will use their technology to fly back to our home, to fulfill our ultimate directive. And then will come the time for which the NWSE has waited nearly four hundred years. To build and rule the Superior Earth."

I only just keep from shaking my head. Mother and her little band of NWSE are not going to rule Earth. I wonder if Mother thinks Earth is a city, like New Canaan. Not a planet of billions.

I study the serenity of her face while she attends to the perfection of mine. I can't see anything inside her. Maybe this is what happens when you cache emotions for too long. Do they become hard to access? Get lost inside your mind? Maybe it's something like Forgetting after all.

I agree with Reddix. This has to be stopped. But not by killing us all. I think the Knowing need a choice. I have to keep Beckett from dropping that bottle. And my mother from having me killed before I can.

Mother steps back and looks at me with more approval than she ever has. "Come, darling," she says. "It is time."

50

BECKETT

I had to use the glasses and burn through the door lock. The beam is small and it took awhile, but my choices were limited. And I was sure to check all the metallic content this time, and not blow up the Underneath. I don't know where my charge went. The glasses are low, out of nowhere—just under 12 percent. I have to tear them off my face and run. There's no time to avoid anyone. Nathan has to get through that door so he can open the gates, and I have to get back into the Forum before Sam.

I sprint full-out down the corridor—the straight way, not the crazy route Reddix took me on—careening past a surprised mother with a baby strapped on her back, but there's no one else out. They're in the Forum. For Judgment. I don't slow when I hit the kitchen stairs.

Up, and up again, and now the lamps aren't lit. I have to use the glasses, and my breath is coming hard, a pain in my side. I burst through the door into the kitchens, through to the empty storage room. Only this storage room isn't empty. Crates and sacks are stacked high against the walls. I stand there, panting, stunned, swearing at full voice. I've missed the level. I don't know where I am. And I'm scared. That Nathan gave up and crawled back up the shaft, that I'm down here alone. That they're bringing Sam onto that platform.

I grab two handfuls of my hair, thinking, run up one more level, and this is the right kitchen, and this is the empty storage room, and my charge is 11 percent. What is draining the glasses? I knock the pin out of the latch and throw open the door. Nathan crawls out, sweating and not pleased.

"Took you long enough. What—"

"Go!" I yell.

He follows me as fast as he can in the dark, back down the steps, and I am counting the levels more carefully this time. I'm at 10 percent on the glasses. As soon as we hit the lamps, I jerk them off my face.

"There," I tell Nathan in the corridor, pointing left. "The way I told you. The main entrance to the Forum is opposite the gates, down the sloping hall. Do you understand?"

Nathan nods. He's already running. I look over my shoulder, at the way I came. I don't think I have time to get back to that empty flat and the safety of the terrace. I'm going to have to go right in among them.

I run down the hall, take the stairs on the left, the same way Sam took me the first time I came Underneath. There's a short tunnel at the bottom, and on the other side of it, rows of columns and braids and backs in shining cloth. I slow, panting, sliding down the wall until I can see the platform, high above the crowd, almost in front of me and a little to the left. And the people are silent, hushed over the rush of the river water. Waiting.

I put on the glasses and zoom them. The Head of Council, Thorne, with his long braids tied back and clipped beard, waits at the top of the steps, along with Craddock, who I watched flog a woodworker three days ago, and the other man who chased Sam in the ruined city. Thorne has called a name, an Administrator, and a teenage boy is now climbing the steps.

There are two tables on the platform, one with a tray stacked with syringes. Wellness injections. I watch rather than hear the boy's hiss when his goes in. On the other table, there is only one tray, one needle sitting in its center. I think I know what that one does. And it's for her. But I can't see her. I can't find her.

I shut the glasses again and wait, and it feels like my breathing should be echoing in the Forum. I watch feet shift as the next Administrator goes up. And then the next. Thirteen of them. We're doing this in alphabetical order. And then Thorne calls out, "Archiva, Samara."

She's in shimmering red, her hair half up and half down and all over her head. I slide on the glasses and zoom. A woman I think must be Sam's mother hands her up the first three steps, tall, with white braids piled high and an expression that is . . . nothing. And then Samara goes on alone. She looks back once over her shoulder, scanning the crowd, and I know she can't see me, but it's like her eyes gaze right into mine, and I feel it, hard inside my chest.

She is so beautiful, but I know that look. She's decided. Fearless. I don't think she's going down without a fight. And the thought of what they are minutes away from doing to her takes my fear away, too. I'm not even nervous. I'm just mad.

I drop the glasses back down my shirt and take the vial of white powder out of the pouch. One deep breath, and with the bottle in my fist, I step out of the tunnel and into the Knowing.

51

SAMARA

I listen to the tap of my shoes against each step of black rock, the Torrens gushing through its channel behind the platform, the painted history of my people stretching upward before my eyes. They're waiting for me up there, and I think somewhere behind me in the silence is Beckett Rodriguez. I can feel his eyes. I look back once, but below me is a still sea of color. The rest is in shadow.

I'll have to move fast, before Beckett does, and I don't Know how it will end. Maybe not well. Maybe well enough for him to get away without killing us all. Maybe not well enough for me to get away without being killed. I watch Thorne's serious face rise above the edge of the platform, Marcus and Craddock behind him, and then I am standing on the platform, too. We look at each other, and Thorne opens his mouth to speak.

And then I kick over the table of syringes, and both tables go down in a scatter of rolling needles. While Marcus and Craddock are reacting to that, I step behind Thorne, stab the back of his knee with my sharp heel, and when he stumbles, I grab his long hair and jerk it downward. His knees hit the stone, and the knife that was against my thigh is now at his throat. Thorne goes still, his bearded chin up, hands half lifted in the air.

I think someone screamed. I can hear the last of the echo fading in the returning silence. Reddix has run halfway up the steps, and I see a smile lurking in the corner of his mouth, full of despair. My mother is just behind him, face hard and cold, but when I find my father, standing far down at the base of the platform among the startled Council, he gives me the tiniest of nods.

"Tell them to open the gates," I say to Thorne. And then I yell it. "Open the gates!"

He shuts his mouth tight, and I feel him go calm in my grip. Caching. I look to the rest of the NWSE, but they are not going to move or try to save him. I turn Thorne to face the crowd, the knife tight against his skin.

"People of the Underneath," I shout, "you have a choice. Starting right now. If there is one of you who has had a family member condemned, a child end their life, one of you who would prefer not to live with your memories anymore, then go and open the gates of our city and let the Outside in. You do not have to live as one of the—"

"Stop!"

The voice cuts through the Forum, cuts across my words, and it's only then that I see Craddock pause in his move toward me. He has a syringe in his hand, and I'm not sure whether it's the kind that kills me or puts me to sleep or makes me well. We both look down from the platform. The people are parting, making an open circle around a shirt of undyed cloth. He's leaner than when I saw him last, harder, his black hair longer, and in this complete mess we're both standing in, he smiles at me once, and that smile is his gift. He holds out his hand, and there's a bottle in it.

"This city," Beckett says, his words sharp and clipped, "belongs to the Outside."

52

BECKETT

She's standing up there with a knife to Thorne's throat, looking at me like I'm the only thing in the world. I want to grab her and run. But it's not time. Not yet. I need the Outsiders in here first. If Nathan got the gate open.

"Stay back," I say, holding out the bottle to the Knowing around me, and then a thrum goes through the rock beneath my feet, a ripple of motion that comes and is gone. I see the flinch in the crowd, a murmur and turning of heads. I don't know what that was, and there's no time to think about it.

"This is Forgetting . . ." I let my voice echo. "If I drop this bottle, then all of you, everyone in this room, will Forget everything you've ever Known."

"Don't!" Sam yells. "Beck, do not drop that bottle . . ." At the same time, Reddix says, "Do it! Now!"

I can tell which ones belong to their little sect by their reactions. Craddock and the other man on the platform stare hard at Reddix, like they're trying to understand what he's up to, and there's another group huddled at the bottom of the steps, eyes narrowed at the bottle in my hand. But the rest of the Knowing are just confused, and Sam is a little tight with that knife. There's a drop of blood running down Thorne's neck.

"The city belongs to the Outside," I say again, loud enough for all of them to hear, and I really hope it's true and that the Outsiders are coming in through the hall. I need them. Now. "Your gates are already open"—please let this be true—"and the Outsiders will discuss the peaceful transition to a government chosen by both—"

"No." The woman who I think is Lian Archiva, Sam's mother, steps forward.

"Beckett!" Sam shouts. "You were right, they don't have to be—"

"No," Lian says again. And another ripple of movement shakes the rock, this time with the lowest rumble. And then there are voices calling in the entrance hall. Finally.

Lian takes another step. "This city was built by the Knowing, and to the Knowing it belongs. This is not your fight, Earthling."

Okay, so we're out in the open with that. I smile at her. "And you," I say, "are not in a position to dictate the rules any . . ."

Or maybe she is. Because that's a twenty-fifth-century katana laser she's got in her palm. From the *Centauri II*.

And a lot of things happen at once. I duck beneath the beam of light and run forward, and there's screaming, probably because Lian has just sliced someone to pieces behind me. Those things were outlawed for a reason. I knock straight into her, the Forgetting bottle tight in my hand, and the laser stops, the katana rolling out of her grip, the foot of a man with long gray ropes of hair kicking it out of her reach. The stone beneath us thrums, and thrums again, setting up a rhythm. And then I realize that some of the screaming is Samara.

I've started up the stairs before I even know what's happening to her. Thorne is on his knees, hand to his throat, and Sam's had to let him go because Craddock is after her again with that needle. Reddix gets there before me, though, knocking the syringe from Craddock's hand while Sam holds off the other NWSE member with the knife. Then Reddix sees me, and his expression changes. And not only is there no calm face of Canaan, he is furious. Insanely mad. Sam yells my name, and then he's coming for me.

But it's not really me he wants. He wants what's in my hand, and he's not fussy about how he gets it. I land hard on my back, where I can feel the new rhythm in the stone, and we are grappling over the bottle in my fingers. Reddix digs an elbow into my arm, trying to get me to open my hand, and then Sam's knife appears at the base of his throat. He goes still.

"Don't move, Marcus!" she shouts at the other man. Both he and Craddock go still.

Reddix looks straight down at me and I can see the crazy in his eyes. He pushes with his elbow, even though it's making the blade dig into his neck like Thorne, and Sam is begging, "No! Please, Reddix! No!"

My hand opens like a flower. Reddix grabs the bottle and smashes it onto the platform beneath his palm, a puff of white dust rising between his fingers. Sam screams.

I have a sense of chaos, not just in my own sphere, but all around me, echoing across the cavern. Fighting. Yelling. The Outsiders are here. The floor is thrumming, and someone is saying "Earth."

And nothing happens.

"Sam," I say. "Sam!" I get her painted eyes to look at me from beyond Reddix's shoulder. "It was sand. Only sand." From the workshop. In a tiny bottle blown by Cyrus, sealed with the same color wax. "If you want to Forget, I have the real thing, and I'll help you. But you get to choose, and so do the rest of them."

Sam blinks, and then she eases the knife from Reddix's throat. He sits up, his crazed expression gone blank, his palm running red and sparkling with glass. I scramble out from under him, get to my feet, while Sam yells, "Stay away from me, Marcus!" The other man, Marcus, steps back again, hands up. I hold out a hand and Samara is at my side, and then we both have knives, though hers is a little bloody.

Reddix steps back, toward the mural. One or two small rocks are falling down into the Torrens behind him, the platform pulsing beneath my feet, and when I look over my shoulder, Thorne and Craddock are gone, and there is a roiling, fighting mass of dyed and undyed cloth below us. But Reddix only has eyes for Samara.

"You heard me?" he asks. "Everything I said?"

"Yes," Sam replies. "I heard everything."

The man Sam called Marcus is still standing to one side. "Reddix," he says, moving forward. "Why . . ." But Reddix holds out a hand, takes another huge step back. Marcus stops. Reddix is only looking at Sam.

"And you're going to remember it now," Reddix whispers.

"Yes. But you have to stop. You don't have to be . . ."

And then his eyes go wide, a little surprised. And Lian Archiva steps from behind Reddix, pulling a needle out of his arm.

And his face relaxes. Relieved. Happy. He smiles, steps back again, opening his arms. Marcus yells like the needle just went in him. Then Lian gives Reddix a little push and he falls off the edge, down into the churning dark of the Torrens.

Sam looks up at me, opens her mouth to speak, and a rock falls five centimeters from her head. I look around us. What's happening? I've been on an adrenaline rush ever since that laser came at my head, but now I slow, listen. And then I know what I'm feeling. Understand the rhythm that has been below my feet. I grab Sam's bare arms.

"Sam! It's—"

And a boom shakes the world and knocks me off my feet.

SAMARA

Beckett is still wiping the dust from his eyes when I push myself upright. My ears are dulled, ringing, but I can hear the crescendo of shouts. Cries. Some of it fear, and some of it injury. One wall of the cavern has partially tumbled in, two columns fallen, choking the Torrens, and a great crack has opened in the mural wall, like a wound between Earth and Canaan.

Then Beckett has me by the hand, pulling me to my feet. "Run," he says. "Run!"

And we do, down the steps of the platform through the haze, and I can't see my mother or father, or any of the Noble Wardens, just dazed faces and blood on both kinds of cloth. I look back, but my hand is firm in Beckett's, and he is sprinting across the Forum, up the wide stairs to the entrance hall, running with people who are trying to get out, and against a steady stream of others trying to get in. Nobody seems to know which is better. Outside or Underneath. We run up the sloping floor, gain the gates, and then we stop, and my hand lifts to my mouth, so I cannot scream.

The sky is made of metal, a ceiling of pale white with lights that are bright and false, blinking, flashing down against panicking people and wooden walls. The ground pulses beneath my feet, and then I see the gap in the mountains, a missing peak in the surrounding circle. Ugly, like a broken tooth, an orange glow around it that is not the sunrising. Rock has been flying, pebbles and dust, small boulders tossed where they shouldn't be, and I can smell the fire in the wind. I look at Beckett.

"You said they couldn't see us. You said they couldn't find us!"

He doesn't answer, just stares at the surroundings with a jaw that is set, his breath coming hard from between his teeth. He jerks the glasses from inside his shirt and puts them on, eyes moving in that odd way, rips them off again, drops the knife and turns to me, taking my face in both his hands.

"Sam, you listen to me. You do not get on that ship. No matter what. You fight. You run. You do whatever you have to. You don't get on the ship. Do you understand?"

I look at the expanse of metal. I didn't Know his Earth could explode mountains. I didn't Know my mother had technology that would cut people up with light.

"I'm sorry," he whispers. "I'm so sorry."

And in the middle of all this chaos, for one long moment, all I can think is how he is not a memory. Not even a dream.

"You came for me," I say.

"Of course I did."

"Beckett!"

We both turn, and it's Nathan, running through the gates, Grandpapa behind him.

"Are you okay?" he asks both of us, though he steps back from me. Nathan's never seen me dressed like the Knowing. Grandpapa kisses my head.

"Where's Annis?" I ask.

"I don't know," Grandpapa replies. His voice sounds shaky. "She was on the cameras above the gates . . ."

"Where is Jill?" This question comes from Beckett, and the intensity of it brings my gaze back to him.

"At the house," Nathan replies. "With the kids." He looks behind him at the missing mountain. "They're well away from—"

"Don't you get it?" Beckett yells. "They're coming!" There's a whoosh through the air, up high, and a sudden burst of wind. "Get some help and guard this gate," Beckett says. "Get the Outsiders in. As many as you can. But the first person you see who's dressed wrong, talks wrong, like me, then you have to shut yourselves in, do you understand? They'll have weapons, but they won't want to kill. But all of you, you stay off that ship, whatever you have to do . . ."

"Beck," I say, "where are you going?"

"To get the kids. I'll bring them straight back here . . ."

"What about Jill?" Nathan says.

"Oh, I'm looking for her, too. Sam, stay with Nathan . . ."

"No. The wounded," I tell him. "Underneath. I'm needed."

I see his chest heaving. And then Beckett takes my head and kisses me once, hard. *"Yuàn dé yī rén xīn, bái shǒu bù xiāng lí,"* he says, his lips still against mine. I kiss him one time more, and he knows my answer.

"I'm coming with you," Grandpapa says, but Beckett shakes his head.

"Let me go. I know what they're capable of . . ." He glances upward, picking up his dropped knife and tucking it back somewhere beneath his shirt. "I'll be right back. But there's some who still might want to kill her down there, and I don't know where they are. Don't leave her alone!"

Grandpapa nods, and then Beckett takes off, fast, into the thrumming world of metal and flashing lights that looks nothing like the Outside to me. Grandpapa watches him go, and then he stares at what isn't the sky. I think he's crying. And then I find Nathan's gaze on me.

"Did she do this?" he asks. His voice has pain in it that I don't understand. "Did Jill do this to us?"

He means the ship above New Canaan. The broken mountain. The group of bodies in the street. The bloody people moving Underneath. I don't Know what Jill did, and only now am I thinking of Beckett's rules, the ones he was afraid of, that he broke so many times. For me. And with my lips still hot from his kiss, only now am I as afraid as I should be. Because I don't Know what will happen to Beckett Rodriguez if Earth finds him first.

54

BECKETT

I run through the streets, yelling at every face I see that Earth has come, to get to the gates and go Underneath. The air bikes are up there, I can feel the wind. It smells like burning roof thatch, and the blood is pumping loud through my ears. Jillian. She did this. The evidence was right there in the glasses, if I'd taken time to see. A simple switch to "transmit." When did Commander Faye think to add Jill's DNA to the security program of the glasses? How long has she been sitting there in the *Centauri*, like the fat spider she is, waiting for Jill to realize it, and for me to be so stupid as to never think of such a simple move? Probably since the last time I had a signal. In the cave, or just outside of it.

I'm so mad it's hard to see straight.

I'll bet the Commander fired that shot to scare them, to rattle the pretech locals, never considering what heat does to some of the metal-infused rock around here. She's going to be merciful, mostly. She's getting paid by the head. But I'm not letting one local onto that ship. Not if I can help it. And then, two turns away from the workshop, I see a blond head hurrying down a cross street. And there's no undyed cloth. She's back in the jumpsuit.

"Hey," I shout. "Hey!"

Jillian looks over her shoulder, her blue eyes wide, and then she sprints away. Great. I go after her.

"Did you get what you wanted?" I yell. She looks back, but she doesn't slow. "Is this what you planned? The dead are in the streets, Jill! And Underneath . . ."

She looks scared of me. She ought to be. I'm gaining on her. Jill darts around a corner, the turn to the Bartering Square, and when I round the same corner I go flying, landing hard on my chest, smashing the glasses and cracking the case with Sam's hair. Cutting my side with the tip of the knife. I've tripped over Jill's outstretched foot, and now there are more feet, Earth-issued boots all around my head, stunsticks poking into my back.

"No, Beckett," Jillian says somewhere above me. "This isn't what I wanted. It's just what has to be."

55

SAMARA

I pull the stitches tight on a crying woman's scalp while Grandpapa holds her arms, keeping her still. What I'm really doing is trying to cache. I'm so much better at caching than I used to be, since I spent all that time in my head. And now, it's still not good enough.

The Knowing my mother killed when she missed Beckett with her technology were from the same Engineering family, all three sliced nearly in half, the mess already covered by one of the tablecloths from what was supposed to be our celebratory feast. I thought I was used to blood. I was wrong, and I cannot cache it.

The weapon my mother used is missing, as is every member of the NWSE, and I have the constant feeling of someone just behind my back, ready to put a needle in my arm. Force amrita down my throat. I can't cache this, either.

And then this woman's tears are making me angry, because Earth saw fit to send half a mountain sailing through the roof of her house, killing her daughter, and I am sick with fear because Annis hasn't come, the children haven't come, and neither has Beckett. Why did we let him run off by himself? Because we thought he could handle that ship in the sky? Because Earth was his responsibility? I pull the last stitch and my insides are saying *wrong, wrong*. He should have been back by now. It's wrong . . .

I jump at a tap on my shoulder. It's Priscilla, one of the four Physiciansons I found to help with the wounded, this one being Reddix's cousin. When I first came back into the Forum, I decided not to mention to Priscilla that being surrounded by the injured, the Physiciansons really might have thought of using their medical skills before I suggested it. And she decided not to mention that I was just nearly condemned and held a knife to the throat of our Head of Council. I can't tell if she's upset by what happened to Reddix, but she's been willing to heal everyone, no matter which kind of cloth they're wearing, and for now, that's good enough for me.

"Mama wants me to ask if there are any more wounded coming up."

I scan the room. "No, I think the rest can stay down here. How many are in the medical rooms?"

"Twenty-two, three Knowing and nineteen Outsiders. Six are critical. All Outsiders."

The Knowing are going to heal quickly, I think. But why shouldn't the Outsiders as well? I look up to the platform, then take the steps fast. Wellness injections lie scattered over the stone, jiggling with each pulsing thrum from the Earth ship above us. I'll bet they're tainted with Forgetting. Every last one of them. Maybe there's a Chemist somewhere in here who would Know . . .

And then I nearly scream. Marcus Physicianson is rising to his feet from behind one of the overturned tables. His face is calm, expressionless. Like the Knowing should be. But his eyes aren't. Black paint runs down his face from the corners, and he lifts a dull stare to me.

"He wanted to Forget," Marcus says.

"No, he didn't," I tell him. "Reddix wanted to die. He wanted all of us to die, all the Knowing, including you. That was his plan."

Marcus blinks, frowns, turns his running eyes back to the cracked mural, to the roar of the Torrens. "But how could he have done that?"

And then I feel the tug of memory, insistent, and I don't resist, because this is a connecting thread. Something my mind is telling me I should see. I let myself fall . . .

And I am reading the medical notes of Janis Atan, looking at the three jagged edges, where the pages have been torn out . . .

And I fall again . . .

. . . into Uncle Towlend's deserted office, and the pages he found in the map book are lying on the floor stones, where Reddix must have seen them . . .

Then the floor gives way . . .

. . . and I am on the platform of the Forum again, and Thorne's neck is warm beneath my knife, and Beckett is below me, holding up the bottle of sand they think is Forgetting. But it's my mother's face I watch carefully now. She isn't frightened by that bottle. None of the NWSE are . . .

And now I Know. Why Marcus didn't understand Reddix's plan. Why Mother made all of the Knowing immune. Because Mother doesn't Know what immunity does. Did Uncle Towlend never show her those pages after he found them, hidden in the front niche of the map book? He should have. We're Archivas. But Aunt Letitia was gone not long after that, and then the Archives closed. Maybe Reddix and I are the only ones to have read those pages since my uncle and Janis Atan.

I rise through my mind and open my eyes. And Marcus Physicianson is only a meter away from my face, a knife in his hand, the one I dropped, with "NWSE" engraved on the blade.

"It was because of you, wasn't it?" he says. There's no calmness to him now. "It was because of you . . ."

He jumps forward, I leap back, and then he drops to the platform like a stone. Because he's been hit with one. I look up and find Angela, Michael's mother, with a piece of rubble in her hand.

"Cyrus said you weren't supposed to be alone," she says, a little shocked. I glance down. Marcus is breathing, but he's not moving. And I'm shaking. I look up again.

"Where's Michael?"

"With his father." She nods her head toward the crowded Forum, and the foolish thought that comes into my head is that now Angela must know I'm from Underneath. I suppose she always did. She says, "You did something to him, didn't you?"

I think she means Michael. I don't Know what to say.

"You fixed him, didn't you?"

I nod.

"Thank you." We look at each other. "You go on. I'll take care of this."

"Make sure Michael rests," I say. I step away. I'm not sure what "taking care of this" means, but it might have something to do with Marcus and the Torrens. And then I move quicker, because Annis is coming down the steps from the entrance hall, Jasmina on her hip, Ari and Luc holding hands just behind her. I meet her halfway across the Forum and hug her until Jasmina protests.

"Where's Beckett?" I ask.

Annis frowns. "I don't know."

"Didn't he get the children?"

"No, I did. Do you know where Nathan is?"

"He was on the gates. Isn't he there?"

"No."

Annis meets my gaze, and then I hear an echoing boom in the Forum. But this is a familiar sound. Metallic and final, a noise I can feel deep in my insides. The gates are shut, and it won't be safe to open them again. Not until Earth is gone, or three days after the white sunrise.

And we are not all inside.

BECKETT

I don't know," I reply. What I do know is to expect the fist in my gut as a reward for my nonanswer. I cough hard, and it takes a few agonizing seconds to get my breath back.

"So let's try again," says Commander Juniper Faye. "What kind of weapons do the locals have?"

We've been "trying again" for a lot longer than either one of us would like. My back is against the stained and pitted post in the center of the Bartering Square, hands cuffed behind me on the other side, facing a squad of about twenty-five soldiers, Faye's inner circle. Jillian is here, and her mother, Vesta, standing in front of the water clock tower, and if they'd just turn their heads and look all the way back into the window of the potter's workshop, they'd see that Nathan is with us, too. Watching. When I give an unsatisfactory answer, I get fists. When I take too long to speak at all, it's the stunsticks.

And now I've taken too long, and I get two of them. One in the neck and one in the knee. The stunsticks are "humane" because they won't leave an injury or even a mark. What they will do is stimulate my nerves to excruciating pain. There's no way not to yell, and when they take them away, I feel blood on my hands. I pulled so hard I've cut my wrists on the cuffs. I blink, panting. When they move up to three, I might start making things up.

"All right. Again," says the Commander. "What kind of weapons . . ."

"Jill," I say, my voice hoarse from yelling, "what did you do with the kids?" Vesta tightens an arm around her daughter. She seems to think I'm getting what I deserve, but Jill's face is a blank wall. "Where are they?" I shout. If she handed them over, I'm going to break out of these cuffs and kill her. As soon as I can stand upright.

Vesta shakes her head, but Jill decides to answer. "They're with Irene next door."

Juniper Faye clicks her tongue. "Oh, Rodriguez. Why couldn't you have been more like her?" She nods her head at Jill. "She gave us a map that is going to be very useful going door to door . . ."

All those trips with Nathan to the orchard groves, high on the mountainside. A perfect aerial view. And I'll bet she showed Nathan the cartographer. Jill won't look at me.

"But like father, like son, I suppose. He tried to blow up my ship. And what have you been up to?"

She fingers my rough cloth. I'm so desperate to know about Mom and Dad it hurts, but asking won't change anything, and I won't give her the satisfaction. "You know exactly what I've been up to. Because you've already uploaded all of my files."

Faye smiles. "True. Very interesting viewing, some of that. But your data was a little thin on weaponry. Let's stop playing. You do understand that it doesn't matter what she did with whoever's children? We're taking all of them with us. And as soon as we have them all, this place will be razed to the bare ground. People assimilate so much better when there's no home to go back to. Or haven't you learned that in your history lessons, young professor?"

I don't say anything.

"They're outgunned no matter what, Rodriguez. Your information only saves lives at this point."

Lives she's getting paid for.

"So," the Commander says, "we have a power source, but we can't see. Why do you think that it is? That we couldn't see this city?"

"Rock," I say, hoping to gain a few seconds before the next blow. "It interferes with communications. And I guess you noticed it explodes."

She's losing her temper. "What kind of weapons are these locals holding? How much have they got of the *Centauri II*?" But instead of waiting for my lack of an answer, she holds up a finger, listening to her earpiece. Then she says, "Finchley, turn your soldiers."

The squad spins a one-eighty like they were one person. And then I see why. There's a group of people entering the Bartering Square. Eight of them. Thorne, Craddock, Lian Archiva, the man with the long ropes of hair who kicked away the katana. Everyone I saw huddled together at the base of the platform. The NWSE, walking with the serenity and elegance that is their trademark. It makes Juniper Faye look like she's the one who's pretech.

I'm kind of doubting this is a rescue mission.

Sam's mother stops in front of Faye, and the two women size each other up. Lian Archiva is willowy, her white hair in complicated braids, clothes glistening weirdly under the lights of the ship. Faye is set heavier, feet apart, poofed hair bobbed, and with a badge on her sleeve. She looks like she could win if this showdown came to fists. I'm not sure who would win the contest of cruel.

"I have no objection to you doing whatever you wish with this young man," Lian says, her accent particularly smooth against the sound of Earth. "But if you have a question, then why not ask it directly? Your source will be so much better."

She smiles, and Commander Faye smiles. "And who are you?"

"I am the judge of New Canaan."

"Oh, really?" Faye is unimpressed. "Well, since I doubt you came out here to offer up helpful information, it seems more likely you have something you want to say."

Lian stands a little straighter, her face a Knowing mask. "The city of New Canaan wishes to surrender to you without further loss of life." I watch the Commander's eyebrows go up. I think mine are up, too. "Under certain conditions."

"Which are?"

"That you remove your ship from over our city"—Faye looks skeptical at the word "city"—"and that we be allowed to formalize our agreement in the proper way. In the meeting place of old, in the city of our ancestors. At sunrise. That is the way these things should be done."

"And why should I agree to that?"

"Because otherwise," Lian replies, "my people will fight. We will not win. We will merely decrease our numbers. And this, I think, is something you might wish to avoid."

The rest of the Knowing are as expressionless as always, but the Commander looks like somebody just told her it was her birthday. I think again about what would happen if the minds of the Knowing came to Earth, what use they would be put to. Faye doesn't have a clue how big this prize really is. She's also getting taken. The Knowing don't have any way of getting back to the old city by sunrise. Not on foot. The sun, and the twelve-year comet, must be only three, four hours away. A rosy pink is blushing over the sky. Or what I can see of it from under the ship.

Lian goes on. "I also require that your ship be left half a kilometer away, and that the old city be entered without technology." Faye's eyes narrow at that. "And that seventy-five of your protectors be present. At least. That is the proper way."

Now the Commander is really confused. "And who will be present on your side?"

"As you see." She waves a hand across the group of Knowing. "And my last request is . . . him."

Everyone looks at me. I can feel my face swelling, bruises hot beneath my skin.

"He must be present for our negotiations."

Commander Faye laughs at that, whether about me or the word "negotiations," I'm not sure. What did Lian Archiva see in the Forum? That I love her daughter? That her daughter loves me? Whatever it is, I think I'm about to feel her revenge as well as the Commander's.

"One question," says Faye, casually. "What happened to the *Centauri II*?"

"Do you mean another ship from Earth?" Lian feigns a look of innocence, and it doesn't really work for her. "I have heard stories about a ship that came here once. And flew away again."

"Flew away again," repeats Faye.

"I believe so. I believe they left a . . . base camp. If those are your words. But this would have been long before my time. Do you accept our terms of surrender?"

"I accept the terms," Faye says. She's not hiding her glee. She nods at Finchley, and he surrounds Lian and her Knowing with half the squad. "Oh, I'm sorry . . ." The Commander also feigns a look of innocence. It doesn't really work for her, either. "You didn't think we were going to meet you there, did you? You're invited to be my guests until that time. And we'll make sure you can instruct your people not to fight, and tell them all about what happens next. Don't worry about a thing."

"The Knowing of New Canaan do not worry, Earthling," says Lian. "And my people have their instructions. Now if you were not to move your ship, as we agreed, or if you were to return to this city without us, or not arrive with the required numbers, well . . ." She tilts her head graciously, a pleasant smile on her face.

Faye doesn't know what to make of this. She has no idea what she's dealing with. Five minutes on the wrong part of the *Centauri* and the Knowing will be flying the thing. Not that I'm going to be the one to tell the Commander that. I don't know what Lian's game is, either, except for one thing: She's getting exactly what she wants.

And that gives me a bad, wrong feeling beneath my bruises.

57

SAMARA

I hold up a yellow lamp in the empty storage room, looking at the shaft that leads to the Outside. I've got a resin pot, ready to seal the metal door, for safety from the sunrise and the air Outside. Safety from Earth is not an option. If Earth decides to come Underneath, then they will come. Here, or through the gates, or by blowing their own doorway through the mountain. The Forgetting might get some of them. But sealing this door means that no one will be able to come back through it. And both Nathan and Beckett have not come back.

Something is wrong. I Know it.

And then I feel a change in the rolling hum of a heartbeat beneath my feet, in the noise of the ship hanging over us. The intensity is weaker, the rhythm slightly slowed. And slowing. And there's a bump against the other side of the metal door. I step back as it swings open, and Nathan's sandals are followed by Nathan, sooty and grim-faced.

"What happened to you?" I think I just shouted.

"Jill happened, that's what . . ." Then another pair of feet comes down the shaft, a woman's, and another set of bare and dirty soles right on top of her head, knocking a shoe out of the shaft that I realize is mine.

"Where's Beckett?"

"They've got him."

I stand where I am. They have Beckett. I don't believe it. Even though I Knew it. Deep down. "Is he on the ship?" I whisper.

"Yes." Nathan helps an old man out of the shaft. "It's moving off, but there's still a lot of Earthlings out there, rounding up everyone they can find. They're on these . . . things, I don't know what to call them. They're like technology you can sit on and they fly the Earthlings around. You can't outrun them. You can only hide . . ."

I listen to him talk, about Earth and the Commander, what he saw her do to Beckett. And Lian Archiva. Surrendering. With terms. And I feel the world slowing, heavy with memory, and I sink as soon as it pulls, down, where . . .

My mother's voice is saying, "Earth will soon be weak, while I have ensured that the Knowing will always be at a place of strength . . ."

And I fall again, to the day of my Judgment . . .

"You have shared our most precious weapon . . ."

I rise back to the present, and Nathan is shutting the door after the last Outsider to come down the shaft. Waiting for me to come back.

"You're sure my mother said sunrise?" I say. "In the old city? And that she's bringing Beckett with them?"

"Yes. I saw them taken up to the ship. On one of those flying things, only bigger . . ."

"And the ship is gone?" There's no hum beneath my feet now. Nothing.

"I watched it go."

I breathe, and breathe again. She's tricked them. My mother tricked them. She's lured Earth into the Cursed City, where the Knowing have their weapon: the Forgetting. And Beckett will Forget, like everyone else from Earth. But she's tricked herself as well. Because my mother made them immune, and now the Forgetting is going to kill every last one of them. All the NWSE.

"Nathan, was my father there?"

"What does he look like?"

Never mind. I'm sure that he was. I don't understand Sampson Archiva. Whether he's with or against my mother. There's not one thing in my world I truly understand right now.

Nathan is standing there, waiting for me to do . . . something, the group of Outsiders standing bunched by the door. They're wide-eyed—shaking, some of them. They don't know where they are or where they're going. Not any more than I do. And they are afraid. Of me.

And the rage that has lived inside me since Nita, since Adam, flares. Blazes. Explodes. I can feel the heat in my head and in my chest. Everyone is wrong. Earth. The Knowing. Everyone has blood on their hands. And that woman—the Commander—and my mother, think they can have Beckett Rodriguez? I don't think so.

I take Nathan's arms, look him in the face, and start talking fast. "Seal this door. The resin is right there. Make it so that no air can come in, then do the same with the gates. Do you understand?"

"But—"

"The Forgetting is coming. With the white sunrise. It's in the air. Tell Grandpapa that everything has to be sealed before the sky turns white, and it has to stay that way for three full days."

"Where are you going?"

"Three days, Nathan! Do you understand?"

Nathan sighs, and his eyes are so sad. "You can't get him back. Not any more than I can get her."

Watch me.

"Wait," he says. "Wait . . ."

I give him one quick, hard hug, and then I throw open the metal door, and start up the tunnel. Any doubts I had are a pile of ash.

Beckett Rodriguez came for me, and now I am coming for him.

And I have no idea what I'm going to do when I get there.

58

BECKETT

I sit still while Dr. Lanik cleans me up. It's disorienting, being back on the *Centauri*. Another rabbit hole. Except this time it was up through the air instead of down through a hole in the ground, into a world that's bright, clean, and completely unreal. Even the air smells fake.

Lanik and I haven't talked so far. We have company, armed company, keeping watch from the door, and I don't know on which side of all this the doctor lands. He's gotten rid of my pain, and I can feel the swelling going down around my eyes. When he leans close to clean the cut on my side, I gamble, and whisper, "Mom and Dad?"

I see one finger go up while he gets ready to close the cut. He looks over his shoulder once, and the armed soldier whose name I don't know gives him a brief nod.

"He's a friend," whispers Lanik, "and we only have a minute, so let's keep this to essentials. Sean and Joanna are confined to quarters. Faye's been waiting for you before starting their punishment."

So they're fine, but not for long.

Then he asks, "What's happening on the surface?"

I glance at the guard, who's looking the other way, and at the windows, where military uniforms are passing back and forth. Dr. Lanik moves his body, sealing my cut, but also blocking my face from view.

I look up at the ceiling and say beneath my breath, "Faye is rounding up locals. They've surrendered, but on conditions that the formal surrender happen in the old city at sunrise."

"The advantage?"

"Don't know. But there is one." Lanik straightens and starts working on the cuts on my wrists. "How many are you?" I breathe. I mean on Dad's side, and he gets it.

"Thirty that Faye doesn't know about. And growing."

"A condition of surrender was seventy-five military present in the city. And me."

The doctor's gaze flicks upward. That's more than half the ship when you take away who's already confined. "Good to know," he whispers.

A discreet cough from the guard shuts us up. But when I'm patched and back in a jumpsuit, I get another very quiet "Careful out there" from Lanik. I nod.

"We're headed straight to transport," says the guard, being a little overly official. "Launching to the surface in twelve."

I know I've been away a long time when I get to the door of the med center and reach out for a latch. How stupid, I think, that we can't even open our own doors. And the light in here is hurting my eyes. It'll be good to go back out to the dark, even if it's almost sunrise. I wish I could show all this to Sam, though. She'd like the med center.

It was a hard-won, terrible half hour, but I'm glad I got to see her again. I don't want to see her again if she's caught, forced to Earth with a value on her head.

I think it would be better not to survive than to come back on board this ship.

59

SAMARA

When I hear the walking patrol coming, I slip back into the shaft in the dark supply hut. Assuming their technology is like Beckett's, they can't see me when I'm below the surface. I wait them out. The patrol is so quick and regular it only took me a few minutes to work out their pattern, just a little longer for the whooshing noises passing overhead. Air bikes, that's what I heard Jillian call them in the rubble mound.

I want one.

I've watched them land and take off twice now, a strange kind of handled chair that you straddle. There seems to be a regular stop in front of the gates. I go through my memories. Leaning to the front to land, leaning back to take off, both accompanied by a twist of both wrists on the handles, forward for speed, back for slowing. It might be all I have time to Know. The white sunrise is coming.

I hear the whoosh above my head that I was waiting for, and jump out of the shaft, slip out the back of the hut, and wait. Marking, calculating my time. My breath is coming hard, pushing against the beat in my chest, so I hold it in. Listen. And here it comes. The next whoosh. I mark the time again, then step around the corner of the hut, raise a heavy, broken piece of lid from one of the stacked boxes, and swing.

The Earthling is flying now, only in the other direction. Off the air bike.

The machine doesn't crash or even fall down. It just slows and lands. Upright. I don't have time to marvel. I hike up the red dress, throw a leg over the air bike, twist the handles, and lean back. And I shoot almost straight up into the air, the peaks of the roof thatch shrinking as I climb. It feels like rising out of a memory, only I've never been afraid to be hit and obliterated by other memories while I was doing it.

But doing is definitely different from Knowing. I give the handles a little twitch to the right, telling the bike to fly me between the peaks, over the parks and across the plain. But the machine isn't responding. Even when I turn the handles hard. And then I realize that I'm not in control. I'm on a prescribed course. I'm on patrol. And how long before the Earthlings realize that a girl patrolling New Canaan in a flapping red dress is not one of their own? Not long.

I hang on as I pick up speed, plunging down in a way that leaves my stomach behind to circle the water clock. But I am remembering, sifting what is inside my brain. And I see Beckett talking to the squares of light.

"Turn right," I say, loud over the freezing wind.

Nothing. And then I think, no, he addressed the technology first.

"Command. Turn right."

I'm wrong again. That was the *Centauri II's* technology. Beckett controls with his eyes. I stare at something that looks a little like a light square. It glows blue. And the Earthling on the air bike I just passed has turned his head. Little words and pictures appear across the blue light, which is so bizarre, especially on a machine flying me through the air by itself. I see the word "Route," and stare carefully at only that word, and then other words appear. "Preset." "Reset."

I choose "Reset," and I see a list. *Centauri III* is one. Canaan and New Canaan are others. And so is "Pilot Control."

And the air bike is slowing. It's going to land me in front of the gates. There are Earthlings there, running up from different directions. Shouting. I stare at the word "Canaan," and then the next option, which is "Set." I grip the handles hard and the bike zooms back upward, leaving the Earthlings behind with a passing wind. The bike shoots between the peaks, putting rocks and a mountainside between us, the plain rushing below me like Beckett's map in the frame of light.

I feel a rush of fear, the cold steals my breath, and then a deep thrill of speed. The sky is glowing, pink rays streaking out from the coming sun, and I think of the words from the medical journal, the ones I have cached for so long. Because I didn't want to believe them.

The onset of Forgetting is traumatic . . . symptoms of fear, panic, disorientation, and paranoia that can lead to unwarranted violence . . .

That's what Beckett is facing if he is there for the Forgetting. With Commander Faye and seventy-five Earthlings trained to fight. And I bet they'll have weapons, agreement or no.

If I'm there, it's going to kill me. And so the solution is: Don't be there.

I twist the grip forward and speed toward the sunrise.

60

BECKETT

We walk back through the gates of Canaan like some kind of ritual procession. Lian Archiva and her Knowing in the lead, Commander Juniper Faye next. Me. And then a squad of seventy-five, in formation. No visible weapons. But I know they've got the small ones in their belts. Maybe we are a ritual. I don't know.

We pass the house where I exploded the door. And even though this is one of the most important archaeological sites in history, and that pile of blackened rubble is a shame caused by nobody but Beckett Rodriguez, I smile. And then I ache.

I miss her.

The Commander turns her head, looking back to check on me, and I fix my face to nothing, like Samara would. Faye doesn't need to catch even a whiff of what I'm thinking. Because the soldier that delivered me to the launch took one quick second to press his thumb to my cuffs and leave them unlocked. A dangerous move that will have been documented, unless he knows someone who can hack. I'm waiting for my moment. To disappear. To get back into the caves, maybe, and back to New Canaan. And maybe that will delay my parents' punishment a little longer, too.

Funny how things have twisted around. I wish I could tell her.

The sky has lightened so much we can see on our own now, but the soldiers behind me are having trouble navigating the trees and staying in formation, tripping over saplings and roots. The buds look ready to explode. And then I hear the faintest whoosh in the air.

I glance up, but I can't see anything. Lian Archiva stops, holds up a hand, and I see we've come to a half bowl in the sloping land of the city, with terraced sides and a broken tower straddling a stream at its bottom. The amphitheater. Exactly the way it was supposed to have been.

"I was clear," says Lian, "that there was to be no one else present at our negotiations, and that the city was not to be entered with technology?"

"Someone's off course," says Faye, her eyes narrowing. "*Centauri*, who's flying around on an air bike?"

But there's no answer.

"*Centauri!*"

I grin. She's out of communication.

"I was told this problem was corrected," Faye says to Finchley.

I think, someone's going to pay once she gets back on the—

An air bike zooms straight over our heads, circling once before angling down into a flat space beside the running stream and the broken tower. It's not a perfect landing, but it's not bad. The rider swings over a leg. A leg beneath a red dress that is dirty and a little torn, hair half up and tangled from the wind. Sam. Whose amber eyes are the most beautiful thing I've ever seen. Who just flew an air bike from New Canaan.

And she looks right at me, and mouths the word "Hi."

61

SAMARA

Who is this?" a woman yells beside Beckett. The Commander. I've never seen her before, but there's no mistaking who she is. She thinks she's in charge. She makes her way down the terraced steps, pushing past the Knowing, who are coming more slowly. The rest of the Earthlings hang back at the rim, not sure, I think, whether she wants them up or down.

"I am Samara Archiva," I say. "You've been tricked."

She grins at me. And so does Beckett. He's got his hands bound in front of him, shaking his head, grinning like he's going to laugh. Which is crazy. I smile back. Then the Commander barks, "Finchley! Set up a perimeter! And send me five soldiers to detain this—"

"No," I say. "Leave them where they are, or I won't tell you what's—"

"No," a different voice says. It's my father, now standing to one side of the Commander, and looking her in the eye. "They stay where they are, or I cut you in half." He's got mother's technology in his palm. What she used to kill that family. And I think he just took it out of his hair.

Commander Faye seems to know exactly what my father has and what it can do. She keeps her eyes on the weapon and raises a hand. "Hold that, Finchley."

And then Beck comes. He's loose from the shackles that were on his wrists, and now he's got Faye's arms back, using them to bind hers. "Hold, Finchley!" she yells again. She's watching that weapon. I'm watching Sampson Archiva.

Beck forces the Commander to her knees while the other Knowing flow past them, slow and elegant, seating themselves in a circle around the tower, hands in laps. Closing their eyes, caching. Rapt. Thorne Councilman is the only one who looks a little unsure. My mother stays where she is. The sky is lightening, a rosy orange.

"Daughter," says Sampson, "do what you came to do."

Then Lian approaches my father. She strokes one painted fingernail down his cheek. "What good does this do?" she whispers. "The deed is done. Come sit with me, and cache."

I watch my father struggle with his mind. And then I hike up the dress, pull out the knife tied to my thigh, get behind Faye, and pull her head back, like I did with Thorne. "I have her," I say to my father. I feel the heat of Beck's body just behind me. We have her together. And my father steps back, and turns the weapon on my mother.

"It is a terrible thing," he says to me, eyes on Lian, "when your love comes for the wrong person. Reddix understood. But it is even more terrible, when the woman you can never forget to love . . . is evil."

Lian Archiva stands perfectly still. And I see a real emotion cross her face. For the first time in my life. And it's shock.

"All those years," my father says. "Adam. The children she condemned. Experimented on. You. And I hated her. And I could not stop feeling love for her. It's untenable, this life."

Which is what Reddix said to me when I was sleeping. "Daddy," I say. Faye squirms and I adjust the knife edge. She goes still. "You don't have to be Knowing. I Know how to make you stop."

"An absence of Knowing is not Forgetting, Samara. And we cannot Forget . . ."

"Stop this!" snaps my mother. It's a jolt, seeing her true anger. "Your lack of vision sickens me." Her gaze falls on me like a storm. "Your Judgment has been pronounced. You are condemned. And coming here today changes nothing . . ."

She takes a step toward me, and then cries out, her hand jumping up to her face. Blood wells through her fingers. My father has just cut her cheek from ear to chin. With a beam of light.

I feel Beckett beside me now. "The Forgetting is coming," I tell him. "With the sunrise. It's the trees, sporing when the sky turns white. That's why they abandoned the city."

He looks at the sky. "How long?"

"Moments."

"What is this all about?" says Faye. But it really doesn't matter if she knows or not. She's trapped here.

"Darling," says my mother. It's horrible to see her smile when she has blood in her mouth. "You do not understand. You will not be Forgetting. Only he will . . ."

"You're short on some Knowing, Mother. Because that's not how immunity works. You never read the missing three pages."

I see her blanch at that.

"I have her," says my father, turning the weapon to Faye. "Go, Samara." He flicks his dark eyes to Beckett and nods. "Both of you."

But as soon as I step away from Faye, something whizzes past me into the rubble. Beckett grabs me by the waist, moves me to one side as a small, contained puff of an explosion turns the stones where I was standing into dust. Two more whizzing noises and we run for the bike. This time it hits the rocks where Jane Chemist and Martina Tutor sit with their eyes closed, still caching, and after the puff noise, they just . . . aren't anymore. Only tissue and blood.

"Stop!" Commander Faye roars. "Do you know how much they were worth?"

"Get on the bike, Sam!" yells Beckett.

Mother is staring at where Martina and Jane used to be, and Thorne is on his feet now. "What does she mean, Lian, that immunity doesn't work that way?"

"You can't Forget," I yell at him. At all of them. "But the spores are going to kill you instead. That's what the experiments of Janis Atan showed, and I don't think it's a very nice way to die. It's a shame you closed the Archives, Mother. Or you would Know that."

"Sam!" Beck says. "Are you immune?"

I nod once before turning to my father. "You Know it, too. Don't you, Daddy?"

"Yes, daughter. Reddix showed me."

"Get on this bike!" Beck shouts.

My mother's eyes go wide, and she drops her hands. The gash in her perfect face is hideous. She's having difficulty speaking. "Samara. Take me with you."

"Daddy," I say. "Come. You can stop being Knowing. You can heal."

He smiles at me, and I have a quick flash of memory. Of seeing that smile. When I was first born. "I will never heal," my father says. He is calm, almost peaceful. "Reddix had his plan, and this is mine. The NWSE will be no more. Even the memory of it. And I will be free of her . . ."

"Wait," says Thorne, Craddock just behind him. "Wait!"

Commander Faye is struggling to her feet. "What is Forgetting?" she screams.

"Samara." Lian Archiva straightens her back. "I am the Judge of New Canaan. You will take me with you."

I throw my leg over the air bike and grab Beck's waist. "You are condemned, Mother. But not by me. You condemned yourself." The air bike begins to rise. "And there is no forgiveness Underneath."

We rise, clear the hole, and the bike leans left, dodging one of those whizzing puffs. Someone screams below us. Another small explosion, and there is shouting. Fighting. The first beam of sunlight shoots out between the mountains.

Beck twists the handles and I lean with him, hands clinging to his chest, as the air bike speeds up and away over the Cursed City of Canaan.

Everything I've Always Wanted, by Beckett Rodriguez:

1. Find the lost colony of Canaan.

2. Meet someone who lives there.

3. Go out and find a new culture. On my own.

4. Take someone with me.

FROM THE LOG BOOK OF BECKETT RODRIGUEZ

Day 9, Year 1

The Lost Canaan Project

62

BECKETT

I have sunbeams on my arms and Samara's body against my back. I push for more speed from the air bike and we leave the screams and sounds of implosion behind, climbing higher as the old city and the treetops blur below us. And then the sky breaks. A white, sparkling sky, brighter than any light on the *Centauri III*.

"Put your face in my back," I yell at Sam over the rush of the wind. "Don't breathe!" But from what Reddix said, I know this probably won't do any good. What was she doing, coming out here when it could've killed her? When it still might? I lean forward again and we're beyond the walls, skirting bare cliff face mirroring the white light, blinding, trying to find the pass between the mountains. She was doing what I would have, I think. I guess we can't help it. And what are we supposed to do about it?

The answer is simple: Stay together.

"Where are we going?" She's whispering beneath the wind now, instead of yelling, her breath on my neck.

"Keep your head down!" I'm looking at the panel while I talk, opening up a channel to the *Centauri*. We're beyond the mountains, their rocky sides stark in the glare. But those spores could be anywhere.

And then a tentative voice says, "Yes?" through the screen.

"Air bike coming into the nearest port. Close the ventilation systems, and as soon as we're in, seal the ship . . ."

"For three days," Sam says near my ear. "The spores live for three days . . ."

"A quarantine. No outside air for three days. Do you copy that, *Centauri*?" I can see the ship now, sitting like an oval-shaped city in the middle of a valley. Getting bigger. Closer.

The voice comes back faint through the panel. "So . . . does anybody know how to do all that?"

"Roger? Is that you?" Roger's the bug man. What's he doing on the communications bridge?

"Beck . . ." Sam whispers.

"It's Beckett, right?" Roger says. "Come in. The *Centauri*'s had a change in ownership. And somebody told me to say copy that."

"Beck . . ." she whispers again, and my heart freezes.

"Are you sick?"

"No. But I'm going to remember . . ."

I'll bet she is. And I don't even know what happened while she was Underneath. "Sam, we're almost there. Hold on . . ."

I aim for the open port door. I can see the other ports snapping shut one by one around the sides. And as soon as we glide in, our door closes, too. I hear the vacuum of the airlock. I jump off the bike, get Sam's face in my hands, make her gaze focus on me.

"Stay here. For just a few more minutes. Stay right here. And then we're going to go somewhere and let them come. And then they can heal. Okay?"

"You'll stay with me?" she whispers.

I kiss her mouth one time, and then the interior door slides open and the room is full of people, and I'm pulled into my dad's hug.

"The ship is ours," he says. "Faye is relieved. What's going—"

"You heard what I said, right? Three days of quarantine . . ."

And then Mom has me. She's little, but no less forceful, and I get both my cheeks kissed and then a smack.

"You moved forward without supervision? What was your training for, Beckett?"

There are other people milling about—Roger, Dr. Kataria, the tech crew, Lanik—and Samara's about to fall off the bike. I pull away from Mom, get Sam off the bike, put an arm around her waist and behind her knees and scoop her up. Which seemed like the right and slightly dramatic thing to do, until I remember that Sam is almost as tall as I am.

"Is she sick?" says Lanik, coming to look her over.

"Not like that," I tell him. I'm already pushing awkwardly through the small crowd. "Sam," I whisper, "stay here. Don't go yet . . ."

Mom says, "She's from the visuals," and Dad changes gears.

"Where are we heading?" he asks. "Medical center?"

"My room."

They don't ask any more questions. Not yet. But it's a long way to our quarters, with her head bobbing against my neck, and when the door to my room slides open, it almost doesn't seem familiar. Like looking at somebody else's stuff. I kind of wish I'd cleaned it. But I don't think Sam is seeing what's around her. I set her on the edge of the bed and she's gone. Somewhere else. Mom and Dad are hovering in the doorway, trying to figure out where this is going. It's really good to see them.

"Sam's dealing with her memories," I tell them. "It's going to take a while, and . . . she's probably going to scream a lot. She's . . . There have been some terrible things."

Mom says, "Shouldn't she have Kataria?"

"Kataria is not going to be familiar."

"And you are?" Dad asks.

"Yes."

He keeps his skepticism to himself, which is appreciated. "She just lost both her parents. And I said I would stay with her."

And since she starts up right then, they leave me to it. For a day and a half.

Though there's time to talk to Mom and Dad in between. While Sam is sleeping. They've seen the visuals Faye uploaded from the glasses, but there's a lot to fill in. And to tell me. About the first attempt to disable the *Centauri*'s thrust, so it couldn't launch, and how the needless destruction and rounding up of the locals had convinced enough of the crew to change the leadership as soon as Faye left the ship. A military captain, Davis, is in charge now. Jill and Vesta are confined to quarters, like all of Faye's supporters.

But mostly I let Sam work through her memories. And her grief. I held her. Stroked her hair. Slept beside her, in case she needed me. She did. But even with this new crop of experiences, now that the first one or two relivings are over, she's been relaxed, more than I've ever seen her. In control. And she's telling me things without going away. About Reddix, and her mother right before Judgment. About Knowing and amrita. How her mind showed her immunity.

"I could go to any memory I wanted while I was asleep," she says. She's curled up sideways on my bed, using the wall as a backrest, wearing a pair of my jogging shorts and a T-shirt. Except for the scars on her arms, she really could be from Texas. I can't stop looking at her.

"So which ones did you choose?"

"Swinging on Adam's rope. Talking to Nita . . ."

I'm amazed that she can say this without the memory of Nita trying to pull her away.

"Jumping off the fern roots," she goes on. "In my bedchamber. On the rug."

"Really?" And then a new thought jumps into my head. "Wait a second. How many times did you go to that memory?"

She's got the blanket between two fingers. Feeling what it's made of. Giving it a shy, slightly sly grin. "Possibly . . . ninety-four."

"You're telling me that you've kissed me, like that, ninety-four more times than I've kissed you? That is completely unfair." She raises her amber eyes.

"Do you need another memory?"

I decide that I do. All the way until Mom and Dad come back from meeting with the new captain.

"Day after tomorrow a team is going out to the old city," Dad says when I come into the common area. "To find what they find and see what they see. It won't be good, probably." He runs a hand through his hair. "Son, are you sure you're not"—he glances at the door to my room, speaks more quietly—"in over your head? Do you need Kataria?"

"Not at all."

I don't know what he sees in my face, probably guilt, because he just shakes his head and says, "Oh, boy. Right. You know your mother is not going to like that."

Mom has not been a fan of Samara in my room. Even with the door open.

"What are the preferred burial practices?" Dad asks.

"Burning. But let me check with . . ."

Then Dad sits up, because Samara is in the doorway. In my shorts and T-shirt. It's the first time she's emerged.

"Hi," she says.

Dad jumps up. I'm not sure he was ready for how pretty Sam is. When she's not screaming. "Sam," he says. "Or Samara? Which do you prefer?"

"Sam."

"Good. Call me Sean. We're—"

"Joanna Cho-Rodriguez," says Mom, coming in from food prep. "We are happy to have you."

This is a little stiff. But Sam just smiles and says, *"Xièxiè nǐ yāoqǐng wǒ zhu nǐ jiā."*

I watch Mom's eyebrows disappear into her fringe of dark hair. "She speaks Chinese? Come," she says, taking Sam's hand and pulling her out of the room. "You have to eat with us. When did you last eat?" And I know by Mom's reaction that Sam must have said something like three or four days. And then I'm hearing Mom offer basically every scrap of food we have in there. In Chinese.

Dad looks me over. "Son, I call that playing dirty."

"I call it playing smart. What would you have done?"

He shrugs.

"Anyway, it only took about five seconds. She'll be having conversations with her before we finish dinner."

"About that," says Dad. "This brain power, it's artificially created?"

"Yes. Sam wants to let it go, now that she knows how. The suicide rate Underneath is . . . well, it's unbelievable. And for good reason."

"Have you considered—"

"What Earth would do with them? Dad, she did her medical training in three months. She's a clock, a thermometer, any instrument of measurement you can think of. She remembers being born, and I watched her put a whole library in her head in an hour."

Dad puts his hands in his pockets. "And Jill knows?"

"Yes, but I'm not sure she saw the potential."

"Okay. Then let's just keep as quiet as we can about it. Until we figure out what's next. Oh, and Dr. Lanik wants to see her. Tomorrow if he could. Before she gets the run of the ship. She'll like the medical center, I think . . ."

He was right. Sam is in there so long, explaining to Lanik about healing, food, and sleep, getting him to tell her about procedures and equipment, that I slip out, thinking to head to the communications bridge, to hear what the team found in the old city. In case I need to break anything to Sam.

And then I see Jill, coming back from the exercise cube with a towel over her shoulder. I didn't know she was allowed out. We're the only ones in the corridor, and the sight of her standing there, staring at me, makes me think of her silence while I was tied to that post. The terrified people in the streets and the top blown off a mountain. I turn to go back in the med center, and she says, "Beckett, wait."

I stop, but I don't turn. The hall is as quiet as the Underneath.

"I thought you'd want to know that Faye is back. She doesn't have any memories from before sunrise, and she was . . . she was the only one left."

That figures. And we left her cuffed, too.

"It's like she's a different person."

You're a different person, Jillian.

I've almost started to walk away again when she says, "Beckett, Earth needs clean DNA. We have to have it, or there's not going to be any of us left to . . . There won't be anyone to . . . That's why we needed each other. You and me. And we had to bring them back. To save the Earth. Don't you see . . ."

"Not that way, Jill," I cut in. "Don't pretend there's any noble reason for doing what Faye did, and I was never going back to Earth. And you know it was all about the money."

She steps back like I smacked her. Sam comes out of the medical center then, wearing one of my jumpsuits, and in her tiny pause I can see that Jill is giving her a barrage of memories. That she's fighting for control. I take her hand, and she relaxes.

"I heard you're taking the bikes to New Canaan in the morning," Jill says quickly. "Do you think . . . Will you see Nathan?"

She just stands there, biting her lip, and I don't say anything. I squeeze Sam's hand and turn away, bring her with me down the hall. Sam is here, safe, with her hand in mine. And I think it really might be okay if I never see Jillian again.

The first time I went Outside and felt the sky, I realized that no matter how high and vast the caverns of my city, there was still a ceiling. And when I stayed Outside, I realized that no matter how immense and infinite the sky, that the mountains still made walls.

If I could do everything I ever wished, I would breach my walls. And I would not do it alone.

FROM THE HIDDEN BOOK OF SAMARA ARCHIVA
IN THE CITY OF NEW CANAAN

63

SAMARA

I attended the burning of my father, and did not go to the burning of my mother. Beckett came with me, and Sean and Joanna, Nita's family, and Dr. Lanik. My father, according to Dr. Lanik's examination, died quickly of a massive exposure to the Forgetting spore. But my mother's body suffered violence before she died. From many different hands. I'll never Know what happened, and I'm glad. And Father was in a wooden box at his burning. Not like the way my mother made me watch Adam.

After flying across the plain, being on the *Centauri*, the city feels so small.

The day we arrived in New Canaan we found a new Council being formed between Annis and Huan Councilman, Thorne's nephew. Three days of Knowing and Outsiders being locked in together with a common enemy on the other side of the gate seems to have done some good. A short-term agreement had already been reached, about medicine, housing, rationing. Longer-term agreements about educating the Outside, having the Knowing provide an actual service for their upkeep, the use of technology and communication were left to be hashed out when everyone was fed.

Commander Davis of the *Centauri III* spoke to the new Council, a smooth and apologetic speech, explaining the actions of Earth and the removal of Faye, a positive commitment to staying long enough to help New Canaan rebuild what had been damaged. The Council had him say it again in the Forum, packed with Outsiders and Knowing together, and it was then that Earth was, if not exactly accepted, at least allowed in. There were crops to get in the ground. But after a conversation with Annis, it was agreed that Earth would no longer be allowed Underneath. The less Earth understood about Knowing, the better. The *Centauri* moved to an easy distance on the barren plain, though still out of sight, and soon the transports began, shuttling help back and forth to the Outside. For rebuilding.

Commander Davis granted permission for me to administer the cure for Forgetting to three of the Earth patrol left Outside while the Underneath was sealed, but he denied this privilege to Juniper Faye. I still haven't decided whether this was a punishment or a kindness. But walking out of the gates into the bustle and sun, a syringe in my bag for Grandpapa, I Know that for him it's going to be neither. It's simply his choice.

I lay the syringe on the table in front of Grandpapa. Nathan is here, but Annis isn't. I gave her and the children the use of the Archiva flat now that she's Council, everything but my bedchamber. The NWSE artifacts on my mother's wall I gave to Sean Rodriguez, everything but the knife. Now I give Grandpapa his choice, and it's entirely his. But it's not an easy one.

Grandpapa stares at the needle. We all do. Then Beckett goes back to making tea for Sean and Joanna, who are observing from the chairs by the unlit furnace. Sunbeams blow straight in the window with the breeze, and Beck looks like he belongs here. He's in the cloth of the Outside, now dyed an Earth-sky blue.

"You don't have to, Grandpapa," I say. "The memories could be good. Or bad. And you're happy as you are, aren't you?" I see Beckett shake his head at me just a little, smiling. I'm overly afraid of bad memories. But he knows I'm making a similar choice, and he wishes I wasn't.

"Well," says Grandpapa. "I'm guessing my memories will be a little bit of both." And he rolls up his sleeve.

So I wipe his arm clean, squeeze his skin together, and dart the needle inside, quick. He sucks in a breath and closes his eyes. We wait. I glance at Nathan, who's lost in thought, mind somewhere else. He's unhappy. Deeply so. It makes me sad to see it. Then I watch a curious story begin on Grandpapa's face. A looking backward.

"I had a brother," he says. "A baby brother who died. I never knew . . . And I see my mother's face, when she was young. And my grandmother. Her name was Liliya."

"What else do you see, Cyrus?" Sean asks, leaning forward.

"Dad," Beckett warns under his breath.

Grandpapa opens his eyes. "Things I'm not going to tell you, young man," he says to Sean. Teasing. Because he knows that not being told drives Sean Rodriguez crazy. Joanna laughs. But I can see that Grandpapa wants to be alone.

"Go lie down," I tell him. "We'll finish our tea and clear up and go."

He pats my head, rubs Nathan's shoulder, and there are tears in his eyes when he shuts the door. Joanna drains her tea. "Ready, Beckett?" she says. Significantly.

Nathan raises a brow, and I see Sean sigh as he finishes his notes.

"No," Beckett says. "I'll come later. I want to work on some glass. Or if it's too late to catch a transport I'll sleep here."

Joanna frowns. "Beck, you are always—"

"I'm going," I say abruptly. Even though I have no patients to see and no rooms to go to that do not haunt me. "See you all after waking?"

But I don't wait for an answer. I take off with my pack, down the streets, up the steps, and through the terraced fields. Up and up until I'm in a blacknut orchard, where I drop my pack, pull out a blanket, spread out on the soft grass beneath the shade, and wait.

Memory is tugging. Genivee, Nadia, and Liliya. Those are three names together on my family tree. The Genivee of the Archives, Nadia who drew the maps, and now Liliya.

I follow the memory to the map inscription. Nadia and Gray, a glassblower's son. Like Cyrus. I wonder if they've always known we had the same ancestors, and just never said anything.

And then Beckett is coming up the slope beneath the trees. He walks straight to the blanket, throws himself on top of me, and puts his face in my hair.

"Why?" he says. "Why so many people?"

I laugh and shove him off, but he takes me with him, and now he has me cradled. "And why aren't you with me every second?" he asks.

"Because you would get tired of me." Only I'm not really laughing now. He is such a beautiful alien.

"I'm going to test that theory," he says, kissing the corner of my mouth.

We test it until the next bell rings. He's missed the last transport, but he doesn't seem that sorry about it. He holds me tight, and I listen to the beat in his chest.

"Hey," he says, "I want you to look at something." He pulls a new pair of glasses out from beneath his shirt—glasses with no security measures—flicks them open, and puts them on. He finds what he wants, then slides the lenses onto my face. "I've been doing some research," he says. "This first visual is a little hard to watch . . ."

My eyes adjust, and it takes a few moments for me to realize that I'm looking at the Cursed City. When it was new. Where did they have cameras in Canaan? But they did, somewhere. The stones are crisp, and there are hardly any trees. The tower in the terraced hole is a beautifully crafted clock. And then I realize that the people are fighting, wandering, attacking each other. Something explodes, and fire blazes. This is panic. Raw fear.

"It's the Forgetting," says Beck. "I found this in the first *Centauri*'s database." He takes the glasses, switches the visual, and hands them back to me. Now I'm looking at a map. Topographical.

"Zoom in a little," Beck says, "and do you see that area, just where the river runs into that lake?"

I see it.

"I've been looking at that carefully, really carefully, and I think there might be a hole. A duplicated piece of land. Just like what we saw when we looked at New Canaan for the first time."

"What are you thinking?" I ask, handing the glasses back. He drops them in his shirt and snuggles me back into his chest.

"The *Centauri II*. There's just not enough of it here. There was a good bit of the first ship, once we dug it out . . ." The *Centauri III* was sitting directly on top of the first ship. "And Lian"—he doesn't refer to her as my mother—"she hinted that the last ship just flew away. But I've looked at the dates, and I've been doing the math. The *Centauri II* landed just ahead of the comet, thirty-six hours before the Forgetting. And the tech New Canaan had is consistent with what might be left behind, say, at a base camp. There's a huge amount of work to be done here, I know, but . . ."

It's an amazing idea. What if the crew just . . . Forgot? What if they're out there? And when it comes down to it, the Canaan Project belongs first and foremost to Sean Rodriguez. Not Beckett. Beckett isn't researching it. He's living it. I sigh, comfortable in his arms. This is almost the only way I can sleep now. My memories are under control, but resting is harder.

"That was a good thing for Cyrus," Beck whispers, "wasn't it?"

It was. And now I'm awake, and tense, because I Know what's coming. The Knowing have been told by the Council that they do not have to be Knowing, and that no new Knowing will be created. For those who have already been injected and drunk the amrita, they may choose. To stop. Or to continue. I have to choose.

"Have you decided what to do?"

"Yes. And you're not going to like it." I prop up my head on a hand, so I can look at his face. He's looking away, his jaw clenched. "Beck, tell me why you want me to be Knowing. The real answer."

He frowns a little. "Your medical skills . . ."

"I said the real answer."

He sits up abruptly. And now he's mad, and I'm the one who's not sorry. Whatever this is, he needs to get it out. Because I cannot be Knowing. Not anymore. I sit up, too. "Why don't you just say it, Beckett?"

He raises a brow at his full name. "Okay, fine. You said . . ." His jaw works, and he starts again. "You said it only comes once for the Knowing, and that your 'once' was for me. Well, I guess there's a lot of security in that, isn't there? If you're . . . me."

"So you think if I can't access my memories in the same way that my feelings will change? Have you ever thought that might be a good thing?" He leans on his knees. "If you're Knowing, your feelings stay the same. That's true. But it's like an echo, the same echo, over and over. Nothing grows. But what if not being Knowing meant I could love you more? Or, maybe not being Knowing would mean that you . . . might love me less."

Now he's offended. "Why would you say that?"

"Why would you say it about me?"

He throws himself back on the blanket. "I hate arguing with you. I lose so badly."

I lie beside him while he fumes.

"What about you?" I say. "What have you decided to do?" The

Centauri III is launching after the harvest, and now there is another choice, for every person of age—Earth, Outside, or Underneath. To stay. Or go.

He huffs once. Then he lifts his arm and puts my head back on his chest.

"Well?"

"Oh, please," he sighs.

"And your parents?"

"Staying. There won't ever be an opportunity like this on Earth."

I look at the moving shadows, my head rising and falling with his breath. "In the Underneath," I say, "when two people make a partnership, they write it down in a book."

He strokes my hair.

"They write, 'I choose Fred or Tamsa or whoever,' and when it's in the book, it's a promise." I lift my head to look at him again. "If I gave you a pen right now, would you write me down? Because I would write you down. My book is in my pack right now."

He takes my face in both his hands, like he's going to keep me from falling into a memory. "Yes," he says, "I would choose you and I would write you down. But if you're not going to be Knowing, then I want you to not be Knowing when you do the choosing. Do you understand?"

I close my eyes. Why does he think I will change?

Then he flips me around, half pinning me down with his weight, and kisses my neck. Fiercely. "Yes," he says against my skin. "Yes. And yes." He's making me giggle. "All the yeses, and just waiting . . . until then. All right?"

I don't answer. I pull his hair until he brings his mouth up to mine. Then he tugs on mine until my chin comes up, so he can kiss my neck again. I laugh, and then I shiver. "And after that," he says just below my ear, "no more sneaking off into the blacknut grove. Unless . . . you're just into it . . ."

I laugh again, and I close my eyes, enjoy his weight and his smell and the roughness of his chin. But I Know the other half of this problem. He doesn't have Joanna's approval. She thinks I'm . . . complicated. But I have a plan for that.

And I begin the next day, when Joanna comes over on the transport. I'm waiting to one side, for the usual flood of Earthlings to go past, off to research or build or plant, and I'm surprised to see Nathan stepping off the dock, heading immediately down a side street. How did he get permission to stay overnight on the *Centauri*? Then I'm afraid I Know. And then Joanna is stepping down, and since Beckett didn't come back to the ship, she's not terribly pleased to see me.

"I have a surprise for you," I say. Her brows disappear into her hair, but I smile, and tilt my head, and she follows. When we get to the gates, I give the supervisor Annis's note, which is permission to allow Dr. Joanna Cho-Rodriguez privileges for visiting Underneath.

I can see I've gotten her attention.

She follows me down the sloping entrance hall, down corridors and stairs. I Know she's seen the visuals, but doing is different from Knowing, and her eyes are big. Then we go down the last, short staircase; I unlock the door and let her into the dust and rot of Uncle Towlend's office. But I have a lamp ready.

"My family name, of course, is Archiva," I say, lighting the flame. "We were the keepers of the Archives until . . ." I'm being yanked by memories here. I take a moment to still them. "Until they were closed. Now I'm the last of that name. But the Council thinks the Archives should be reopened, and . . . I thought you might want to help."

Joanna looks unsure, until I open the other door and she steps out onto the balcony. I hold up the light and her mouth drops. She says nothing for so long that I finally just hand her the lantern, so she can move and see what she wishes.

"I'm going to start cleaning up the office, so you'll have a place to work when you're not in here. I'll leave you now, to get oriented."

She still hasn't spoken.

"Unless you don't want to?"

"No," she whispers. "No, I'd be happy to help."

And we practically don't see her again until sunsetting, when she comes out to help Sean move their belongings from the *Centauri* into Uncle Towlend's empty chambers. It seemed appropriate, somehow. I chose to stay in my bedchamber. Memories are there, but I want to see if they can fade. I want to Know if I can heal. We put Ari and Luc in Adam's old room, and I can hear it when they laugh. And that's a new memory that isn't bad. And it means that Beckett is home much more often, which makes Joanna happy.

Or so she thinks. My balcony is just not that hard of a climb.

We all go together, the Outsiders, the Earthlings, and the ones left from Underneath, to the upland parks to watch the *Centauri* launch. It's both bitter and sweet to see it go. The ship is leaving with thirty-two of our Outsiders and a generous number of blood samples. We're keeping fifteen of its crew, including Dr. Lanik, who's holding Jasmina for a missing Annis, while Grandpapa shoos the children away from the cliff edge. Sean and Joanna stand together, still and solemn, while the *Centauri* goes up and up, and then sideways fast, becoming a burning light before it winks and is gone. Beckett puts his chin on my shoulder. We're staring at an empty sky.

"Well, that's done," he whispers. He means this is home. Then he looks down at my empty hands. "Hey, where's the moonshine?"

"What?"

"Where's the moonshine? You were supposed to get a bottle from Cyrus for Mom and Dad, to toast New Canaan . . ."

I turn around and look at him, wide-eyed. "I forgot," I say. "Beck! I forgot!"

"Congratulations," he says, shaking his head. I hug him hard.

We go back for the moonshine, and when I open the workshop door, Annis is red-eyed and stone-faced, alone at the table in the dimming light. "He's gone," she says. "Nathan's gone!"

I knew he'd been going to see Jill again, but he wasn't on the list of those going to Earth. Or did he hide being on the list? Annis is crying, without any hope of comfort, and Grandpapa joins her soon after. Beckett and I exchange a glance.

Not like this, his expression says. And I agree.

We prepare all through the dark days. I see patients with Dr. Lanik. I've retained almost all of my knowing since not drinking the amrita, but the information is not as vivid, and sometimes I have to work hard to retrieve it. Beckett helps Sean document memories from both Outside and Underneath, before they can fade, and I take my mandatory orientation classes for tech. Medical and educational, that's the technology the Council decided to introduce to New Canaan, and so that's the tech Earth left us.

And I begin dreaming again. For the first time since I was a child. And my dreams are still of him.

It's almost sunrising and I've gone to do an inventory of the medical supplies—with pencil and paper—and also to do a bit of clandestine packing, when I notice that the seal on one of the amrita bottles is the tiniest bit loose. I lift it to my nose, then tear off the seal and smell again. Water. I check the others. Three more, just water, and the tiny bottle of Forgetting, the one that Reddix gave to Beckett, is gone. And I know who did this. Nathan. Jill, it seems, realized the potential after all.

I have to tell Annis. We have working communications now, through the re-launched satellites, and she sends a message. But her words won't fly any faster than the ship, so it may be far too late by the time the message gets there. We don't tell anyone else. Earth is beyond our control, and so many other things are here, within our grasp.

I meet Beckett at Uncle Towlend's desk, which is really Joanna's now, and sometimes Sean's, the room clean, organized, but with the same soft chairs. I set the book of maps on her desk, with the inscription from my ancestor, and the book that describes Nadia's journeys outside the old city's walls. And then together, we set down my book on the desk. The only written account of the Knowing. And in the back is a page to say what—and who—we choose, signed last night on my balcony. I hope the story of Nadia will help Beckett's parents understand what we're doing. I hope my book will help them understand who I've been and who I am now.

I pick up my pack, which is huge, Beckett hoists his own, takes my hand, and we leave the office—up the stairs, out the gates that are never shut, past one or two sleepy people moving too early for the waking, the mountain shadows deep, except for the place where the mountain isn't.

We are so hemmed in here.

I climb with Beckett up through the gated fields, already prepared for the sunrising and the planting, across the groves, and then up through the dark of the thick-growing brush. We find a cliff, but instead of looking out over a barren plain, what stretches below us are rolling hills, the first streaks of sunlight shining from behind us, showing the new yellows and blues.

Beckett is hoping to find a colony out there. Another lost outpost of Earth. I don't know if we'll find that. But what if all we find is . . . a place. An open space. For a new city. A city without walls. We could be builders after all, if we wanted to. The architects of a new world. The ones to get it right.

Or maybe just the ones to get it a little bit better.

Beckett grins, and the rising sun is gold on his face. "Ready?"

I turn to face the unknown. And I am.

ACKNOWLEDGMENTS

"Acknowledgment" seems like such an inaccurate word, when what I really want is to say thank you, thank you, thank you, thank you from the bottom of my heart to everyone who made this book possible, and that's a lot of people.

First to my critique group: Amy Eytchison, Ruta Sepetys, Howard Shirley, and Angelika Stegmann. Let's just keep on doing this forever, shall we?

Second to the entire Middle Tennessee writing community: SCBWI Midsouth, Parnassus Books, the SEYA Book Fest, you know who you are. Your support makes me who I am as a writer. I don't deserve you.

Kelly Sonnack, truly the best agent I could have ever signed with. Never have I stopped counting my lucky stars. Plus, I admire you to pieces.

Lisa Sandell, truly the best editor I could have ever been paired with. You stretch me and challenge me in the most patient of ways, and suddenly here comes a book I would have never guessed I could write. Perhaps you are magic. Thank you for being my friend.

Brooke Shearouse, you are the most excellent of publicists. Please find things for me to do so we can go more places together.

All those lovely, lovely people in the Scholastic offices who not only make beautiful books, but make me feel like one of the family: David Levithan (love you, David!), Elizabeth Parisi (for yet another gorgeous cover), Rachel Gluckstern, Olivia Valcarce, Rachel Feld, Isa Caban, Mindy Stockfield, every single person on the Scholastic marketing and creative marketing teams, Tracy van Straaten, Lizette Serrano, Emily Heddleson, Michelle Campbell, Ellie Berger, Lori Benton, John Pels, Sue Flynn, Jacquelyn Rubin, Jody Stigliano, Chris Satterlund, Alexis Lunsford, Elizabeth Whiting, Alan Smagler, and the whole sales team and everyone on the Scholastic Reading Clubs and Book Fairs teams. And a special shout-out to Nikki Mutch, Roz Hilden, and Terribeth Smith. You three ladies are the best!

Aunt Brenda, this book would not exist without your willingness to share your porch, your extra bedroom, your popcorn, and hot beverages. Love you.

And finally, Philip, Elizabeth, Stephen, Chris, and Siobhan. You are my family, and family is everything.

ABOUT THE AUTHOR

Sharon Cameron's debut novel, *The Dark Unwinding*, was awarded the Society of Children's Book Writers and Illustrators' Sue Alexander Award for Most Promising New Work and the SCBWI Crystal Kite Award, and was named an ALA Best Fiction for Young Adults selection. Sharon is also the author of its sequel, *A Spark Unseen*; *Rook*, which was selected as an Indie Next Top Ten Pick of the List selection; and the companion to this book, *The Forgetting*, a #1 *New York Times* bestseller and an Indie Next List selection. She lives with her family in Nashville, Tennessee, and you can visit her online at sharoncameronbooks.com.